westland ltd

THE ROZABAL LINE

Ashwin Sanghi's first novel, *The Rozabal Line*, was self-published in 2007 under his pseudonym, Shawn Haigins. The theological thriller based upon the theory that Jesus died in Kashmir was subsequently published by Westland in 2008 in India under his own name and went on to become a bestseller, remaining on national bestseller lists for several months.

Ashwin Sanghi's second novel, *Chanakya's Chant*, a political thriller with roots in ancient Mauryan history, shot to the top of almost every bestseller list in India within a few weeks of its launch. The novel went on to win the Crossword-Vodafone Popular Choice Award 2010, and film producer UTV acquired the movie rights to the book. The novel continues to dominate the fiction charts.

The Krishna Key, A paced and riveting thril of the Vedic age and th

Ashwin is an entre historical fiction in t and hobby. Ashwin was educated at the Cathedral & John Connon School, Mumbai, and St Xavier's College, Mumbai. He holds a masters degree from Yale and is working towards a Ph.D. in Creative Writing. Ashwin lives in Mumbai with his wife, Anushika, and his son, Raghuvir.

To connect with Ashwin on email or social media please visit his website at www.sanghi.in.

'Sanghi's flair for religion, history and politics is clearly visible as he takes the reader across the world spanning different decades. A mixture of comparative religion, dangerous secrets and a thrilling plot makes for an esoteric read.' - Aditi Vij, *The Statesman*

'A provocative, clever and radiant line of theology Sanghi suggests is that the cult of Mary Magdalene has its true inspiration in the trinity of the Indian sacred feminine — thereby outthinking and out-conspiring Dan Brown.' - Pradeep Sebastian, *The Hindu*

'...a must-read for all those who enjoyed Dan Brown's *The Da Vinci Code*. A fine combination of history, religion, spirituality and mystery, the book is thought-provoking and definitely not for the faint-hearted.' - Chethana Dinesh, *Deccan Herald*

'The ultimate reward that *The Rozabal Line* holds for the reader is the treasure-house of surprises that lie in store, as history gets presented ... as delightful, jaw-dropping trivia.' - L. Suresh, *Indian Express*

'One must remember that this is a work of fiction. Provocative, but commanding attention!' - M.V. Kamath, *Free Press Journal*

'Though Dan Brown's *The Da Vinci Code* may still be the uncrowned king in conspiracy theory fiction, he has got an Indian challenger in Ashwin Sanghi.' - Mandira Nayar, *The Week*

'Sanghi dishes out a heady mixture of terrorist attacks, secret societies, murdered professors, hallucinating priests and seductive femmes fatales.' - *The Telegraph*

'*The Rozabal Line* asks that really fun question — what if ?' - Divya Kumar, *The Hindu*

'If you are one of the millions who lapped up every page of *The Da Vinci Code*, here's a book that's even better... Ashwin

Sanghi takes us into a world of intrigue and conspiracy, almost having us believe that all religions in the world are linked.'
-Mid-Day

'Ashwin Sanghi's book is a pot-boiler, despite the somewhat incredible claims... A thrilling read for all fans of the genre!'
-Hindustan Times

'... a well-researched theological thriller that fictionalises the myth that Jesus travelled to Kashmir...' *-Sakaal Times*

'I found *The Rozabal Line* quite gripping ... it unfurls a possible life of Jesus the Christ in India, and traces this life all the way to twenty-first-century descendants...' - Kala Krishnan Ramesh, *Metro Plus*

'With a religio-historical sweep, it explores the reason to believe that Christ did not die on the cross and went on to live in India...' - *Mumbai Mirror*

'... and the end result is a book that will have you biting your nails ever so often...' - Siddharth Srikanth, *The Hindu*

'Cut from the same cloth as Dan Brown's *Angels and Demons* and *The Da Vinci Code*, and with shades of Vikram Chandra's *Sacred Games—The Rozabal Line* is a thriller.' - Mint **WSJ**

'Of late, a flood of literature, including a Da Vinci Code-type potboiler called *The Rozabal Line* by Ashwin Sanghi, and documentaries have led to renewed interest [in the Rozabal shrine]' - *The Telegraph*

'And so Dan Brown's *The Lost Symbol* comes two years too late. Conspiracy thrillers swamped the market, reaching even Indian shores with *The Rozabal Line*, and offered us so much meat, that we couldn't relish chewing anymore.' - Pradeep Sebastian, *Deccan Herald*

'Westland has had a hit with Ashwin Sanghi's *The Rozabal Line*, a modern-day Dan Brown-style thriller that revolves around Christ and whether he lived in Kashmir.' *-The Telegraph*

KIMAYA KAMAT.

The Rozabal Line

Ashwin Sanghi

𝒲
Westland Ltd

westland ltd

61, Silverline Building, Alapakkam Main Road, Maduravoyal, Chennai 600 095
No.38/10 (New No.5), Raghava Nagar, New Timber Yard Layout, Bangalore 560 026
93, 1st Floor, Sham Lal Road, Daryaganj, New Delhi 110 002

Originally published in the United States of America as *The Rozabal Line*
by 'Shawn Haigins' by Lulu Press Inc. 2007

Revised edition first published by westland ltd 2008

Copyright © Ashwin Sanghi 2008

This edition published by westland ltd 2010

All rights reserved

18 17 16 15 14

ISBN: 978-93-81626-82-5

Typeset in BakerSignet BT by Art Works, Chennai

Printed at Manipal Technologies Ltd, Manipal

Author's Note

This book is a work of fiction. Names, characters, places and incidents are products of the author's imagination or are used fictitiously. Religion, history and factual narrative have been liberally interspersed with the fictional narrative in order to give context and colour to the plot.

Any resemblance to actual events, locales, organisations or persons—living or dead—is entirely coincidental. Any publicly recognisable people or historical or mythological personalities are used as characters in fiction and the author does not believe that the events around, or dialogues attributed to them actually happened.

Wherever possible, notes have been provided at the end of the book to explain, justify, attribute or acknowledge. One does not, however, need to refer to these notes to enjoy the story itself.

I am obliged to my wife and son who ungrudgingly tolerated my persistent absence from their lives while I was writing this book, while juggling the rest of my life. I am beholden to my family, which supported me in my endeavours—including my writing. I am thankful to various authors and producers of original or derived works. A separate acknowledgements section in the back lists these in detail.

I am grateful to my editor, Prita Maitra, and my publisher, Westland Limited & Tranquebar Press, especially Gautam Padmanabhan, without whom none of my novels—including this one—would have seen the light of day.

Finally, I am fortunate to be the grandson of the late Shri Ram Prasad Gupta, and grandnephew to his brother the late Shri Ram Gopal Gupta. Their blessings move the fingers that hold my pen.

Chapter One

The onset of winter in idyllic Kashmir meant that the days were gradually getting shorter. Even though it was only three in the afternoon, it felt like nightfall. Icy winter winds, having wafted through the numerous apple and cherry orchards of the area, sent a spicy and refreshing aromatic chill to the man's nostrils. The leather jacket and lambswool pullover underneath it were his only comfort as he knelt to pray at the tomb.

Father Vincent Sinclair rubbed his hands together to keep warm as he took in the sight of the four glass walls, within which lay the wooden sarcophagus. The occupant of the tomb, however, resided in an inaccessible crypt below. Standing in front of a Muslim cemetery, the tomb was located within an ordinary and unassuming structure with whitewashed walls and simple wooden fixtures.

Vincent's blond hair, blue eyes, together with his athletic build and pale skin clearly marked him out as separate and distinct from the locals. The goatee and rimless spectacles completed the slightly academic look.

The sign outside informed visitors that the Rozabal tomb in the Kanyar district of old Srinagar contained the body of a person named Yuz Asaf. Local land records acknowledged the existence of the tomb from AD 112 onwards.[1]

The word 'Rozabal', derived from the Kashmiri term *Rauza-Bal*, meant 'Tomb of the Prophet'. According to Muslim custom, the gravestone had been placed along the north-south axis. However, a small opening to the true burial chamber beneath revealed that the sarcophagus of Yuz Asaf lay along the east-west axis as per Jewish custom.

Nothing else was out of the ordinary here—except for the carved imprint of a pair of feet near the sarcophagus. The feet were normal human feet—normal, barring the fact that they bore marks on them; marks that coincided with the puncture wounds inflicted in crucifixion.

Crucifixion had never been practised in Asia, so it was quite obvious that the resident of the tomb had undergone this ordeal in some other, distant land.

⚇

Mecca, Saudi Arabia, 2012

The thousands of male pilgrims to Mecca during the Islamic month of Dhu-al-Hijjah were dressed identically in Ihram—a simple white, unhemmed cloth. It was impossible to distinguish one pilgrim from another in the white sea of humanity.

After all, this was Haj, and all of Allah's followers were meant to be equal before Him. Some, however, were more equal than the others.

The simple face and ordinary features did not reveal the secret depths of this particular pilgrim as he performed the Tawaf—circling the holy Kaaba—swiftly, four times, and then another three times at an unhurried pace.

This was Ghalib's second visit to the Kaaba. A week ago he had already been through the entire routine once. After completing the Umrah, Ghalib had stopped to drink water from the sacred well of Zamzam. He had then travelled to Medina to visit the mosque of the Prophet before performing the final three acts of Haj—journeying over five days to the hill of Arafat, throwing stones at the devil in the city of Mina, and then returning to Mecca to perform a second Tawaf around the Kaaba.

Ghalib was praying: *Bismillah ar-rahman ar-rahim. Allah, the most kind and the most merciful.* Please do not show your legendary kindness or mercy to my enemies.

He felt refreshed. Blessed. Purified.

The Lashkar-e-Toiba, the Army of the Pure, had been fighting a bloody jihad in Kashmir for the restoration of an Islamic caliphate over India. The outfit was on the radar of most intelligence agencies around the world. Ghalib, however, was not yet even a blip on the screen.

Unknown to most intelligence agencies, the Lashkar-e-Toiba had spun off an even more elite group within itself called the Lashkar-e-Talatashar, the Army of Thirteen, consisting of twelve elite holy warriors who would deem it an honour and privilege to die for the cause of Allah. They were not confined to Kashmir but scattered across the world.[2]

Their leader, the thirteenth man, was their general. His name was Ghalib.

London, UK, 2012

The Department for the Study of Religions was part of the School of Oriental and African Studies which, in turn, was part of the University of London. The school boasted a vast library located in the main school building just off Russell Square.

On this damp morning, faculty librarian Barbara Poulson was attempting to prepare the library for its first wave of students and faculty members at the opening time of 9 am.

Most students would start their search with the library catalogue, which indicated whether the library had the required item. In the catalogue one could find the class mark—a reference number—of the item one wanted and this could be used to find the exact location of the book.

The previous day, Professor Terry Acton had been attempting to locate a copy of the Hindu treatise, *The Bhagavad Gita*, published in 1855 by Stephen Austin. The absentminded professor had been unable to locate it and had requested Barbara's assistance. She had promised to find it before his arrival that morning.

She mechanically typed the words 'Bhagavad Gita' into the library's computerised catalogue. There were only two books displayed, neither of which was the one that the professor wanted. She then recalled the professor mentioning that the *Bhagavad Gita* was actually part of a broader epic, the *Mahabharata*. She quickly typed 'Mahabharata' into the computer and saw 229 entries. The twelfth entry was 'The Bhagavad Gita, A Colloquy Between Krishna and Arjuna on the Divine'. She clicked on this hyperlink and she had it—the book by Stephen Austin, published by Hertford in 1855. Noting the class mark—CWML 1220—she looked it up on the location list.

Items starting with 'CWML' were located on level F in the Special Collections Reading Room. The extremely efficient Barbara Poulson headed towards level F, where she started moving in reverse serial towards CWML 1220.

CWML 1224 . . . CWML 1223 . . . CWML 1222 . . . CWML 1221 . . . CWML 1219 . . . Where was CWML 1220?

In place of the book was a perfect square, crimson box about twelve inches in length, width and height. It had a small, white label pasted on the front that simply read 'CWML 1220'.

Barbara was puzzled, but she had no time in her efficient and orderly world to ponder over things for too long. She lifted the box off the shelf, placed it on the nearest reading desk and lifted off the cardboard lid to reveal the perfectly preserved head of Professor Terry Acton, neatly severed at the neck. On his forehead was a yellow Post-it that read 'Mark 16:16'.

The cool and extremely efficient Barbara Poulson grasped the edge of the desk for support before she fainted and fell to the floor.

The passage Mark 16:16 of the New Testament reads as follows: *He that believeth and is baptised shall be saved; but he that believeth not shall be damned.*

Waziristan, Pakistan-Afghanistan border, 2012

Waziristan was no-man's-land, a rocky and hilly area on the Pakistan–Afghanistan border, and a law unto itself. Even though Waziristan was officially part of Pakistan, it was actually self-administered by Waziri tribal chiefs, who were feared warriors, as well as being completely indomitable and conservative.

The presence of the lanky, olive-skinned man wearing a simple white turban, camouflage jacket and holding a walking cane in his left hand was a little out of place in this region. The man was extremely soft-spoken and gentle in his ways. His overall demeanour was that of an ascetic, not a warrior. So what was he doing in this harsh land where swords and bullets did most of the talking?

He was sitting inside a cave on a beautiful Afghan rug. His few trusted followers sat around him drinking tea. He was talking to them. 'As for the World Trade Center attack, the people who were attacked and who perished in it were those controlling some of the most important positions in business and government. It wasn't a school! It wasn't someone's home. And the accepted view would be that most of the people inside were responsible for backing a terrible financial power that excels in spreading worldwide mischief!'[3]

'Praise be to Allah!' said one of the followers excitedly.

'We treat others merely like they treat us. Those who kill our women and our innocent, we kill their women and innocent until they desist.'

'But Sheikh, we have already achieved a sensational victory. What else is left to achieve?' asked one of his followers.

'We started out by draining their wealth through costly wars in Afghanistan. We then destroyed their security through attacks on their soil. We shall now attack the only thing that is left— their faith.'

'How?' wondered the followers.

'Ah! I have a secret weapon,' said the Sheikh in his usual hushed voice.

Vatican City, 2012

Popes had ruled most of the Italian peninsula, Rome included, for over a millennium, until 1870. Disputes between the Pope and Italy had been settled by Mussolini in 1929 through three Lateran Treaties, which had established the Stato della Città del Vaticano, more commonly known as Vatican City. It instantly became the world's smallest state, with an area of just 0.44 square kilometres.

His Eminence Alberto Cardinal Valerio was just one among 921 other national citizens of the Holy See but was extremely important among the 183 cardinals.

He now sat in his office wearing his black simar with scarlet piping and scarlet sash around his waist. The bright scarlet symbolised the cardinal's willingness to die for his faith. *To die or to kill*, thought His Eminence.

He picked up the sleek Bang & Olufsen BeoCom-4 telephone that contrasted dramatically with his Murano antique desk and asked his secretary to send in his visitor.

The young woman who entered his office had delicate features and flawless skin. It was evident that she possessed a beautiful blend of European and Oriental features. Her bright eyes shone with fervent devotion and she knelt before His Eminence.

'Bless me, Father, for I have sinned. It has been a year since my last confession.'

'Go ahead, my child,' whispered His Eminence. He motioned for her to talk by waving his podgy hand. On his ring finger sat a pigeon-blood-red Burmese ruby of 10.16 carats.

Swakilki began. 'I severed the professor's head and left it in the library as a lesson to those who mock the sanctity of Christ's suffering. He deserved it for his blasphemy.'

'And are you repentant for this terrible sin?'

'Oh, my God, I am heartily sorry for having offended Thee and I detest all my sins because of Thy just punishments, but most of all because they offend Thee, my God, who art all good and deserving of all my love. I firmly resolve, with the help of Thy grace, to sin no more and avoid the near occasions of sin. Amen.'

His Eminence pondered over what she had said for a few seconds before he spoke. 'May our Lord Jesus Christ absolve you; and by His authority I absolve you from every bond of excommunication . . . I absolve you of your sins in the name of the Father, and the Son, and the Holy Spirit. Amen. *Passio Domini nostri Jesu Christi, merita Beatae Mariae Virginis et omnium sanctorum, quidquid boni feceris vel mail sustinueris sint tibi in remissionem peccatorum, augmentum gratiae et praemium vitae aeternae.*'[4]

Valerio made the sign of the cross and looked squarely at the young woman. Swakilki looked up at the cardinal. He was seated on a large leather sofa in the luxurious office.

'Do you reject sin so as to live in the freedom of God's children?' asked Valerio.

'I do,' replied Swakilki.

'Do you reject Satan, father of sin and prince of darkness?'

'I do.'

'Do you believe in God, the Father Almighty, creator of heaven and earth?'

'I do.'

'Do you believe in Jesus Christ, His only Son, our Lord, who was born of the Virgin Mary, was crucified, died, and was buried, rose from the dead, and is now seated at the right hand of the Father?'

'I do.'

'Do you believe in the Holy Spirit, the Holy Catholic Church, the communion of saints, the forgiveness of sins, the resurrection of the body, and life everlasting?'

'I do.'

'Then it is time to eliminate all those who make people believe otherwise. Now listen carefully . . .'

Zurich, Switzerland, 2012

In 1844 Johannes Baur opened his second hotel in Zurich, right beside the lake and with an open view of the mountains. The hotel would soon become one of the most luxurious hotels of Zurich, the Baur au Lac.

Nestled within one of the deluxe suites of the Baur au Lac, with a beautiful view of Lake Zurich, sat Brother Thomas Manning. He was quite obviously a very valued regular patron. Why else would the hotel specifically stock Brunello di Montalcino, his favourite Tuscan wine?

There was a discreet knock at the door. The brother commanded in fluent German, '*Kommen sie herein*!' and the door opened.

The visitor was a thin, spectacled man.

Mr Egloff was the investment advisor from Bank Leu, the oldest Swiss bank in the world. Bank Leu had started out as Leu et Compagnie in 1755 under its first chairman, Johann Jacob Leu, the mayor of Zurich. The bank's clients had soon included European royalty such as the Empress Maria Theresa of Austria.[5]

'Herr Egloff, under instructions from His Eminence Alberto Cardinal Valerio, I require a sum of ten million dollars to be transferred from the Oedipus trust to the Isabel Madonna trust,' said Brother Manning.

'Very well, Brother Manning,' replied the banker.

Unknown to the outside world, the strange sounding offshore trusts managed by Herr Egloff for his clients had anagrams as the beneficiaries. Brother Manning chuckled to himself.

After all, the beneficiary of the Oedipus trust was Opus Dei and the primary beneficiary of the Isabel Madonna trust was Osama-bin-Laden.

Chapter Two

Dmitriy Novikov was tired.[6] His expedition from Srinagar through the 3,500-metre-high Zoji-la Pass into Ladakh had been exhausting in spite of several men taking on the burden of luggage and equipment. The onward trek to Leh, the capital of Ladakh, and thereon to Hemis had sapped all his energy. To make matters worse, he had injured his right leg as a result of a fall from the mule that was carrying him.

Hemis was one of the most respected Buddhist monasteries in Ladakh, and their visitor was welcomed as an honoured guest. The monks quickly carried him into their simple quarters and began tending to his injury. While he was being fed a meal of apricots and walnuts washed down by hot butter tea, he met the chief Lama of the monastery.

'I know why you are here, my son,' said the Lama. 'We too honour the Christian Son of God.'

Dmitriy was dumbfounded. He had not expected such a forthright approach. 'Would it be possible for me to see the writings that talk of Issa?' he began cautiously.

The wise Lama smiled quizzically at Dmitriy and then quietly continued, 'The soul of Buddha certainly was incarnate in the great Issa who, without resorting to war, was able to spread the wisdom of our beautiful religion through many parts of the world. Issa is an honoured prophet, who took birth after twenty-two earlier Buddhas. His name, his life and his deeds are noted in the texts that you refer to. But first you must rest and allow yourself to heal.'

Dmitriy's leg was throbbing with pain. The Buddhist monks applied a wide assortment of herbal remedies and packs, but they were of little help. He attempted to ignore the pain and continue his animated conversation with the Lama.

The Lama was turning his prayer-wheel when he stopped and said, 'The Muslims and Buddhists do not share commonalities. The Muslims used violence and battles to convert Buddhists to Islam. This was never the case with the Christians. They could be considered honorary Buddhists! It's truly sad to see that Christians decided to forget their roots and wander further and further away from Buddhism!'

Dmitriy was sweating profusely. The Lama's words seemed to be questioning years of conventional wisdom. He realised how momentous his discovery was, but he also knew the danger of exposing his knowledge to the Western world. He would be branded a traitor and a liar. His words would be considered blasphemous. He would need to proceed carefully.

Dmitriy quickly asked again whether he would be able to see the sacred writings that the Lama was referring to. The Lama looked at him and smiled. 'Patience is a Buddhist virtue, my son,' he said. 'Patience.'

ᨢ

Dmitriy was as patient as could be. He waited for several days to see the writings that the Lama had spoken of, the ones about Issa. It was difficult to conceal his anticipation and he had been sorely tempted to ask for the manuscripts without further delay. Today his patience had finally paid dividend. The Lama brought him a number of ancient scrolls written in Tibetan by Buddhist historians.

An interpreter was called for and began to translate the scrolls while Dmitriy attempted to make copies of them.

The scrolls told the story of a boy called Issa, born in Judea. The story went on to explain that sometime during the fourteenth year of his life, the boy arrived in India to study the teachings of the Buddhists. His travels through the country took him through Sindh, the Punjab and eventually to Maghada, the ancient kingdom of Ashoka, where he studied the Vedas, the Hindu texts of knowledge. However, Issa was forced to leave when he began to teach those whom the Hindu Brahmins considered 'untouchables' under the rigid caste system of Hinduism.

Issa then took refuge in Buddhist monasteries and began learning the Buddhist scriptures in Pali, the language of the Buddha. Thereafter he headed home to Judea via Persia. In Persia he made himself unpopular with the Zoroastrian priests. They expelled him into the jungles, hoping he would be eaten alive by wild animals.

He finally reached Judea at the age of twenty-nine. Because he had been away for so long, no one seemed to know him. They asked, 'Who art thou, and from what country hast thou come into our own? We have never heard of thee, and do not even know thy name.'

And Issa said, 'I am an Israelite and on the very day of my birth, I saw the walls of Jerusalem, and I heard the weeping of my brothers reduced to slavery, and the moans of my sisters carried away by pagans into captivity. While yet a child, I left my father's house to go among other nations. But hearing that my brothers were enduring still greater tortures, I have returned to the land in which my parents dwelt, that I might recall to my brothers the faith of their ancestors.'

The learned men asked Issa, 'It is claimed that you deny the laws of Moses and teach the people to desert the temple of God.'

And Issa replied, 'We cannot demolish what has been given to us by God. As for Moses's laws, I have striven to re-establish them in the hearts of men, and I say to you that you are in ignorance of their true meaning, for it is not vengeance, but forgiveness, that they teach.'[7]

Dmitriy was excited. Then petrified. He knew there was no going back on his discovery. He now knew that he held in his hands one of the most stunning revelations in two millennia.

A revelation about *Issa*, the Arabic form of the Hebrew name *Yeshua*, also known as *Jesus*.

Chapter Three

Srinagar, Kashmir, India, 1975

The house of Rashid-bin-Isar was overflowing with joy. His wife, Nasira, had just delivered a baby boy. The proud father had announced that he would feed all the poor and homeless in the city for a week. Large vats filled with lamb biryani, a spicy and aromatic rice pilaf, overflowed into the streets as beggars and street children flocked to Rashid's home to feast.

Rashid cradled his firstborn in his arms as he recited the Islamic prayers, Adhan in the right ear and Iqaamah in the left ear of the child, as he awaited the Khittaan, the ritual circumcision.

Father and son appeared on the balcony a few moments later as cheers erupted from the throngs in the street. 'I want all of you to bless my son. By the will and grace of Allah, he will be great. His name shall be Ghalib, the Victorious One!'

Gulmarg, Kashmir, India, 1985

Ten years later, the members of the Indian Army who burst into the weekend home of Rashid-bin-Isar were convinced that he had financed the activities of those responsible for the bomb blast in the market the previous day.

He pleaded his innocence, but his cries and protestations were to no avail. His terror-stricken family watched as their beloved *abba* was arrested on the spot.

He was quickly handcuffed and dragged away to prison, where he was punched and kicked till he could barely see, hear, talk, or walk. The next day he was found hanging in his cell; he had used his own clothes to fashion the noose around his neck.

The family had been allowed to take away his body to give him a burial. As per Islamic custom, in preparation for burial, the family was expected to wash and shroud the body.[8] However, this step was to be omitted if the deceased had died a martyr; martyrs were to be buried in the very clothes they had died in. Rashid-bin-Isar was going to be buried in the clothes he had died in. He was no less than a martyr.

The mourners carried his body to the burial ground where the Imam began reciting the funeral prayers, the Salat-i-Janazah. Prayers over, the men carried the body to the gravesite. Rashid's body was laid in the grave without a coffin, as per custom, on his right side, facing Mecca.

Standing by the grave was little ten-year-old Ghalib, tears streaming down his cheeks. The Imam placed his hands on Ghalib's shoulders and said, 'Son, you should not cry. You are the son of a hero. Your father's death was not in vain. You will avenge his death. Henceforth, you shall not shed tears. You shall shed blood!'

Little Ghalib was confused. How could he possibly take revenge? He was merely a ten-year-old boy.

'Come with me, my son,' said the Imam, and taking Ghalib by the hand he led him to the mosque. The next day, the Imam journeyed across the Line of Control to get to Muzaffarabad on the Pakistani side of Kashmir. Here the boy was enrolled into the Jamaat-ud-Dawa Madrasah, an Islamic school of learning.

The lanky, olive-skinned Imam wearing a simple white turban bid him goodbye. 'See me after you have completed your studies,' he said simply.

ૐ

Muzaffarabad, Pakistan, 1986

During the next few years in Pakistan, Ghalib would go through two separate courses of study. In the Hifz course, he would memorise the holy Qur'an. In the 'Aalim course he would study the Arabic language, Qur'anic interpretation, Islamic law, the sayings and deeds of the Prophet Muhammad, logic and Islamic history. At the end of his study, he would be awarded the title of 'Aalim, meaning scholar.

One day, when he was in his Islamic history class, his teacher told them about the Islamic conquests of India.

'The first was the invasion by Mohammed-bin-Qasim from Syria in the seventh century. This was followed by the eleventh-century incursions of Muhammad of Ghazni. Ghazni was followed by Mohammed Ghori, who left India to be ruled by his Turkish generals. Then came the attacks by the Mongol hordes of Chenghiz Khan. Then, in AD 1398, came one of the most successful attacks of all, under the Mongol Taimur,' continued the teacher.[9]

Little Ghalib argued, 'But none of these people stayed in India. They were mostly interested in looting rather than ruling.'

Whack! The cane was swift on his palm,

'You must never say that again. Babar, Taimur's descendant, invaded India in 1526 and established Mughal rule over India for the next 300 years. In fact, it was God's will that India be ruled by Muslims. Till then, Hindus had continued to indulge in idolatry. The Muslim invasions made them realise the greatness of Islam!'

'So why do Muslims not rule over Kashmir today?' asked Ghalib.

'This is the reason that you must fight,' explained the teacher. 'It is your duty to do so. Fight a jihad to restore Islamic rule over Kashmir and then over the whole of India! Allah-o-Akbar!' he shouted.

'Allah-o-Akbar!' shouted the children in unison, including little Ghalib.

Waziristan, Pakistan-Afghanistan border, 2010

The lanky, olive-skinned Imam wearing the simple white turban who had escorted the ten-year-old was now Ghalib's controller. Everyone simply called him 'Sheikh'.

He was sitting on an intricately woven rug inside his cave in Waziristan, located on the Pakistan–Afghanistan border.

On his right sat Ghalib-bin-Isar, the thirty-five-year-old leader of the Lashkar-e-Talatashar. He was here with his army of the dirty dozen.

The host first looked at Ghalib. He then swept a glance over Ghalib's men—Boutros, Kader, Yahya, Yaqub, Faris, Fadan, Ataullah, Tau'am, Adil, Shamoon, Yehuda and Fouad. Each of these veterans had crossed the Khyber Pass from different parts of the world and had enrolled in the Khalden Camp run by Al-Qaeda as fresh recruits, who were now toughened and battle-ready.

Khalden was a mishmash of tents and rough stone buildings. It used to take in about a hundred recruits at a time. Each group consisted of Muslims from Saudi Arabia, Jordan, Yemen, Algeria, France, Germany, Sweden, Chechnya and Kashmir. Ironically, the Al-Qaeda Khalden Camp was using teaching and training methods originally adopted by the American CIA in training the Mujahideen guerrillas to fight the Soviets.[10] Even text books— in Arabic, French and English—on terror techniques had been made available to the recruits, courtesy of the CIA.

Each morning at Khalden, the group would be called to parade and then asked to pray. After the morning meal, they would go through endurance training followed by strength training. They would also be taught hand-to-hand combat using a variety of knives, alternative forms of garrottes and other weapons. They would learn to use small firearms, deadly assault rifles and even grenade-launchers. The science of explosives and landmines was also part of their study. Representatives of Islamic terror groups, such as Hamas, Hezbollah and Islamic Jihad would regularly visit the camp in order to teach the recruits more about the practical applications of their knowledge.

The final result of the efforts at the Khalden Camp had been this elite Army of Thirteen, the Lashkar-e-Talatashar. The Sheikh was happy with the output.

These men would help the Sheikh's Master teach the whole world of infidels a lesson that they would not forget. The 9/11 attack on America in 2001 would seem like a tea party in comparison. The Sheikh's Master was convinced that it was time to re-establish the supremacy of the Islamic Caliphate.

The Sheikh wondered how it would affect the Crux Decussata Permuta.

Chapter Four

Osaka, Japan, 1972

Pink Floyd performed live at the Festival Hall in Osaka on 9 March. Among those in the audience was a pretty young woman, Aki Herai. She had a job in the large Daimaru store in the Shinsaibashi district of the city but was now on leave because she was eight months pregnant. The concert tickets were a present from her friends at the store. The delicate subject of the child's father was never discussed.

Pink Floyd's *Dark Side of the Moon* was a big hit with the Japanese youth attending the concert. The show was reaching its finale when Aki felt her water break. Her friends rushed her to Osaka National Hospital, where the doctors performed an emergency caesarean section.

Her daughter, Swakilki, arrived six weeks short of a normal forty-week pregnancy. Luckily she weighed five pounds, was 12.6 inches tall, and had fairly well-developed lungs, enabling her to survive.

On Swakilki's sixth birthday, her mother threw a party. Aki entertained the guests inside the cramped shoebox home while one of her friends took little Swakilki to the garden for some fresh air. As the woman cuddled the little girl in her arms, she felt the shock from the hot blast that ripped through Aki Herai's home.

The cause of the explosion would later be diagnosed as an accident—a gas leak.

It was a gas leak; an accident, it was not.

Yes, Swakilki was indeed a survivor—born without a father, and alive without a mother.

⚜

Tokyo, Japan, 1987

Orphaned at the age of six, Swakilki had been transferred to the Holy Family Home, an Osaka orphanage run by kind, gentle and caring nuns. She would spend the next six years here.

During these six years she would eagerly await the monthly arrival of one of the jovial and rotund Fathers from Rome. His name was Alberto Valerio, and he would always bring her candy. For Swakilki, he was her Santa Claus.

She was one of the 'lucky' ones to get adopted at the age of twelve by a fairly well-off couple in Tokyo. What she could not have known was that the adoption would come at a price. Little Swakilki was abused and raped by her adoptive father at the age of fourteen; he told her it was their 'special little secret'.

Scared and confused, she ran away a year later to take up a job in an *oppaipabu*, one of the sleazy establishments on the outskirts of Tokyo where customers were allowed to fondle the female staff to their hearts' content. It was at the oppaipabu that she met an older man, Takuya.

She shared his bed on the first night they met, and he shared with her his knowledge of anandamides.

⚜

Anandamides are naturally occurring neurotransmitters in the brain whose chemical make-up is very similar to cannabis. The word 'anandamide' is derived from the Sanskrit word *ananda*, which means bliss.

Swakilki learnt how to enjoy the rush of anandamides within her brain when she killed. She then learnt how to make men experience the same rush when she had sex with them.

Takuya trained her well over the next few years. First came the techniques of killing——suffocation, strangulation, drowning, garrotting, poisoning, explosion, shooting, stabbing, castration and ritual disembowelment.

Next were the techniques of seduction. Tantric sex and the *Kama Sutra* became her daily study rituals. Self-grooming, dressing, conversation, cuisine and wine selection were next on the menu.

The friendship between Takuya and Swakilki was one of mutual dependence. Takuya was closely linked to Aum Shinrikyo, a lethal religious cult. He was member of a small group that carried out assassinations of important and influential people who were considered enemies of Aum Shinrikyo. Swakilki was an ideal recruit. She was gorgeous, ruthless and, most importantly, emotionally barren. The final product was sexy, seductive, sultry, silent, and sharp. Razor-sharp.

Her first assignment would be Murakami-san, one of the most outspoken critics of Aum Shinrikyo.

Tokyo, Japan, 1990

Swakilki and Murakami-san had dined at a very expensive Kaiseki restaurant. Kaiseki cuisine was historically vegetarian owing to its Zen origin, though not anymore. Only the freshest seasonal ingredients were utilised, and these were cooked in a delicate style aimed at enhancing their original flavours. Each dish was exquisitely prepared and carefully presented along with elaborate garnishes of leaves and flowers.

They were now in his penthouse on the top floor of a skyscraper in the neon-filled district of Shunjuku in northwest Tokyo. They lay entirely naked on the king-sized bed; she had worn him out completely. Swakilki knew some of the finest techniques in the art of pleasuring a man. Her petite frame, perfectly rounded breasts and delicate features only accentuated her oozing sex appeal.

She had taken Murakami through several waves of near orgasm using different styles of stroking and stimulation. She knew that after coming close to orgasm a few times, without releasing themselves, most men experienced very strong and sometimes very lengthy orgasms.

The art of Tantra had taught her that it was possible for a man to experience the feeling of orgasm without actually ejaculating. She had made Murakami experience several of these 'dry' orgasms in a row. When she allowed him a final release, the actual orgasm was so intense that it was a full body tremor lasting over a minute.

It was thus no surprise to Swakilki that the ancient Indian sex treatise, the *Kama Sutra*, was still a bestseller even though its author, Vatsyayana, had written it way back in AD 600.

She looked at Murakami-san, who was gently snoring, and sleeping like a contented baby. Quietly, she lifted her pillow and brought it down on his face. It was time for Murakami-san to sleep deeper.

Tokyo, Japan, 1993

Seishu Takemasa was sound asleep.

Swakilki had just given Seishu a hot, sensual mineral bath in the luxurious sunken marble tub of the Imperial Suite.

The legendary grande dame of Tokyo, the Imperial Hotel, had 1,057 rooms, including 64 suites, which were mostly reserved for statesmen, royalty and celebrities.

Seishu Takemasa was all of the above. His proximity to His Imperial Majesty Akihito, the 125th Emperor of Japan, was well known. He was also close to the political establishment, including three successive prime ministers—Tsutomu Hata, Tomiichi Murayama and Ryutaro Hashimoto. His photographs with Madonna, Oprah, Prince Charles, Bill Gates, Tom Cruise and Bill Clinton appeared regularly in the society pages. The media empire he owned was second only to that of Rupert Murdoch and he had used it to launch a frontal attack on Aum Shinrikyo.

Over the years, Swakilki had grown even more attractive. She was built like a beautiful and graceful Japanese doll. Her pale ivory skin was flawless. Her dark black hair had just a hint of auburn and cascaded down all the way to the curve of her hips. Her face was exquisite, with deep pools for eyes, an aquiline nose and delicate but full lips. She looked every inch a princess.

After giving Seishu his bath, she began to massage him. Her intention was to tune him inward while deepening his awareness. Her knowledge of Tantra allowed her to focus on all the seven chakras, the nerve centres, starting from the base of his spine, to his genitals, onward to his belly, upward to his heart, further on to his throat, northward to his forehead—the mystical third eye—and finally to the top of his head. Her pampering ministrations had turned him into soft clay that she could mould in any way she wanted.

Her present focus was on his prostate gland. This was purportedly one of the access points for Kundalini energy, which was supposed to lead to enlightenment.

As she massaged him, he began to experience a deep emotional release. Tears ran down his cheeks. He was laughing. Then crying. It was wave after wave of immense pleasure. He looked up at her gentle smiling face to express his gratitude for her incredible skills.

He barely noticed the flash of the extremely sharp razor as it swiftly slit his throat.

Osaka, Japan, 1995

On 20 March 1995, during the morning rush hour, ten members belonging to the Aum Shinrikyo cult boarded five trains at different stations. At a predetermined time, they punctured bags of sarin gas. Twelve people died and thousands were incapacitated. The Japanese police thought that the attack had been perpetrated by ten members of the gang. It had actually been twelve.

Osaka, Japan's third largest city, with a population of 2.5 million, was the economic powerhouse of the Kansai region. Higashi-Osaka, or East Osaka, was a residential suburb and its industrial district produced electric appliances, machinery, clothing fibre and paper. It had also produced Swakilki and Takuya.

Takuya had been born in 1955, the same year as Asahara Shoko, the notorious founder of the Aum Shinrikyo sect. Like Asahara, he had failed the entrance exam at Tokyo University and had turned to studying acupuncture. Both Asahara and Takuya had joined Agonshu, a new religion that stressed liberation from 'bad karma' via meditation. Asahara had visited India in 1986 and upon his return to Japan had claimed to have attained enlightenment in the Himalayas. He had named his new group Aum Shinrikyo.[11]

In Aum, a believer could eliminate bad karma by enduring various sufferings. As a result, members of the cult were free to justify the abuse of other members.

As Asahara's cult grew, so did his power and wealth. All new entrants had to sever ties with their families and contribute their wealth to the cult. Aum Shinrikyo became infamous for bloody initiations, involuntary donations, threats and extortion. Takuya was the brains and muscle behind many of these activities, although purely for commercial motivations.

As Asahara became crazier, he felt the need to convince the world that an apocalypse was about to happen and that he was the world's only salvation. In 1994 he ordered clouds of sarin gas to be released in the Kita-Fukashi district of Matsumoto. This was soon followed by the horrible train attack.

Asahara was eventually found hiding in a secret room in the village of Kamikuishiki. He had in his possession a huge amount of cash and gold bars. Many of his followers were also found—comatose, under the influence of pentobarbital, an anaesthetic. Asahara and 104 followers were indicted. Two were not.

Unlike the others, Swakilki and Takuya had been with Asahara for commercial reasons alone. They had no emotional or spiritual ties to Asahara or to Aum Shinrikyo, and they were now free to do as they pleased.

⚜

Tel-Aviv, Israel, 1995

On 4 November, Yitzhak Rabin, the prime minister of Israel, was assassinated by Yigal Amir, a right-wing activist. The popularly accepted version of the killing was that the assassin had felt betrayed by Rabin's signing of the Oslo Accord, which prompted him to take Rabin's life.[12]

No one knew of the two other international conspirators who had taken the Thai Airways flight 643 from Tokyo to Bangkok and the connecting El Al flight 84 from Bangkok to Tel Aviv.

⚜

Madrid, Spain, 1998

Lopez Tomas, president of the Spanish Constitutional Court, was in his office at Madrid Autonomous University when a gunman rushed into his office and shot him at point-blank range. The commonly accepted view was that the Basque separatist group, ETA, was behind his murder.

The camera-slung Asian couple that had arrived in Frankfurt on Lufthansa's flight 711 from Tokyo had not bothered to shoot any photographs in Germany. Instead, they had taken the connecting Spanair flight 2582 to Madrid the very same day.

There had been much more to shoot in Madrid.

⚜

Dushanbe, Tajikistan, 2001

On 27 October, Otakhon Khairollayev, a journalist of repute from Tajikistan, was shot dead at point-blank range. The same day a Japanese woman had entered the capital, Dushanbe, wearing an Afghan burqa.

⚜

Asunción, Paraguay, 2002

On 27 June, Luis Santa Cruz, the finance minister of Paraguay, was gunned down in his car. He had been a likely candidate for President. A Japanese woman had been visiting all the tourist spots, including Asunción, for a week around the same time.

⚜

Athens, Greece, 2005

On 16 June, David Roberts, a British military attaché in Athens, was shot dead by gunmen on motorcycles who belonged to N17, the Marxist revolutionary organisation. A honeymooning couple from Japan had been on a cruise of the Greek islands at that time.

⚜

Manila, Philippines, 2007

On 26 February, Filemon Montinola, an upcoming left-leaning politician in the Philippines, was assassinated.

A young Japanese woman visited the Minor Basilica of the Immaculate Conception, more commonly known as the Manila Cathedral, in order to light a candle the next day.

⚜

Belgrade, Serbia, 2010

On 9 May, Draginja Djindjic, the foreign minister of Serbia, was shot twice in the chest at 11:28 am inside a government building. His assassin, Vojislav Jovanoviæ, had fired the bullets from another building in the area. The same building had been visited by a Japanese woman that morning.

Yes, business was good for Swakilki and Takuya. They could now work entirely for themselves, given the fact that Asahara and Aum Shinrikyo were history. It also seemed that no one was really looking for them. Actually, someone was. Swakilki's Santa Claus. His name was Alberto Valerio.

⚴

Vatican City, 2012

Alberto Valerio was busy reading a dissertation by the renowned scholar Professor Terry Acton, head of the Department for the Study of Religions at the University of London. The good doctor had built up a cogent case to prove that Jesus Christ had not died on the cross at all. Alberto Cardinal Valerio took a sip of his Valpolicella, and continued reading:

> If the vested interests of the temple Jews had wanted to kill Jesus, they had the power to do so by stoning him to death without taking any permission from Rome. Why did this not happen?
>
> Instead, Jesus was punished by the Romans under Roman law and then crucified—a punishment meted out to enemies of the Roman Empire. Why punish a man under Roman law if he had no political agenda, only a religious one?
>
> Under Roman law, he would have first been flogged, causing a significant loss of blood. In this weakened state, his arms would have been fastened by thongs or nails to a solid wooden beam placed across his shoulders and neck. He would then have been made to walk to the final place of crucifixion while continuing to bear the weight of this beam.
>
> At the place of crucifixion, the horizontal beam would have been attached to a vertical one, with the victim still

hanging. Thus suspended, the victim would have been able to survive for a couple of days provided that his feet remained fixed to the cross. His feet remaining fixed would have enabled him to keep breathing by reducing the pressure on his chest.

Eventually, the victim would have died from exhaustion, thirst or blood poisoning caused by the nails. The victim's protracted agony could have been brought to an end by breaking his knees, causing the entire pressure to shift to the victim's chest, resulting in immediate asphyxiation. Thus, contrary to popular opinion, the breaking of the knees was not malicious—in fact, it was an act of mercy. Jesus's knees were never broken, yet he died within a few hours on the cross. Why?

During his suspension from the cross, Jesus said that he was thirsty. Popular opinion tells us that he was sadistically offered a sponge soaked in vinegar instead of one soaked in water. It is worthwhile to note that vinegar was used to revive exhausted slaves on ships. In fact, the vinegar should have revived him temporarily. Instead, he spoke his final words and died immediately upon inhaling the vinegar fumes. Why did it have this opposite effect on him?

There is one possible explanation. The sponge might not have contained vinegar. Instead, it may have contained a compound of belladonna and opium. This would have made Jesus pass out completely, only making it appear that he was dead. This would have prevented the guards from carrying out the final act of breaking his knees, leading to death from actual asphyxiation.

Roman law specifically prohibited bodies of crucified victims being given back to the family. Bodies were meant to remain on the cross to decay or to be consumed by birds of prey. Why did Pontius Pilate, the Roman governor of Judea, decide to ignore Roman law and allow Jesus's body to be handed over for burial to Joseph of Arimathea?[13]

Alberto Cardinal Valerio smiled a contented smile as he took another measured sip of his delightful Valpolicella. It was time to send another heretic to burn in hell!

♱

Alberto Cardinal Valerio was a jovial, rotund and gregarious individual. His smiling eyes, his pink face and his Buddha-belly gave him the demeanour and appearance of a jolly Santa Claus. The position that he occupied, however, was sombre and serious. He was head of the Archivio Segreto Vaticano, more commonly known as the Secret Archives of the Vatican.

The Vatican Secret Archives were the central repository for all documents that had been accumulated by the Roman Catholic Church over many ages. The Archives, containing thirty miles of bookshelves, had been closed to outsiders by Pope Paul V in the seventeenth century and they had remained closed till the nineteenth.

Alberto Valerio had been born in 1941 in Turin. Ordained in 1964, he had soon been offered his first appointment in the Roman Curia and had rapidly risen through various positions in the Sacred Congregation for Seminaries and Universities till he had eventually become its undersecretary in 1981.

After taking some time off to pursue a doctorate in theology from the Catholic University of Leuven in Belgium, he had returned to the Vatican to become secretary for the Congregazione per le Chiese Orientali, or the Congregation for the Oriental Churches, at which time he had travelled extensively within Japan. He had held several positions within the Curia till he was given charge of the Archivio Segreto Vaticano, a position he relished immensely.

What was common knowledge was his membership in the Priestly Society of the Holy Cross, an association of the clergy who were completely supportive of Opus Dei and its activities. What was not common knowledge was Valerio's membership of the Crux Decussata Permuta.[14]

While a standard crucifix hung prominently around his neck, a much smaller pendant hung underneath his robes. It had a rather curious design.

He picked up the Bang & Olufsen telephone on his antique Murano desk and began to dial: +81 . . .3 . . .

After a few rings a female voice answered at the other end. His Eminence began '*Ohaya gozaimasu . . .*' in fluent Japanese. 'I have an assignment for you. Can you meet me in London sometime in the next two days?'

'*Hai, wakarimasu,*' said Swakilki respectfully. 'Where shall I meet you?'

'The Dorchester. We'll meet in my suite.'

'*Domo arigato gozaimasu.*'

'God bless you, my child.'

Swakilki looked across the table at Takuya as she put the phone down. She absentmindedly ran her fingers over the strange tattoo on her left forearm.

● ● ●

The tattoo had been placed there by her mother, Aki, when Swakilki had turned five. It was identical to the one that Aki had also possessed on her own arm.

Swakilki remembered the Sisters of Charity of St Vincent de Paul who had taken such good care of her during her six years at the Holy Family orphanage in Osaka. She also remembered the jovial Santa Claus who had brought candy for all the kids in the orphanage in those years. She had always thought of him as Santa Claus ever since; his real name of course had been Alberto Valerio.

He had taken special interest in her due to his personal friendship with Swakilki's late mother, Aki. After her adoption she had continued to receive postcards from him for the next two years, but she had lost contact with him after she ran away from her abusive adoptive father. He had somehow managed to track her down several years later. She had confessed her plight to him, revealing the most intimate details of her life. He had then said to her, 'I absolve you from your sins in the name of the Father, and of the Son, and of the Holy Spirit.'

Swakilki could only remember how relieved she had been to unburden herself to him. Henceforth she would no longer kill for Aum Shinrikyo.

Only for Christ.

London, UK, 2012

Virgin Atlantic's flight 901 from Tokyo's Narita airport took off on the dot at 11am and landed at London Heathrow a few minutes before the scheduled arrival of 3:30 pm local time. On board in Virgin's Upper Class cabin was a Japanese couple who had spent the entire twelve-and-a-half-hour flight sleeping soundly.[15]

They had not asked for any reading material, nor did they turn on the personal entertainment screens. When the elaborate dinner consisting of shrimp with fish roe, zucchini in miso paste, egg yolk crabmeat rolls, buckwheat noodles and green tea, had been served, they had continued to sleep. They were certainly the freshest passengers to emerge from the Airbus aircraft in London.

Just another camera-slung Japanese tourist couple, the immigration officer thought of Mr and Mrs Yamamoto while cursorily checking their passports. The landing cards they had filled in on the flight indicated that they were staying for a week at the Grosvenor House Hotel on Park Lane. He stamped their passports matter-of-factly and waved them through.

They had no checked-in luggage, only onboard strollers, so they did not need to wait at the conveyor belts that were being crowded by hundreds of bleary-eyed passengers. Instead, they passed through the green channel at Heathrow's Terminal Three and walked straight through the arrival area to the taxi departure point without raising any suspicion. There were four London cabs waiting and they got into the first one in line.

'Where to, guv?' asked the cheerful cabbie.

'The London Hilton on Park Lane, please,' came the reply. Not the Grosvenor House.

At the reception desk of the London Hilton, the uninterested receptionist required their passports and a credit card. Takuya was happy to give her two false passports, one belonging to him and one to his wife, along with a Visa card.

Upon reaching their room on the Executive Floor, Swakilki took off her curly wig and Takuya removed his clear-glass spectacles and his neat little moustache. They got out of their casual travelling clothes and showered vigorously before putting on fresh formals. Swakilki then put the curly wig back on her head while Takuya once again put on his clear-glass spectacles and moustache.They then took the elevator to the lobby and walked out of the hotel onto Park Lane, turned right, and walked from the Hilton at 22 Park Lane, to 54 Park Lane, which housed The Dorchester Hotel, just a few blocks away.

Once there, they were to receive their formal assignment from His Eminence Alberto Cardinal Valerio.

Chapter Five

On 20 July, the first television transmission from the moon was viewed by 600 million people around the world. Matthew Sinclair sat riveted on a well-worn sofa and watched Neil Armstrong become the first man to walk on the moon. Also watching the incredible spectacle was his wife Julia, along with their three-week-old baby boy, Vincent Matthew Sinclair.

Another important event had taken place a year before Neil Armstrong's arrival on the moon and little Vincent's arrival on earth. Terence Cardinal Cooke had become the archbishop of New York. On the day of Cooke's installation, Martin Luther King Jr was assassinated, leading to bloody riots in many American cities.[16]

Cooke's tenure as archbishop would be difficult. Between 1967 and 1983 the number of diocesan priests in New York would decline by around 30 per cent, infant baptisms would fall by around 40 per cent, and church weddings would decline by around 50 per cent. It seemed that Catholicism was quickly going out of fashion in New York.

In the midst of this turmoil within the archdiocese of New York, the Sinclairs, who were extremely religious, hoped that their son would eventually make them proud by entering Saint Joseph's Seminary.

Vincent's demeanour, even as a child, was one of piety, and the priesthood seemed preordained.

Thus it was preordained by God and ordained by his parents that Vincent would become one of the rapidly shrinking minority groups—that of diocesan priests.

◊

New York City, USA, 1979

Vincent Sinclair at the age of ten was just another kid. He was playing with Kate, the neighbour's daughter, in the backyard. They were on a swing that his father, Matthew, had rigged to a sturdy branch of a strong tree in the yard. Vincent had already had a go at sitting on the swing and being pushed by Kate; it was now her turn to sit and be pushed.

Boys will be boys. A mischievous glow was on Vincent's face as he began pushing the swing for Kate. As the momentum increased, he found that he could send her higher and higher into the air with less and less effort. The resultant effect was a look of panic on Kate's innocent face.

Pushing was certainly more fun than being pushed.

Then the inevitable happened. The final push was too strong and Kate lost her balance. Poor little Kate fell to the ground and grazed her knee. Vincent's mother, Julia, and his aunt, Martha, ran out to apply an anti-bacterial ointment on the little girl, who was lying on the ground with tears streaming down her rosy cheeks.

Vincent was standing next to her, feeling apologetic and offering his hand to help her up.

While holding out his hand, he was repeating the words, '*Talitha koum. Talitha koum. Talitha koum.*'

◊

The Biblical passage of Mark 5:41 reads as follows:

He came to the synagogue ruler's house, and he saw an uproar, weeping, and great wailing. When he had entered in, he said to them, 'Why do you make an uproar and weep? The child is not dead, but is asleep.' They ridiculed him. But he, having put them all out, took the father of the child, her mother, and those who were with him, and went in where the child was lying.

Taking the child by the hand, he said to her, 'Talitha koum!' which means, 'Girl, I tell you, get up!' Immediately, the girl rose and walked, for she was twelve years old.[17]

New York City, USA, 1989

Four years of high school, four years of college and four years of theology later, Vincent Matthew Sinclair would be called to ordination by the archbishop at St Patrick's Cathedral.

Construction of St Patrick's Cathedral, located on 50th Street and 5th Avenue in the heart of Manhattan, had been completed in 1879. However, it was only in 1989 that the cathedral received a new amplification system as well as modernised lighting. Due to this technology upgrade, Father Vincent Sinclair's ordination to the Roman Catholic priesthood was seen and heard clearly by all who were present.

Present among the crowd were two very proud parents, Julia and Matthew Sinclair, as well as a bored but dutifully present aunt, Martha Sinclair.

His Eminence John Cardinal O'Connor, the Archbishop, had imposed his hands on Vincent's head and had repeated the words from Psalm 110:4: 'Thou art a priest forever after the order of Melchizedek!'

This marked the beginning of Vincent's new life as a diocesan priest in the Church of Our Lady of Sorrows in White Plains, New York. His duties included celebrating Mass on Sundays and other days, hearing confessions, anointing the sick, baptising newborns, marrying the marriageable and burying the dead.

Besides his church duties, Vincent also began teaching history to a class of Catholic boys at the nearby Archbishop Stepinac High School.

White Plains, New York, USA, 1990

The school's oldest fixture was a grizzly old janitor, Ted Callaghan. On Vincent's first day at school, Ted had cornered him in the schoolyard. 'Father, can I ask you a few questions regarding some serious matters that have been bothering me?' asked Ted slyly.

Without waiting for an answer, Ted plodded on, 'You see, the Bible's Leviticus 15:19-24 tells me that I am allowed no contact with a woman while she is in her period of menstrual uncleanliness. Problem is, how do I tell? I have tried asking, but most women take offence!'

Vincent chuckled.

Ted, blowing an ugly puff of acrid smoke from a cheap cigar, continued with his 'serious' issues. 'Also, Father, Exodus 21:7 allows me to sell my daughter into slavery. What do you think would be a fair price?'

Vincent was getting the idea.

Pretty much oblivious to Vincent's reactions, Ted went on, 'Leviticus 25:44 also says that I may possess slaves, both male and female, provided that they're from neighbouring countries. Do you think this applies to both Mexicans and Canadians?'

By now Vincent was laughing uncontrollably. Ted paused for effect and then continued, 'I have a neighbour who insists on working on the Sabbath. Exodus 35:2 clearly states that he should be put to death. Am I morally obliged to kill him?'[18]

Ted had reached the climax of his joke and guffawed loudly as he delivered his punch line while dramatically brandishing the now dead cigar stub in his hand. Vincent couldn't help doubling up with laughter. From that day onwards, Ted and Vincent were firm friends.

White Plains, New York, USA, 2006

They would remain friends for the next sixteen years that

Vincent remained ensconced in his uneventful little world. However, things were about to change.

'So when we think of Abraham Lincoln as the sixteenth President of the United States, we often forget that he worked on a riverboat, ran a store, thought about becoming a blacksmith and studied law. We tend to forget that he was unsuccessful in many of his pursuits. He lost several law cases, failed in his effort to become the Republican Party's vice-presidential nominee, and lost again when he ran against Stephen Douglas for the US Senate. The important thing to remember is that he didn't let these defeats stop him. He ran for President in 1860 and won,' concluded Vincent.[19]

The boys were impatiently waiting to get up. The bell announcing lunch break had sounded a full thirty seconds earlier, but Vincent's concluding remarks had overrun. He hastily picked up his books and headed to the staff lounge, where stale coffee awaited him.

The lousy coffee was a small price to pay for a job that he now loved. There was nothing more refreshing than opening up young minds. Moreover, he was passionate about his subject. This passion allowed him to transport his young audience into times bygone with flair. It was no wonder that Vincent had become one of the most admired teachers at Stepinac High.

Vincent had been able to settle down in Westchester quite easily. His parishioners at the church were decent people and his flock continued to grow along with his own stature within the diocese. His casual and comfortable style had immediately put people at ease within the first months of his arrival.

After one of his Sunday sermons, one of the middle-aged male attendees had come up to him and had congratulated him for a 'short and sweet sermon, so unlike the long and boring ones' delivered by his predecessor. Vincent had quickly retorted that a sermon was meant to be like a woman's skirt, long enough to cover the essentials and short enough to keep one interested! The word had soon got around that the new boy was actually quite a lot of fun, in spite of being celibate!

The coffee that greeted him was stale but hot. He had just settled down in one of the armchairs in the lounge and opened his newspaper, when janitor-of-the-year Ted Callaghan walked in.

'Phone for you, Vincent,' he said.

Vincent looked up and asked, 'Who's calling?'

'Dunno. Probably some chick that you blessed with holy water,' chuckled Ted.

Vincent ignored the sarcasm and got up to take the call at the phone located near the lounge entrance. He picked up the receiver and spoke, 'Hello?'

'Is that Mr Vincent Sinclair?' asked the female voice at the other end.

'Yes, it is. Who's calling?'

'I'm Dr Joan Silver from Lenox Hill Hospital. I'm afraid I have some bad news for you.'

Vincent was immediately alert. He knew that something was seriously wrong. He pressed on, 'Please do go on.'

'Mr Sinclair, this morning at around 8 am, a car accident took place. Your father died on the spot, I'm afraid. Your mother suffered head wounds but by the time she arrived here, it was too late. She was dead, too.'

Father Vincent Matthew Sinclair let go of the receiver and knelt down to pray, but he was unable to; all he could do was weep.

⚕

Queens, New York, USA, 2006

In 1852, a city law forbade burials within Manhattan. Manhattanites could be born in Manhattan, could study or work in Manhattan, could get married in Manhattan, could die in Manhattan, but could not be buried in Manhattan.[20]

The rain made the burial a rather messy affair. Both Matthew and Julia Sinclair were to be buried in St John Cemetery in Queens County, where they would join Vincent's paternal grandparents, who had also been buried there.

The presence of Vincent's aunt, Martha, was of great comfort to him. Martha was the significantly younger sister of Vincent's father, Matthew, and had been more of a friend than an aunt to Vincent.

Martha Sinclair had remained a spinster. At the age of thirty-two, she had given up a career in interior design so she could pursue her study of Iyengar Yoga in India. Her travels in India and Nepal had lasted for three whole years and she had grown fond of the subcontinent. This had been followed by a few years in England, where she had become a practitioner of past-life healing, working in the Spiritualist Association of Great Britain.

After spending another year back in India, she had returned rather reluctantly to New York to set up her own yoga academy. Her tryst with India had opened up her mind to philosophy, religion, meditation and spirituality; this fact made her seem eccentric to most men.

She now stood next to Vincent, trying to be the best comfort possible in his grief.

Vincent stood silently in prayer with folded hands, ignoring the rain pouring down his face as his friend and colleague, Father Thomas Manning, read from Psalm 23:4, 'Yea, though I walk through the valley of the shadow of death, I will fear no evil for Thou art with me.'

Vincent's eyes were closed in prayer-induced stupor. Everyone was holding umbrellas and trying as best as possible to stay dry. The light showers were becoming ugly and there were occasional flashes of lightning in the skies above the cemetery. The coffins were being lowered into the ground. Vincent's eyes were tightly shut. He was merely following the words being recited by Father Thomas.

'Daughters of Jerusalem, stop weeping for me! On the contrary, weep for yourselves and for your children!' Vincent snapped out of his trance and opened his eyes wide. These words were totally out of place for a funeral.

The words were not from Father Thomas. His Bible was closed and his lips were not moving. The prayer was already over. Who had said that?

Flash! He felt a camera flash bulb go off inside his head. *'Eloi, Eloi, lema sabachthani?* Vincent was in a daze. Was he hearing things? Was he going mad?

Flash! *Jerusalem. Why was he holding a wooden cross?* Flash! *Wailing women. 'Impale him! Impale him!'* Flash! *Blood. 'Eloi, Eloi, lema sabachthani?* The scenes were flashing through Vincent's head at a dizzying pace, much like a silent movie reel.

Vincent stood pale and frozen. He then bent over while standing and drew both his arms close to his right shoulder. He resembled a man carrying a heavy wooden object on his right shoulder. *Simon! Alexander! Rufus!* What were these names? Vincent fell awkwardly to the ground.

Sympathetic friends assumed that grief had overtaken the young man and attempted to help him up and comfort him.

Vincent had passed out.

The Biblical passage of Mark 15:34 of the New Testament reads as follows:

And at the ninth hour, Jesus shouted in a loud voice, *'Eloi, Eloi, lema sabachthani?* which is translated as 'My God, my God, for what have you forsaken me?'

Vincent woke up in a brightly lit room of Queens Hospital Center. He first saw the anxious face of Father Thomas Manning. He then saw a nurse standing with his Aunt Martha. Next he saw the white light fixture on the ceiling.

An intravenous line was attached to his arm. Patches were attached to his torso to monitor his heart rate, blood pressure and lung function.

Vincent was mumbling incoherently. Father Thomas put his ear close to Vincent's face to understand what he was trying to

say. He was uttering a few words sporadically. '. . .impressed . . .
service . . . passer-by . . . Simon . . . Cyrene . . . country . . . the
father . . . Alexander . . . Rufus . . . lift . . . torture . . . stake . . .'

Father Thomas immediately recognised the Biblical passage
that spoke of Jesus's journey through the streets of Jerusalem
on his way to Golgotha to be crucified. Since Jesus had become
physically too weak after the trauma that he had endured, the
Romans had ordered a man called Simon to help him bear the
burden of the cross.

The passage that Vincent seemed to be muttering was: 'Also,
they impressed into service a passer-by, a certain Simon of
Cyrene, coming from the country, the father of Alexander and
Rufus, that he should lift up his torture stake.'

Why was Vincent sputtering these words? 'Relax, Vincent.
You have been subjected to trauma, shock and exhaustion. You
need rest. You collapsed at the cemetery and we had to bring
you here to recuperate,' began Father Thomas.

Vincent couldn't care less. His shoulder was hurting. His
arms were aching. He could hear screams and jeers. He was
sweating. He was walking on blood! He was carrying a cross!

Aunt Martha was lying down on the sofa in the hospital
room when Vincent stirred. The doctor had prescribed Dalmane
shots to ensure that he slept calmly. It was around eleven in the
morning.

'Good morning, sweetheart,' said Aunt Martha as she
sat up on the sofa. Even though she had been up all night,
Martha still looked fresh. The years of yoga and meditation had
obviously helped her; she certainly did not look to be in her
mid-forties. Her youthful skin, auburn hair, pert nose and her
well-toned 34-24-34 figure ensured that she did not look a
day over thirty-five.

Vincent responded. 'Hi, Nana. What's happened to me?
Am I sick?' Martha was relieved to hear Vincent calling her by

the name that Matthew's entire family had for her—Nana. It obviously meant that Vincent was recovering. Martha got up from the sofa and walked to the side of the bed.

'You had a shock during the funeral, Vincent. You passed out. Poor baby, you've been in and out of consciousness for the past two days. We couldn't feed you through your mouth so we had to nourish you intravenously.'

Vincent thought back to the funeral and said, 'Nana, where's Father Thomas? I need to speak to him.'

Martha replied, 'He was here last night, baby. He left rather late. I think he'll come back to see you around lunchtime. What did you need to ask him?'

'Nana, I think I'm going crazy. At the funeral, before I fainted, I thought I saw visions. They were so real it was scary. I was even more scared because I thought I saw myself in some of the pictures that flashed before my eyes,' said Vincent.

Martha held Vincent's hand as she said, 'Vincent, sometimes when we confront shocks in our lives, they tend to electrify portions of our brain that we normally don't use. This can sometimes bring older memories to the forefront, memories that have been long suppressed.'

'This wasn't an older memory, Nana. I have never been to Jerusalem, yet I could see it in vivid detail. This wasn't a memory. It was something else . . . I just can't explain it. The scary bit is that I saw myself carrying the cross of Jesus!'

Martha looked straight into Vincent's eyes and asked, 'It could be your imagination . . . As a priest you have read virtually everything there is to learn about Jesus. Some of those stored facts could trigger visualisations. Possible, isn't it?'

'You're absolutely right, Nana. It's the shock that's causing hallucinations. It's nothing for us to really worry about,' said Vincent, just about convincing himself.

Martha rang the bell at Vincent's side so the nurse could sponge him and arrange for some breakfast. Though she didn't comment any further, she couldn't but help remember Vincent as a small boy standing next to the sweet little Kate, mumbling something in another language that only she had been able to understand.

'Talitha koum. Talitha koum. Talitha koum.'

New York City, USA, 2012

It had now been six years since his parents' death. Martha Sinclair and Vincent Sinclair were sitting together in the trendy York Avenue studio of Martha's yoga academy. Since Vincent had been discharged from hospital six years ago, Martha had succeeded in convincing him that he needed to recharge himself by practising Pranayama, the ancient yogic science of breathing.[21]

Since the passing of his parents, Vincent had made it a point to visit Aunt Martha each week. He looked forward to these visits because she was a lot of fun. Moreover, she was the only real family he had left.

Aunt and nephew were sitting with legs crossed facing one another. The classic yogic position called Padmasan was not as easy as Nana had made it out to be. The right foot had to be under the left knee, and the left foot was to be kept under the right knee. Easier said than done!

'Breathing is life. But how much do we notice it? For example, do you observe or notice that you use only one nostril at a time to breathe?' said Martha to her student. Vincent was sceptical.

Martha quickly continued, 'At any given moment, only the right or left nostril will be breathing for you. Did you know that the active nostril changes approximately every ninety minutes during the twenty-four-hour day? It's only for a short period that both nostrils breathe together. The ancient Indian yogis knew all this and much more. They discovered and explored the intimate relationship between one's breath and one's mind. They knew that when the mind is agitated, breathing almost certainly gets disturbed. They also knew that if one's breath were held too long, the mind would have a tendency to get disturbed.

Since the yogis were fundamentally attempting to control the mind, they figured that controlling the breath could possibly regulate the mind,' she concluded.

She had succeeded in holding his interest. Slowly but surely, Vincent Sinclair began to learn how to breathe and relax.

Not for long.

ॐ

Central Park covers 843 acres or around 6 per cent of Manhattan. The park stretches from 59th Street in the south, to 110th Street at the northern end, and from 5th Avenue on the east side, to 8th Avenue on the west.

As a child, Vincent had loved visiting the Central Park Zoo. In later adult years, he had enjoyed attending performances at the park's Delacorte Theatre and indulging in the occasional culinary treat at the park's most famous restaurant, Tavern on the Green.

Martha's regimen of yoga and meditation was working wonders for him and he was feeling energetic as he headed for a quiet spot in the park's Reservoir. The Reservoir, located in the heart of Central Park, was quite a distance away from any of the bordering streets and was one of the most tranquil areas within the park. It was here that Vincent found a bench to try out the Vipassana techniques that Martha had been teaching him for the past few months.[22]

In Pali, the original language of Buddhism, Vipassana meant 'insight'. It was also more commonly used to describe one of India's most ancient meditation techniques, which had been rediscovered by the Buddha.

Vincent sat down on the bench and then drew up his legs so that he could assume the Padmasan position that Nana had taught him. He then closed his eyes and began to focus on his breathing. Inhale. Exhale. As he settled into a relaxed state of mind there was a familiar flash! The same damn flash from the funeral six years ago!

Damn! Vincent thought. I thought that the craziness was over and done with!

Blood. Flash! *Wounded soldiers . . . bandages.* Flash! *A blood-red cross with equal arms.* Flash! *A Bassano portrait . . . an elegant lady.* Flash! *A stately house . . . reception rooms on the ground and first floors.* Flash! *Number 18.* Flash! *London streets.* Flash! *Iron fencing . . . an 'S' logo.* Flash! *Indian antiques.* Flash! *Parties, food, musicians, soldiers.* Flash! *An old LaSalle ambulance.* Flash! *Buckingham Palace.* Flash! *Bell . . . Grave . . . so soon?*

What was that? Vincent opened his eyes in mortal fear. Why was this happening to him? *Bell . . . Grave . . . so soon?* What in heaven's name did that mean? Was he to die? Was this a premonition? And why was he seeing images of London streets and stately homes? Vincent Sinclair was convinced more than ever that he was going mad.

He got up and started running wildly. Luckily he was on the periphery of the reservoir of Central Park, which was mainly used by joggers.

No one found it odd to see him running. They thought he was running to exercise himself. How could they possibly know that he was running from himself?

'Help me, Nana4. I'm going stark, raving mad. Either that, or I'm possessed. Do you think I should call Father Thomas Manning for an exorcism? What is wrong with me? Why am I seeing strange things and hearing strange words?' Vincent was on the verge of hysteria.

Nana realised she needed to calm him down. 'Relax, sweetheart. It isn't uncommon to have recollections of events, things, people or places that are hidden in our brains. In fact, it isn't strange to remember past lives either. Unfortunately, you're a Catholic priest . . . how on earth can I possibly discuss past life issues with you when you have closed your mind to such possibilities?'

Vincent's eyes widened. 'You think I could be having past-life recollections? But surely that's nonsense, Nana. The Bible says it is appointed unto men to die once, and after death comes judgement.'

'Listen, Vincent, I know I will always be the eccentric, esoteric, Eastern philosophy-espousing crazy aunt to you, but isn't it possible that what you have learnt so far is not the whole truth? Isn't it possible that there are things that you are yet to learn?' asked Martha rather innocently.

'Sure, Nana, but I can't question my faith. My faith is all that I have.'

Martha said, 'Okay. Let me try to help you see things my way. We all know the bit from the Bible about the blind man . . . you know, the bit when Jesus's disciples asked him: "Rabbi, who has sinned, this man or his parents, that he should be born blind?" Tell me, Vincent, why would the disciples have asked this question if there was no belief in a past life? Huh?'

Vincent remained silent in thought.

Martha continued, 'You probably remember the passage where Jesus says: "I tell you the truth, no one can see the kingdom of God unless he is born again." Tell me, sweetheart, how is it possible to be born again unless you have more than one life?'

Vincent was ready with arguments of his own.

'Nana, the fact that the disciples asked Jesus about the reasons for the blind man's condition only means that reincarnation as a concept was alive in his era. It does not mean that Jesus believed in it. Also, when Jesus talked about being born again he was referring to spiritual awakening, not birth in the literal sense.'[23]

Martha was just as determined to have her way. She countered defiantly, 'So what else do you think can explain your strange visions and flashes?'

Vincent was quiet. He really didn't have a logical answer.

'May I suggest something? Sometimes, a past-life memory can be triggered by a place or an object. Is there something that you can recall from your recent flashes?'

'The only thing I can recall seeing in today's visions is Buckingham Palace. I've never been there . . . but I've seen it on postcards. Let me think . . . what else? At Mom and Dad's funeral, I remember seeing flashes of Jerusalem—at least I think it was Jerusalem. The rest of the stuff that I saw can't really be pinned down to a definite place.'

Martha quickly cut in. 'I think it's time you and your aunt had a vacation in London. What do you say, Vincent?' She winked at him, a wide grin on her face.

'I thought I was the crazy one! Are you out of your mind, Nana? I don't believe in this past life nonsense. In any case, I can't afford it; I'm a priest, remember? We don't really earn all that much!'

'Oh shut up, Vincent! Your Nana has made some serious money from her Eastern mumbo-jumbo. I'm paying. So you damn well get your holy ass on that blessed flight, Father Vincent Sinclair!'

Chapter Six

Harare, Zimbabwe, 1965

Terry Acton was born on 11 November, the very day that Ian Smith, Prime Minister of Rhodesia, made a unilateral declaration of independence for the country.

Terry's father had moved to Rhodesia from England upon being offered a position at the De Beers Mining Company. He had married the daughter of his British supervisor a year after moving and had decided to make Rhodesia his home. Terry had been born two years later.

Unfortunately, Rhodesia was in turmoil. The government of Prime Minister Ian Smith was a white minority running an apartheid regime. The country was in civil war with the rebels being led by Robert Mugabe, who eventually seized power in 1980.

Mugabe's regime was one of corruption, sleaze, torture, and dictatorship.[24] The Actons were forced to leave the country and return to England in 1991.

London, UK, 1991

Terry's parents ended up losing their lifesavings when they fled Zimbabwe. Circumstances made them poor East-Enders, living in the working-class borough of Hackney.

The economy was in recession and Terry's father was lucky to get a blue-collar factory job at Lesney's. Lesney's factory was located in Hackney Wick, and produced Matchbox toys such as miniature cars and trucks. Lesney's was the main employer in the area; in fact, it was pretty much the only employer in the area.[25]

Senior Acton had not taken the knocks well. He became an obnoxious, red-nosed drunk who excelled at beating his wife often and his kids occasionally, depending upon the level of alcohol in his bloodstream. Little Terry was a frail and frightened little boy who suffered from asthma, a chronic respiratory condition that weakened him further.

Terry's mother was an angel from heaven who somehow managed to lock away her emotional and physical scars to produce the finest Yorkshire pudding, rhubarb crumble and shepherd's pie in England for her son. Terry loved returning home from school to his mother, but he hated his father coming home.

He was relieved when his father shot himself when the Lesney's factory, one of the last few remaining businesses in Hackney, shut shop and made him redundant.

Knocks in his early years would make Terry even more determined to succeed at school and eventually in life. The Rhodes Scholarship to Oxford two years later was his ticket to the future.

He silently thanked Cecil John Rhodes.

⚜

Cecil John Rhodes, the founder of the state of Rhodesia, which eventually became Zimbabwe, had made his millions by shrewdly investing in the diamond mines of southern Africa. In 1880, he had created the De Beers Mining Company, which would eventually bring him great power, fortune and recognition.[26]

In 1877, Rhodes would contend: 'We British are the finest race in the world; and that the more of the world we inhabit, the better it is for the human race.'

47

Rhodes would die young at the age of just forty-nine. In his last will and testament, he would leave his fabulous wealth to create a secret society: one that would allow Britannia to rule the world. It was projected by Rhodes that by 1920 there would be around 2,000 to 3,000 men in their prime scattered all over the globe, each having been mathematically selected to achieve the goals set out by Rhodes.

Rhodes had confided to a close friend that it was necessary to create 'a society copied . . . from the Jesuits . . . a secret society organised, like Loyola's, supported by the accumulated wealth of those whose aspiration is to do something . . . a scheme to take the government of the whole world!'

The Rhodes Scholarships, which would become very famous, would merely be a tool to recruit the most promising and bright future leaders—in whichever arena they chose to work—in politics, business, government, banking, finance, arts, science, medicine, technology or social work.

The forty-second President of the United States, Bill Clinton, would be a Rhodes Scholar. His administration alone would have more than twenty other Rhodes Scholars.

In 1993, one of the new recruits into Rhodes' secret society was Terry Acton. He was one of the youngest and brightest members of this elite group, accepted into Oxford to pursue an undergraduate degree in psychology. Another recruit was an incredibly intelligent American woman. Her name was Alissa Kaetzel.

Two years into his Oxford degree, Terry was offered the opportunity of a lifetime—a chance to obtain an advanced degree in clinical psychology at Yale. Terry grabbed it with both hands.

Alissa stayed on at Oxford to complete her M.Phil in political theory, comparative government and international relations.

New Haven, Connecticut, USA, 1993

Terry's Rhodes Scholarship had opened a new door, not only to Oxford and Yale, but also to Yale's secret society—The Order of Skull & Bones.[27]

The previous year, he had climbed to the tower of Weir Hall overlooking the Bones courtyard and had heard blood-curdling cries from within the structure as fifteen newcomers were put through their initiation.

Terry's moment had arrived on 'tap night' when fifteen seniors led by Stephen Elliot arrived outside his room and pounded on the door. When he opened his door, Stephen slammed Terry's shoulder and shouted, 'Skull and Bones: Do you accept?'

Bewildered, Terry mumbled, 'Accept.'

He had been handed a message wrapped with a black ribbon and sealed with black wax with the skull-and-crossbones emblem and the number 322. The message mentioned a time and a place for Terry to appear on initiation night.

On initiation night, he had been taken by Stephen Elliot to a special room which had a question written in German on its walls: *'Wer war der thor, wer weiser, bettler oder kaiser? Ob arm, ob reich, im tode gleich.'*

Translated, the German sentence meant: 'Who was the fool, who the wise man, beggar or king? Whether poor or rich, all's the same in death.'

The origins of that particular riddle were very old indeed. They could be traced back to 1776.

In 1776, the Bavarian Illuminati had come into being at the University of Ingolstadt in Germany. The Latin word *Illuminati* meant 'the enlightened ones'.[28]

These were people for whom the illuminating light came, not from an authoritative source such as the Church, but from elevated spiritual consciousness. The secret society would have elaborate initiation rituals. The initiate would be shown a skeleton, at the feet of which would be a crown and sword. The initiate would then be asked whether the skeleton was that of a king, nobleman or beggar. Unable to answer, the initiate would be told that it was unimportant . . . the only thing of importance was the character of being a man.

At the end of the day, all humans were merely skull and bones.

☗

Terry Acton had realised he had a 'spiritual gift' after the death of his wife, Susan.

Terry and Susan had been university sweethearts at Yale. She had been working as a waitress in Romano's, the pizza hangout for Yallies and he had tried the most ridiculous pick-up lines on her each day till she agreed to go out with him. They got married during his final year at Yale. Stephen Elliot, who had initiated Terry into Skull & Bones, had been his best man.

While Stephen had introduced Terry to Skull & Bones, Terry returned the favour by introducing Stephen to Alissa Kaetzel. Alissa returned home after completing her M.Phil from Oxford and had dropped in to meet Terry in New Haven. She had ended up staying on for two weeks after meeting Stephen Elliot.

The two couples were on a vacation in the Pocono Mountains when Terry's car swerved off a wet road. Stephen and Alissa survived along with Terry, but Susan did not.

Stephen and Alissa had been arguing about whether a woman or African–American could ever become President of the United States. Terry had been totally absorbed in the rather heated discussion and had not noticed the sharp bend in the road a few yards ahead.

Terry's life came to a standstill. He mourned the loss of Susan. He mourned the loss of the children they had planned together but did not have.

America was no longer attractive. It reminded him too much of Susan. Terry took the first available flight back to London. He did not bother to inform anyone of his decision, except for his close friend and confidant Stephen Elliot.

🔱

London, UK, 1996

Lonely and miserable in London, Terry was left with no alternative but to fill the vacuum. He began to fill it with a bottle of Bell's whisky each day.

He realised he needed discipline in life. So, he disciplined himself into walking into the Star Tavern pub at 11:30 sharp each morning.

Terry was sitting at his usual table in the Star Tavern when a young lady walked into the pub and started going up to each table and hurriedly asking the men, 'Excuse me. Is your name Terry?' After several failed attempts she finally reached Terry's table.

'Excuse me. Is your name Terry?' she enquired. Terry continued to stare at the glass in his hand and nodded his assent without looking up.

'I have a message for you from Susan,' she said.

Terry's hand dropped the glass and the whisky and ice spilled on the table. 'Who the fuck are you?' he demanded in a sudden fit of rage.

'Please listen to me. I'm not a crank. I know that Susan's dead. I work next door at the Spiritualist Association. I'm a psychic medium,' she pleaded.

'Fuck you! You sick, perverted bitch! Bugger off.'

Terry was furious. The mere mention of Susan had reopened raw, unhealed wounds.

The woman was equally determined and stood her ground. 'Listen, you pathetic drunk, I have no inclination to carry on a conversation with you. I do, however, suggest that you let Sabrina and Jonathan go to summer camp.'

With those words, the woman did an about-turn and stormed out of the pub.

Terry's jaw dropped and his throat went dry. Since the day that Susan and Terry had started planning for children they had zeroed in on two names, Sabrina and Jonathan, for their yet-to-be-born children. Susan used to joke that she would pack the children off to camp each summer so as to get some respite from motherhood, much to the consternation of Terry, who could not bear the thought of his kids ever being away from him.

No one else had ever shared this private conversation between husband and wife.

The Spiritualist Association of Great Britain, or the SAGB, sat inside a charming Victorian building in southwest London. The ninety-two-year lease had been purchased by the association in 1955 for the unbelievably low price of £24,500.[29]

The building housed several independent rooms that were bare except for two chairs facing one another in each room. One of these chairs would be used by the visitor, and the other would be occupied by any of the several psychic mediums who worked there. Each room had a glass skylight to allow energy to flow in and out of the room. The SAGB offered one-on-one sittings with psychics for spiritual healing, psychic workshops as well as regression sessions.

Terry Acton had come to the SAGB looking for the woman who had approached him in the pub. He was unable to recall her name. Actually, he was quite sure he had not even given her a chance to introduce herself.

Luckily, the SAGB lobby had a bulletin board with the names and photos of all the psychic mediums working there and he recognised her picture on it. The photo was obviously one of her at a younger age, but it was unmistakably her. Martha Sinclair.

He had gone up to the reception and hesitated. The elderly receptionist looked up and said, 'Yes? May I help you, sir?'

'Yeah. I uh . . . was wondering whether Martha Sinclair would be available for a psychic session today?' he asked.

'You're in luck. She is presently in a session that should be over in around fifteen minutes. Shall I book you for a sitting? The cost of a thirty-minute private appointment is £30,' the receptionist had added helpfully. Terry had thought about it only for a moment and then quickly shelled out the thirty pounds for the sitting with Martha.

'Could you please wait in room number six? She'll be with you shortly.'

Terry had never imagined he would be at the SAGB waiting for a psychic sitting. This was so unlike him. In a short while, Martha walked in. He had not known that this one sitting would change his life forever.

त्रिशूल

He had expected her to be mad at him for the way he had behaved at the pub. Instead, she was gentle, warm, friendly and genuinely concerned for him. By being so nice, she ended up making him feel even guiltier about his obnoxious attitude at the pub.

'Please don't be sorry,' she said to him. 'It's important to let go of your guilt. Life puts us in situations so that we can learn from them. Once we have learned, it's time to throw away the guilt and move on,' she said.

She continued. 'Everyone is endowed with psychic gifts. These gifts could be empathy, prophecy, cognition or vision. Each of us has some of these in lesser or greater quantities. They are the various ways in which psychic perception is possible. As you open yourself to these offerings, spiritual energy becomes your teacher and you become more acutely aware of your sixth sense.'

She then lowered her voice and said, 'During the past few weeks, I have been feeling the presence of a spirit which is not completely at peace. A few days ago, when I was meditating, I heard a female voice telling me that her name was Susan and that I should give a message to her husband, Terry, who was at the pub just next door,' she said. Martha paused to look into Terry's eyes for disbelief—she found none.

'She wanted me to tell you she is happy. She is in a place where she is in the midst of happiness and love. She wants you to understand that our lives on earth are merely illusions. Each life is nothing but a change of clothes. Bodies die and decay, what remains unchanged is the soul; that is eternal,' she concluded.

Terry's eyes had turned moist. He started feeling the healing touch of a soothing balm on his tired and aching spirit. Her gentle voice was comforting him, like a mother's lullaby.

Martha continued, 'She knew you would not believe me and that's why she gave me the children's names. She said you have a clean and pure heart and that you can easily help others by looking inside yourself and discovering your spiritual self.'

Martha only stopped when she saw Terry looking up at the skylight in the room, sobbing and laughing alternately, as he felt the warmth of Susan's spirit enveloping him.

༢༥

Being a student of psychology, Terry had some basic understanding of the past-life therapy pioneered by Dr Brian Weiss. However, he was quite unprepared for the regression Martha put him through a few days later.

In 1980, Dr Brian Weiss, head of the Department of Psychiatry, Mount Sinai Medical Center, in Miami Beach, had started the treatment of a patient, Catherine. Catherine was a twenty-seven-year-old woman, completely overwhelmed by moods of depression, anxieties and phobias. Weiss had used hypnosis to help bring to the surface forgotten or repressed incidents, traumas and memories from her infancy and childhood.

Catherine had not only remembered incidents from her childhood, but also successfully provided detailed descriptions from several of her eighty-six previous lives.

Catherine's phobias had eventually been eliminated because the process of recollecting her past lives had made her realise the reason for these phobias in her present life. Past-life therapy had now become a medical term.[30]

Martha wanted to heal Terry's wounds by using past-life therapy on him.

Martha said, 'Past-life therapy is a great way to heal old wounds or to understand the cause of certain ailments or developments in our present lives. For you to be able to heal anyone else, Terry, it is first necessary to heal yourself. I am going to try to make you understand how the entire process works by making you the subject. Fine?'

Terry had nodded his assent.

'Okay, let's just start by getting you comfortable, physically comfortable. Settle back in your chair and begin to relax . . . that's right . . . just . . . relax.' The voice was soothing but firm.

Terry actually began to let go and concentrate on Martha's voice. 'Look up now, and observe the skylight. You can see a little green dot on the skylight. A green dot is simply what it is. Its shape is round and its colour is green. The shape and colour are really quite irrelevant. All that I want you to do is to completely focus your concentration on that spot for a while as you continue to listen to my voice.'[31]

Martha continued, 'A peaceful, easy feeling is settling over you like a comfortable quilt. Relax. Allow yourself to drift. As you focus on the dot, something will begin to happen. The dot may move. It may change shape. It may change colour. As you notice these transformations, you will also begin to feel changes within yourself. Your eyes are tired. They're fed up of focusing on the dot. Your eyes and your eyelids want to close. That's fine.'

She continued in the same soothing voice, 'Now drift deeper with every breath you take. Feel your body getting heavier and sinking further. You're comfortable and relaxed, but you're heavy and sinking. Deeper. Deeper. Okay, now I want you to allow your mind to drift back in time . . . drift back to this morning . . . drift back to last night . . . drift back to university . . . to your high-school days . . . drift back to your infancy . . . drift back beyond your infancy . . . that's right.' Martha now began to probe with gentle questions.

'Where are you now?'

'I'm on a farm somewhere in northern India.'

'Who are you?'

'I'm a landlord. I own lots of land in the area.'

'So you're a farmer?'

'No. I only own the land. I rent it out to landless farmers who till the land and share the produce.'

'Where do you live?'

'I have a palatial house which is on the banks of a beautiful river. It has a very nice outdoor veranda where I sit and smoke a hookah.'

'What is a hookah?'

'It's a big copper pipe. My servants fill it with tobacco, saffron, cardamom, hot coals and water. I sit and smoke it all day long while gazing at the river.'

'Do you have many servants?'

'Yes. One's importance is determined by the number of servants one has and the head of cattle one owns.'

'Are you married?'

'Yes. My wife is very beautiful. We got married when we were children.'

'So you fell in love with her?'

'No. Our marriage was arranged by our families. I had to marry her because my father insisted. I was lucky that I eventually fell in love with her. I would do anything for her. I worship her . . . I am hopelessly devoted to her.'

'Do you have children?'

'Three. A daughter and two sons.'

'Do you love them?'

'Yes, but I had to give my daughter away in marriage when she was just thirteen.'

'Why?'

'Because child marriage is the norm. I love her and want her to be happy—but she's just a child! She misses me terribly.'

'What about your sons? Do you love them?'

'Yes. But the eldest one is reckless. I get very angry with him. I sometimes have to beat him to knock some sense into his head.'

'How does that make him feel?'

'I think he resents me.'

'How old are you?'

'I am quite old. I do not know my exact age because no one noted the date or time when I was born. Unfortunately, I am quite ill.'

'Why?'

'The tobacco has given me a terrible cough. It never goes. And I am hopelessly addicted to the hookah. I cannot stop smoking.'

'Do you think this could be the reason for your asthma and breathing disorders in your present life as Terry?'

'Yes. Probably.'

'Why are you addicted?'

'I have been under a great deal of pressure. My youngest son is a teacher and has written a book questioning the caste system of the Hindu religion. Many Brahmins and priests have turned against him.'

'What is this *caste* that you talk about?'

'Hindus believe that your position in society is determined by birth. Many people are treated unfairly due to this. Untouchability is a direct consequence of this system.'

'You must be very proud of your son for having written about the problem.'

'No. I dissuaded him from doing it. Why rake up contro-versies? Let sleeping dogs lie. He is very upset with me.'

'Do you see any familiar faces from your present life?'

'Yes.'

'Who?'

'My mother, in my present life as Terry . . . she was my wife in my previous life.'

'Anyone else?'

'My father in my present life . . . he was my eldest son in my previous life—the one I used to hit quite often.'

'Any other faces that look familiar?'

'Susan. My wife in my present life.'

'Who is she in your previous life?'

'She was my daughter in my previous life—I arranged to have her married off to someone when she was just thirteen! Poor kid!'

'What can you learn from all this?'

'My mother gave me intense love in my present life. It was because I had intensely loved her when she was my wife in my previous life. She was merely returning the favour.'

'And?'

'I used to take out my anger on my eldest son in a previous life by hitting him. He became my father in my present life to teach me how dreadful it feels to be at the receiving end of a parent's anger.'

'Anything else?'

'I ensured that my daughter was parted from me at an early age as a result of her early child marriage. She became my wife, Susan, in my present lifetime. She taught me the intense sorrow and despair of separation—through her early death.'

'Anything that your younger son taught you? You know, the one who wrote about the evils of caste discrimination.'

'One should never let sleeping dogs lie.'

London, UK, 2012

Professor Terry Acton looked unkempt. His hair was finger-combed and his face had a permanently unshaven look. His jeans and sweater had certainly seen better days. Strangely enough, all of this only enhanced his appeal to the opposite sex. There was pain in his eyes and this seemed to make him more attractive to women.

The sixteen years since that fateful day of his session with Martha Sinclair had produced positive healing for Terry Acton.

Terry had decided to use his background in psychology and combine it with past-life therapy and a comparative study of religion at the Spiritualist Association. Terry had first started out by being a spiritual medium. He then mastered the art of hypnosis. He moved on to practise regression when Martha moved back to New York to start her yoga academy.

After his first few sessions with Martha, Terry began attending lectures on spirituality at the Department for the Study of Religions at the University of London. His teachers awoke Terry's interest in religion and spirituality. This eventually led to a prestigious teaching assignment at the university.

Today, Terry was delivering a lecture on Hinduism and its twin pillars of reincarnation and karma.

'It's impossible to place a date on the origin of Hinduism, but even way back in 4000 BC, it was being practised in the Indus Valley. Hinduism is the third largest religion in the world with approximately 940 million followers,' started Terry.[32]

Without consulting any notes, he continued. 'Hinduism is similar to many world religions. For example, the Holy Trinity exists in Hinduism. The trinity is that of Brahma the creator, Vishnu the preserver, and Shiva the destroyer. The Trinity is also repeated in the divine Hindu Mother Goddess, with Lakshmi, Saraswati and Kali being three manifestations of the supreme feminine force. Hindu mythology has an abundance of gods. This is quite similar to the ancient Greek and Roman mythologies. However, unlike the Greeks or Romans, Hindus hold the view that all their gods are merely different manifestations of the same supreme God. Thus, Hinduism is mono-theistic, not polytheistic.

'Hinduism talks of Brahman, or the one supreme and divine entity. The fundamental belief is that every living thing has a soul which is connected to the greater being, Brahman. Hindus believe that they have eternal life due to their fundamental belief in reincarnation.' Terry noticed a student in the front looking sceptical. He paused and asked, 'Any questions?'

The sceptical one raised her hand and said, 'Professor Acton, in your recently published book you have said that the word *reincarnation* is derived from the word *carnate,* which translates into *flesh.* Therefore, *incarnate* means *entering the flesh* and hence *reincarnate* means *re-entering the flesh.* You say that the soul enters the body at birth and leaves the body upon death, and that this is a continuous cycle. Why? What is the purpose of such a cycle?'

Terry smiled at the rather lengthy but fundamental question and replied, 'With each life, the soul learns something more until the soul reaches the stage of Mukti, or complete enlighten-ment. This is the goal that all Hindus must work towards. At the stage of Mukti, which happens after many lifetimes, the soul is reunited with Brahman. Now, you may ask, what determines when and where a soul is reborn?

'This brings us to the theory of karma. Karma literally means *deed,* and as a theory it outlines the cause-and-effect nature of life. Karma is not to be confused with fate. Man has free will and creates his destiny based upon his actions. The most dramatic illustration of karma is found in the Hindu epic, the *Mahabharata.* The Hindu concept of karma was also adopted by other religions, such as Buddhism.[33]

'The theory of karma is not really crazy when one thinks about it. Almost all religions have at some point of time in their histories believed in reincarnation—including Christianity. References to reincarnation in the New Testament were deleted only in the fourth century when Christianity became the official religion of the Roman Empire. It was sometime in the year

AD 553 that the second Council of Constantinople declared reincarnation as heresy. These decisions were intended to increase the power of the Church by making people believe that their salvation depended solely on the Church.'[34]

Chapter Seven

'*Tah-shi de-leh. Khe-rahng ku-su de-bo yin-peh?*' asked the leader of the search party. Little Tenzin Gyatso looked up innocently and replied, '*La yin. Ngah sug-po de-bo yin.*'[35]

Dalai Lamas were manifestations of Buddha who chose to take rebirth in order to serve other human beings. The thirteenth Dalai Lama had died in 1933. The Tibetan Government had not only to appoint a successor but also to search for and discover the reincarnation of the thirteenth Dalai Lama.[36]

In 1935, the Regent of Tibet travelled to a sacred lake near Lhasa. The regent looked into the waters and saw a vision of a monastery with a jade-green and gilded roof and a house with turquoise tiles.

Soon, search parties were sent out to all parts of Tibet to search for a place that resembled the vision. One of the search parties went east to the Tibetan village of Amdo, where they found a house with turquoise tiles sitting dwarfed by the hilltop Karma monastery. The monastery had a jade-green and gilded roof.

The leader of the search went into the house and found the child, Tenzin Gyatso, playing inside. He had been born to his parents on 6 July 1935.

'Hello. How are you?' asked the leader of the search party to little Tenzin Gyatso in Tibetan. Tenzin looked up innocently and replied, 'I am fine.' Then the little boy immediately and authoritatively demanded the rosary that the leader of the search was wearing. It was a rosary that had belonged to the thirteenth Dalai Lama.

※

Born to a peasant family, His Holiness Tenzin Gyatso was recognised at the age of two, in accordance with Tibetan tradition, as the reincarnation of his predecessor the thirteenth Dalai Lama. The tradition of wise elders seeking out the reincarnation of their spiritual leaders had continued through the ages. In fact, a similar search had been carried out in Bethlehem in 7 BC by three wise men.

※

Bethlehem, Judea, 7 BC

A triple conjunction of Jupiter and Saturn in a given year was very rare indeed. This conjunction, in which the two planets seemed to almost touch one another, occurred on 29 May, 3 October and finally on 5 December in the year 7 BC.[37] The three Buddhist wise men observing this astronomical miracle were convinced. A reincarnation had indeed arrived on earth and it was finally time to meet Him. They would then need to convince themselves that He was indeed the one they were looking for. They would then embark on the task of preparing Him for His mission in this life. They needed to visit Jerusalem.

※

Jerusalem, Judea, 5 BC

King Herod was livid; Judea was impossible to rule. To add fuel to the fire, there were these three strangers who claimed they had seen Jupiter and Saturn kiss each other in the heavens and thought it was some idiotic celestial signal. Damn them!

They now wanted to find a two-year-old boy who was supposedly an incarnate of some spiritual leader or the other from India. They wanted to take him back so that he could be schooled by them. Damn them!

He hated the fact that he was forced to be a friend and ally of the Roman Empire. He hated being looked down upon by the Jews because of his Arab mother. At times, he even hated Octavian and Mark Antony for putting him in charge of Judea in the first place, even though he had wanted so desperately to be king. Damn them all![38]

And then it struck him! Kill all the two-year-olds that he could find. At least it would give him something to do. Damn them all!

'Kill them,' said Herod to his generals.

Cairo, Egypt, 5 BC

'Kill him,' said the governor of Cairo. He had heard that the little boy had entered the temple of Bastet, the lion goddess, and that the idols had just crumbled to the ground before him. He was quite certainly evil.

After Herod's decision to kill all two-year-olds, the boy's parents had realised that the only way to save his life was to flee from Bethlehem to Egypt. They had made their way from Bethlehem to Rafah, on to Al-Arish, further on to Farama and then on to Tel Basta.[39] This was the city of the lion goddess Bastet. When the child had entered the temple of the lion goddess, the ground had shaken and the idols of the temple had crumbled in submission before him.

The family had then proceeded to old Cairo where they took refuge in a cave. When the governor of the region heard the stories of crumbling idols in Tel Basta, he started planning the boy's murder and this prompted the family's premature departure to Maadi.

They went on board a sailboat that took them to Deir Al-Garnous. From here the family moved on to Gabal Al-Kaf and rested in a cave before heading towards Qussqam, home to the Al-Moharraq monastery.

This was one among many monasteries in Egypt that would play a role in the boy's education.

Egypt, AD 4

The little boy who had fled with his parents from Judea did not know that he owed his education to developments that had taken place 200 years earlier.

A mystical revolution had happened among the Jews of Egypt and Palestine about two centuries before. In Egypt, these mystics called themselves 'Therapeuts' and their spiritual counterparts in Palestine called themselves 'Nazarenes' and 'Essenes'.

The Therapeuts, Nazarenes and Essenes had remarkable similarities to Buddhists. For example, they were vegetarians; they abstained from wine; they chose to remain celibate; they lived monastic lives in caves; they opposed animal sacrifice; they considered poverty to be a virtue; they worked towards attaining knowledge through fasting and extended periods of silence; they wore simple white robes; and they initiated novices through baptism in water.

The origins of ritual immersion in water were Indian. Two millennia later, one would still see millions of Hindus practising this ancient rite each day on the banks of their sacred river, the Ganges.[40]

The boy's teachers were experts. Many of them had extraordinary powers, such as those of levitation, clairvoyance, teleportation and healing. The fruits of their labours were similar to the results achieved by exponents of yoga in ancient India. The boy was made to study various ancient texts in preparation for his future studies in India.

Many of the teachings in those texts had arrived in Egypt because of a brutal murder that had taken place in India in 265 BC.

Kalinga, Northeast India, 265 BC

'Murderer! Killer of innocents! You are the devil incarnate!' the crazy old woman cried while sobbing uncontrollably. She was old and haggard; dried tears caked her face and her hair was strewn across her features like that of a witch. In her lap was the body of a young boy, probably her grandson, who had been killed by Emperor Ashoka's army.

Ashoka, the emperor of Maghada, had killed 1,00,000 people in a massive show of strength when he invaded and overran the neighbouring kingdom of Kalinga in eastern India.[41]

War over, Ashoka had ventured out into the city. Corpses littered the streets. Once happy homes lay completely destroyed. 'What have I done?' thought Ashoka. This was far too high a price to pay for victory. Enough of war; his future conquests would be those in quest of love and peace.

The great king converted to Buddhism and decided to spread its message of peace, compassion, non-violence and love to every person in his kingdom, and beyond.

Among the recipients of Ashoka's missionaries of love and peace would be King Ptolemy II Philadelphus of Egypt.

Egypt, 258 BC

Ptolemy II Philadelphus sat on the throne. Next to him sat his wife and sister. In fact, his wife was his sister.

He was listening to missionaries who had been sent by the Indian King Ashoka to spread the word of some man who called himself the Buddha.[42]

They called themselves Theravada monks. Curiously, Egypt would soon become home to a set of monks with a name that was suspiciously similar—they would be known as the Therapeutae. These were the famous reclusive monks of Egypt, devoted to poverty, celibacy, good deeds and compassion; everything that the Buddha, who was also known as Muni Sakya, stood for.

Ptolemy II could not have possibly known that 500 years later, the great Egyptian port of Alexandria would have its own Muni Sakya—Ammonius Saccas.

2️⃣

Alexandria, Egypt, AD 240

Ammonius Saccas was dying. After many years of study and meditation, he had opened his school of philosophy in Alexandria. The school lived on but he was fading. History would record his name as Ammonius Saccas. His name was derived, in fact, from Muni Sakya, the Buddha's commonly accepted name.

His most famous pupil would be Origen, one of the earliest fathers of the Christian Church. Origen's writings on reincarnation would be considered heresy by the Church three centuries later.

Ammonius Saccas was a follower of Pythagoras. Pythagoreans were philosophers, mathematicians and geometricians. They were famous for their belief in the transmigration of souls. They would perform purification rituals and would follow ascetic, dietary and moral rules, which would allow their souls to improve their ranking.

Of course, Ammonius Saccas could not possibly have considered the fact that Pythagoras had derived a great deal of his knowledge from an Indian sage who had lived in 800 BC.

2️⃣

India, 800 BC

Baudhayana, the great Indian sage, was sitting in the forest attempting to figure out the right dimensions for the holy fire. The fire would burn inside a specially constructed square altar. Into this fire would be poured milk, curds, honey, clarified butter, flowers, grain, and holy water as offerings to the gods. He was attempting to figure out the resultant effect on the area of the altar as a result of changes in the dimensions of the square. His mind was calm, but one could almost hear the humming of the machinery inside his head. Yes! He had it. He wrote carefully, 'The rope which is stretched along the length of the diagonal of a rectangle produces an area which the vertical and horizontal sides make together.'[43]

Around 250 years later, a mathematician and philosopher from the Greek island of Samos would further revise the theory propounded by Baudhayana. He would write the Pythagorean Theorem as: 'The square of the hypotenuse equals the sum of the squares of the sides.'[44]

Five hundred years later, a Gnostic school in Aegea would be solely focused on teaching Pythagorean theories. A branch of the Essenes, the Koinobi, would teach the philosophy of Pythagoras in Egypt. A Gnostic college in Ephesus would be flourishing where the principles and secrets of Buddhism, Zoroastrianism and the Chaldean system of mystical numerology would be taught along with Platonic philosophy. While in Alexandria, the Therapeutae would spend lifetimes in meditation and contemplation; the Essenes and Nazarenes would be perpetuating many of these schools of thought back home in Palestine.

By the time the boy who had fled Judea was ready for school, Gnosis, or the ancient wisdom of self-knowledge, would be flourishing in Gnostic groups and mystery schools all over Egypt. The boy would be able receive his education in some of the best Gnostic schools of the time. It wouldn't matter whether they followed Pythagorean, Chaldean, Platonic, Essene, Therapeut, or Nazarene teachings, or anything else. The fundamental knowledge would be derived from the same source: Buddhism.[45]

It would remain buried thereafter till 1947.

Qumran, Israel, 1947

'Stupid goat!' muttered Muhammed. The damned goat had wandered inside the cave and Muhammed picked up a stone to pelt it in order to bring the dumb animal running out. This stone was about to make him famous.

In 1947, a young shepherd by the name of Muhammed edh-Dhib threw a stone into a cave in an effort to coax a wandering goat out of it. His stone flew inside and ended up striking a ceramic vessel. This vessel was just one among many earthen clay jars that contained ancient scrolls that would later come to be known as the 'Dead Sea Scrolls'. Subsequent efforts by the local Bedouins and archaeologists would recover 900 documents during the period between 1947 and 1956. Based on carbon dating, it would soon be established that the scrolls had been written between the first century BC and second century AD.[46]

The scrolls were quite obviously from the library of a Jewish sect and may have been hidden away during the Jewish–Roman war in AD 66. It is believed that this sect was that of the Essenes. Christian theologians would be quite perplexed to discover that most of the Beatitudes in the Sermon on the Mount, which were attributed to Jesus, were already present in the Dead Sea Scrolls, many of which had been written several years before Jesus lived.[47]

This seemed to indicate that much of the knowledge imparted by Jesus to his disciples had emerged from earlier works of the Essenes; who themselves had derived significant spiritual wisdom from Buddhism.

It was this spiritual wisdom that had been reflected in the Gnostic gospels discovered in Egypt in 1945.

Nag Hammadi, Egypt, 1945

'*Shukran li-l-láh!* Thanks be to Allah!' cried Muhammad as he saw the jar that was buried in the ground.

His brother Khalifa-Ali watched curiously. '*Tawakkaltu `ala-l-lláh!* But what if this contains an evil genie that pops out and destroys us?' he asked.

It was a hot December day in Upper Egypt. The two peasants, Muhammad and Khalifa-Ali, had been digging for fertiliser and had stumbled upon an old but large earthenware jar. They were hoping to find hidden treasure but were scared that the jar would contain a bad spirit!

'*In shá' Alláh*, it will be all right!' said Muhammad as he eagerly opened the jar, only to be disappointed as well as relieved. While he was disappointed that the jar did not contain treasure, he was also relieved that it did not contain any form of magic. The jar contained around a dozen old papyrus books bound in golden-brown leather. These had been placed there hundreds of years before. The fifty-two sacred texts contained in the jar were the long-lost Gnostic texts that had been written several hundred years previously in the earliest days of Christianity.[48]

The Gospel of Mary Magdalene. The Gospel of Thomas. The Gospel of Judas. The Gospel of Philip. Gospels that would be shut out by the Church fathers, in the same way that they had tried to shut out Dmitriy Novikov.

Paris, France, 1899

Dmitriy Novikov just couldn't believe it! He was finally being accepted into the Societé d'Histoire Diplomatique, the most exclusive and famous association of celebrated historians, writers, and diplomats. He could not believe that he was here among them all; he was both proud and relieved. He couldn't but help think back a dozen years to 1887 when he had discovered the ancient Issa manuscripts in Ladakh.

After his discovery, his intention had been to immediately publish the manuscripts. The archbishop of Paris had tried desperately to dissuade Dmitriy from doing so. Dmitriy had then gone to Italy to seek the opinion of a high-ranking cardinal, who had been equally and vehemently opposed to any such publication.

Dmitriy had, however, remained steadfast, and succeeded in getting a French publisher for his book, *Les Années Secrètes de Jésus, The Secret Years of Jesus,* which had eventually rolled off the press in 1896.

After publication, Dmitriy made a trip to Moscow, where he was immediately arrested by the Tsar's government for literary activity that was 'dangerous to the state and to society'. He remained exiled, without trial, for the next several years.

His book had stirred a hornet's nest of criticism. The renowned German expert, Max Müller, had led the critics who protested against any notion that Buddhism had influenced Christianity. Some critics had argued that Dmitriy Novikov had never visited the Hemis monastery in Ladakh and that the Issa manuscripts were a figment of his imagination.

Dmitriy Novikov had become a pariah and an untouchable. For a pariah to be accommodated into the Societé d'Histoire Diplomatique just a few years later was a rare honour indeed. Probably the Societé knew something that Max Müller didn't. Possibly, they had read the works of Hippolytus.

Rome, Italy, AD 225

Hippolytus, a Greek-speaking Roman Christian, wrote: 'Buddhists were in contact with the Thomas Christians in southern India . . . who philosophise among the Brahmins, who live a self-sufficient life, abstaining from eating living creatures and all cooked food . . . they say that God is light . . . God is discourse.'[49]

Trade routes between the Graeco-Roman world and the Far East were flourishing during the age of Gnosticism, and Buddhist missionaries had been active in Alexandria for several generations after Ashoka had first sent his emissaries to Ptolemy II.

The Thomas Christians of ancient India were named after Thomas Didymus, one of the twelve apostles of Christ. He had been speared to death in AD 72. No, he wasn't killed in Palestine or Egypt. He was killed near Mylapore, in southern India.

Before reaching the south, he had visited King Gondophares, whose kingdom lay in the northwest regions of India. He had even written about it in his *Acta Thomae* or *The Acts of Judas Thomas*.[50]

Historians and Church authorities alike had dismissed the very existence of any king called Gondophares. There was no record of any such king having ruled the northwest of India around that time. By 1854 all of them would have to eat their words.

⚇

Calcutta, India, 1854

Sir Alexander Cunningham, the first director of the Archaeological Survey of India, would report that King Gondophares could no longer be dismissed as fictitious.

Cunningham would report that, since the commencement of a British presence in Afghanistan, more than 30,000 coins had been discovered. Some of these coins had been minted by King Gondophares, who was now miraculously transformed from myth to reality.[51]

Suddenly, the *Acta Thomae* was no longer a work of imagination and copies of the book had necessarily to be moved from the fiction to the non-fiction shelves. In which case, one would also have to believe the rest of the book, right up to AD 72.

⚇

Mylapore, south India, AD 72

Thomas Didymus was praying in the woods outside his hermitage when a hunter, who belonged to the Govi clan, carefully aimed his poisoned dart and hit him. The wound was critical and St Thomas died on 21 December, AD 72.[52]

Thomas had arrived in Cranganore, just thirty-eight kilometres away from Cochin, India, in AD 52. He had begun preaching the gospel to inhabitants of the Malabar Coast and had soon established seven churches in the region. Sometime before his arrival in southern India, he had been at the court of King Gondophares. The court had been celebrating the wedding of the king's daughter. Besides the wedding, there had been another celebration in the king's court. The apostle, Thomas, according to his own words in the *Acta Thomae,* had been able to meet and reunite with his master, Jesus, who was also present at the wedding,[53] looking quite well and surprisingly relaxed for a man who had been crucified!

Chapter Eight

Balakote, Line of Control, Indo-Pakistan border, 2012

Balakote, a remote village on the India–Pakistan border, was literally sitting on the fence. It was neither here nor there. The river, Jallas Nullah, flowed through the middle,[54] hence the village lay half in Pakistan and half in India. It was here that Ghalib was celebrating Id, having just returned from another meeting with the Sheikh.

He first checked the animal's eyes and ears to ensure that it was healthy. After all, only a healthy animal could be considered suitable for sacrifice. He then gave it water to drink and pointed the animal towards Mecca. He chanted, '*Bismillah, i-rahman, i-rahim*—in the name of Allah, most gracious, most merciful. *Sibhana man halalaka lil dabh*—praise be upon He who has made you suitable for slaughter.' He slaughtered the lamb using the halaal method—cutting the animal's neck arteries with a single swipe of a non-serrated blade. He then watched the blood drain from the beast. As per religious law, he did not touch the animal until it died.

It was Id ul-Adha and animal sacrifice was part of the festival. It was the tenth day of Dhul Hijja as per the Islamic calendar, and seventy days after the end of Ramazan.

Ghalib-bin-Isar, leader of the Lashkar-e-Talatashar, sat with his army around him in a semicircle. In the centre, the lamb was being roasted over a roaring fire, and another smaller fire was being used to bake naan.

Ghalib was overcome with emotion. He looked around him— at his team; these were his fiercest, most loyal companions. They would die for him willingly. He needed to show them that he not only loved them, but also respected them. He stood up and took off the Pathan-suit he was wearing and tied a coarse cotton cloth towel around himself. He filled the iron tub meant for the utensils with warm water. He called his comrades one by one and washed their feet, patting them dry with the towel. Boutros was reluctant to accept the ministrations of his leader, but Ghalib insisted.

Feet duly washed, they sat down and were served the lamb. Ghalib took the hot naan and, breaking it into pieces, lovingly served it to each of his men. He then spoke to Yehuda. 'In Srinagar, there is a Japanese woman looking for me. You will go, find her, and tell her that you will deliver me to her.'

The *kahwa* tea was boiling in the samovar. He poured it into a large bowl and passed it around. His young men would leave for each of their destinations within a few days. He knew his time had come.

⚜

Jerusalem, Judea, AD 27

Knowing that his time had come, Jesus asked that the Passover feast be organised. Before supper, Jesus got up from the table, took off his outer garment and tied a towel around himself. He then poured water into a basin and, one by one, washed his disciples' feet; he then wiped them dry with the towel. Simon Peter hesitated but Jesus insisted. He soon finished washing everyone's feet, put on his clothes and sat down at the table with his disciples.

While eating, Jesus remarked that he would be betrayed by one of the men around the table. Judas asked Jesus whether he was alluding to him. 'You have said it,' replied Jesus.

During the meal, Jesus broke the bread into pieces and offered them to his disciples while saying, 'Take this and eat; this is my body.' He then took a cup of wine and gave it to his disciples, saying, 'Drink from it, all of you. For this is my blood, the blood of the covenant, shed for the forgiveness of sins.'

Balakote, Line of Control, Indo-Pak border, 2012

Because the river Jallas Nullah flows through the centre of Balakote, either side of the landscape is dotted with rocky hills. Ghalib-bin-Isar wanted to explain the reasons and motivations behind his intended actions to his men as well as to the extended army. He stood atop one of the hillocks closest to the river and began to speak.

'Your being poor does not mean that God does not love you. Thousands of rich Americans died in the Twin Towers on 9/11 by the will of Allah. He protected you! Not them!' he said as his army looked up at him in awe.

He continued, 'The families of those who died in New York mourned. They said, "Had we known the evil that America does all around the world, we would never have supported our government." Let me tell you, Allah will protect these people who have now understood our cause. God will protect and comfort these mourners.'

He carried on in the same vein. 'The Americans say that we Muslims do not like their way of life and that we wish to destroy their free society. I ask you, why do we attack America and not Sweden? Sweden is as free as America. The difference lies in America's arrogance. Doesn't America know it is the meek that shall inherit the earth?'

The mood was jubilant and members of his team were getting charged up. Ghalib raised his voice a little. *'Bismillah, i-rahman, i-rahim,* in the name of Allah, do we not fast in the holy month of Ramazan and savour the delicious taste of food and water after the fast is over? That is precisely the way I want you to hunger and thirst for the word and for the will of Allah! The hungrier and thirstier you are, the more worthy you are in the eyes of God!

'Our brothers and sisters in Palestine, Lebanon, Kashmir, Iraq, Afghanistan and Chechnya have been murdered, looted and raped. Yet we have not done the same to the infidels who perpetrated these ghastly crimes. Instead, the will of Allah showered terror and fire on the perpetrators almost automatically.

We are Muslims. We are merciful even in the most trying of circumstances!' thundered Ghalib.

His words were met by chants of 'Allah-o-Akbar!'

Ghalib's voice softened. 'All that God asks of us is to have a clear conscience. Our hearts should remain clean and pure. Only this can ensure that we are victorious. *A'uzu billahi minashaitanir rajim!'*

'The Qur'an[55] tells us in Chapter 4, Verse 90: "Thus, if they let you be, and do not make war on you, and offer you peace, God does not allow you to harm them." Don't you think that Muslims all over the world would prefer peace to war? Islam is a religion of peace and the peacemakers are beloved of Allah! Unfortunately, the infidels do not want peace!' shouted Ghalib.

Ghalib's voice was now choked with emotion. He continued, 'The Noble Qur'an 49:13 says that "the most honoured of you in the sight of Allah is the most righteous of you". For years we have been persecuted and have continued to remain righteous. This is why we are beloved of Allah! Our friends who led the attacks on 9/11 willingly allowed themselves to be martyred for the cause of righteousness.'

He then drew to his conclusion. 'Do not worry if the world calls Ghalib a terrorist, or if my enemies hurl insults at you. As long as you do Allah's will, you shall have His reward. Keep this in mind when we execute our plan,' he said as he stood on the hill and looked at his followers with pure, raw emotion.

☩

Sea of Galilee, Capernaum, AD 27

He stood on the hill and looked at his followers with pure, raw emotion as he delivered to them a sermon on the mount.[56] High on a mountain, towards the north end of the Sea of Galilee, near Capernaum, Jesus spoke to his disciples and to a large gathering of followers:

'Blessed are the poor in spirit, for theirs is the kingdom of heaven. Blessed are they who mourn, for they will be comforted. Blessed are the meek, for they will inherit the land. Blessed are they who hunger and thirst for righteousness, for they will be satisfied. Blessed are the merciful, for they will be shown mercy. Blessed are the clean of heart, for they will see God. Blessed are the peacemakers, for they will be called the children of God. Blessed are they who are persecuted for the sake of righteousness, for theirs is the kingdom of heaven. Blessed are you when they insult you and persecute you and utter every kind of evil falsely against you because of me. Rejoice and be glad, for your reward will be great in heaven.'

ॐ

Balakote, Line of Control, Indo-Pak border, 2012

Ghalib lay on the resplendent shahtoosh shawl that was carefully laid out over the mattress inside his tent. In one corner sat a rose-water jar that had been sprinkled with Jannat-ul-Firdaus, literally, 'perfume from heaven'. Resting her head on his shoulder was his wife—his one and only wife, Mariyam. She had borne him a beautiful daughter, Zahira.

Unlike some Muslim men, Ghalib had remained devoted to a single wife. While the Qur'an sanctioned polygamy, Ghalib's view was that the Surah An-Nisa of the Qur'an actually said, 'Marry other women of your choice, two or three, or four, but if you fear that you shall not be able to deal evenly with them, then only one . . . '

Ghalib had decided on only one. She was the most exquisite creature that had ever lived, and he was hopelessly devoted to her. He lovingly ran his fingers through her silky reddish-brown hair as she nestled her head on his shoulder.

Presently, she got up to retrieve a small phial that she had prepared during the day. It was an intense, warm and fragrant musk that she had extracted from the fibrous spindle-like needles of the *nalada* plants that grew in the area.'This is just a small token of my love,' she said to Ghalib as she opened the phial and poured it over his feet. She applied the perfume to his feet and then lowered her head over them. Her soft hair trailed along his soles and produced exquisite sensations throughout his entire body. She then began kissing his feet and gently licking his toes. She playfully sucked on his toes while her hair continued to caress his skin. She guided him to her already wet and warm core and once he was fully inside, she kissed him passionately.

Gar bar-ru-e-zamin ast; hamin ast, hamin ast, hamin asto. The Persian couplet, uttered by the Mughal Emperor Jehangir to describe the beauty of Kashmir, meant, 'If there is a paradise on earth, it is here, it is here, it is here!'[57]

Ghalib remained in paradise with the wonderful scent of nalada wafting through his tent.

Bethany, Israel, AD 27

The Latin name *nardostachys jatamansi*[58] was derived from the Sanskrit word *nalada*. This tough and hardy herb grew in the Himalayan foothills. The fibrous spindles of the plant grew underground and were rich in oil. This oil was made into a dry rhizome oil extract called nardin. This was the source of nard.

Six days before the Passover, Jesus arrived at Bethany, where Mary Magdalene took a pint of pure nard, an expensive perfume, poured it on Jesus's feet and wiped his feet with her hair. The house in which he sat was filled with the aromatic fragrance of the perfume.

Chapter Nine

New York, USA. 2012

British Airways flight BA 0178 left John F. Kennedy airport at 9:15 am and was scheduled to reach Heathrow at 9 pm GMT. Occupying two seats in the second row of World Traveller Class, with 351 other passengers and 39,900 pounds of luggage on the 747-400, were Martha and Vincent Sinclair.

The customary drinks and salted peanuts had arrived, and aunt and nephew were getting into the mood of the trip. 'Vincent, you must write down whatever you saw in your visions. Very often we tend to forget things like that,' said Martha.

Vincent replied, 'Actually Nana, I've already done that. In fact, I've brought along my notes of the images that I saw during Mom and Dad's funeral, as well as what I saw when I had those crazy flashes in Central Park.'

Vincent got up, opened the overhead luggage bin and pulled out his duffel bag. Unzipping it, he quickly found his leather-bound notebook. Taking it out, he zipped up the bag and returned it to the overhead storage before sitting down. Opening it, he turned to a page that had been tabbed with a yellow Post-it. He gave the notebook to Martha. There were several notations on the page:

'St John Cemetery: Daughters of Jerusalem. Eloi, Eloi, lema sabachthani? Jerusalem. Wooden cross. Blood. Wailing women. Impale him. Simon. Alexander. Rufus.'

These entries were followed by: 'Central Park: Blood. Wounded soldiers. Bandages. Greek cross. Red. Bassano portrait. Stately house. Number 18. London street. Iron fencing with an "S" logo. Indian antiques. Parties. Food. Musicians.

1940s' La Salle ambulance. Buckingham Palace. Bell. Grave. So soon?'

'Excuse me, ma'am. Would you prefer the chicken casserole or the sliced roast beef?' enquired the flight attendant. 'Neither. I've pre-ordered a vegetarian meal,' said Martha. The stewardess referred to a list and immediately pulled out an appropriate tray from her cart. Stir-fried vegetables with basmati rice, pasta salad and fresh fruit yoghurt for Ms Martha Sinclair.

Vincent tucked into a meal of sliced roast beef with scalloped cheese potatoes and green beans, garden salad with ranch dressing, and blueberry cheesecake; not bad for airline food. For a while at least, they forgot about the notebook and its contents.

⚱

London, UK, 2012

The ridiculous name, Airways Hotel, belonged to a nineteenth-century period home that was located just a stone's throw away from Buckingham Palace. It had now been converted into a forty-room bed-and-breakfast priced at £45 a night. It was just one of the many little family-run places that one saw in the oddest parts of London. They all looked identical to one another—in fact, without the signboards outside, one wouldn't be able to tell any given Victorian townhouse-hotel, with its pillars and white façade, from another.

This is where Martha and Vincent checked in upon arriving in London. Vincent had decided that he would rather be near Buckingham Palace in order to experience the area a little better. They had boarded the Piccadilly Line from Heathrow to Hammersmith and had then taken the District Line to Victoria Station, which was just a short walk away from the hotel.

The front desk was supervised by a middle-aged matron. She was the proverbial English landlady with rosy cheeks, wide matronly hips and checked apron. She quickly rattled off the deal to Vincent: 'Your bedrooms have independent bathrooms. Both rooms have a telly, hairdryer, fridge and tea-coffee maker. Direct dial in your room gets billed to your account. The tariff includes traditional English breakfast served downstairs in the morning between eight and nine o'clock. VAT included. Any questions, luv?'

The traditional English breakfast the next morning was essentially a full-blown frontal cholesterol attack. Besides toast, marmalade, fruit and porridge was the fry-up which included sausages, bacon, kippers, black pudding, fried eggs, mushrooms, tomatoes, baked beans and hash browns. Vincent couldn't believe the amount of grease the English consumed each morning, until Martha told him that not all English people ate like that every day. While Martha attempted to rid herself of her jet lag, Vincent settled for some tea and toast. He then quickly made his way to Buckingham Palace.

During the journey from New York to London, Vincent had succeeded in convincing himself that his trip to London was going to be a waste of time—this talk about past-life experiences was humbug. He now headed along St George's Drive till he reached Warwick Square where he turned left and started walking down Belgrave Road. When he reached the intersection with Buckingham Palace Road, he turned right and kept walking until he reached Buckingham Gate. The walk had taken him less than thirty minutes. It was only when he reached Buckingham Palace that it struck him.

He hadn't asked for directions. He hadn't referred to a map. He hadn't visited London ever in his life. And yet he had walked effortlessly from his hotel to the palace as if he had lived there his entire life!

Buckingham House had originally been built in 1703 as the private residence of the Duke of Buckingham. In 1762, the house had been purchased by George III to be used as one among many homes belonging to the royals. George IV had subsequently engaged the services of architect John Nash, who had redesigned Buckingham House with a marble arch as its entrance; this would later be relocated to Hyde Park. In 1837, Queen Victoria had made Buckingham House her principal residence in London and Buckingham House had now officially been rechristened Buckingham Palace.[59]

The Household Troops had guarded the monarchy since 1660, their foot guards attired in the familiar uniforms of red tunics and bearskins. In summer, the main attraction for tourists continued to be the changing of the guard, which happened in the forecourt of the palace at 11:30 each morning. The forty-five-minute, minutely choreographed ceremony involved the new guard marching to the palace from Wellington Barracks accompanied by a band, and taking over duty from the old guard.

It was only around 10:30 in the morning when Vincent arrived and the forecourt was quiet at this hour except for a few enthusiastic tourists. Vincent just stood and surveyed the façade of the palace, attempting to see whether it stirred any latent memories inside him. Nothing. So it was a false alarm after all, a complete waste of time, as he'd expected.

After half an hour of wandering about, Vincent decided to make his way back to the hotel to check on Martha. He walked along Buckingham Palace Road and turned right into Eccleston Street. He kept walking till he reached a lovely Victorian residential quarter. For some uncanny reason, Vincent walked further towards it. He now found himself in Belgrave Square.

Bell . . . Grave . . . so soon? It struck him like a thunderbolt! It was one word—*Belgrave*, not two! Belgrave had been the word hitting his brain cells during his memory flashes in Central Park. If the past-life theory held true, and if Vincent had indeed lived in this area earlier, he would have passed Buckingham Palace often. His primary recollection should have been of Belgrave Square, but he would also have a fleeting memory of the Buckingham Palace environs. Yes, that made sense.

Vincent looked around the square. The grand white-stuccoed townhouses with their uniform pillared façades gave him a sense of déjà vu. He felt a chill run down his spine. He trembled; this was eerie. All the terraced houses had the same Victorian 'period feel' to them. The house that he had mentally seen in his visions in Central Park was very much like these homes.

He quickly consulted his notebook. Number 18. Could that mean a house number? He kept walking along the side of the square that he had entered until, about halfway along, he saw Number 18. It had a sign outside which read 'The Royal College of Psychiatrists'. This couldn't be what he had seen—a psychiatric college? No. He had clearly seen a residential house, not a college. Vincent was about to do an about-turn when he noticed the 'S' logo that had been delicately incorporated into the iron railings running along the boundary.

It was the same 'S' design on the ironwork that he had seen in his flashes. He was feeling faint with excitement and anticipation. He felt the sweat running down his back. He felt compelled to go in and find out more about this place.

In the reception area there was a help desk for visitors, and a lounge with some comfortable chairs arranged around a low-level coffee table. He noticed a few glossy brochures on the coffee table and casually picked one up. It was about the Royal College of Psychiatry. He quickly leafed through the sections about the college's courses, career options for students, publications, college events, faculty, and fees, until he finally reached the section on the history of the college. It read:

> The district of London known today as Belgravia was developed in the 1820s. Previously it was called Five Fields and was a rural area between London, as it was then, and the village of Knightsbridge.
>
> In the early 19th century the landowners, the Grosvenor family, began developing the area. The name 'Belgrave' comes from their property of that name in either Cheshire or Leicestershire.

The square is ten acres in size. Belgrave Square was laid out in 1826. The corners of the square are on the points of the compass and number 18 is part of the south-west terrace line, the last to be completed.

The development was a success from the start, probably helped by George IV's decision to convert nearby Buckingham House into a palace for his residence. Later, Queen Victoria rented number 36 for her mother and this was considered to be a royal seal of approval for the square.

Many of the tenants were members of the aristocracy and people of political importance. The first tenant of number 18 was Sir Ralph Howard, who was himself MP for Wicklow, with extensive property in Ireland . . .

The next tenant was Clementine, Lady Sossoon. She too had overseas connections; her husband's family, the Sossoons, came originally from Baghdad and India. She lived here from 1929 until 1942 and kept open house for the troops during the Second World War. She is said to have had parties here for soldiers during the war; also, part of the property was used as a Red Cross supply depot during this war. Lady Clementine left in 1942 but retained the tenancy until she died, aged over 90, in 1955.

Number 18 was taken over by the Institute of Metals in 1956 and the College came in 1974.[60]

Vincent quickly consulted his notes from Central Park: Blood. Wounded soldiers. Bandages. Greek cross. Red. Bassano portrait. Stately house. Number 18. London street. Iron fencing with an "S" logo. Indian antiques. Parties. Food. Musicians. 1940s' La Salle ambulance. Buckingham Palace. Bell. Grave. So soon?'

Well, this place was very close to Buckingham Palace. It was in Belgrave Square. It certainly was a stately house, with all the elements of Victorian architecture. It did bear the number 18. The 'S' was definitely a part of its grillwork. Coincidence? Imagination?

The lightbulb flashed inside Vincent's head . . . *Bell* . . . *Grave . . . so soon. Sossoon!* The house in Belgrave Square had been occupied by Lady Sossoon. It wasn't 'so soon'. It was Sossoon! That also explained the 'S' in the iron grills! Vincent was now sweating profusely. He went over the bit about Lady Sossoon again:

The next tenant was Clementine, Lady Sossoon . . . kept open house for the troops during the Second World War . . . said to have had parties here for soldiers during the war . . . also part of the property was used as a Red Cross supply depot during this war.

'What is wrong with you, Vincent?' he said to himself irritably. 'Don't you realise that every cross is not a cross of Jesus? An equal-armed cross is not only a Greek cross, it's also the symbol of the International Red Cross!'

Vincent stepped outside the house at 18, Belgrave Square. His mobile phone had run out of power. Looking around, he located a phone booth and managed to get through to Martha. Before she could get a word in, Vincent said, 'Listen, Nana. I need to talk to you very urgently. There's a pub quite close by. I saw it this morning while getting here. It's called the Star Tavern, I think. It's on the mews adjoining Belgrave Square. Can you meet me there ASAP?' Vincent then quickly made his way to the rendezvous.

The pub was located at the end of the secluded cobbled mews that was just off Belgrave Square. The pub had probably been built sometime in the early part of the nineteenth century to meet the needs of the domestics who served in the aristocratic homes of Belgravia. The mews, quite obviously, had been created to provide horse stables as well as accommodation for coachmen. Of course, in the present day, the mews housed neither stables nor servants' quarters, merely millionaires' homes. The pub was furnished with comfortable benches and scrubbed pine tables, and Vincent also noticed a friendly-looking room upstairs, which seemed to be a dining area. Vincent sat down and ordered himself a Fuller's London Pride and waited for Martha.

The table next to his was occupied by an unkempt but handsome man. Professor Terry Acton had just finished his morning sessions with his patients at the Spiritualist Association and had wandered over to the pub for a relaxed lunch of fish and chips washed down with a pint of Chiswick Bitter.

About fifteen minutes later, Martha walked in. Vincent waved to her to let her know where he was seated. Martha walked over, took off her coat, folded it over the back of her chair and sat down. 'So, Vincent, what's this about?' she began.

'Martha, is that you?' came the incredulous voice from the next table.

Martha looked sideways at the occupant of the table next to theirs and saw the smiling face of Terry Acton. It took a few seconds to sink in. 'Terry!' she exclaimed.

'Martha, sweetheart! It's great to see you after so many years! You're looking great. Where on earth have you been?' asked Terry.

'It's been almost ten years since we went to the Igatpuri silent zone, hasn't it?' said Martha jokingly. Terry and Martha had visited India around the same time after their regression sessions in London but for different reasons. While Martha had been interested in brushing up on advanced yoga techniques, Terry had enrolled in the Bharatiya Vidya Bhavan—a university of ancient sciences in Mumbai which taught astrology and a few other occult sciences. During their Indian sojourns, both had independently decided to enrol for a course in Vipassana meditation at Igatpuri, a sprawling but serene Buddhist meditation centre located five hours away from Mumbai.[61]

Igatpuri had certainly not been for the faint-hearted. The school had required them to sign a solemn oath that they would not leave mid-course, the course itself being twelve days long.

Each day, they would meditate for ten hours on an average and live the life of Buddhist monks. They would maintain perfect silence and were allowed the luxury of talking only on the twelfth day of the course.

Terry and Martha had, by pure chance, been allotted sleeping quarters that were next to each other. Ironically, they would be unable to talk to one another at all for the next eleven days. On the twelfth day, when they had eventually been given permission to talk, talk they did—starved as they'd been of conversation for the previous 264 hours! They had driven back to Mumbai together after the course and continued to remain in touch while pursuing different vocations in India. Six months later, Martha had left India to return home to New York, while Terry returned to London, to the Spiritualist Association and his university research. They had lost contact completely thereafter. It was truly a wonderful surprise for both to meet like this, by sheer luck.

Martha continued, 'By the way, Vincent, this is one of my closest friends, Professor Terry Acton.'

'Nice to meet you, Professor,' said Vincent. 'I am Father Vincent Sinclair. I have heard a lot about you from my aunt, who talks about you very fondly.'

After a few pleasantries, Terry asked, 'Martha, I always thought you were going to settle down in India permanently. What happened?'

Martha replied, 'I moved back to New York. I now teach yoga at my own centre in Manhattan. How about you?'

Terry responded. 'I owe my life to you, Martha. Without you, I would never have overcome the grief of losing Susan. My degree in psychology from Yale would have been worthless if it weren't for your introduction to the Spiritualist Association. I not only practise my art at the Association here in Belgrave Square, I also use it as the basis of psychiatric therapy. I also teach and research in the fields of spirituality and religion at the University of London. To that extent, I'm more theoretical than you.'

Vincent couldn't hold himself back. 'Mediums? Please don't think I'm being rude, but what exactly do you people do, Nana?'

Martha hesitated. She had deliberately kept her Spiritualist Association connections concealed from Vincent because of his possible reaction. She reluctantly spoke up. 'Well, as you probably know, the concept of reincarnation tells us that when we die, we shed our mortal bodies but the soul lives on. This soul generally finds another body and another life from which it can continue to learn. Once a soul has completely learned everything there is to learn about life, it reunites with the Supreme Being in a state of Nirvana or bliss. In between the various lives that it takes rebirth in, the soul also takes rest. It is possible to tap into this spiritual energy through a spiritual medium and contact one's lost loved ones who may no longer be present in the flesh but certainly are in spirit.'

Terry suddenly spoke up. 'I never believed in this stuff till I lost my wife many years ago. Your aunt, Martha, helped me reach out to my wife's spirit. I now help people reach out to their loved ones. Besides being spiritual mediums, your aunt and I are also certified regression therapists; we help people who want to know more about their previous lives so that it can help them understand and deal with their present ones a little better.'

Vincent had many questions to ask. He was reluctant to ask all of them for fear of seeming rude. Martha cut short his mental debate by telling Terry, 'Vincent obviously doesn't believe in reincarnation since he's a priest in the Roman Catholic Church.'

'Ah. Then I had better be careful about what I say,' said Terry light-heartedly, 'I wouldn't want to get into a theological debate with the clergy!'

Quite unexpectedly, Vincent turned to Terry and said, 'Please help me. Maybe God has guided me to you by providence! I want to know more.'

Vincent, Martha, and Terry were sitting in St James's Park, probably the most beautiful park in London. The tourists and locals were out in full force, strolling through the green, feeding the ducks, watching the pelicans, viewing Buckingham Palace from the bridge, supervising their kids in the playground, or enjoying refreshments in the park's café.

The three of them had eaten a quick lunch at the pub and then walked over to the park so they could discuss the issues surrounding the concept of reincarnation and regression. Martha had attempted to fill Terry in on the broad details of what Vincent had been going through since the death of his parents six years earlier, as well as the flashes and visions that he had been experiencing.

Terry took over. 'Listen to me, Vincent. Even if the entire idea of reincarnation is anathema to Catholicism, it doesn't mean that you can't believe in it. There are indeed many Christians who believe that reincarnation is not incompatible with Christianity. Consider this: homosexuality is not approved by the Roman Catholic Church, but does that mean there aren't any gays who continue to be Roman Catholic, culturally at least?'

Terry continued. 'The Roman Catholic Church tried Galileo in 1633 and held that his view of the planets revolving around the sun were rubbish. Can you be certain that the present view on reincarnation will not change at some time in the near future? There are several non-canonical texts in the Nag Hammadi finds, the Dead Sea Scrolls, as well as the Gnostic gospels, that do, in fact, support reincarnation.'

Vincent listened to Terry patiently and then spoke. 'The fact is that for the first time in my life, I find some parts of myself in conflict with my faith.'

Martha suddenly cut in. 'Can I suggest something? You are obviously familiar with the concept of *gnosis*, or personally experienced knowledge. If someone is born blind and we ask him to describe the colour red, he will be unable to do so. He has not experienced red, green, blue, or any other colour, for that matter. Reincarnation, as a theory can be debated endlessly.

Instead, if you were to experience some part of the theory yourself, maybe through a regression session, your ability to accept or reject a certain point of view may become much easier.'

Vincent was in his hotel room, semi-reclining on the bed with several pillows propping him up. Terry had pulled up a chair next to him and had sat down. Martha was downstairs in the hotel lounge.

'Okay, I'm going to try to take you into a state of deep relaxation. I want you to make yourself comfortable, settle back and relax . . . if you find that any limb or muscle is uncomfortable, just move it into the most comfortable position and then relax it.'

Vincent settled in and Terry continued. 'I now want you to focus on your breathing. Feel your breath going in . . . and out . . . in . . . and out . . . imagine that with every exhalation you are breathing out all your toxins, your stress, your worries and your fears. With every inhalation, you are breathing in life-giving energy. Now visualise a beautiful light . . . it is just above you . . . it's entering your body and healing you . . . all that's important to you is my voice . . . a peaceful, easy feeling is settling over you like a wonderfully soft blanket . . . I will now count backwards from five down to one. You will feel yourself floating into a deeper and deeper trance with each number. Five . . . four . . . three . . . two . . . one.'

Vincent seemed to be semi-comatose so Terry went on. 'Now visualise that you are walking down a flight of stairs . . . with every step you take, you go deeper and deeper into a relaxed state . . . at the bottom of the stairs is a peaceful, tranquil oasis filled with energy, happiness, love, peace, joy, contentment . . . your mind is now so relaxed that it can allow itself to open up and remember almost everything.'

Terry paused before continuing, 'Now think back to a childhood memory . . . it could be anything . . . something nice and happy . . . just be a neutral observer of the memory . . . it doesn't matter if your mind wanders a little . . . just experience the sensation of the memory . . . I will now count backwards from five down to one and you will become a child once again . . . Five . . . four . . . three . . . two . . . one.'

'Where are you?'

'I'm in the backyard of my parents' home in New York. There's a slight chill, but it isn't cold . . . it's probably autumn.'

'What are you wearing?'

'It's a baseball jacket and cap—New York Yankees. My father and I both love the Yankees.'

'Who are you with?'

'My dad and I are playing catch in the backyard. My mom is barbequing hot dogs in the corner. I love the smell of hot dogs. She puts on extra mustard, relish, ketchup, chopped onions and sauerkraut for me!'

'Are you enjoying yourself?'

'Oh, I love the days that my dad doesn't have to go to work. We play catch and my mom barbeques. I love every minute of it. My parents are the most wonderful parents in the world. They take me to the movies, to the zoo and buy me cotton candy.'

'Okay, just enjoy the love and warmth you are experiencing. Just relish the memory, savour it. I now want you to float above it a little and when I count backwards from five, I want you to go back deeper beyond the womb . . . think you can go deeper? Okay . . . five . . . four . . . three . . . two . . . one . . . where are you now?'

'It's a lovely Victorian house. It's definitely London. But the street is a mess. There's tension all around . . . I think there's a war going on.'

'Are you fighting in the war?'

'No. I'm a doctor. I make trips back and forth between the supply depots and the hospitals. The hospitals are overflowing with wounded soldiers and civilians. The Germans have been bombing London incessantly. I also drive the ambulance.'

'Really? What sort of an ambulance is it?'

'It's a sturdy 1940s' Chevy . . . it's been modified . . . I think it's a La Salle. It's seen a great deal of action. The front fender is badly bent, but we have no time to fix it.'

'So why are you in this Victorian home?'

'Oh, it's a Red Cross supply depot. The house belongs to a wealthy Jewish lady who has allowed part of it to be used by the Red Cross. She is very kind and generous. She often hosts parties for the soldiers. I have attended some of them. Music and some food, whatever is possible, what with the war rationing.'

'Do you know her personally?'

'I have met her many times. She's very elegant. Her portrait is in the lounge downstairs, done by a famous artist. Bassano, I think. The lounge opens into a beautiful square. The front door and grilles have the family crest emblazoned on them . . . "S", I think.'

'Do you remember her name?'

'Sossoon, I think.'

'Sure?'

'Yes. Sossoon. The house is on Belgrave Square. I have to pick up my Red Cross supplies from there. I often go past Buckingham Palace to the hospitals, where I unload the stuff. Their family is quite famous. They made their wealth in Baghdad and then India.'

Sossoon Ben Saleh was born in 1745 and around thirty years later was appointed Sheikh of Baghdad. Since the lion's share of Baghdad's earnings was derived from Jewish business, the Governor of Baghdad used to always appoint a Jewish finance minister.

In 1821, a new anti-Semitic Governor of Baghdad caused the departure of many Jewish families, including the Sossoons, who would eventually settle down in the Indian port of Mumbai, or Bombay, as it was then known.

Sossoon Ben Saleh's son, Matthew, was born in 1791. Matthew acquired British citizenship and set up Matthew Sossoon & Co. in Bombay, one of the most profitable firms exporting Indian opium to China.

His son, Jonathan Sossoon, moved to London to set up J.D. Sossoon & Co., which soon owned interests in shipping, real estate and banking. Jonathan died in 1885, leaving behind a widow, Clementine, Lady Sossoon, who would continue living at 18, Belgrave Square, in London.

Alexander Bassano, one of the most famous photographers of the time, turned out portraits of some of the most aristocratic and beautiful women of the time. Among these had been Clementine, Lady Sossoon.

'Okay. Forget the Red Cross and the Sossoons. Is there anyone important in your life? Parents? Brothers? Sisters? Wife? Kids? Lover?' asked Terry. Vincent was still lying peacefully on the bed in his hotel room.

'My parents aren't alive. I have no wife or kids. The only person dear to me is Lady Clementine. She has everything—wealth and power. But she will soon die.'

'You must love her very much?'

'She is everything to me in an otherwise dreary world. Unfortunately, she has cancer. It's a matter of time . . . she will soon die.'

'Do you remember what she looks like?'

'She's beautiful, graceful, and delicate. But she is withering away. The hospitals are overloaded and medicines are a problem. I'm trying really hard to look after her as best as I can.'

'Can you see anyone who is from your present life?'

'Clementine—she's Nana in my present life.'

Vincent was still in a deep hypnotic state. Terry gently probed, 'So why do you think she is here with you again in this life?'

Vincent paused and then replied, 'She seems to be taking care of me, nurturing me, much the same way that I took care of her in our previous lives.'

'Can you see anyone else you recognise?' asked Terry.

'My parents.'

'Present-life or past-life parents?'

'My present-life ones. In my previous life, they were strangers who were simply crossing the street and I was in a hurry to get some wounded soldiers to the hospital. My ambulance knocked them down!'

'What are you doing?'

'Not much I can do. They are dead. There is a young boy standing at the edge of the road. He's crying! I think he's their son. Oh God! What have I done?'

'Relax, Vincent. What do you think you can learn from what you have done?'

'I caused someone to lose his parents by my carelessness . . . my parents were lost by me in exactly the same circumstances—a car accident!'

'Vincent, I now want you to once again hover above the memories. I will again count backwards from five, and I want you to go deeper, beyond the lifetime that you have just recounted . . . much further . . . five . . . four . . . three . . . two . . . one . . . and what do you see? Where are you now?'

'In Ireland, I think. They have no food.'

'Why? Who are they?'

'There is a famine. The Catholic farmers are starving. I am the Protestant tax-collector. I have betrayed them all. I collect taxes from them that they cannot possibly pay, even if they were to sell themselves!'

'Anyone familiar?'

'Yes, I think so.'

'You think so?'

'Yes. I have a friend. Father Thomas Manning. It's him.'

'Who is he?'

'He's one of the poor Catholic farmers. I have persecuted him.' Vincent fell silent.

Terry realised he was not getting much out of Vincent, so he quickly shifted gears. 'Let's go deeper, Vincent . . . five . . . four . . . three . . . two . . . one . . . where are you?'

'A farm in rural India, a palatial house which is on the banks of a beautiful river.'

'Who are you?'

'I'm the son of a landlord. I am a teacher. I have just written a book.'

'Do you love your father?'

'Yes . . . no . . . I don't know. He is supporting the view of the village elders. He does not want me to tamper with the traditions and caste equations of the village. I feel very let down.'

Terry could feel the sweat building up on his forehead as he asked the next question.

'Do you see anyone familiar?'

'Yes. It's you! You! Terry! You are my father! I hate you! You sided with them!'

'Anything to learn?'

'For you. Not me.'

'What?'

'You prevented the truth from emerging. You blocked my path. You will make amends in another life, maybe this one. You will go to any lengths to ensure that the truth emerges.'

Terry digested this information and decided it was time to move on. 'Vincent, hover above the memories again . . . I will again count backwards from five . . . go deeper . . . much further . . . five . . . four . . . three . . . two . . . one . . . and what do you see?'

'*Abwûn d'bwaschmâja nethkâdasch schmach têtê malkuthach nehwê tzevjânach aikâna d'bwaschmâja af b'arha.*'

'Which language are you speaking in? Is this your native tongue?'

'*Hawvlân lachma d'sûnkanân jaomâna waschboklân chaubên aikâna daf chnân schvoken l'chaijabên wela tachlân l'nesjuna ela patzân min bischa metol dilachie malkutha wahaila wateschbuchta l'ahlâm almîn.*'[62]

'Vincent, I cannot understand what you are saying. I want you to float above the scene and see it as an impartial observer . . . I need you to tell me what it is that you see.'

'I am in Yerushalem. I am here on a visit to the great city.'

'Where have you come from?'

'Cyrene. It's in North Africa.'

'What are you doing? Can you see who is around you?'

'The streets are filled with people. The rough stones that line the street have blood on them. There is a lot of shouting. I can see Roman soldiers everywhere.'

'What does Jerusalem look like?'

'Yerushalem? It is the most magnificent city between Alexandria and Damascus, with almost 80,000 people living here. Almost 250,000 visitors are here right now because of the Passover!'[63]

'Is it very crowded?'

'The pilgrims share the roads with teams of oxen who are hauling huge blocks of limestone. Large-scale construction work is going on. As you approach the city, on the left side is a massive wall around 150 feet high. It's not the temple, merely the platform of the temple! To my right is the upper city where the Jewish priests live in splendour.'

'So the city is being rebuilt?'

'Herod is a great builder. He has built forts, palaces, cities and an artificial harbour. He has rebuilt all the existing meandering streets on a paved grid and has created a palace that is surrounded by a moat and boasts of wondrous water gardens. He wants to outdo King Solomon.'

'How?'

'Tradition forbids enlarging the temple beyond the size originally constructed by Solomon. Herod has added this gigantic thirty-five-acre platform, on which the temple sits. Some of the stones weigh more than fifty tonnes each.'

'Can you describe the temple?'

'The temple mount has seven entrances, but the main entry is from a stairway on the south side. At the foot of the

stairs are shops selling sacrificial animals. There are also baths
for ritual purification.'

'What do you do at the temple?'

'Sacrifice. A lamb for Passover, a bull for Yom Kippur, two
doves for a child's birth.'

'So, one buys the animals and sacrifices them?'

'Yes, but to buy animals, one has to first change Roman
denarii for shekels.'

'What are shekels?'

'Shekels are temple currency—coins that have no portraits
on them. They do not contradict Jewish law.'

'What is the temple like?'

'There are thousands of priests and scholars. There is smoke
from the pyres as well as the screaming of terrified beasts that
are about to be sacrificed. The abattoir smells terrible and there
is blood everywhere.'

'How did you come to Jerusalem?'

'Caravan. Goods come in caravans from Samaria, Syria,
Egypt, Nabatea, Arabia and Persia. Yerushalem is very cosmo-
politan. Greek, Aramaic and Hebrew are spoken here.'

'Are the Romans in charge of the city?'

'Yes, but they do not really control things. In one of the
corners of the temple is the Antonia, the great Roman garrison
that houses about 3,000 soldiers. Many do not like what Herod
has done by virtually demolishing the old temple. He has more
or less built a Roman temple. People seem to hate being under
Roman rule.'

'Which religions are under Roman rule?'

'Most of the temple elite consists of the Sadducees and the
Pharisees. The Zealots are rather militant in nature whereas the
Essenes live in monastic groups outside the city. There is a lot
of tension among these groups.'

'What is causing the crowds on the streets?'

'I know the reason . . . I saw it myself. Caiphas, the high
priest of the Sanhedrin, has asked Pontius Pilate to crucify this
man who is bleeding. People are lining up in the streets to see

him. He is being made to carry his crossbeam to Golgotha. The crowds are shouting, "Barabbas! We want Barabbas released!"'

'Anything else?'

'Εβραίος! βοηθήστε αυτό το κάθαρμα να φέρει το σταυρό του!'[64]

'Vincent, you are again slipping into a language I cannot understand. What did you just say?'

'Greek! They are calling me a Jew in a contemptuous way and are asking me to help him with the cross.'

'Who is telling you this?'

'The Roman soldiers coming down the Mount of Olives.'

'What are you doing?'

'I am lifting up the crossbeam for him. I can see the man's face and body. He has been beaten so savagely that his features have been rendered almost indistinguishable. He is stooping even though I am now taking the entire load of the crossbeam. He is trying to say something to me.'

'What?'

'*Nayim mayod Simon. Toda. Hashem Yaazor!*'

'You're again speaking in an alien language. I need you to float above the scene so that you can be a neutral observer. Now, what is he saying?'

'Nice to meet you, Simon. Thank you. God shall help. It's Hebrew. How in heaven's name does he know my name?'

'What else can you see around you?'

'The Jewish leaders. They seem to be very excited. They are hurling insults at him. Some women are crying. He is saying to them, "Daughters of Jerusalem, stop weeping for me. On the contrary, weep for yourselves and for your children! In the days ahead the childless woman will be considered lucky. When the end-time comes, men and women will be calling on mountains and the hills to cover them. If they do this when the tree is green, what will they not do when it is dry?"'

'What else can you see or hear?'

'Eloi, Eloi, lema sabachthani.'

'What are you saying, Vincent? What does that mean?' asked Terry.

Vincent continued animatedly. 'I have seen his agony as the hammers pound nails through his body. It's excruciatingly painful when the crossbeam is hoisted by ropes up the vertical post. They have placed two criminals on either side of him.'

Vincent had been in a hypnotic state for close to an hour. Terry was sweating profusely and his pulse was racing. Could this be real? A person in the present day having seen Jesus upfront and alive in a previous life?

'"My God, my God, why hast thou forsaken me?" is what he is saying. They have put a sign over his head.'

'What does the sign read?'

'*Iésous o Nazóraios o Basileus tón Ioudaión.*'

'What is that?'

'Greek. Jesus the Nazarene, King of the Jews.'

'What else can you see?'

'The soldiers are dividing his clothes among themselves. The crowd is taunting him. They say that he saved others but cannot save himself.'

'Is he replying to them?'

'Τους συγχωρήστε τον πατέρα επειδή δεν ξέρουν τι κάνουν.'

'What's that?'

'Forgive them, Father, for they know not what they do.'

'What else does he say?'

'Σας υπόσχομαι ότι σήμερα θα είστε στον παράδεισο με με.'

'Okay. To whom is he saying that and what does it mean?'

'He is talking to one of the criminals. He is promising him that he will take him to Paradise. Two men are sharing a private joke near the cross. One man is commenting that the crucified king of Jews is calling for Elijah. The other fellow is saying, "Let's stay and see if Elijah helps him down!"'

'Anything else?'

'He's thirsty. They aren't giving him water. They are putting something that looks like vinegar. Is it vinegar? I can't quite make out. No wait, it's a combination of a couple of things that they are putting on the sponge at the end of a long stick. They are now putting it to his lips. He's groaning. Wait! He's saying something . . . "Father, I commit my spirit to your hands. It is finished." He seems to have passed out.'

'Is he dead?'

'I can't be sure. He has definitely fainted. He certainly *looks* dead. The centurion seems nervous. "Surely that good man was a son of God," he is saying. The crowd that has been standing around is now beating their chests with their fists. They are going away.'

'So everyone is leaving?'

'Since it's the day of preparation for the Passover, the temple clergy doesn't seem to want the bodies to stay on the crosses over the Sabbath. They've sent representatives to Pilate to ask that the legs of the crucified men be broken so as to bring death quickly. This will allow for their bodies to be removed in good time.'

'Are they breaking the legs?'

'They have broken the legs of the two criminals but they are checking to see whether Jesus is dead. One of the soldiers is raising his spear and thrusting it into Jesus's side . . . blood and water! He must be alive for blood to spurt like that! They seem to think he's dead. "No point breaking the legs of a dead man," they're saying.'

'Where are you?'

'I am standing a little distance away. Near me are his mother and Mary Magdalene. I'm going closer to the cross. I want to see his condition. What's that smell? It isn't vinegar. It's some sort of opium . . . opium and belladonna? I can't be sure.'

'What time is it?'

'It's evening. I'm hanging around to see what happens. There's this rich man called Joseph of Arimathea. He's been to Pilate and has obtained permission to take down the body and bury it. I wonder whether he realises that the man could be alive?'

'Who is this Joseph?'

'Well, the people here say that he's a secret follower of Jesus. He's also very rich and has his way with Pilate. Pilate was apparently quite surprised that Jesus died so quickly. I wonder whether he knows anything?'

'What's happening now?'

'They're carrying the body to a tomb that Joseph has hewn from a rock close to Golgotha. It's quite surprising that Pilate has allowed them to bury the body . . . Roman law does not allow for burial of crucified men. Joseph and another man, Nicodemus, are taking the body down. They have brought a long linen winding-cloth and about a hundred pounds of crushed myrrh and aloe vera.'

Pittsburgh, USA, 2004

The scientists of the University of Pittsburgh finally made the breakthrough in 2004. They proved that an extract from the leaves of aloe vera could preserve organ function in rats that had lost massive amounts of blood. Indications were that aloe vera could possibly end up becoming the ideal treatment for battle wounds because the extract could help buy time until blood became available.[65] Accelerated loss of blood was quite difficult to replenish rapidly and this often led to organ failure. Aloe vera could step in at such times.

Dr Mitchell Fink, the author of the Pittsburgh study, formally indicated that the study revealed that when the human body lost large quantities of blood, it would go into haemorrhage shock because blood would get diverted from the rest of the body to critical organs such as the heart, brain and liver. This would cause a drop in blood pressure.

The University of Pittsburgh team found that the juice of aloe vera leaves actually reduced the force required by blood to flow through blood vessels, thus increasing the chances of survival. Some of these properties had been known to Indian sages since 1400 BC.

North India, 1400 BC

The great sage, Vyasa, was writing on Ayurveda—the 'science of life'—by combining relevant medical texts from various ancient Indian books of wisdom. The sage was presently engrossed in the properties of a herb called *heerabol*. Heerabol had a long history of therapeutic use in Ayurveda; it was routinely used to treat inflammations and infections.

The uses of heerabol were later introduced by Ayurveda into the Chinese and Tibetan medicinal systems during the seventh century. The *Gyu-zhi*, or the 'Four Tantras', was one of the first Indian medical texts to be translated into Tibetan. As a result, in Tibetan and Chinese medicine, heerabol began to be used in the treatment of impact injuries, wounds, incisions and bone pain.

Subsequent research by the Memorial Sloan-Kettering Cancer Centre found that heerabol had anti-inflammatory and antipyretic properties when used on mice. According to the Centre, a constituent of heerabol was a potent inhibitor of certain cancers.[66] The scientific name for heerabol is *commiphora molmol*. It is also known by its more common name, myrrh.

'Joseph and another man, Nicodemus, are taking the body down. They have brought a long linen winding-cloth and about a hundred pounds of crushed myrrh and aloe vera.'

⚶

London, UK, 2012

Vincent was still in his hotel room, semi-reclined on the bed. The pillows propping him up were damp from his perspiration. Terry continued to remain frozen on the chair next to the bed, and Martha was waiting downstairs in the hotel lounge.

The regression session had been going on for over an hour, and even though Terry was overwhelmed with the richness of detail that Vincent had been able to recall, he realised that he needed to terminate the session and continue it another day, for the sake of his own health as well as for Vincent's well-being.

Terry began the process of bringing Vincent back into the present. 'Vincent, it's time for you to return to waking consciousness. I will now start counting upwards from one to ten. Let each incremental number awaken you more. By the time I reach ten, you will open your eyes and be fully awake, remembering everything that you saw . . . one . . . two . . . three . . . you're awakening . . . four . . . five . . . six . . . you're feeling good . . . seven . . . eight . . . you're nearly awake now . . . nine . . . ten . . . you can now open your eyes. You are now fully awake and are fully in control of your body and mind.'

Vincent's eyes adjusted themselves to the dimly lit room. It had become dark outside and the light that had been filtering in through the window when they had started the session was no longer available. Terry reached out to the bedside lamp and switched it on.

'So, how do you feel?' asked Terry.

Vincent's words came gushing out, 'Awesome! Terry, I am truly blessed to have been able to see the Lord. I had only read about the cross-bearer Simon of Cyrene, but I'd never ever imagined that I could have been that person in a previous life. I am truly blessed. Thank you for helping me experience this.'

Terry thought for a moment and then, lowering his voice, he said, 'Vincent, I must tell you I am as excited as you are. I have never been through a more nail-biting regression therapy session than the one I just put you through. It's only natural that you will want to share this experience with others. My advice is that you should be selective in choosing the people you share this information with. You should be prepared that many will think you a lunatic if you tell them what you just experienced.'

'Thanks for the advice . . . tell you what, let's go someplace where we can have a drink and I can share this with Nana!' said Vincent, excitedly kicking his feet off the bed and picking up his jacket that lay folded on the armchair in the corner.

Terry stopped him. From his pocket he took out a folded envelope and handed it over to Vincent. On the face of the envelope were two words, 'Bom Jesus'.

Vincent was confused. 'What's this?' he asked.

Terry replied, 'I have spent the last few years studying virtually every religion around the globe. Inside this envelope is a document that will have dramatic consequences for the world. I do not expect you to understand it. Just keep it safe and promise me that you will research it further in the event that your regression experiences point you in a certain direction. Having held you back from the truth in a previous life as your father, I need to ensure that the truth prevails in this lifetime! I can't let sleeping dogs lie, my friend!'

Even though Martha was curious about the outcome of the regression session, she suppressed her eagerness. The three of them headed to the White Horse. The White Horse, located at Parsons Green, was probably London's best pub, precisely because most Londoners did not know about it. The pub's cellar man, Mark Dorber, was internationally acknowledged as one of the best artists in the storage and serving of English casked beer. The pub's menu was wide, but the hot favourites were bangers and mash, red bean soup and goat's cheese salad. The pub was one of Terry's regular haunts.[67] Having settled in and ordered their drinks and food, Martha finally spoke, 'Well, Vincent, how did it go?'

Vincent recounted what he had seen during the hour-long session that Terry had put him through. Martha was wide-eyed with amazement as he attempted to recall each detail between gulps of Gales Trafalgar, a deep amber beer. Vincent couldn't help pondering over the fact that Jewish burial customs had not changed in almost 3,500 years and that Jewish burial simply involved washing the body and burying it. Embalming the body with herbs such as aloe vera and myrrh was never employed.[68]

So why were crushed myrrh and aloe vera used on Jesus after he was taken down from the cross? And why did the soured-wine-vinegar sponge smell of opium and belladonna? Why was Pontius Pilate willing to give the body of Jesus to the influential Joseph, even though Roman law did not allow those sentenced to crucifixion to be given a burial?

There were just too many questions and not enough answers. 'I have to discuss this with someone who can possibly help me reconcile what I have just seen with my faith,' thought Vincent. He helped himself to another succulent sausage with creamy mashed potatoes and thought of his friend, Thomas Manning.

Thomas Manning and Vincent had attended St Joseph's seminary together and had been ordained to the priesthood at the same time. When Vincent's parents died, it was Thomas who had taken care of all the funeral arrangements. He had continued to visit Vincent each day in the hospital while he was recovering. Yes, Thomas was just the person to give him direction and advice. But hadn't he seen Thomas Manning in Ireland in a previous life? Would he be doing the right thing by trusting him? Yes, he was sure he could trust Thomas—a past life incident was certainly no reason to mistrust someone.

As they were getting up from their table, they saw a petite Japanese woman sitting, along with a Japanese man, at a table by the window. She was sipping red wine and speaking rather softly, despite the din of the noisy customers. Vincent couldn't help thinking to himself: 'What a delightful creature!'

He did not notice her fixed gaze on Terry while they were inside the restaurant. He also did not notice her following Terry as he headed over to the university to pick up some reference material from the library later in the evening. Most significantly, he did not notice his aunt, Martha, staring intently at the young Japanese woman. Just like he'd never noticed the barely perceptible little tattoo on his aunt's wrist.

Chapter Ten

Ireland, 1864

The Great Famine of Ireland had been caused by the failure of a single crop, the potato, which was the staple diet of Irish peasantry. Even though Catholic peasants were able to grow enough potatoes, most of their crop had to be sold off in order to pay the exorbitant land rents that were demanded by the Protestant tax collectors.[69] One of the poor Catholic families that fell victim to the Great Famine was the illustrious Ó Mainnín clan, descendants of Mainnín, a great chieftain of Connacht. They were left with no alternative but to immigrate to America in 1864—all because of the damned spud!

The Catholics who left Ireland and arrived in America never forgot the hunger that they had experienced. They clung to their faith with fervent devotion but they also clung to their hatred of the Protestant minority which had caused their hunger in the first place.

Middle Village, New York, USA, 1968

One could not escape death in Middle Village. It was a neighbourhood in west-central Queens that had grown precisely because of the cemetery business. Middle Village had begun as a cluster of English families and had derived its name because of its central position between Williamsburgh and the Jamaica Turnpike. In 1879, St John Cemetery had been established just east of 80th Street by the Roman Catholic Church. The hamlet's economic progress had soon become inextricably linked to death.[70]

Ninety years later, Thomas Manning had been born to parents who lived in a simple nondescript house along Metropolitan and 69th Street. Thomas's father worked for *The Ridgewood Times,* the local newspaper, which had been around since 1908. Their family name *Manning* was simply the English equivalent of the Gaelic *Ó Mainnín.*

In 1853, the bishop of New York had observed that there were many Catholics who were without a church in the Middle Village area. He had commenced the construction of St Margaret's Church and school in 1860. Thomas Manning would be baptised here in 1968.

The church and school would become the centre of Thomas Manning's early years growing up in Middle Village. His favourite teacher, who taught the students science, economics and mathematics, made sure that he inculcated the right values among his wards. His favourite lessons and teachings were taken from a book of 999 sayings, or maxims. The book of 999 maxims, entitled *The Way* had been written by Josemaría Escrivá, the Spanish priest who had founded Opus Dei. Yes, Thomas Manning was a very good student.

⚜

Einsiedeln, Switzerland, 1988

In fact, Thomas Manning was an excellent student. After preaching for several years at St Catherine in Virginia, Father Thomas Manning had settled down in Switzerland in the Benedictine abbey of Einsiedeln some years later. Even now, the book of 999 maxims continued to remain by his bedside. His affiliation to the Priestly Society of the Holy Cross continued to be strong—much like the foundations of Einsiedeln. Father Thomas Manning had morphed into Brother Thomas Manning.

Einsiedeln traced its origins back to AD 835 when Meinrad, a Benedictine monk, had withdrawn as a hermit into the Dark Forest. Many more hermits had followed him. Around a century later, Eberhard, a priest from Strasbourg, had assembled the hermits into a monastic community and had founded the Benedictine monastery of Einsiedeln.[71]

Einsiedeln would eventually become extremely important for Swiss Catholicism as also an international site of pilgrimage. Einsiedeln would spur the creation of monastic foundations in North and South America, some of which would go on to become significantly bigger than Einsiedeln itself.

In fact, it was one of these American foundations that had found Thomas Manning and arranged for him to meet Cardinal Alberto Valerio in Italy. Valerio had discreetly spoken to the master of Einsiedeln and ensured that the Oedipus trust had its way in recruiting the right man for the job.

When Manning had first arrived in Einsiedeln, it had taken him a while to become acquainted with daily monastic prayer and work. This had been followed by a novitiate year during which he was introduced to the Rule of St Benedict, monastic spirituality, prayer, and community life. He then took vows for three years. During these three years, he was required to study either philosophy and theology or 'work in his craft'.

Brother Manning had chosen to apply his knowledge of mathematics and economics to better manage the finances of the monastery. Unknown to the other brothers of Einsiedeln, he was also managing several secret numbered accounts in Zurich for his mentor, Cardinal Alberto Valerio. It was indeed true that it was no longer sufficient to slip into a monk's habit and sing the *Gloria Patri*. The skills required by Brother Manning were of an altogether different magnitude.

London, UK, 2012

In the UK, the commonly accepted joke was that *The Times* was read by the people who ran the country; the *Mirror* was read by people who thought they ran the country; the *Guardian* was read by the people who only thought about running the country; the *Mail* was read by the wives of the people who ran the country; the *Daily Telegraph* was read by the people who thought that the country needed to be run by another country; the *Express* by those who were convinced that, indeed, it was; and the *Sun* was read by people who couldn't care less who ran the country as long as the naked girl on page three had big tits.[72]

Vincent was sitting in the pathetically small lobby of the Airways Hotel reading the *Sun.* He was blissfully unaware of the big tits on page three. He was staring at the photograph of his new friend, Professor Terry Acton, on page one. The news story that followed was filled with gruesome details of the discovery of the severed head of Professor Terry Acton in the library of the School of Oriental and African Studies at the University of London. It quoted a visibly shaken librarian, Barbara Poulson, saying she 'could not believe that any human being could do this to another'. Obviously, Ms.Poulson was not up-to-date with global crime.

The story quoted a detective chief superintendent saying that a note had been found along with the severed head and that it had been decided to keep the contents of the note confidential to avoid public misconceptions about the nature of the crime. He went on to say that efforts were ongoing to locate the rest of the body and to track down the perpetrators as soon as possible.

Vincent was trembling. Why was God doing this to him? Why bring Terry Acton into his life and then eliminate him? Why open up secrets of previous lives through Terry? Why place the Bom Jesus documents in his hands? And who in the world would want to kill Terry, a kind, gentle and mild-mannered professor?

Vincent continued sitting in the lobby of the Airways Hotel, not bothered that the furniture and décor had seen better days. He continued staring at Terry's photograph until he made up his mind. He got up, walked over to the front desk and asked the middle-aged matron behind the desk to lend him the phone. He pulled out his AT&T USA Direct calling card from his wallet and dialled the local access number in London, 0800-89-0011. The electronic English voice that answered prompted him to enter the area code and the seven-digit number in the United States. He entered 718-777-2840 for the number in Queens, New York. He was then prompted to enter his international calling card number, which he quickly did. He heard the single, long and straightforward ring tone that was so different to the local English hyphenated one. After four rings, Thomas Manning answered the phone.

'Hello?'

'Tom! I'm glad I caught you in New York. I wasn't sure whether I'd find you there or in Switzerland.'

'Vince, where are you? It's been ages.'

'I'm in London.'

There was a pause at the other end. After a moment, Thomas asked, 'Why are you in London?'

'Well, why not? Listen, Tom, I have to tell you something . . . I'm wondering whether it's such a great idea to have this conversation over a phone, but I don't know when I'll get a chance to meet you . . .'

'Vince, is something wrong? Has something happened?' Thomas sounded genuinely concerned.

'Before I say anything else, I need your promise to keep this conversation confidential,' said Vincent.

'Sure, but *what* exactly is the matter? You're beginning to worry me.'

'Okay, here goes . . . as you know, I had been having strange visions after the passing away of my parents. In fact, you were there by my side in the hospital, right? I needed to explore these strange visions. Don't ask how . . . but that's why I arrived here.'

'I don't understand, Vince. Why this phone call?'

'Tom, yesterday I met a person by sheer chance—Terry Acton, a professor of spirituality and religion. He helped me explain some of the confusion surrounding the odd flashes that were going off in my head.'

The pause at the other end was much longer.

'Tom, are you still there?' asked Vincent.

'Yes, sorry, Vince, my mind had wandered off elsewhere. You were talking about this professor.'

'Precisely. We spent an entire day together and he was killed the very same night!'

'What? How did that happen?'

'I have no idea. Tom, I'm really scared. Could God have punished him for opening up my past lives to me?'

'Whoa! Hold it right there, Vince. What past lives?'

'It's a long story.'

'Go ahead . . . I'm all ears,' said Thomas Manning as he pressed the automatic recording button that was built into his phone while absentmindedly playing with the small pendant that hung around his neck.

New York City, USA, 2012

Thomas Manning picked up the phone and dialled the number in Vatican City.

The Bang & Olufsen phone buzzed gently. His Eminence answered it on the first ring. He pressed the button on the SV-100 scrambler that was attached to the line; one couldn't be too careful nowadays.

When the voice answered, Thomas quickly spoke in Latin, '*Salve! Quomodo vales?*'

The voice answered, '*EGO sum teres. Operor vos postulo ut sermo secretum?*'

Thomas replied in hushed tones, '*Etiam Vincent Sinclair postulo futurus vigilo.*'

The voice was concerned. '*Quare?*'

Thomas began explaining the situation to His Eminence,'*Is orator volo . . .* we have a problem . . .'

His Eminence was on alert.

'Professor Terry Acton may have spoken with someone before his death,' continued Thomas.

His Eminence was getting angry and he spoke sharply, 'Who?'

'Father Vincent Sinclair. Apparently they spent the entire day together before Acton was killed.'

His Eminence was turning crimson red, the colour of his robes, but he controlled his rage.

'Do you think he knows about Terry Acton's research? Is Vincent Illuminati?' asked His Eminence.

'I don't think he knows as yet. And no, I don't think that Vincent is Illuminati. Terry Acton was definitely Illuminati, but I don't think Vincent is. Terry Acton's connections to the Illuminati only happened because of his Rhodes Scholarship and his membership of the Skull & Bones,' explained Thomas Manning.

Valerio cut in, 'Thomas, let me be more specific. Do you think that Acton would have shared the Bom Jesus records with Vincent Sinclair?'

Thomas Manning was quiet for a moment. He then replied, 'It's very likely. It seems that Vincent believes he saw Jesus Christ in a previous life.'

'Blasphemy!' shouted His Eminence.

'True. But he genuinely believes it. I have the recording of the conversation I had with him over the phone. I am quite sure that Terry Acton also believed it. It's thus quite possible that they discussed the Bom Jesus papers,' replied Thomas.

'Then there's only one solution. I will meet you in Zurich to decide the final steps to rid ourselves of this Illuminati menace!' shouted one loyal member of the Crux Decussata Permuta to the other.

Virgin Atlantic's flight VS 900 from London's Heathrow to Tokyo's Narita airport took off at 1pm. The camera-festooned Japanese tourist couple, Mr and Mrs Yamamoto, were in Virgin's Upper Class cabin, having received their professional fees for the library job from their mentor, Alberto Valerio, at The Dorchester Hotel. His Eminence had subsequently checked out on the same day and left for Vatican City. Mr Yamamoto did not know that Mrs Yamamoto had received a fresh assignment involving Mr Yamamoto.

Unknown to them, another flight from Rome was taking off fifty-fifty minutes after their departure. Swiss International Airlines flight LX 333 was on its way to Zurich. Since the airline did not have a first-class section on this flight, His Eminence Alberto Cardinal Valerio had no option but to settle for business class.

The previous evening, Brother Thomas Manning had boarded American Airlines flight 64 at JFK airport. He had arrived in Zurich at 7:05 the next morning, a full nine hours before His Eminence. He had proceeded to Einsiedeln only to return to Zurich on a forty-seven-minute train ride leaving Einsiedeln for Zurich at 3 pm Swiss time, with a single change at Wädenswil.

Mr and Mrs Yamamoto arrived in Tokyo twelve hours after their departure from London. Takuya was tired and decided to soak himself in the bathtub while Swakilki dutifully unpacked for both of them. Swakilki thought about the specific instructions that she had received from His Eminence. Future activities were going to be extremely delicate. Duets were out; solo performances were required. Takuya was a liability.

She needed to calm herself. Where the hell was the marijuana? She steadied herself and walked over to the steamed-up bathroom and opened the medicine cabinet. She rolled herself a joint using the cannabis stored in the innocent-looking vitamin jar. With trembling hands she lit it and inhaled long and hard. As she inhaled, she felt the easing of the tension and the onset of mild euphoria.

She was fine. She was beautiful. She didn't need Takuya. He needed her. The enemy had to be killed. She turned around and saw that he had fallen asleep in the tub and was snoring gently.

She took out the hairdryer from her travel kit and plugged it in. She then flipped on its switch and released it casually into the tub. She then watched with a blank expression as the electric current raced through Takuya's body. As his breath escaped him, she regained hers.

Zurich, Switzerland, 2012

The two men sat together at His Eminence's favourite place, Sprüngli's café on Paradeplatz. His Eminence had ordered hot chocolate for both of them. As they sipped the rich brew, they discussed the latest complication, and two decisions were taken over two rounds of hot chocolate.

Let Swakilki handle the pest, Vincent Sinclair. Let Brother Thomas Manning represent the Oedipus trust to negotiate a settlement with the Isabel Madonna trust as soon as possible.

Chapter Eleven

The convent chapel of the Church of the Holy Ghost at 36, Nightingale Square had been dedicated in 1890. The present church building opened seven years later, in 1897.

Vincent and Martha were seated among the several students, colleagues, friends and family who had assembled inside the church to attend the special Memorial Mass for Professor Terry Acton. Vincent still found it hard to believe that someone could brutally murder a simple and harmless man for no apparent reason. The manner of his death seemed to indicate something far more sinister.

Martha was thoroughly shaken. The depth of her loss could be seen in her moist eyes that would well up every few minutes. They sat quietly listening to the sermon. 'The faith that Jesus had in God allowed him to look at death in a detached way. Death was simply a door that led to a far better existence,' the pastor was saying.

Memorial Mass over, Vincent and Martha stepped out of the cool, dark interiors of the church into a sunny afternoon. Vincent tried consoling a devastated Martha.

'Why should you be sad? You are one of the most ardent believers of life after death. Terry has simply moved on. He's probably with his wife, Susan, right now. C'mon, Nana, be brave,' said Vincent.

Vincent continued, 'Terry gave me a document after our regression. He specifically asked me to follow up on the regression because it might possibly prove a theory of his. Nana, I'm going to need your help.'

'Vincent, I'm in no condition to help anyone. I can barely manage myself,' snapped Martha.

Vincent shot back, 'Listen, I know this is difficult for you, but if you are Terry's friend, you will do what he wanted you to do . . . you owe it to Terry.'

⚱

Vincent and Martha took the stairs to the third floor of the SAGB, which was used for conducting healing therapies such as Reiki, spiritual healing and regression, and borrowed a room. Martha was still remembered affectionately by the administrative staff and they were happy to oblige.

'Okay, get yourself comfortable, physically comfortable. Settle back and relax . . . that's right . . . just . . . relax,' started Martha. 'Look up and observe the skylight. You can see a little green dot on the skylight . . . completely focus your concentration on that spot for a while as you continue to listen . . . a peaceful easy feeling is settling over you . . . your eyes want to close. That's fine. You want to go deeper and relax. Your eyelids are heavy . . . your eyes will close on their own just to rest themselves . . . I will now count backwards from five down to one. You will feel yourself floating into a deeper and deeper trance with each number. Five . . . four . . . three . . . two . . . one. Okay, Vincent, where are you?'

'I think I'm in France.'

'What can you see?'

'There are public executions going on. I'm in the crowd, but in front of me is the Place de la Revolution. There is a guillotine in the centre.'

'What sort of guillotine is it?'

'It has two large upright posts joined by a beam at the top. It sits on top of a platform that is reached by two dozen steps. The whole machine is blood-red. There is a huge blade that has a weight on it. This blade runs in grooves that have been greased with tallow.'[73]

'Are people being killed at this guillotine?'

'The reign of terror has already killed 30,000 people. In this month alone over a thousand people have been beheaded.'

'Are you in the middle of the French Revolution?'

'I think so. It's 1794.'

'Who are you?'

'I am Jean-Paul Pelletier. I'm watching the public spectacle. Right now they are about to execute a young woman called Charlotte Lavoisier.'

'Why?'

'She has been condemned by trial for stabbing and wounding me, Jean-Paul Pelletier, a great leader of the Revolution.'[74]

'Is she waiting for the blade to fall?'

Non, elle a juste arrivé dans le tumbrel normal . . . elle demande à Sanson, le bourreau, voir la guillotine. Elle est courageuse!

'Stop there, Vincent. Float above the scene. I need you to repeat what you just said in English, not French.'

'She has just arrived in the usual tumbrel . . . she has got off . . . she's asking Sanson, the executioner, to be allowed to take a closer look at the guillotine . . . she hasn't seen one before and is curious to see how it works . . . my word, she is brave!'

'What's happening now?'

'She is being strapped to the bascule and the bascule is being hinged horizontally to bring her head into the lunette.'

'Go on.'

'Sanson is pulling the cord . . . the blade is released . . . the head is off! It is rolling into the bloody oil cloth in the wicker basket in front of the guillotine!'

'Okay, Vincent, I need you to go deeper into your previous lives. I'm going to count backwards from five, and when I finish counting you will be in an even older life . . . five . . . four . . . three . . . two . . . one . . . where are you now?'

'I am in Tahuantinsuyu.'

'Where is that?'

'South America. I am a respected warrior under the command of Sapa Inca Pachacuti.'

'Are you an Inca warrior?'

'Yes. Sapa Inca Pachacuti has vastly expanded and created the Tahuantinsuyu. He is the head of four provincial governments—Chinchasuyu, Antisuyu, Contisuyu and Collasuyu. These are located at the four corners of his vast empire. At the centre is Cuzco, the capital.'[75]

'Are you in Cuzco?'

'No. Sapa Inca Pachacuti has built a huge retreat in Machu Picchu. I protect his family there.'

'What is Machu Picchu like?'

'Oh, it is the most beautiful place on earth. It is located on a high mountain ridge, very high up in the clouds. It has a huge palace and several temples. About 750 people can stay in Machu Picchu at a given time. The mountain ranges in the background of Machu Picchu resemble an Inca looking up at the sky . . . the tallest one, Huayna Picchu, is the Inca's nose.'

'What else can you tell me about Machu Picchu?'

'We Incas believe that the solid foundation of the earth must never be excavated, so we have had to build this place entirely out of loose rocks and boulders! Many of our buildings have no mortar . . . it is our extreme precision in cutting that allows this to be done.'

'What do you see around you?'

'Temples for Apo, the god of the mountains; for Apocatequil, the god of lightning; for Chasca, the goddess of dawn; for Chasca Coyllur, the goddess of flowers; for Mama Coca, the goddess of health; for Coniraya, the moon god; for Ekkeko, the god of wealth; for Illapa, the god of thunder; for Kon, the god of rain and for many, many others . . .'

'Is the king a just person? Does he treat you well?'

'*No ladrón, no mentiroso, no ocioso. Tal como estimes a otro, otros también te estimarán.*'

'What language is that, Vincent? Sounds like Spanish.'

'Quechua. It is the language we speak here.'

'So what did you just say?'

'The king is a just man. His motto is, "Do not steal, do not lie, don't be lazy." He also believes that just as you love others, they will love you.'

'What is your role?'

'I am the bodyguard for Mama Anawarkhi.'

'Who is that?'

'She is the wife of Sapa Inca Pachacuti.'

'What do you have to do?'

'I am supposed to protect her. Instead, I am going to kill her because she is plotting against the Sapa Inca.'

'Vincent, I need you to go even deeper . . . I'm once again going to count backwards five . . . four . . . three . . . two . . . one . . . where are you now?'

'我是在中國。我是在宮殿裡面。'

'I take it that you're somewhere in Asia?'

'我有很多痛苦。我是在極度痛苦。痛苦是可怕的。'

'Vincent, I need you to distance yourself from the scene. Can you pull away slightly so that you can tell me in English?'

'I am in China . . . inside a palace. I have a lot of pain. I am in agony. The pain is terrible.'

'What has happened to you?'

'The empress, Wu Zhao, is the evil power on the throne. She had my limbs shattered and then had me placed in a large wine urn to die a slow death in agony!'

'Why would someone be so cruel?'

'I was an advisor to Emperor Gaozong while he lived. I advised him to be wary of Wu Zhao, who was the emperor's chief concubine. After the death of Emperor Gaozong, Wu Zhao has seized the throne and wants to eliminate me.'[76]

'Has she succeeded?'

'我認為不如此。'

'Sorry?'

'I do not think so. Even though I am a cripple for life, I was saved by one of the other concubines, Xiao. I am lucky.'

'Can you tell the time period—which year is this?'

'I think it is AD 689.'

'So where are you? Why are you still in the palace?'

'The kind concubine Xiao has arranged for me to be transported to my ancestral village. Hopefully, I will be able to live the rest of my life there without being detected by Wu Zhao's spies.'

'Vincent, much deeper now . . . I'm once again going to count backwards—five . . . four . . . three . . . two . . . one . . . where are you now?'

'I am in Yerushalem. I'm outside the tomb into which Joseph and Nicodemus have taken Jesus.'

'Who else is there?'

'Mary Magdalene and his mother followed. I was behind them. But it's close to sundown and the women have returned home for the Sabbath.'

'What are you doing?'

'I am now waiting outside the tomb. Temple guards have been sent here to secure the tomb. The Pharisees are worried that the followers of Jesus may try to steal Jesus's body and then claim that he has risen from the dead. They are placing their own guards.'

'Now what?'

'I am hiding behind some bushes. I don't know why I am unable to tear myself away from here. Night has fallen. In the middle of the night, there was a visitor. He looked like an angel because of his white robes . . . I think he was an Essene monk. He rolled away the stone. The guards collapsed with terror.'

'And?'

'The Sabbath is over, and the two Marys have come here to roll away the stone to the tomb, but they are rather surprised to see it open. They are going inside. I'm following at a discreet distance.'

'What do you see?'

'There are two men in white robes. They look like Essenes. They are saying that Jesus is alive, not dead! They are asking the women to go and tell the disciples this news.'

'And do they?'

'They are running out. I'm waiting here to see what happens.'

'Anyone there?'

'The two Essenes are still there. The third person is not recognisable; he has come out of the bushes. Someone's coming . . .'

'Who?'

'Jesus's disciples—Peter and John. Both are looking around inside . . . no, wait, they are coming out. They seem bewildered. They are returning to the city. Ah. Here comes Mary.'

'Which Mary?'

'Mary Magdalene.'

'What is she doing?'

'She's looking inside the tomb. She seems very nervous. She's staring at the two Essenes inside the tomb. She now sees the third man in the bushes. Is it the gardener? No. It's Jesus! Mary is talking to him.'

'Can you hear what they are saying to each other?'

'Not really. I think he is asking her to go and tell his disciples that he is alive. She is walking away. Whenever I see Mary Magdalene, I see three blurred images that seem to fuse together. Jesus is also walking away, but not with her.'

'What are you doing?'

'I am following Jesus.'

'Where is he going?'

'He is following two of his disciples who are on their way to Emmaus. He is catching up with them. He is now walking alongside them and is talking to them. They do not realise that it's him.'

'What is he saying?'

'He is telling them that prophets must necessarily go through pain and suffering. Ah! They have reached Emmaus. They have entered the house and are having dinner. Jesus is picking up a piece of bread, giving thanks and breaking it into pieces before giving it to them. Finally! They have finally realised that it's Jesus!'

'Okay. What are they doing now?'

'The two disciples are heading back to Yerushalem and are meeting the apostles and some others in a secret place. They are telling the others of their experience. Ah! Jesus has arrived here also.'

'They must be happy, right?'

'They are scared. They think he's a ghost. Jesus is telling them not to doubt him. He's pulling his robe to one side to show them his wounds. They seem reassured but not quite certain. He's asking them for food. They've given him some broiled fish. He's eating it. Now they seem to understand that he's real.'[77]

'Go on.'

'Jesus is leaving. I'm still here with the apostles. Oh, it seems that Thomas wasn't here. Here he comes now.'

'What are they saying?'

'The apostles are telling Thomas about Jesus being alive. He doesn't believe them. He's telling them that unless he sees and feels the scars for himself, he cannot believe.'

'Has Jesus returned?'

'Ah, today both Thomas and Jesus are here. Jesus is calling out to Thomas and asking him to touch his wounds. Now Thomas seems to believe that this is indeed Jesus in the flesh. Jesus is calling him "doubting Thomas" because he seems to believe something only when he has actually observed it for himself.'

'Now what's happening?'

'I'm following Jesus to Lake Galilee. Peter, Thomas, Nathaniel, James and John are here. They are fishing through the night with no luck. Jesus is waiting for them on the beach. He's asking them whether they have any fish. They're telling him they have not caught anything at all. Jesus is telling them to cast their nets to the right because he knows there are some fish there. They are trying. They catch a huge load of fish! Jesus has started a charcoal fire and is making breakfast for them. He's asking Peter some questions.'

'And?'

'He's walking away with Peter. John's following. I'm behind them.'

'Where are they going?'

'To a mountain in Galilee. Jesus has arranged a meeting there with all his apostles.'

'What is happening at this meeting?'

'Jesus is telling them to go to different parts of the world in order to recruit disciples in every nation. They are kneeling down as he speaks. They are now getting up and he's leading them to the outskirts of Bethany. He's blessing them. He's walking away towards Bethany . . . the town of Martha, Lazarus and Mary Magdalene.'

Chapter Twelve

The term *Shinto* is simply a combination of two words: *Shin*, meaning *God*, and *Tao*, meaning *path*. Shinto is thus the *path to God*. Shin is the Chinese symbol for God and was rendered into *Kami* by the Japanese.[78] Kami were generally seen as divine spirits that were still caught in the cycle of birth, death and rebirth.

The Meiji restoration had resulted in Shinto becoming the state religion of Japan. State Shinto, however, had ended with the Second World War. To many it appeared that the divine spirits, or Kami, had been unsuccessful in creating a *kamikaze*, a divine wind, to repel the foreign attacks! Shortly after the end of the war, the emperor renounced his status as a living god. In modern Japan, however, Shinto continued to flourish even with the passing of the divine status of the royal family. Shinto shrines continued to assist ordinary people in maintaining their relationships with the spirits of their ancestors and with Kami.

When Swakilki was born, her mother, Aki Herai, had Swakilki's name added to the list kept at the Sumiyoshi Jinja, one of the oldest Shinto shrines in Osaka, and had her declared *ujiko*, a named child. It was a way of making sure that the divine Kami protected Swakilki during this lifetime and beyond.

Swakilki was now at the Sumiyoshi Jinja. Even though she was Catholic, Shinto belief and rituals had remained with her and she desperately wanted comforting. She had just killed the only man whom she had ever come close to loving. She was now well and truly alone, except for the company of the divine Kami.

After electrocuting Takuya, she had spent the next six hours meticulously cleaning the apartment until she had removed all traces of herself. She had then packed all her belongings, loaded Takuya's lifeless body into the trunk of her Toyota Sprinter and driven out of Tokyo along the Toumei Express Motorway to Nagoya. She had then transferred to the Meishin Express Motorway to Osaka. Soon she was driving towards Kansai International Airport. She stopped for a brief moment on the three-kilometre bridge connecting the mainland to the artificial island airport to throw the body into Osaka Bay. She had cringed while doing so. She longed to bring him back to life and hold him in her arms again. She checked into a room at Osaka's Hyatt Regency Hotel where she placed a 'Do Not Disturb' sign on the door and slept for the next seven hours. It was when she woke up and saw the emptiness of her bed that she once again realised how much she missed him.

Swakilki now walked through the Torii, the double-columned gate of the Sumiyoshi Jinja, and crossed over the beautiful bright red staircase bridge within the complex. Swakilki stopped at the water fountain to wash her hands and mouth, a symbolic purification expected before entering a shrine. She needed to find Yoshihama Shiokawa.

Yoshihama was a Shinto priest who had become quite famous in the area. His claim to fame was his combination of Shinto principles with Reiki, the ancient Japanese art of spiritual healing—a formula that Swakilki desperately needed.

Reiki was an alternative therapy developed during the latter half of the nineteenth century by Mikao Usui in Japan. The word *reiki* was a combination of two Japanese words, *rei*, implying the cosmos, and *ki*, meaning energy. It was, therefore, the energy of the cosmos.

Practitioners such as Yoshihama Shiokawa believed that they could direct Reiki energy through their palms into specific parts of the patient's body. More importantly, Yoshihama had combined Reiki with Shinto and Buddhist principles in order to handle mental healing along with physical healing. He believed that he could treat even deeply ingrained issues such as addiction, anxiety, and depressive tendencies by absorbing 'visions' of incidents in the present and past lives of his patients while he energised them.

Yoshihama urged Swakilki to lie down and relax. Once she was relaxed, he began to apply the healing energy of his hands to various areas of her body. Reiki energy would enter Swakilki through her seven chakras. Her body would absorb the required Reiki energy to heal itself while unwanted energy would be dissipated.[79]

Swakilki began to feel varying sensations: hot flushes, cold waves and pressure. The Reiki energy was flowing. Her energy deficiencies were being filled; her energy meridians were being repaired and opened; blocks of stale energy were being slowly melted away.

His hands stopped in the air over her pelvic region. He was certain. This girl had definitely faced sexual trauma in her life; probably child abuse, but he didn't make any comment.

His palms were feeling warm—too much heat. An explosion? What sort of explosion? A gas leak? Why was he seeing a cardinal in scarlet robes?

Yoshihama gradually moved his palms over Swakilki's head and continued moving them down towards her shoulders. He stopped at the base of her neck. 'You have a severe energy blockage here,' he said, as a vision flashed before him. In the vision he saw a young woman's head being chopped off by a guillotine in eighteenth-century Paris. In his vision, Yoshihama did not see the faces of either the victim, Charlotte Lavoisier, or the executioner, Sanson. The original faces must have been different. What Yoshihama saw was Swakilki being executed at the guillotine by Professor Terry Acton. Swakilki had cut off Terry's head in her present life because he had cut off her head in a previous avatar!

He moved his palms further down to her stomach. It was definitely tight and constricted. She had something to hide. Guilt? She had killed. Who? Another vision—an electric chair at Sing Sing prison in New York in 1890. The woman prisoner was killed by the flick of a switch that sent 2,450 volts of electricity through her. The switch was flicked by the state executioner whose face Yoshihama could not recognise. Actually, the face was that of Takuya, recently electrocuted by Swakilki. Tit for tat!

Another vision—an Inca palace in Machu Picchu. Mama Anawarkhi, the wife of the king Sapa Inca Pachacuti, is being strangled by her bodyguard. Yoshihama saw that the queen's face was that of Swakilki, but the bodyguard's face was not known to him. The face was that of Vincent Sinclair. Yoshihama moved his palms along her arms and onwards to her hands. The hands had evil energy flows. Murder? Was this a killer that he was healing? In his vision, Swakilki morphed into Empress Wu Zhao, the evil power on the Chinese throne, shattering the limbs of Vincent Sinclair in revenge for having killed Mama Anawarkhi.

Wu Zhao and Mama Anawarkhi were simply Swakilki in previous lives. She then morphed back into Swakilki as she killed again and again and again.

Chapter Thirteen

Medina, Saudi Arabia, AD 632

All the wives of Prophet Muhammad took care of him during his illness. Lady Ayesha was always by his side. She would only withdraw when his daughter, Lady Fatima, came to visit him. After a short illness, Prophet Muhammad died at around noon on Monday, 8 June, AD 632, in the city of Medina at the age of sixty-three.[80] The Qur'an had been revealed to him by the angel Gabriel over an extended period of time before his death. The Prophet, in turn, had dictated the revelations to his secretaries. One of the passages (4:155-159) that was among the several dictated by the Prophet was:

'They said in boast, "We killed Jesus the son of Mary the Apostle of Allah." But they killed him not nor crucified him. But so it was made to appear to them. And those who differ therein are full of doubt with no knowledge but only conjecture to follow. For sure they killed him not!'[81] Could the Prophet possibly have heard of Irenaeus of Lyons?

Lyons, France, AD 185

The intriguing paragraph written by Irenaeus in Book II, Chapter 22, of his treatise, *Against Heresies*, reads as follows:

On completing His thirtieth year He suffered, being in fact still a young man, and who had by no means attained to advanced age . . . from the fortieth and fiftieth year a man begins to decline towards old age, which our Lord possessed while He still fulfilled the office of a Teacher, even as the Gospel and all the elders testify.[82]

In this rather strange paragraph, Irenaeus was telling his readers that Jesus was very much alive and teaching at the age of fifty, even though he was no longer the youthful man that he had been at the time of his crucifixion at around the age of thirty. Was it possible that Irenaeus had read an Indian book of history called the *Bhavishya Mahapurana* that spoke of a meeting that had happened in AD 115?

North India, AD 115

The man sitting on the mountain had a peaceful and tranquil expression. Peace and love seemed to radiate from within him. King Shalivahana was enraptured by this man's serenity.

Shalivahana was a brave and effective ruler. He had vanquished the attacking hordes of Chinese, Parthians, Scythians and Bactrians. One day, Shalivahana went into the Himalayas. There, in the Land of the Hun, the powerful king saw a man sitting on a mountain who seemed to promise auspiciousness. His skin was fair and he wore white garments. The king asked the holy man who he was. The other replied, 'I am called a son of God, born of a virgin, minister of the non-believers, relentless in the search of truth.'

The king then asked him: 'What is your religion?' The holy man replied, 'O great King, I come from a foreign country, where there is no longer truth and where evil knows no bounds. In the land of the non-believers, I appeared as the Messiah. O King, lend your ear to the religion that I brought unto the non-believers. Through justice, truth, meditation and unity of spirit, man will find his way to Issa in the centre of light. God, as firm as the sun, will finally unite the spirit of all wandering beings in himself. Thus, O King, the blissful image of Issa, the giver of happiness, will remain forever in the heart; it is for this that I am called Issa-Masih.'[83]

The Hindus had eighteen historical books called the *Puranas*. The ninth book was the *Bhavishya Mahapurana*. Unlike the Gospels, which could not be accurately dated, the *Bhavishya Mahapurana*'s date of origin was clearly known. It was authored by the poet Sutta in the year AD 115. The historical passage on King Shalivahana and the holy man was from the *Bhavishya Mahapurana*. Could the *Bhavishya Mahapurana* have possibly influenced Hazrat Mirza Ghulam Ahmad?

Qadian, India, 1835

Hazrat Mirza Ghulam Ahmad was born in the year 1835 in a small town called Qadian in India. He became famous in the Islamic world and before his death in 1908 he published a book titled *Masih Hindustan Mein*.[84] He later went on to found the Ahmaddiya sect of Muslims. In his book he wrote:

> Let it be noted that though Christians believe that Jesus, after his arrest through the betrayal by Judas Iscariot, and crucifixion, and resurrection, went to heaven, yet, from the Holy Bible, it appears that this belief of theirs is altogether wrong . . .
>
> The truth rather is that as Jesus was a true prophet . . . he knew that God . . . would save him from an accursed death . . . he would not die on the cross, nor would he give up the ghost on the accursed wood; on the contrary, like the prophet Jonah, he would only pass through a state of swoon.
>
> Jesus, coming out of the bowels of the earth, went to his tribes who lived in the eastern countries, Kashmir and Tibet, etc.—the ten tribes of the Israelites who, 721 years before Jesus, had been taken prisoner from Samaria by Shalmaneser, King of Assur, and had been taken away by

him. Ultimately, these tribes came to India and settled in various parts of that country.

Jesus, at all events, must have made this journey; for the divine object underlying his advent was that he should meet the lost Jews who had settled in different parts of India; the reason being that these in fact were the lost sheep of Israel.

Of course, Hazrat Mirza had not heard of the Bnei Menashe, who would only come into prominence several years later.

Israel, 2005

The report filed at the BBC World News desk in early April was crisp and concise:

An Indian tribe called the Bnei Menashe have always claimed that they are one of the ten lost tribes of Israel. Now, one of Israel's chief rabbis has recognised this Indian tribe as the lost descendants of ancient Israelites.

Lalrin Sailo, convenor of the Singlung-Israel Association, an organisation representing the Jews of India, said: 'We have always said we are descendants of Menashe (son of Joseph) so it is great to hear that our claims have been authenticated.'

According to the community, the Bnei Menashe are one of the lost ten tribes of Israel who were exiled when the Assyrians invaded the northern kingdom of Israel in the eighth century BC. The community's oral tradition is that the tribe travelled through Persia, Afghanistan, Tibet, China and on to India.[85]

The report spoke about the journey made by the lost tribes of the eighth century BC, but failed to mention the journey St Thomas had made to India in AD 52.

India, AD 52

Acta Thomae, or T*he Acts of Judas Thomas*, was written in several languages, including Syriac, Greek, Latin, Armenian and Ethiopic. According to *Acta Thomae*, after the crucifixion, the apostles had met in order to allocate the various countries of the world among themselves. The Middle East and India had fallen into the lot picked by St Thomas.

The book went on to say that a merchant by the name of Habban arrived in Jerusalem searching for a carpenter needed by the Indian king Gondophares. Jesus apparently met Habban, introduced himself as Jesus the carpenter, and sold his 'slave', Thomas, to Habban for twenty pieces of silver.

Habban enquired of Thomas whether Jesus was truly his master. Thomas quite naturally answered, 'Yes, he is my Lord.' It was then that Habban told Thomas, 'He has sold you to me.'

Jesus had taken the twenty pieces of silver from Habban and given them to Thomas, who then left on Habban's boat. The sea route to India had taken them via the port of Sandruk Mahosa, and they eventually reached the kingdom of Gondophares in India.

Thomas then proceeded southwards to Kerala. In Kodungallur, several families of Kerala were converted by him to the Christian faith. After establishing several churches, Thomas moved on to the east coast of India. He was eventually martyred for proselytising near Mylapore.

The St Thomas Christians continued to flourish in Kerala after Thomas's death. This position would remain unaltered till 1498.

Calicut, India, 1498

It was 20 May 1498. The fleet of three ships that had left Lisbon around a year earlier, the *São Gabriel*, the *São Rafael*, and the *São Miguel*, succeeded in going around the Cape of Good Hope and arrived in Calicut on the west coast of India.[86]

Vasco da Gama had arrived on Indian shores. Over the next 450 years, the Portuguese influence over their Indian colonies would be brutal, ruthless and extremely profitable.

The 170 expedition members had arrived in India assuming they would need to preach Christianity to the 'faithless' natives. They were shocked to see that there were already an estimated two million Christians spread across the land, and that they had 1,500 churches under the jurisdiction of a single Metropolitan of the East Syrian Church.[87] St Thomas had done his job well.

The St Thomas Christians were considered high-caste members of society along Hindu caste lines. Their churches were modelled on the lines of Hindu temples. The East Syrian Church of the St Thomas Christians was Hindu in culture, Christian in religion and Syro-Oriental in worship.

This was not very palatable to the visitors from Portugal. Portugal was Roman Catholic and everything outside the Roman Catholic Church was considered heretic. In order to bring the Indian Christians under his control, Pope Paul IV would declare Goa an Archdiocese in 1557.

This was easier said than done. It was not possible to change hundreds of years of worship, culture, practices and customs that had evolved locally. A possible solution was to bring the Inquisition to India. The Goa Inquisition would be formally inaugurated in 1560, and by the time it would end around 1774, it would succeed in torturing and executing thousands.

The first inquisitors were Aleixo Dias Falcão and Francisco, who took the first formal action of banning Hindus from practising their religion. Any contravention was made punishable by death. In 1599, the Thomas Christians were forcibly converted by the inquisitors to Roman Catholicism. This also implied severe restrictions on their Syriac and Aramaic customs. Again, violations were punishable by death. Condemned Hindus were tortured and put to death.[88]

The Inquisition gained momentum and went on to ban Indian musical instruments, the dhoti—the Indian loincloth favoured by men—and the chewing of betel leaves, a traditional Indian habit. Hundreds of Hindu temples were either destroyed or forcibly converted into Christian churches. Thousands of Hindu texts were burned with a view to ensuring the supremacy of Roman Catholic texts.[89]

It was amidst this turmoil that Alphonso de Castro arrived in Goa in 1767, towards the end of the Inquisition.

⚔

Goa, India, 1767

Alphonso de Castro arrived in Goa ostensibly to give further impetus to the Inquisition, but he was a bad choice for the task. He was more of a scholar than a religious fanatic and was more likely to be found studying the Hindu foundations of Goa's churches than burning heretics at the stake.

This obviously created a problem. The chief inquisitor wanted Castro to be sent back to Lisbon but this could not be done because of the excellent rapport that Castro's father enjoyed with King Joseph I of Portugal.

The next best solution was to give him a project that would keep him busy and, more importantly, out of the way. He was asked to make an exhaustive list of ancient texts that had been found in the homes, temples, churches, mosques and synagogues of the Hindus, the Thomas Christians, the Muslims and the Sephardic Jews. Any text that did not suit the sensibilities of the Roman Catholic Church would eventually have to be destroyed.

It was while going through an old set of manuscripts discovered in the bowels of the Church of Bom Jesus that Castro found a document that would change his life forever.

The Church of Bom Jesus contained the tomb of the Spanish missionary St Francis Xavier, who had begun his mission in Goa in 1542. This, however, was not its principal claim to fame. History recorded that this church had been constructed in 1559. It had actually been in existence well before 1559. Not as a church, but as a mosque.[90]

Within one of the pillars that had been discarded in favour of non-Islamic stonework was a cavity. The cavity contained a bundle of documents that had been written in Urdu. These documents had been found by a Hindu worker, Lakshman Powale, at the site where the mosque was being torn down to make way for the church.

Unaware of the significance of the documents, Lakshman had carried them to his home in the city of Damao, where they had continued to lie unattended for many years. He passed the bundle down to his son, Ravindra Powale, who buried them under his house for fear of the Inquisition. When Ravindra died in 1702 at the ripe old age of eighty-four, his house was requisitioned by the Portuguese administration to facilitate the construction of quarters for visiting missionaries.

The houses in the area had been acquired in 1705 but construction was stopped for lack of funds. Construction recommenced almost forty-three years later, in 1748. It was while the ground was being broken for a new foundation that the old bundle of papers was discovered. The bundle was immediately transferred to the archives of the Portuguese viceroy where it continued to stay until it was taken up for cataloguing by Alphonso de Castro nineteen years later.

The bundle contained eleven texts, of which ten were earmarked for destruction. The eleventh would not be formally catalogued by Castro. It was called the *Tarikh-Issa-Massih*.[91]

For fear for his own life, Alphonso de Castro decided that it would be better for him to leave the document in India prior to his departure for Lisbon in 1770. He was, however, determined to store the document in a place where it would be preserved so that it may be discovered by future generations.

He first set out on a trip to northern India, including Kashmir. Upon his return a few months later, he visited the Church of Bom Jesus and knelt down to pray before the perfectly preserved body of St Francis Xavier, just before boarding the ship that would take him back to Portugal.

'Agradeça-o Deus para dar me a força poupar este livro,' he thought to himself as he prayed fervently.[92]

Chapter Fourteen

London, UK, 2012

Vincent was reading the document that had been entrusted to him by Terry Acton. It was a photocopy of an English translation of the *Tarikh-i-Kashmir*, a history of Kashmir written by a person called Mullah Nadri in 1421.[93]

> . . .Raja Akh came to the throne. He ruled for sixty years. Thereafter, his son, Gopananda, took over the government and ruled the country under the name of Gopadatta. During his reign, many temples were built.
>
> On top of Mount Solomon the dome of the temple had cracked. Gopadatta deputed one of his ministers, named Sulaiman, who had come from Persia, to repair it. The Hindus objected that the minister was an infidel.
>
> During this time Yuz Asaf, having come from the Holy Land to this holy valley, proclaimed his prophethood. He devoted himself, day and night, in prayers to God, and having attained the heights of piety and virtue, declared himself to be a messenger of God for the people of Kashmir. He invited people to his religion.
>
> Because the people of the valley had faith in this Prophet, Raja Gopadatta referred the objection of Hindus to him for a decision. It was because of this Prophet's orders that Sulaiman was able to complete the repairs of the dome.
>
> Further, on one of the stones, Sulaiman inscribed: 'In these times Yuz Asaf proclaimed his prophethood,' and on another stone, he also inscribed that Yuz Asaf was Yusu, Prophet of the Children of Israel.

I have seen in a book of Hindus that this prophet was really Jesus, the Spirit of God, on whom be peace and salutations, and had also assumed the name of Yuz Asaf. The real knowledge is with God. He spent his life in this valley. After his death he was laid to rest in Mohalla Anzmarah. It is also said that lights of prophethood used to emanate from the tomb of this Prophet. Raja Gopadatta died after having ruled for sixty years and two months.

Vincent came to the end of the page. Turning it over, he found another photocopied document. It was called the *Tarikh-Issa-Massih* and had originally been written in Urdu sometime around the eleventh century. The tedious passage read much like the sixteen verses of Matthew in the Bible, outlining the royal lineage of Jesus:

Abraham was the father of Isaac, and it was Isaac who fathered Jacob. In turn, Jacob's son was Judas. The children of Judas and his wife, Thamar, were Phares and Zara. Phares would have a child—Esrom, and Esrom would have a child—Aram. Aram's offspring was Aminadab who sired Naasson. Naasson would become the father of Salmon. Salmon had a child with Rachab by the name of Boaz. Boaz would father Obed with Ruth. Obed would produce Jesse. Jesse was the immediate predecessor of David, the great king.

The great King David married the woman who had been a previous wife of Urias and fathered the great Solomon. Solomon's offspring was Roboam, who fathered Abia. Abia's child was Asa. Asa's son was Josaphat, who sired Joram. Joram fathered Ozias, whose lineage would be continued through Joatham. Joatham's son was Achaz, and his grandson was Ezekias. Ezekias continued the dynasty with Manasses, who fathered Amon who, in turn, produced Josias. Josias had a son by the name of Jechonias around the time that they were carried off in captivity to Babylon. It was in Babylon that Jechonias had a son, Salathiel.

Salathiel continued the unbroken line with his son Zorobabel, who fathered Abiud. Eliakim was the son of Abiud. Eliakim produced a child by the name of Azor. Azor's progeny was Sadoc. Sadoc's offspring was Achim. Achim produced Eliud, who fathered Eleazar. Matthan was his son. It was Matthan who sired Jacob. Jacob was the father of Joseph, the husband of Mary, of whom was born Issa . . .

The Bible, of course, stopped right there. This document, however, went further:

Jacob was the father of Joseph, the husband of Mary, of whom was born Issa, who married Mary Magdala. Issa and Mary had a child by the name of Sara, who was born to them in India but was later sent to Gaul with her mother. Issa remained in India, where he married a woman from the Sakya clan on the persistence of King Gopadatta and had a son, Benissa. Benissa had a son, Yushua, who fathered Akkub. Akkub's son was Jashub. Abihud was the son of Jashub. Jashub's grandson was Elnaam. Elnaam sired Harsha, who sired Jabal, who sired Shalman. Shalman's son Zabbud converted to Islam. Zabbud fathered Abdul, who sired Haaroon. His child was Hamza. Omar was Hamza's son and he produced Rashid. Rashid's offspring was Khaleel.

Vincent's mind was in a panic. His head was reeling with this information overload. He needed to assimilate what he had just read. At the bottom of the page was written in Portuguese:

Satis est, Domine, Satis est, os dois anjos ditos. Mastrilli sem dúvida fêz a mais melhor cama de prata. Mas para guardar com cuidado um segredo dos mortos. O copo do ouro de Ignatius' é melhor do que uma cabeça de prata. A cidade é ficada situada entre o' norte 15°48' e 14°53'54 e entre 74°20' e 73°40' para o leste.

Translated into English, it meant:

It is enough, O Lord, it is enough, the two angels said. Mastrilli, without doubt, made the best silver bed. But to carefully guard a secret of the dead, Ignatius's gold cup is better than a silver bed. The city is located between 15°48' and 14°53'54' north and between 74°20' and 73°40' east.

Chapter Fifteen

The Federalnaya Sluzhba Bezopasnosti is an unfortunate choice of name, even when it is abbreviated to FSB. Particularly when one considers the fact that its brand equity was much greater when it used to be called the Komitet Gosudarstvennoy Bezopasnosti, or the KGB.[94]

Lavrenty Edmundovich Bakatin was sitting in his office, halfway through his customary bottle of vodka, when the phone rang. He picked it up and listened for a few seconds. He then said abruptly, 'I'll meet you at St Louis on the Malaya Lubyanka,' and hung up.

Quickly putting on his overcoat, he headed downstairs to Lubyanka Square, which was where the FSB's headquarters, and his office, were located. Just in front of the drab FSB building stood the Church of St Louis.

It was November, and the average daily temperature in Moscow ranged from 24°F to 32°F. The heavy woollens made Bakatin look even fatter than he actually was. He made his way inside the church and sat down clumsily on the last pew.

Throughout the glasnost era of Gorbachev, millions of dollars had been funnelled by the Vatican into Moscow using the good offices of Bakatin. This had been necessary in order to ensure that Poland be released from the Warsaw Pact.

The provider of those funds came and sat down next to Bakatin. Brother Thomas Manning looked closely at Bakatin, and then sniffed. 'Have you been drinking the stuff or swimming in it?' he remarked as he smelled the vodka.

'*Vali otsyuda*!' grunted Bakatin to Thomas in Russian.

Thomas grinned. 'Fuck you too, old man!' The two men enjoyed an excellent rapport that had been strengthened over the years by the continuous flow of cash. Thomas Manning prided himself on being greater than any other freedom fighter. His backdoor collaboration with Bakatin and Moscow had resulted in the independence of predominantly Catholic Hungary, Czechoslovakia and Ukraine from Russia as well as the independence of Slovenia and Croatia from Yugoslavia. All of this had been achieved at the behest of Alberto Valerio.

Luckily, the entire American security establishment had been ultra-conservative from the Reagan years onwards. They had been quite happy to encourage Manning's efforts, even partially fund them. In the post-glasnost era, Bakatin had become Manning's conduit to the Sheikh.

'So. Are they willing to deal?' asked Manning.

'*Pacheemu ti takoy galuboy*?' asked Bakatin. Thomas was getting fed up with the insults. Bakatin was asking him why he looked so gay! '*Perestan' mne jabat' mozgi svojimi voprosami*!' shot back Manning. 'Stop fucking my brain with your stupid questions!'

Manning continued, 'It's vital that we get access to him, either in Kashmir or anywhere else. If that means purchasing equipment for the Sheikh from the Pakistanis or North Koreans, so be it.'

Bakatin looked at him through glazed eyes. He then turned serious and said, 'The Sheikh wants it all. The reactor, the raw material, delivery systems, the drawings——and the cash. In return he will hand him over to you.'

He then held Manning's face in his gloved hands and planted two stinging Russian vodka-breathed kisses on his cheeks before he got up and left.

Thomas thanked his lucky stars for having preached for some years at St Catherine of Siena in Virginia before moving to Switzerland. Otherwise he would never have met Bakatin through the FBI.

The Fox News anchor was saying, 'There's now disturbing information regarding the FBI operative being held for espionage on behalf of the Russians. Apparently, his activities, which were supposed to help the Russians, also succeeded in helping Osama-bin-Laden . . .'[95]

The report continued: 'He sold the Russians a highly classified and secret piece of American technology, and by all accounts it seems that the Russians, in turn, may have passed on the technology to bin-Laden's Al-Qaeda terrorist network.'

The FBI agent in question had been born in 1957 in Chicago. After attending Southern Illinois University, he had joined the Chicago police and then moved on to the FBI's counter-intelligence wing. After fifteen years of selling secrets for a gross remuneration of $2.1 million, he had finally been arrested in his Virginia home. Throughout his years of treachery, he had continued to attend Mass daily and was a regular parishioner of St Catherine of Siena, a church in a Virginia suburb. One of the regular preachers at St Catherine of Siena was a priest called Thomas Manning. Thomas Manning would soon become friends with Bakatin through his parishioner.

⚜

Bakatin would receive millions of dollars from accounts in Switzerland operated by Brother Thomas Manning for Valerio. The *Pacific News* of May 2001 would write:

> Rivers of money, much of it provided by Bill Casey's CIA, poured into Warsaw and Moscow, and the Vatican found ready support from the US because the security establishment . . . was packed with conservative Catholics. The Vatican's political work with Moscow paid off handsomely with the independence of Catholic-dominant Hungary, Czechoslovakia, Ukraine, and later, from Moscow's nominal ally Yugoslavia, of Slovenia and Croatia.
>
> Intelligence experts and congressional committees are puzzling over what motivated the FBI agent to spy for

Moscow over the past fifteen years. Money does not seem to be the answer because he lived in an ascetic style. The search for a motive is complicated by the fact that his colleagues say that he was fiercely anti-communist and a devout member of Opus Dei, an ultra-conservative Catholic organisation. He was a regular parishioner of St Catherine of Siena Church, in a Virginia suburb of the capital. It may seem paradoxical that he would spy for the Soviet Union, a moral adversary and indeed a Satanic force in the eyes of Opus Dei. During Gorbachev's glasnost era, however, there is evidence of behind-the-scenes collaboration between the Vatican and Moscow. In particular, Cardinal Alberto Valerio, a powerful Opus Dei supporter, pursued a policy of reaching out to Moscow with the aim of gaining Poland's release from the Warsaw Pact.

The entire process of securing the independence of Poland had made one man very powerful: His Eminence Alberto Cardinal Valerio. Alberto Cardinal Valerio had earned his doctorate in theology from the Catholic University of Leuven in Belgium.

☩

Kahuta, Pakistan, 2012

Someone else had earned a doctorate from the Catholic University of Leuven at around the same time. Not in theology but in metallurgy. His name was Dr Dawood Omar, one of the members of the scientific team reporting to Dr Abdul Qadeer Khan, the father of the Pakistani nuclear bomb.[96] Dr A.Q. Khan and Dr Dawood Omar had attended the University of Leuven at the same time as Alberto Cardinal Valerio.

Dr Dawood Omar looked at the photographs of his nuclear facilities longingly, the way a parent looks at his child with love. He had nurtured the Khan Nuclear Research Laboratories in Kahuta since 1976. Twenty-five years later, they had succeeded in closing the nuclear gap with India. Omar had every reason to be proud, even though he was now rather old.[97]

Omar had received his engineering degree from the University of Karachi before moving on to Germany and Belgium, where he had finally earned his doctorate in physics from the Catholic University of Leuven, in 1972—the same time as Alberto Valerio, later to become His Eminence Alberto Cardinal Valerio, who was on his way to Pyongyang.

༢༠

Pyongyang, North Korea, 2010

International intelligence agencies had begun to observe regular flights between Pakistan and North Korea, accelerating at the beginning of the 1990s when there were about nine flights per month. These flights reportedly followed the visit of high-level North Korean officials to Pakistan. Dawood Omar had also made thirteen visits to North Korea, beginning in the 1990s. This particular flight, however, was not clandestine.

North Korea's official carrier, Air Koryo, flew into Pyongyang on only two days of the week—Tuesdays and Thursdays. Both flights were from one origin, Beijing. Air Koryo's flight JS 152 from Beijing to Pyongyang had taken off at 11:30 am and arrived in Pyongyang at 2 pm. On board was His Eminence Alberto Cardinal Valerio, travelling under an alias. His visa to the Democratic People's Republic of Korea had been organised through FBI channels. For all intents and purposes, he was merely a consultant to the World Health Organisation. He was met at the airport by a member of the Ministry of Public Health. At customs, he was asked to hand over his mobile phone, for which he was issued a receipt. He would be allowed to take it back upon his departure. He was quickly escorted to the Yanggakdo Hotel along with his car, driver, ministry representative and official interpreter.

Another flight had arrived in Pyongyang the same day. Its lone Pakistani occupant had visited Pyongyang several times before as part of the delegations led by Dr A.Q. Khan. His name was Dr Dawood Omar.

He did not have a visa. He didn't need one. He had valuable technology to sell; not only to Iran, Libya and North Korea, but also to Al-Qaeda. The bill would be paid by Thomas Manning on behalf of His Eminence Alberto Cardinal Valerio from the Oedipus trust.

🔱

The world's longest railway journey without changing trains is of 10,214 kilometres. The train, operated by the Trans-Siberian Railway, starts in Moscow and ends in Pyongyang. It is the route least used for entering Pyongyang, and it was precisely for this reason that Lavrenty Edmundovich Bakatin was on it, along with the Sheikh.

Bakatin had drunk vodka throughout the journey. His friend, the Sheikh, had prayed to Allah throughout it.

🔱

The *Washington Quarterly* would report that:

> The most disturbing aspect of the international nuclear smuggling network headed by Dr Abdul Qadeer Khan, widely viewed as the father of Pakistan's nuclear weapons, is how poorly the nuclear non-proliferation regime fared in exposing and stopping the network's operation. Despite a wide range of hints and leads, the United States and its allies failed to thwart this network throughout the 1980s and 1990s as it sold the equipment and expertise needed to produce nuclear weapons to major US enemies, including Iran, Libya, and North Korea.[98]

US intelligence had, at least partially, penetrated the network's operations, leading to many revelations and ultimately, the dramatic seizure of uranium-enrichment gas-centrifuge components bound for Libya's secret nuclear weapons programme aboard the German-owned ship *BBC China*. Libya's subsequent renunciation of nuclear weapons led to further discoveries about the network's operations and the arrest of many of its key players, including Khan himself. Suspicions remain that members of the network may have helped Al-Qaeda obtain nuclear secrets.

The University of Leuven had spawned an interesting partnership between the Oedipus trust and the Isabel Madonna trust. Alberto Valerio and Dawood Omar.

🕉

Waziristan, Pakistan-Afghanistan border, 2012

The Sheikh's Master, the ultimate beneficiary of the Isabel Madonna trust, was performing Salah, his daily prayer, for the fifth time that day. He had already completed his Wudu, the ritual ablution, during which he had washed his hands, teeth, face, nose, arms, hair, ears and feet, three times in specific order. He had started his Salah with the Niyyah, or the intention to pray, by reciting the first Surah of the Qur'an. He had then bowed, recited something, stood upright again, then sat on his legs. He had placed his hands and face down on his prayer mat and had then sat up, repeating this action once more before standing up and running through the entire sequence, or Raka'ah. He was now nearing the end of his prayers by looking right and left, saying, 'Peace be unto you, and on you be peace.'[99]

Prayers duly completed, he sat down on his rug, turned around and stared into the eyes of the Sheikh, who was present along with Bakatin. He asked, 'So what do the crusaders of the cross demand?'

'They want him . . . you know, our man. In return they have paid for and have arranged for the nuclear weapon. Besides, they have transferred ten million dollars from their Oedipus account to our Isabel Madonna account.'

'What if I do not give him to them? What if I decide to use him for some greater calling?'

'We promised them that we would give him up,' said the Sheikh, shifting his weight uneasily on his own prayer rug.

'Have Christians kept their promise to Muslims that we should now honour a promise made by a Muslim to a Christian?' asked the Sheikh's Master.

Bakatin was surprisingly sober; he could not drink in the presence of the Sheikh's Master. In his newfound sobriety he said, 'Muslims have always been kind and gracious. I know that you are no less than the great Saladin!'

Flattery always worked. Bakatin's sobriety helped.

Jerusalem, 1192

Saladin, or Salah al-Din Yusuf, had recaptured Jerusalem for the Muslims in 1187. When his army entered Jerusalem, his soldiers were strictly prohibited from killing civilians, looting or plundering. Saladin's victory came as a shock to Pope Gregory VIII, who had commissioned Richard the Lionheart to mount the Third Crusade to recapture the holy city.

Richard had marched on Jerusalem in 1192. Unfortunately, his fever got in the way. His men were dying of hunger and thirst, so he appealed to the great Saladin to provide him with food and water. Saladin had duly obliged. Being a devout Muslim, it was his duty to help the needy. He sent frozen snow and fresh fruit to Richard in abundance.[100]

Richard had eventually been unable to recapture Jerusalem and finally sued for truce with Saladin. Saladin agreed to let Christian pilgrims continue to visit the holy city without being troubled in any way by his Muslim brothers. Neither Richard nor Saladin had been too happy with the uneasy agreement, but both had realised that it was in their respective interests to work together.

An alliance between Christianity and Islam.

Vatican City, 2012

'Wearing traditional papal robes, the 265th Pontiff appeared Tuesday on a Vatican balcony as tens of thousands gathered in St Peter's Square to listen to him deliver his Easter address,' said CNN.[101]

Sitting along with the other cardinals was His Eminence Alberto Cardinal Valerio. That morning he had been reading an article that was culled from the *Arab News*. The author was someone called Amir Taheri, who had written:

> At the start of the last century there were just six more or less independent Muslim states. By the year 2000 that number had grown to fifty-three. When John Paul II became Pope, Islam was no longer the religion of a neighbouring civilisation of Europe but a significant and growing presence within the continent.[102]

It was the next paragraph that had held Valerio's rapt attention:

> The history of the past three to four decades is one of intense competition between Islam and Christianity, especially the Catholic version, for converts. In 1980, John Paul II ordered a review of relations with Islam. This was based on the idea of a grand alliance between the Catholic Church and Islam. In western Europe, the heartland of Catholicism, the Pope saw Islam as an ally on such issues as homosexual 'marriages', abortion, euthanasia, human cloning, and the status of women. John Paul II pursued his

quest for an alliance with Islam in 1986, by becoming the
first Pope to visit a Muslim country. During that visit to
Morocco he had this to say: 'We believe in the same God,
the one and the only God, who created the world and
brought its creatures to perfection.'

Valerio smiled a smile of quiet satisfaction and made up his
mind that on critical issues, it was advisable to work alongside
the enemy. They had done it for hundreds of years in the Crux
Decussata Permuta.

Chapter Sixteen

Port Pipavav, located in the Saurashtra region of the state of Gujarat in western India, was one of the smaller ports, certainly much smaller than Mumbai, which handled the bulk of India's cargo flows. Phase I of Pipavav Port had resulted in three dry cargo berths and one liquid cargo berth. The three dry cargo berths had been constructed as a single-length jetty of 725 metres, employing equipment capable of handling containers as well as bulk cargo.[103]

The cargo ship that was docked at Pipavav was a standard 65,000-dwt Panamax vessel, one that represented the largest acceptable size to transit the Panama Canal—a length of 275 metres and a width of 32. It bore the name *M/V Namgung*, a North Korean registration.

It was unloading a rather nondescript container. The container held an important piece of cargo that needed to be cleared through customs with minimum fuss. This was precisely the reason the cargo had been sent to the port of Pipavav, and not to Mumbai.

The certificate of origin indicated that the 'construction jig' inside the container was from China and was headed to Himachal Pradesh in northern India. This was not entirely true. It had actually travelled from Pakistan to China, onwards to North Korea and then to Pipavav. At each stage, some critical components had been added.

From here, it would be loaded onto a massive truck that would eventually transport it by road to its final destination. The recipient was shown on the bill of lading as a company with its registered office in Himachal Pradesh.

The 'construction jig' was very similar to the 13-kiloton uranium gun-type device that had been used in Hiroshima. It consisted of four simple elements. First, there was a uranium target. Second, there was a rail on which this uranium target sat mounted at one end. Third was the gun that would shoot a 'uranium bullet' and was mounted on the other end of the rail. And fourth was the uranium bullet itself.[104]

Neither the target nor the bullet individually contained adequate uranium-235 to start a chain reaction. However, critical mass and a nuclear reaction could be started if these two elements were slammed together with sufficient force. After all, uranium-235 was radioactive. This meant that it was emitting neutrons spontaneously. If sufficient uranium-235 could be held together, each of the released neutrons could strike a uranium atom, releasing another pair of neutrons, thus setting off the chain reaction that could cause the massive detonation needed. The sort that Nostradamus had written about in 1547.

Salon, France, 1547

Michel de Nostredame was working on over a thousand different prophecies. Some years earlier, he had met some Franciscan monks while travelling through Italy. Nostradamus had thrown himself down on his knees and had reverentially clutched at the habit of one of the monks, Felice Peretti. When the monks had asked him why he was showing such reverence for an ordinary monk, Nostradamus had replied, 'I must yield myself and bow before His Holiness.'[105] The ordinary monk of lowly birth, Felice Peretti, would become Pope Sixtus V, nineteen years after the death of Nostradamus.

Nostradamus' quatrains spoke of three powerful and tyrannical leaders called 'anti-Christs', who would each lead their nations and people into terrible bloodshed.

Nostradamus wrote about the first, Napoleon:

'An emperor shall be born near Italy, who shall cost the empire dear . . . from a simple soldier he will rise to the empire . . . a great troop shall come through Russia . . . the exhausted ones will die in the white territory . . . the captive prince, conquered, is sent to Elba.'

Nostradamus then wrote about the second anti-Christ, Hitler:

'Out of the deepest part of the west of Europe, from poor people a young child shall be born, who with his tongue shall seduce many people . . . he shall raise up a hatred that had long been dormant . . . the child of Germany observes no law . . . the greater part of the battlefield will be against Hister.'

Nostradamus went on to write about a third, one who would follow Hitler:

'Out of the country of Greater Arabia shall be born a strong master of Mohammed . . . he will be the terror of mankind . . . never more horror . . . by fire he will destroy their city, a cold and cruel heart, blood will pour, mercy to none.'

Nostradamus could not have imagined how devastatingly accurate his predictions would be.

⚜

Paris, France, 2011

Ataullah al-Liby read the note in his pathetic little flat in the Banlieue, the poorest section of suburban Paris, home to the highest concentration of Muslim immigrants. In 2006, Paris had burned as disenchanted Muslim youths had gone on a rampage. The French Intifada,[106] as it would come to be known, had been masterminded by the young Ataullah.

Born in the wretched squalor of the Banlieue, the Muslim-dominated suburb of Paris, Ataullah had learned to fight for survival at a very young age when he had beaten up two other children who had tried to rob him of his only pair of shoes. Ataullah had not only kept his shoes, he had given the two would-be thieves a black eye, several broken teeth and two broken ribs between them.

153

For the average American, the word 'suburb' evoked images of an idyllic, leafy home to a community best depicted in *Desperate Housewives*. The French Banlieue, however, had developed rather differently, to say the least. If one took a train ride from Charles de Gaulle Airport to the centre of Paris, one saw the miles of depressing, stark, dehumanising and ominous concrete buildings that constituted the Banlieue. If one added, to this terrible landscape, a high rate of unemployment and a seething resentment against the perception that even French-born Muslims would never really be accepted as French, one had an explosive formula, ideally suited for the indoctrination of young and angry Muslims by Al-Qaeda.

The well-indoctrinated Ataullah now looked closely at the note he had received from Ghalib.

21 January 2012.

⚱

La Triple Frontera, TBA, South America, 2011

The almost inaccessible jungle and hilly terrain nestled between Brazil, Argentina and Paraguay was known as the TBA, the Tri-Border Area, or La Triple Frontera.[107]

Terror groups such as the Hezbollah, al-Gama'a al-Islamiyya, Islamic Jihad, Al-Qaeda, Hamas, and the Lebanese drug mafia had been sending their recruits to this region for many years precisely because it was inaccessible and out of reach for most government authorities.

The kingpin of the TBA was Boutros Ahmad. Positioned here by Ghalib, he had masterminded the attack on the Israeli embassy in Buenos Aires as well as the attack on the Jewish Community Centre.

Boutros Ahmad commanded money power. The Black Market Peso Exchange, the largest and most sophisticated system of laundering money in the western hemisphere, along with *hawala*, an Islamic form of money transfer, was entirely controlled by

Boutros in the La Triple Frontera region. Boutros had also been accused of cocaine-trafficking through a cartel of drug smugglers in the sizeable Muslim immigrant communities of the region. None of the charges had ever been proved and Boutros didn't really care. Boutros was a member of the al-Murabitun, the most popular missionary movement of Latin America, an international Sufi order founded in the seventies by Sheikh Abdel Qader as-Sufi al-Murabit, a controversial Scottish Muslim convert. Religious zeal, drug money and terrorism made for a lethal combination.

The product of that lethal combination now read the message from Ghalib. Finally, some serious action.

21 February 2012.

⚑

Xinjiang, China, 2011

The East Turkestan Islamic Movement had been seeking independence for the Chinese province of Xinjiang since the 1990s. The group was radically Islamist but extremely popular among the Uighur population of Xinjiang.[108]

Even countries that had originally held the view that the East Turkestan Islamic Movement was a genuine independence movement had been left speechless when it had come to light that 1,000 Uighur men had undergone training by Al-Qaeda in Afghanistan.

The group had raked up an impressive score: 200 attacks with 162 dead and more than 440 injured. Faris Kadeer enjoyed his work.

Faris Kadeer had been born an Uighur Sunni Muslim. As a child growing up in Xinjiang, the *mahalla* had been the centre of his life. Daily life had been based on these local residential cooperatives, the mahallas, and the centre of each mahalla had inevitably been the local mosque where daily prayers were conducted. It was at one of these prayers that Faris Kadeer had been recruited and sent to the Khalden Camp. Faris was now one of the most dedicated members of Ghalib's team.

He looked at the note from Ghalib—wonderful! *Bek esil boldi!*[09]

21 March 2012.

⚑

London, UK, 2011

Fouad al-Noor was reading the note in his cramped studio in Wembley. Next to him sat a cup of steaming hot tea and a plate of mutton kebabs.

He had just finished his prayers when the note arrived. It had been delivered by the old gatekeeper of the Wembley mosque on Ealing Road.

At times Fouad found it difficult to remember his old self. Where had the east Londoner's spiky haircut, the Gucci shoes and the Armani clothes gone? Fouad, a British-born Pakistani, had lived most of his life as a Londonstani, the popular term given to Asian youth of England, staying out late with his friends, and missing prayers quite often. All that had changed after he went for Haj to Saudi Arabia.

He had found himself in Mecca, wandering among 23,000 Muslim pilgrims from Britain. His head had been shaven, and he had grown a beard. His only clothing was the simple white robe signifying that all Muslims were equal before God—quite a radical departure from Gucci and Armani.

As he jostled with the hundreds of thousands filtering out of the Grand Mosque in Mecca, he joined them in raising his hands to the heavens and chanting *'Labbaik Allah humma labbaik!* Here I am, O Lord!' That was when he knew that he was a Muslim first, last, and to the end. The subsequent meeting with Ghalib had convinced him of his mission in life. The training at Khalden had been a cakewalk.

Fouad had been waiting impatiently since. Good. The date was final.

21 April 2012.

🔱

Kuala Lumpur, Malaysia, 2011

Tau'am Zin Hassan read the note. The strategist behind Darul Islam had spent many months waiting to see his dream fulfilled, setting up the Daulah Islamiah Nusantara, or the Islamic Caliphate of Indonesia, Malaysia and Southern Philippines.[110]

He remembered the call to prayer at the Al Mukmin Islamic boarding school in Ngruki, Central Java. On that fateful day, he had left his wife and headed towards the mosque and the Taklim councils in the surrounding villages. He had not returned for five years. From Ngruki, he had run from one town to another—Semarang, Bandung, Jakarta, Lampung and Medan—before finally settling down in Malaysia. Tau'am Zin Hassan had fled Ngruki because of his refusal to accept Pancasila as the sole state-sponsored ideology in Indonesia. Little had he imagined that he would one day become the most dreaded Islamic hardliner in all of Malaysia, Indonesia and the Philippines. Ghalib was a bonus.

The note was one more step in the direction of the Islamic Caliphate.

21 May 2012.

🔱

Katra, Jammu & Kashmir, India, 2011

Nearly five-and-a-half million devotees paid homage to the divine Goddess in 2003. An average of 14,794 visits each day of the year. A pilgrimage to the holy shrine of Vaishno Devi was considered to be one of the holiest pilgrimages by one billion Hindus in the world. So why was Bin Fadan, one of the key operatives of the Jaish-e-Mohammed,[111] present in this Hindu pilgrimage town? He read the note from Ghalib:

> Longitude: 74°57'00'. Latitude: 32°59'00'. Phase of Moon: 0.274. Planet, Longitude, Latitude, Right Asc., Declination. Sun, 29 Sgr 31'38', -0°00'03', 17:57:56, -23°26'09'. Moon, 08 Ari 00'14', 3°24'56', 00:23:59, 6°18'43'. Moon's Node, 25 Sco 35'58', 0°00'00', 15:33:04, -19°09'27'. Apogee, 29 Tau 47'12', -0°22'58', 03:50:44, 19°43'42'. Mercury, 14 Sgr 00'41', 0°27'53', 16:50:52, -22°01'02'. Venus, 06 Sgr 00'19', 1°07'28', 16:17:19, -20°11'56'. Mars, 26 Cap 03'52', -1°09'54', 19:53:11, -22°04'38'. Jupiter, 08 Gem 57'20'R, - 0°44'40', 04:29:29, 21°03'14'. Saturn, 08 Sco 37'09', 2°18'24', 14:27:59, -12°11'14'.Uranus, 04 Ari 38'16', - 0°42'47', 00:18:09, 1°11'18'. Neptune, 00 Psc 48'11', - 0°36'39', 22:12:18, -11°45'30'. Pluto, 08 Cap 55'59', 3°20'47', 18:37:56, -19°47'46'. Chiron, 05 Psc 36'53', 5°16'39', 22:21:54, - 4°32'17'. Quaoar, 23 Sgr 58'46', 7°32'28', 17:35:11, -15°45'55'. Sedna, 22 Tau 52'08'R, -12°02'07', 03:34:04, 6°49'24'. Sgr A*/GalCtr, 27 Sgr 01'52', -5°36'34', 17:46:29, -29°00'38'[112]

An astrologer was immediately summoned; someone who could interpret the planetary positions. 'Can you tell me what this means?' asked Bin Fadan.

Pandit Ramgopal Prasad Sharma was just another ordinary visitor to Katra on a pilgrimage to the divine Mother, but he always carried his Panchaang, the Indian ephemeris, wherever he went. After all, planetary positions were the tools of his trade.

He looked in his ephemeris and said, 'These are planetary positions on a given date at a particular location. Judging from my ephemeris, I would say that these positions would be attained in Katra on 21 June 2012.'

Bin Fadan smiled at Pandit Ramgopal Prasad Sharma as he remembered growing up in Pakistan.

During his eleven-year reign over Pakistan, General Zia ul-Haq had enforced his policy of Islamisation, and eventually the madrasa infrastructure had been institutionalised. Zia had empowered the mullah who eventually became the sword of Islamisation. Bin Fadan was the product of one such madrasa. He was, in effect, a product of the Pakistani military, which had developed the top-down strategy of the expansion of the madrasa system for political gain. The main objective of the madrasa infrastructure was to use Islamist militancy as an economical tool for Pakistan's geopolitical interests in Afghanistan and India.

Bin Fadan's education had been a hybrid mix of the ultra-conservative Deobandhi version of Islam in the Indian subcontinent, the Saudi desert version of Wahabism, and the Middle-Eastern revolutionary version of Islamic Brotherhood. A few years later, he had been selected to secretly infiltrate the Pakistan-India border and assimilate himself among the millions of Indian Muslims.

Now his preparation would come in use.

21 June 2012.

Baghdad, Iraq, 2011

Kader al-Zarqawi had been born in Zarqa, Jordan. In fact his name, 'al-Zarqawi', literally meant 'the man from Zarqa'. The man from Zarqa was now the man from Baghdad. He was the most dreaded and feared Islamic terrorist in Iraq and the American government was offering a reward of US$ 50 million for his capture.[113]

Kader al-Zarqawi had spent his youth as a petty criminal in Jordan. Quick-tempered, and barely literate, al-Zarqawi had been quick to volunteer as an Afghan Arab, to lead fighters against the Soviets in Afganistan in the eighties. The defeat of the Soviets in Afghanistan had resulted in Kader returning to Jordan with a radical Islamist agenda. He would spend the next six years in prison there, accused of conspiring to overthrow the monarchy. He had managed a daring escape and, at Ghalib's behest, moved to Iraq and established links with Ansar al-Islam—a group of Kurdish Islamists from the north of the country.

Sitting inside a decrepit old house located close to the Al-Noor Hospital in the Al-Sho'la neighbourhood in Baghdad, virtually under the very noses of the American forces, Kader al-Zarqawi calmly read the handwritten note in Arabic that had come directly from Ghalib. Good. He cursed, '*Ebn el metanaka*'[114]

'Those American sons of bitches will now realise what it really means to be blown up,' he exclaimed.

21 July 2012.

New York, USA, 2011

Shamoon Idris sat inside the Masjid Abu Bakr on Foster Avenue in Brooklyn. Around him were other members of the Islamic Jehad Council.[115]

Looking at Shamoon, one could not tell that he was a terrorist. His faded jeans, his Hugo Boss sunglasses and the clean-shaven smiling face were not things one associated with a fundamentalist. A hapless Wall Street investment banker would realise that the hard way.

The investment banker had been clicking photos of his girlfriend in front of the Masjid At-Taqwa Mosque in the Bedford-Stuyvesant section of Brooklyn. She had been 'inappropriately dressed' and this had roused the ire of Shamoon. The banker had been huddled off to a basement beneath the mosque, where he had been grilled by Shamoon who had remained surrounded by his ardent fan following. It was only when the banker claimed that he was an admirer of Islam and wanted to learn about this religion of peace and tolerance, that Shamoon's grimace turned into a smile.

Shamoon was patiently discussing the note he had received from Ghalib. It had a date mentioned.

21 August 2012.

Jakarta, Indonesia, 2011

Jemaah Islamiyah was a militant Islamic terrorist outfit with a one-point agenda: the establishment of a fundamentalist Islamic caliphate in Indonesia, Singapore, Brunei, Malaysia, Thailand and the Philippines. The Jemaah Islamiyah had carried out the Bali bombing in which suicide squads had murdered 202 people in a busy nightclub.

Yaqub Islamuddin, the intellectual director of the Jemaah Islamiyah, sat inside his jail cell, which he had occupied for the past few months, reading his Qur'an.[116] Yaqub had been a techno-nerd running a computer business in Jakarta. It was the two weeks he had spent studying the Qur'an at a pro-Afghan training centre in Peshawar, that had led him to create a small core of young Muslims who wanted the introduction of Islamic law, or Sharia, as the basis of Indonesian law. He had always been more of an intellectual than a muscleman. Unfortunately, his words and thoughts were often more dangerous than the blows of a thug.

Among the correspondence that he had been allowed to receive was a single note from Ghalib. It contained a verse from the holy book. 'Their Lord gives them good news: mercy and approval from Him, and gardens where they rejoice in everlasting bliss.' Yaqub Islamuddin knew the verse.

Chapter 9, Verse 21.

9/21.

21 September 2012.

Sydney, Australia, 2011

Muslims in Australia had a long history. Adil Afrose's ancestors had come to Australia as Afghan camel drivers in the 1800s.[117] They had played an important role in the exploration of Australia's endless dry terrains by carrying people and telegraph poles to points that could only be reached on camelback. But had they been appreciated? The white man didn't give a camel's ass about them.

Adil had done quite well for himself in life. He had succeeded in setting up a trading firm that specialised in the export of halaal meat to very discerning customers in the Middle East. In 2005, a delegation of young Muslim leaders from Australia had travelled to Jakarta to explore Islam in Indonesia. The Australian ambassador to Indonesia had said, 'It's important for young Australians to gain a better understanding of the role of religion in Indonesia and to share their views on how Islam contributes to diverse, democratic societies like Australia and Indonesia.' The Ambassador had obviously not known what exactly it was that Adil had learnt during that trip!

Adil surveyed the beautiful Lakemba Mosque where he prayed each day. Today he was praying that Allah would give him strength to do His will as per the note from Ghalib.

21 October 2012.

Grozny, Chechnya, Russia, 2011

Grozny's four administrative districts included Leninsky, Zavodskoy, Staropromyslovsky and Oktyabrsky. While Staropromyslovsky was the main oil-drilling area, it was Oktyabrsky that housed the industries and the economy, including the mafia. It was here that Dzhokar Raduev sat inside a luxuriously appointed house, blissfully unperturbed by the $10-million reward on his head.[118]

Dzhokar Raduev was not merely a Chechen warlord. No. He was also a shrewd politician, a dangerous terrorist and, above all, Chechnya's most adored national hero. In his early youth, Raduev had changed his name; his new name was Yahya Ali, much more in keeping with his Islamic roots.

In 1992, when Boris Yeltsin sent his troops into Chechnya, Yahya had hijacked an Aeroflot aircraft travelling from Mineralnye Vody in Russia to Ankara in Turkey. He had threatened to blow up the flight unless Yeltsin lifted the state of emergency. Yahya had then travelled to Afghanistan, and had developed and strengthened his bonds with Al-Qaeda. Thereafter, he had moved back to Chechnya to carry on the struggle.

He now read the note from Ghalib. A smile of satisfaction spread over his face.

21 November 2012.

Bakhtaran, Iran, 2011

The truck had done its fair share of travel. From the port at Pipavav, it had headed to Jammu, where the consignment marked for the recipient had been 'officially unloaded', even though the actual machinery had continued to remain on board.

The truck had then been stripped of all its accessories and had been repainted a dirty military green. The cargo container had been covered with a khaki canvas and the licence plates had been changed to a series used by the Indian Army. A military pass was glued to the top left-hand corner of the windscreen.

The truck had proceeded in its new identity along the inter-state Punjab-Kashmir border westwards and stopped short of the town of Rajouri on the Indian side. From here, Azad Kashmir or POK—Pakistan Occupied Kashmir—was just a stone's throw away. The truck waited at a quiet point along the Line of Control, the line dividing Kashmir into POK and Indian Kashmir. It was awaiting a signal from across the border.

Even though Indians had constructed over 734 kilometres of fencing along the Line of Control, significant portions of the border remained unfenced. This suited the Pakistan-trained militant outfits perfectly because it enabled them to send armed groups of terrorists across the border at will.

At 11 pm sharp, on observing five quick flashes of light, the truck's engine was restarted and it began the crossing. The road was non-existent and it required considerable skill to negotiate the dirt track. At 11:27 pm, the truck was firmly in Pakistani territory, and a few hours later it was in Mirpur.

A team of ten truck detailers from Rawalpindi awaited the vehicle in Mirpur. Over the next twenty-four hours, the truck would be repainted with floral designs, bright colours, and Urdu poetry. The canvas top would give way to a hardwood body with carved motifs. This would be further enhanced by little mirrors, reflectors, ornamental brass fittings and jingling bells and chains.[119]

Truck art had become a very critical part of Pakistani folk art and this particular team specialised in what was referred to as 'disco painting' in which almost every square inch of surface area would be covered with decorations in the form of images or ornaments. Newly embellished, the truck would become part of the Pakistani landscape and would not be noticed. The new licence plates read 'KAE 5675'. The number was from a Karachi number series.

The truck now moved northwards to Muzaffarabad and from there westwards to Mansehra. From Mansehra it headed in a gentle south-westerly direction towards Peshawar in the North-West Frontier Province of Pakistan where it waited to cross the famous Khyber Pass.

The Khyber Pass between Afghanistan and Pakistan's North-West Frontier Province was probably the most evocative border crossing in the world. The border, the Durand Line, had been frozen by the English in 1893 and had ended up dividing the ethnic Pashtuns, resulting in the ongoing Pashtunistan issue, which had pretty much determined relations between Pakistan and Afghanistan throughout history.[120]

The tribal areas of Pakistan continued to be mostly outside federal control, thus creating an entirely porous Pak–Afghan border, and a smuggler's delight.

The truck's papers indicated that it was carrying construction equipment needed for upgrading the Kabul highway. An armed guard from the Khyber Agency had been generously tipped to accompany the truck to Torkham on the border. Stamped out of Pakistan, the truck reached the small border post on the Afghan side and then proceeded to the main immigration post a further 500 metres ahead. The customs officers had already been taken care of. No checks.

The truck proceeded into Afghanistan and into the town of Jalalabad. From Jalalabad it took the road to Kabul and on to Chaghcharan. From Chaghcharan it progressed further towards Herat which, at one point in history, used to be at the crossroads of civilisations. Its north-south axis was part of the old Silk Route, while its east-west axis was the gateway to Europe. Afghanistan's border with Iran continued to remain mostly on paper and maps—the ground realities being rather different along the 900-kilometre border. The long stretches of desert sand did not lend themselves well to being policed.

At Herat, the truck underwent another cosmetic surgery. The images were removed. The garish colours were painted over with dull shades of grey. The Urdu poems were replaced by Persian proverbs of religious hue. The new licence plates were yellow and read 'THR 77708', a Teheran registration number.

No one gave a second glance to the truck as it crossed the border from Afghanistan into Iran. It was simply a truck carrying a miniscule part of the materials needed for a $38-million road construction project. Having reached Iranian territory, the truck headed southwards to Zahedan, from where it started a westward sweep through Kerman, Yazd, Esfahan and Arak till it reached Bakhtaran, which lay just across the Iran–Iraq border from Baghdad.

The driver was tired, but he forced himself to stay alert. He had yet to cross Iraq and Syria before he reached his final destination. Ghalib decided to take a short nap. His friend, El-Azhar, would take up the watch while he slept. He needed to be prepared for the final act on 21 December 2012. Eleven other events would precede it, one each month. And each event would wreak havoc.

The Sheikh's Master would have the last laugh. The world had been waiting for this day since 500 BC.

21 December 2012.

⚕

Guatemala, 500 BC

The royal astrologer was looking up at the heavens from his observatory, which formed part of the temple honouring Kukulcan.

He was looking rather worried. He had determined the exact end of the great cycle of the Long Count Maya calendar, a 26,000-year planetary cycle. The date would have massive repercussions. It would coincide with the geomagnetic reversal of the poles of the earth, having last occurred 780,000 years ago! The date was definite; an extremely close conjunction of the winter solstice sun with the crossing point of the galactic equator and the ecliptic path of the sun. More commonly known to Maya civilisation as the Sacred Tree.[121]

21 December 2012.

⚕

Langley, Virginia, USA, 2011

The compass had sixteen points, and it symbolised the search for information from all over the world. This information had to be brought back and centralised at one place where it would be stored, catalogued and analysed. The compass rested on a shield—a shield that was meant to defend America. This was

166

the familiar crest that welcomed visitors to the Central Intelligence Agency's headquarters in Langley.

Hidden within the miles of corridors was a small office that housed the SAS, or the Special Activities Staff. A division of the Directorate of Operations, the SAS handled covert paramilitary exercises which the American Government did not wish to be publicly associated with. Members on missions strictly avoided carrying anything on their person that could even remotely link them to the United States Government.

The division had less than a few hundred personnel, most of them former operators of Delta Force and Navy SEAL teams, although, on occasion, they were known to employ civilians for paramilitary activities. The division used RQ-1 Predator Drones equipped with high-resolution cameras and AGM-114 Hellfire antitank missiles as part of their wide arsenal. The division was known to be a major part of the US's unconventional war in Afghanistan and Iraq.[122]

The real strategic advantage of the SAS was ADA, or Agility, Deniability and Adaptability. More often than not, SAS agents would operate individually and all alone, undercover, and that too in inhospitable areas behind enemy lines. They would carry out all types of assignments including counter-intelligence, espionage, handling hostage situations, deliberate sabotage, and targeted assassinations.

One of the SAS's most prized agents was simply known by the agency nickname of 'CIA Trois'. He was of Arab–Algerian stock and a devout Muslim. His areas of operation were Afghanistan, Pakistan and Kashmir and since he was equally familiar with all three regions, he had the nickname 'Trois', or 'Three'.

Stephen Elliot, head of the SAS, was his controller. Stephen was one of the brightest stars within the agency. He had been recruited into the intelligence service during his final year at Yale, the same year he 'tapped' Terry Acton for the Skull & Bones membership.

Elliot was at the SAS headquarters deciphering the encrypted message that had reached him from CIA Trois. It read simply:

N 45:50 E 6:52 S 11:00 W 66:00 N 31:00 E 112:00 N 51:07 E 1:19 N 3:09 E 101:41 N 32:59 E 74:57 N 33:20 E 44:30 N 44:98 W 110:45 S 06:09 E 106.49 S 33:00 E 146:00 N 43.2 E 45.45 N 31:34 E 34:51.

It ended with: Q 17:16.

The N, S, E and W obviously meant North, South, East and West. Trois had provided the locations. The Langley computers quickly looked up the coordinates and spat out the results.

N 45:50 E 6:52	–	Rhone Alps, France
S 11:00 W 66:00	–	Riberalta, Bolivia
N 31:00 E 112:00	–	Hubei, China
N 51:07 E 1:19	–	Dover, England
N 3:09 E 101:41	–	Kuala Lumpur, Malaysia
N 32:59 E 74:57	–	Katra, Jammu & Kashmir, India
N 33:20 E 44:30	–	Baghdad, Iraq
N 44:98 W 110:45	–	Wyoming, USA
S 06:09 E 106.49	–	Jakarta, Indonesia
S 33:00 E 146:00	–	New South Wales, Australia
N 43.2 E 45.45	–	Grozny, Chechnya, Russia
N 31:34 E 34:51	–	Tel Megiddo, Israel.

But Q 17:16? Elliot pulled out of his desk an English pocket Qur'an and looked up Chapter 17, Verse 16. It read:

'And when We wish to destroy a town, We send Our commandment to the people of it who lead easy lives, but they transgress therein; thus the word proves true against it, so We destroy it with utter destruction.'

Elliot was confused. He knew about the first eleven locations, but how had Megiddo entered this plan? He needed to discuss this one on one, with the President.

Megiddo, Israel, 2012

A hill near the modern settlement of Tel Megiddo was made up of twenty-six layers of ruins of ancient cities. Megiddo, however, was famous for another reason. The New Testament's Book of Revelation had prophesied that the final military showdown of the world would happen in Megiddo. Soon, the word 'Megiddo' had become synonymous with the end of the world. In fact, the word 'Armageddon' was derived from the name 'Megiddo'.

Ghalib's truck was on its way there. Ghalib asked El-Azhar for his Thuraya satellite phone and began dialling a number in Pakistan: +92 51 . . .

Chapter Seventeen

Mumbai, India, 2012

Swakilki had followed Vincent from London to Mumbai via Delhi. Indian Airlines flight IC-887 had ferried her from New Delhi to Mumbai within one hour and fifty-five minutes. The Mercedes-Benz S350L sent by the Taj Mahal Hotel to receive her at the airport quickly wove its way through the notorious traffic snarls and deposited her at the waterfront paradise of the luxury hotel.

George Bernard Shaw had commented that after staying at the Taj Mahal Hotel, he had no longer felt the need to visit the original Taj Mahal in Agra. Swakilki was staying in the Heritage Wing, where individually themed high-ceilinged suites made one imagine an era when personalities like Somerset Maugham and Duke Ellington had rested their heads on soft pillows in the city's best hotel.

The discovery of the Bom Jesus document given by Terry to Vincent had resulted in endless discussions with Martha. The document seemed to indicate that Jesus had survived the crucifixion and that he had settled in India. Vincent's own past-life regressions in which he had seen Jesus had seemed to confirm the theory that Jesus had indeed survived the ordeal. They had finally decided that they needed to distinguish fact from fiction. The only way to do this necessitated a visit to India.

Upon their arrival in Mumbai, Martha and Vincent had taken a cab to the Taj Mahal Hotel. They were put up in the business-like Tower Wing of the hotel. They did not observe the young Japanese woman who checked into the adjoining luxurious Heritage Wing.

The Taj Mahal Hotel had something else that was more interesting than the themed suites. Besides the usual 'house doctor' for medical emergencies, it also boasted a 'house astrologer' for far more urgent counselling from the heavens. Vincent had decided to take an appointment. He had noticed the bit about the 'house astrologer' while leafing through the hotel's extensive services directory. Even though he was sceptical about the occult, his last experience with the world beyond, in London, had opened up his mind to newer concepts.

He dropped in at the hotel's reception to book an appointment with Pandit Ramgopal Prasad Sharma, the world-renowned astrologer who practised his art and science from the hallowed portals of the Taj every alternate week. The receptionist was happy to give Vincent an appointment for 3 pm.

Pandit Ramgopal Prasad Sharma turned out to be a wise old man of eighty-one, who spoke wonderful English, not the crazy, half-naked fakir that Vincent had imagined.

'You see, Mr Sinclair, my childhood and growing-up years were spent in the picturesque fields of Hoshiarpur in Punjab. Surrounded by the splendour of nature, I became fascinated with the concept of destiny. This led me to the question: is everything preordained in life? It was this question that led me to the study of the occult, Hindu astrology and philosophy,' explained Pandit Ramgopal Prasad Sharma as he poured two cups of lemon tea, one for Vincent and one for himself.

Pandit Ramgopal Prasad Sharma's father had been a professor of science and mathematics but had remained perpetually absorbed in subjects such as astrology, palmistry, mysticism, and spiritualism. With twenty-four-hour access to his father's texts and scrolls, Ramgopal had read, re-read, absorbed and understood each of them with a voracious appetite. He had become so curious about the metaphysical that he had begun to delve deeper and deeper into the subject. Very soon, there was a perpetual line of waiting visitors at his father's house. People had begun to believe his uncannily accurate predictions. This had led to more enthusiasm and deeper research, eventually resulting in Ramgopal becoming one of the most sought-after astrologers in India and abroad.

'Now, I take it that you do not have a *janam-kundli*, in which case I will need to make one for you.'

'What is that?' asked Vincent.

Pandit Ramgopal explained patiently. 'A janam-kundli is a birth chart. It indicates the planetary positions when you were born. I will need your date, time and location of birth.'

Vincent supplied him with the relevant data: 1 July 1969; 7:15 am; New York City.

The pandit referred to a musty old tome from which he derived the latitude and longitude of New York City. Latitude 40°29'40'N to 45°0'42'N and longitude 71°47'25'W to 79°45'54'W.

Master craftsman that he was, he then started filling in the planetary positions in Vincent's birth chart. Chart duly completed, he looked at it carefully as if he were admiring a work of art.

'I will tell you a few things about your past. Please tell me whether I am right or wrong. This will ensure that the chart I have before me is indeed accurate.'

Vincent meekly nodded his assent.

'You are an only child. No brothers or sisters.'

'Yes.'

'Your parents are dead. They died around the same time. Rather violently and suddenly. An accident?'

'Yes.'

'You are not married.'

'Yes.'

'Even though you are not married, you love children. You work with children in your career. A schoolteacher or paediatrician perhaps?'

'Yes.'

'You are deeply religious. In fact, your work is spiritual in nature.'

'Yes.'

'That's fine then,' said Pandit Ramgopal rather matter-of-factly as if all his accurate readings about Vincent's past meant nothing.

He then became very serious. 'The ascendant of your horoscope is Pisces with the moon in Pisces,' he said.

'Huh?' said Vincent.

Pandit Ramgopal carried on, 'What it means is that in this life you are at the end of your multiple cycles of birth, death and rebirth. This is your final lifetime before you merge with the divine. This is a wonderful horoscope. I am honoured to read it.'

'What does that mean?' asked Vincent.

Pandit Ramgopal replied, 'It means that you have been through several lifetimes in which you have learned various things. In this final lifetime, your soul will have learned whatever there is left to learn. After this, you will not need rebirth. We Hindus call it *moksha*.'

'What else can you tell me?'

'There are three supreme forces in your life. You will need to recognise them before you can attain moksha.'

'How?'

'The first force has Saturn in the ascendant. But in this horoscope the ascendant is Libra, not Cancer. Saturn has its highest power in Libra, driving this person to the very top of wealth and power. Furthermore, the conjunction of Venus and the moon in the second house is a Raja Yog, the astral bounty that has kept this person in public prominence always.'

'Who is this person?' asked Vincent.

'That I cannot tell you. But wait, hear me out. There is a second force which has what is called a Paap-Katri Yog or a Vish-Kanya Yog. The moon is afflicted and is surrounded by malevolent planets such as Saturn, Mars as well as Rahu-Ketu. This makes the person almost maniacal. This person will not hesitate to kill.'

'What can I do?' asked a visibly shaken Vincent.

'Well. This second force has Rahu in the sixth house and Ketu in the twelfth house. This makes the person holy and very religious. Unfortunately, the person's ascendant is a combination of Saturn and Mars. This makes him or her violent and bloody. Thus there is a spiritual side to this negative force.'

'What do you mean by Rahu and Ketu?' asked Vincent.

Pandit Ramgopal answered, 'In Hindu mythology, Rahu is the snake that swallows the sun or the moon, thus causing an eclipse. From the astronomical point of view, Rahu and Ketu denote the point of intersection of the sun and the moon as they move. To that extent, they are the north and south lunar nodes, hence eclipses are bound to occur at these points.'

'So how can I neutralise this negative force generated by Rahu and Ketu?' asked Vincent.

'Use the third force to neutralise the second. This third force has a Gajakesari Yog in the ninth house. Both Jupiter and the moon are without blemish here. There is no aspect of any planet on it, nor any conjunction. This is a person of wisdom and knowledge. Let them cancel each other out!' he commanded as he thumped the table in front of him.

♊

Martha and Vincent were sitting in the Sea Lounge of the Taj, one of the city's favourite tearooms. They had just returned to the hotel after a hectic day of sightseeing and were enjoying the restaurant's specialty, Viennoise coffee.

Vincent had been left rather shaken by the predictions of Pandit Ramgopal Prasad Sharma, and it had taken him a day to recover. In the morning, Martha had suggested that they spend the day seeing a little more of the city.

Vincent had told their guide—who turned out to be a mine of information even other than local—that he wanted to see St Thomas's Cathedral first, and that's exactly where they had headed. In the heart of the business district of Mumbai, St Thomas's Cathedral stood like a quiet oasis in the midst of chaos. The cathedral had been built as the city's first Anglican church in 1718 with a view to improving the 'moral standards' of the growing British settlement.

And then it struck Vincent. Wasn't St Thomas one of the first apostles to come to India? He made up his mind quickly. He needed to go to the southern parts of India in order to understand the context of the Bom Jesus documents.

As they were returning to their hotel they crossed the bustling shopping district of Colaba, filled with shops selling carpets and shawls. Most of the shops were owned by Kashmiri traders. Vincent noticed the names: *Ahmad Joo, Bashir Joo, Muhammad Joo* . . .

Vincent casually enquired of their guide, 'Why is it that so many shopkeepers have the same last name?' Pat came the reply, 'Oh yes, an interesting question, sir. The word *joo* is added as an honorific by local Kashmiri Muslims to the names of elderly persons to show respect, as in, for instance, Muhammad Joo or Ahmad Joo. But the word "joo" is also believed to have been derived from the word "Jew". The names of many tribes in Kashmir have Jewish associations. One of the tribes is called Asheriya, as in Asher; the tribe of Dand could be Dan; Gadha, Gad; Lavi, Levi, and so on.' Vincent realised that the connections between the lost tribes of Israel and the present-day population of Kashmir were much more significant than had ever been discussed by Western scholars.

As they were nearing the hotel, they saw a petite Japanese woman sitting alone by a window table at a café. She was sipping camomile tea and staring out at the ocean. Vincent couldn't help thinking, once again, what a delightful creature she was. Where had he seen her before? She looked familiar, but he shrugged off the feeling.

His aunt Martha didn't.

Cochin, Kerala, India, 2012

Vincent had decided to opt for a package tour that would take him to all the relevant spots on the St Thomas circuit. He would proceed from Mumbai to Cochin on his own by air, while Martha would spend the next few days researching some documents at the David Sassoon Library.

Vincent's tour guide was a young Keralite by the name of Kurien. Kurien did not wait for formalities before plunging into his prepared material. 'St Thomas visited Kerala in AD 52. At that time, Kerala was famous in the ancient trade for spices, sandalwood, pepper, cardamom and cinnamon, and used to routinely trade with the Greeks, the Romans and the Arabs. The trade centres in Kerala were headed by Jews. Gold coins from Rome and Greece of the period 27 BC to AD 80 have been found in ancient port cities of Kerala.'[123]

Kurien continued, '*The Acts of Judas Thomas*, a Syrian manuscript about the voyage of St Thomas to India, and the travelogue of Thomas Canae from Syria, who established Syrian Christianity in AD 372 in Kerala, describe Malabar Christians living along the Kerala coastline. When the Portuguese arrived in India in 1498, they found 143 Christian churches already established in Kerala.'

Kurien pointed out that St Thomas had established six prayer centres in Kerala and that all of them were Jewish. Obviously, it had been much easier for St Thomas to preach to the Jews than to the gentiles.

By the time Vincent returned to Mumbai, he was convinced that St Thomas had indeed visited India. He now had many questions racing around inside his head. Was it possible that Jesus had also visited India along with St Thomas? If so, could a bloodline of Jesus still be surviving in India? Could Terry Acton's Bom Jesus document lead them further in that direction? What about Mary Magdalene and the Holy Grail—weren't they supposed to have travelled to France? Could there be more than one bloodline?

Before proceeding any further, he needed to discuss these matters with Martha, who was still in Mumbai.

Mumbai, India, 2012

Martha was sitting inside the David Sassoon Library. Located in the city's Kala Ghoda district, the library housed over 40,000 books, many of them extremely rare.

Martha's research had led her to a rare Persian work entitled *Negaris-Tan-i-Kashmir*. Also in front of her was a book by Andreas Faber Kaiser entitled *Jesus Died in Kashmir*.[124] In the latter, there was an interesting passage wherein the author related a conversation he had had with Mr Basharat Saleem, a man claiming to be a descendant of Jesus:

> He [Bashrat Saleem] told me that to his knowledge the only written source on this subject of Jesus's marriage was the *Negaris-Tan-i-Kashmir*, an old Persian book that had been translated into Urdu. That [book] relates that King Shalivahana [the same king who met and conversed with Jesus in the mountains] told Jesus that he needed a woman to take care of him and offered him a choice of fifty . . . Jesus had replied that he did not need anyone and that no one was obliged to work for him, but the king persisted until Jesus agreed . . . the woman's name was Marjan, and the same book says that she bore Jesus children.

Martha recalled that Vincent's regression sessions had seemed to indicate that Jesus survived the crucifixion. Martha remembered something else. In 1780, Karl Friedrich Bahrdt[125] had suggested that Jesus had quite deliberately enacted his death on the cross, using drugs that were arranged by the physician Luke. He had done this in order to ensure that his followers would reject the possibility of his being a political messiah and instead would embrace the more desirable alternative of his being a spiritual messiah. According to Bahrdt, Jesus had been resuscitated by Joseph of Arimathea, one of his secret disciples, who was a member of the Essenes, just like Jesus!

Next, Martha pored over the photocopies that she had made of the research done by Karl Venturini.[126] Venturini had suggested that Jesus's fellow members of the secret society had heard groaning from inside the tomb where Jesus had been placed after his crucifixion. They had succeeded in scaring away the guards and eventually rescued Jesus. A scholarly paper by Heinrich Paulus seemed to show that Jesus had merely fallen into a temporary coma and was revived without any external help in the tomb.

A story seemed to be emerging. Martha was yet to read the *Nathanamavali*, a book on the Nath yogis of India.

ॐ

In western India, there existed an extremely austere band of wandering ascetics in white robes. They were known as the Nath yogis. The Nath yogis hailed from a line of historical gurus. Among several others was one called Issa Nath. A book on the history of the Nath yogis, called *Nathanamavali*[27] stated the following:

> Issa Nath came to India at the age of fourteen. After this he returned to his own country and began preaching. Soon after, his brutish and materialistic countrymen conspired against him and had him crucified. After crucifixion, or perhaps even before it, Issa Nath entered *samadhi* by means of yoga.

Samadhi, according to the proponents of yoga, was the final stage of the discipline. Samadhi literally means to 'bring together'. It was the bringing together of the conscious mind and the divine, a union of one's soul with Brahman.

> Seeing him thus, the Jews presumed he was dead, and buried him in a tomb. When Issa Nath's guru arrived, he took the body of Issa Nath from the tomb, woke him from his samadhi, and later led him to the sacred land of the Aryans. Issa Nath then established an ashram in the lower regions of the Himalayas.

Martha recalled Vincent's words when he was under the trance of regression: 'I am hiding behind some bushes. I don't know why I am unable to tear myself away from here. Night has fallen. In the middle of the night, there was a visitor. He looked like an angel because of his white robes . . . I think he was an Essene monk. He rolled away the stone. The guards collapsed with terror. The Sabbath is over, and the two Marys have come here to roll away the stone to the tomb, but they are rather surprised to see it open. They are going inside. I'm following at a discreet distance. There are two men in white robes. They look like Essenes. They are saying that Jesus is alive, not dead!'

Were they Nath yogis? Could it also be that the great prophet 'Nathan' mentioned in the Old Testament had actually been a proponent of the 'Nathanamavali'?

Not completely satisfied with the progress she had made with her research on behalf of Vincent, Martha decided to look up Holger Kersten, the leading authority on the subject of Jesus in India.

In 1983, the book *Jesus Lived in India* had created a mild storm when it had expanded the scope of Russian traveller Nicholas Notovich's experiences in Ladakh. Kersten had set out on the path ten years previously when he had first come across the theory that Jesus had lived in India.

Kersten had found that the Persian scholar F. Mohammed's historical work *Jami-ut-tuwarik*, which spoke of Jesus's visit to Nisibis, Turkey, by royal invitation, had been ignored by Western theology. Kersten discovered that in Turkey, as well as Persia, there were stories of a great saviour by the name of Yuz Asaf, 'Leader of the Healed', who shared several similarities with Jesus in terms of character, lessons and life incidents.

Kersten also drew from the Apocrypha, which were texts written by the Apostles but were not officially accepted by the

Roman Catholic Church. The Apocryphal *Acta Thomae*, or *The Acts of Judas Thomas*, spoke of the several meetings that had taken place between Jesus and Thomas on several occasions after Christ's crucifixion. The *Acta* further spoke of Christ specifically sending Thomas to preach in India.

Holger Kersten had found that stone inscriptions at Fatehpur Sikri, near the Taj Mahal, included 'Agrapha', or 'sayings of Christ', that were completely absent in the Bible. Their grammar resembled the Apocryphal Gospel of Thomas.

Kersten had cited this fact to drive home the point that texts deleted by the Church contained extremely important information about Jesus and his life and that this information, while having been ruthlessly obliterated by the Church, had not been erased from the Indian stone inscriptions.

ॐ

Martha decided that she needed to trace the *Tarikh-Issa-Massih* that had been photocopied by Terry Acton and given to Vincent. In the published *Tarikh-Issa-Massih* that she found in the library, the final paragraph said:

> Issa and Mary had a child by the name of Sara, who was born to them in India, but was later sent to Gaul with her mother. Issa remained in India, where he married a woman from the Sakya clan on the persistence of King Gopadatta, and had a son, Benissa. Benissa had a son, Yushua, who fathered Akkub. Akkub's son was Jashub. Abihud was the son of Jashub. Jashub's grandson was Elnaam. Elnaam sired Harsha, who sired Jabal, who sired Shalman. Shalman's son Zabbud embraced Islam. Zabbud fathered Abdul, who sired Haaroon. His child was Hamza. Omar was Hamza's son and he produced Rashid. Rashid's offspring was Khaleel.

The problem, of course, was that even if one considered the sixteen generations after Jesus that were specifically mentioned in the book, and putting a forty-year lifespan to each generation, the book only had information for around 640 years after Jesus. Where was the lineage after Khaleel?

Martha was now pretty sure that some sort of cover-up was going on. She needed to see the original Urdu work and not the translated version. The library had the original Urdu version—it was a third edition, published in 1862.

The lucky break was that having lived in India for many years, Martha understood Urdu perfectly.

She started reading the work in Urdu. She began by reading each line, first in Urdu, and then translating it into English:

Issa and Mary had a child by the name of Sara, who was born to them in India, but was later sent to Gaul with her mother. Issa remained in India, where he married a woman from the Sakya clan on the persistence of King Gopadatta, and had a son, Benissa. Benissa had a son, Yushua, who fathered Akkub. Akkub's son was Jashub. Abihud was the son of Jashub. Jashub's grandson was Elnaam. Elnaam sired Harsha, who sired Jabal, who sired Shalman. Shalman's son Zabbud embraced Islam.

Zabbud's son was Abdul, and Abdul's son was Haaroon. Haaroon's son was Hamza and Hamza's son was Omar. Rashid's father was Omar and Khaleel's father was Rashid. Rashid had two more children, a son and a daughter. The boy's name was Muhammad and the girl was named Sultana. Muhammad died before his marriage, but Sultana produced a son. The name of her son was Salim. Salim had a son called Ikram. Ikram got married to Raziya and they had a daughter called Bano. Bano produced a son called Ali. Ali had a son, Ghulam, and Ghulam also had a son, Mustafa. Mustafa's son's name was Humayun. Humayun's son's name was Abbas. Abbas had a son called Faiz. Faiz had a son called Javed. Javed had a son, Gulzar.

Gulzar had a daughter. The daughter's name was Nasreen. Nasreen had a son called Akbar. Akbar produced a son called Yusuf. Yusuf's son's name was Mansoor. Mansoor's son's name was Zain. Zain had a son, Faisal. Faisal produced a daughter called Sharmeen. Sharmeen had a son called Ibrahim. Ibrahim's son's name was Alam. Alam's son's name was Mehdi. Mehdi had a son called Bismillah. Bismillah had a son called Hassan. Hassan had a son called Shabbir.

Martha was stunned. Here was a passage that took the lineage almost twenty-five generations further! How could this have been mistakenly omitted from the English translation?

She thought to herself, 'Max Müller is admired all over the world for his translation of many historic Sanskrit works. Unfortunately, his motives are rarely discussed. It was Max Müller who wrote that, "India has been conquered once, but India must be conquered again . . . the ancient religion is doomed and if Christianity does not step in, whose fault will it be?"'

Martha was clear. English scholars had been reluctant to expose any historical Indian works that seemed to portray Indian culture or religions as being older or more advanced than Western Christian thought. Any work that showed Jesus or Christianity as having learned from India, from Buddhism or from Hinduism, would have made the work of Christian missionaries extremely difficult. Indians would have questioned why they needed to convert to Christianity if Christian thought in itself had been derived from ancient Buddhist or Hindu wisdom.

'So the omissions in the English translations were deliberate?' thought Martha to herself. 'There is only one way to tell,' she replied to herself equally quickly. 'We must take up the challenge posed by the Bom Jesus document that Terry gave Vincent.'

Time to visit Goa. Had Vincent arrived in Mumbai yet? Martha pondered over her research and considered the implications of what it meant for her personally.

There were many ways of getting from Mumbai to Goa. The boring way was to take a forty-five-minute flight. The exhausting way was to board an overnight bus. The economical way was by the super-fast Konkan Railways express train that got there in seven hours. The dignified way was called the Deccan Odyssey.

Aboard India's answer to Europe's Orient Express and South Africa's Blue Train were Vincent and Martha. During his visit to Cochin, Vincent had befriended a senior superintendent of India's Western Railways. The two tickets on this super-luxury train were a heavily discounted gift from him.

The Deccan Odyssey was a dark blue train trimmed with gilded stripes. The decadent coaches were named after well-known forts, palaces and monuments of India, names that would become familiar on the leisurely journey from Mumbai to Goa. The journey would also give the duo some time to review all their research.

The Deccan Odyssey travelled at a leisurely sixty miles an hour as it snaked its way through the western peninsula of India, stopping along the way at small towns and beaches.

It was delightful to be awakened in the morning by hot coffee and toast brought by a personal valet, to be served whisky-and-soda by white-gloved bearers in the evenings and to be offered cocoa and biscuits before falling asleep each night.

On the third day they arrived at Sindhudurg, which was famous for its Hindu temples. It was also famous for the Fort of Sindhudurg, which had taken 6,000 workers three years of round-the-clock work to complete. The massive structure sat on forty-eight acres of land, a breathtaking goliath sitting in the water and surrounded by a pristine rocky coastline.

As aunt and nephew drank in the beauty of their surroundings, Vincent spoke. During the train journey, he had been reading a novel called *Guardian of the Dawn* by Richard Zimler,[128] which Martha had managed to procure from the library.

'Nana, do you know that the author of this book was recently interviewed in India? Do you know what he said?'[129]

'What?' asked Martha.

'He said that the Portuguese exported the Inquisition to Goa in the sixteenth century, and that many Indian Hindus were tortured and burnt at the stake for continuing to practise their religion. Muslim Indians were generally murdered right away or made to flee Goan territory.'

Vincent continued, 'Historians consider the Goa Inquisition to have been the most merciless and cruel ever. It was a machinery of death. A large number of Hindus were first made to convert and then persecuted from 1560 all the way to 1812! Over that period of 252 years, any man, woman or child living in Goa could be arrested and tortured for simply whispering a prayer or keeping a small idol at home. Many Hindus, Muslims and some former Jews as well, languished in special inquisitional prisons, some for four, five, or six years at a time.'

Vincent looked at Martha for reactions. None.

He continued, 'The author was horrified to learn about this, of course. He was quite shocked that his friends in Portugal knew nothing about it. The Portuguese tended to think of Goa as the glorious capital of the spice trade, and they believed, erroneously, that people of different ethnic backgrounds lived there in tolerance and tranquillity, but they knew nothing about the terror that the Portuguese had wrought in India. They knew nothing of how their fundamentalist religious leaders made so many suffer.'

'But Islam also spread itself by the sword, Vincent. Why only point the finger at Christianity?' asked Martha.

'Yes. My point exactly. Both Christianity and Islam are religions of peace; however, their mass following today is partly due to blood that was shed over many years of history. On the other hand, we do not see Buddhism or Hinduism having gone to war to spread their faith even though modern-day Hindu nationalists have been responsible for anti-minority riots, and Buddhist monks have taken to the streets in Myanmar.'

'So where exactly are we going with this conversation?' enquired Martha.

'Well, the aggressive competition between Islam and Christianity for converts could possibly have been handled better if they had cooperated rather than fought with each other.'

ॐ

'It now seems entirely probable to me that Jesus, having survived the crucifixion as seen by me in my past-life regressions, could have decided to come here to India to rediscover the ancient knowledge that he had been educated in,' commented Vincent as he put away his clothes in the suitcase in preparation for their arrival in Goa.

'Well, he might have come to India also because of the fact that the Lost Tribes had actually settled down in the Kashmir Valley. Various places in Kashmir have Israeli names, such as *Har Nevo, Beit Peor, Pisga, Heshubon*. These were all names in the land of the Ten Tribes of Israel. The same is true of the names of people. People in Kashmir perform a feast called Pasca in spring, when they adjust the difference of days between the lunar calendar and solar calendar, and the method of this adjustment is the same as the Jewish one. *Hoon* in Kashmiri means a dog, and a wife is called an *aashen*, the same as in Hebrew. Half-roasted fish called *phar* in Kashmir is a favourite dish of both the Israelis and the people of Kashmir. So Jesus may have come here because of this older connection. Right?'

'Right. So, what if his children continue to live here? Wouldn't it be ironic if they were Muslim? After all, Islam came into India rather violently through Muslim invasions from the eighth century onwards.'

'Be that as it may, what is your point, Vincent?' asked an exasperated Martha.

'Well, any such offspring having a bloodline of Jesus and following Islam as a faith today would be a problem for Christians and Muslims alike.'

'Why?'

185

'First of all, the Church would not want to acknowledge that there's a bloodline at all . . . it destroys the fundamental belief that Jesus died on the cross in order to bear the burden of human sin. It means that there was no death, no resurrection, and no divine status. Also, to tell the world that Christ's own bloodline renounced the faith founded by Christ, would be to acknowledge that Islam has won the battle with Christianity!'

'Point taken. But why would such a descendant of Jesus be a problem for Islam?' persisted Martha.

'According to the Qur'an, there is only a single religion that is acceptable to God, and that is one in which there is complete submission to God's will. To that extent, Muslims believe that Islam was also the religion of earlier prophets such as Abraham, Moses and Jesus, because they also submitted themselves completely to the will and obedience of God. Islam not only recognises officially the bona fides of all earlier prophets, including Jesus, but also of any future prophets that may come.'[130]

'So?'

'Wouldn't such a prophet in the present day be a threat to the power structure of Islam? If such a person were indeed to claim prophethood, what would happen to all the present-day Imams?'

ॐ

Goa, India, 2012

Goa, located along the Konkan coastline of India that runs along its western edge, is India's party capital. Flights arrive in the state's capital, Panjim, but its business and commerce are in a town called Vasco, named after the famous explorer Vasco da Gama. The Portuguese traders who had landed here in the sixteenth century had succeeded in colonising Goa, and it had remained a colony of Portugal till it was annexed by an independent India in 1961.

At every bend along the Goa coastline are picturesque coves and bays, each unique in its beauty. Along the sun-washed coast are delightful little sleepy villages with whitewashed churches and uniformly quaint houses with red-tiled roofs. The lush green and verdant miles of coconut and palm trees are breathtakingly beautiful, irrespective of the season. It is precisely because of this Hawaii-like experience, at a fraction of the cost, that many foreign tourists who visit Goa are reluctant to return home.

Towards the northern part of Goa, around eighteen kilometres away from Goa's capital, Panaji, lies Anjuna Beach. Commonly called 'the freak capital of the world', Anjuna is quite notorious for its trance and rave parties as well as the abundance of hippies. Surrounded by dense coconut groves, it is the most happening place on Wednesdays when 'flea market mania' takes over. The market is always a wonderful cauldron of flavours, colours, smells and textures.

Rents in Goa vary from one area to the next, but Vincent's railway friend had succeeded in getting them a very rustic yet functional cottage near Anjuna Beach for about two hundred dollars for the week. It had two small bedrooms, a bathroom, a kitchen, a living room and a delightful sit-out for relaxing evenings. Luckily, their cottage was not in the heart of the trance circuit but nearer the sleepy hamlet. This location offered them best of both worlds—proximity to civilisation as well as the tranquillity of the quiet cove.

As their taxi, which had definitely seen better days, rattled towards their new home, it was overtaken by a fast motorbike. Under the jacket and helmet was a pretty young Japanese woman, who sped off very quickly.

She had stared at Martha.

⚵

Seated on the motorbike and surveying the lush green countryside around her, Swakilki realised that Goa reminded her a great deal of the little village that her mother, Aki, used to take her to on holidays when she was a little girl. The village was called Shingo and was located in the Sannohe district of Aomori in Japan. This had been her mother Aki's birthplace.

Unknown to little Swakilki, the little village of Shingo had been in the eye of a storm in 1935. A gentleman called Kiyomaro Takeuchi had discovered a 1,900-year-old document stored in the Ibaraki prefecture containing evidence that Jesus lay buried in Shingo. The document was considered so authentic and explosive that the Imperial Japanese government had banned the document from public view and had kept it locked in a museum in Tokyo. During the bombing raids of World War II, the museum with all its documents was allegedly destroyed. Rather convenient for the Japanese government.[131]

What was unknown to the villagers was the fact that Jesus had certainly *not* visited them. What was also unknown was the fact that his daughter *had*.

Chapter Eighteen

His Eminence was reading the verses from the Book of Revelation in the Holy Bible.[132] His mind was focused on the seven angels mentioned in the book:

The first angel sounded, and there followed hail and fire mingled with blood, and they were cast upon the earth.

One-third of the trees were burnt, and all green grass was burnt.

And the second angel sounded, and a great mountain burning with fire was cast into the sea.

One-third of the sea became blood. One-third of life in the sea died.

And the third angel sounded, and there fell a great star from the heavens, burning as if it were a lamp. It fell upon one-third of the rivers, which became undrinkable and killed many.

And a fourth angel sounded, and one-third of the sun, moon and stars was darkened so that one-third of the day became dark.

And the fifth angel sounded, and a star fell from heaven unto the earth and to him was given the key of a bottomless pit. And he opened the bottomless pit; and there arose a smoke like that of a great furnace and the atmosphere became black.

Out of the smoke came locusts upon the earth and unto them was given the power to hurt men that did not have the seal of God upon their foreheads.

And the sixth angel sounded, and was asked to let loose two hundred thousand horsemen to kill one-third of humanity.

And the seventh angel sounded; and there were great voices in heaven, saying, 'The kingdoms of this world have become the kingdoms of our Lord, and of his Christ, and He shall reign for ever and ever.'

⚑

Chamonix, French Alps, France, 2012

Chamonix, in Haute-Savoie, offered some of the most stunning views of Mont Blanc. Savoy became part of France in 1860, bordering Switzerland to the north and Italy to the east.[133] The region boasted Mont Blanc, the roof of Europe, rising to a height of 4,807 metres.

No one took notice of Ataullah al-Liby boarding the cable car for the Aiguille du Midi. The first part of the journey, a nine-minute trip to the Plan des l'Aiguille located at a height of 2,263 metres, was not too bad. The second part of the cable car trip to the Aiguille du Midi station at 3,781 metres was nerve-wracking; Ataullah feared heights.

Reaching his destination, Ataullah was around a hundred metres from the peak of Mont Blanc and had a commanding view of the Aiguilles of Chamonix and Vallée Blanche, the largest glacier in Europe. It was here that he would conveniently slip away into the darkness. His ski jacket had been specially fitted with high-powered Semtex. He quickly took it off.

The delayed blast on 21 January 2012 sent a wall of hail and fire ripping through Chamonix, killing 332 people. Assignment completed, Ataullah headed for Chamonix airport to catch a flight to Geneva and thereon to his rendezvous in Frederick County in America.

And the first angel sounded, and there followed hail and fire mingled with blood, and they were cast upon the earth . . .

Riberalta, Bolivia, 2012

The epicentre of the blast was 25 kilometres from Riberalta, 850 kilometres northeast of Bolivia's capital, La Paz.

No one could have spotted the crude IED, the Improvised Explosive Device, fashioned from potassium perchlorate, aluminium powder and sulphur that had been left under the dense cover of the Amazon forest by Boutros Ahmad. The intense heat applied by a welding torch was enough to set off the highly unstable mixture.[134]

The fire on 21 February 2012 would destroy over 4,48,000 acres of tropical forest besides killing 113 people.

Job done, Boutros drove to Gen Buech Airport to catch his Lloyd Aéreo Boliviano flight that took him to his meeting in Frederick County.

One-third of the trees, and all green grass was burnt.

⚇

Hubei Province, China, 2012

The Three Gorges Dam spanned the Yangtze River at Sandouping, Yichang and Hubei. Construction of the largest hydroelectric dam in the world, more than five times the size of the Hoover Dam, had begun in 1993. The dam had become fully operational in 2009. The reservoir now held 39.3 billion cubic metres of water. The twenty-six power generators had a combined generating capacity of 18.2 GW.[135]

The Three Gorges Dam was strong enough to resist terrorist attacks—China had enough manpower and equipment to guard the important parts, such as the dam itself, power plants and the lock of the Three Gorges.

What could not be guarded was the cargo aboard the ships that went through the massive ship lift. The ship lift at the Three Gorges Dam had been designed to lift ships of up to 3,000 tonnes displacement through a vertical distance of 113 metres.

The size of the basin through which ships would ascend or descend was a massive 120 by 18 by 3.5 metres. Each ship would take around thirty minutes to go up or down.

The 3,000-tonne ship *Daiyang* had done this route several times before. No one could have guessed the presence of ammonium nitrate in the diesel. The technical grade ammonium nitrate granules mixed with diesel were extremely porous, resulting in better fuel absorption and thus significantly higher reactivity.[136]

The ship's crew was aware of their cargo. They were all Uighurs ready to die for their leader, Faris Kadeer. The sudden heat application created a reaction: $2NH_4NO_3 \rightarrow 4H_2O + 2N_2 + O_2$

The combination with the diesel resulted in a detonation rate of around 914 metres per second. The dam was strong enough to resist the explosion, but the lift and locks were not.

Some 39.3 billion cubic metres of water began to flow on 21 March 2012 as the manmade mountain, the Three Gorges Dam, was cast into the frothy sea. The death toll was over a thousand people.

Faris was not there. He was on an Air China flight to London. From there he boarded a flight headed for Baltimore-Washington International Airport. This got him to his appointment in Frederick County on time.

And the second angel sounded, and a great mountain burning with fire was cast into the sea . . .

<hr />

English Channel, Dover, 2012

The accident happened around 1.3 kilometres north of the Dover coast on 21 April 2012. It resulted in a hole measuring 15 by 4 metres in the side of the Panama-registered tanker, the *Gulf Princess*. The tanker had been carrying 3,00,000 tonnes of oil from the Middle East to Dover, when the English fishing boat collided with it.

It was one of the worst oil spills in history. More than 2,39,000 metric tonnes of oil poured into the English Channel. The next two months would be hell—putting out oil fires, bringing all shipping through the channel to a virtual halt and pulling out thousands of dead fish from the ocean.

Subsequent enquiries revealed that the English fishing boat that had caused the collision, the *Wilson Flyer*, had been sold for £16,005 by its previous owner in East Sussex through a broker, Powertech Marine, to a wealthy boat enthusiast only the previous week. The money had been transferred electronically to the seller from an account in Guernsey belonging to the Isabel Madonna trust.

Fouad al-Noor had done his job well. He had personally trained his men to do the job of steering the fishing boat into the hull of the tanker. Fouad was now on a British Midland flight headed for the United States. His diary indicated an appointment in Frederick County.

One-third of the sea became blood. One-third of life in the sea died.

Kuala Lumpur, Malaysia, 2012

The Petronas Towers in Kuala Lumpur used to be the world's tallest buildings until they were surpassed by the Taipei-101 in 2004. The twin towers had one very striking feature, though—a sky bridge between the two towers on the forty-first and forty-second floors. The bridge lay 170 metres off the ground. The sky bridge was strategically located on the podium floor because visitors wanting to travel to higher floors necessarily had to change elevators on that floor.[137]

The bridge was open to all visitors but the 1,400 passes that were rationed out each day were only available on a first-come first-served basis. Tau'am Zin Hassan and his men from the Darul Islam had managed to secure over thirty passes that day. Each one of them went up to the bridge and placed a small strip of what looked like modelling clay into the grooves that formed the design element of the supporting pillars. The modelling clay was actually C-4, a deadly military plastic explosive containing RDX. Each little strip had a small NEC credit card-size cellphone hanging from it. Once all the strips were in place, the thirty visitors congregated together at Kuala Lumpur International airport. All thirty of them pressed the speed dial keys on their phones that had been pre-set on the letter 'A'. Each cellphone was calling its partner phone inside the Petronas sky bridge.

As the miniphone rang inside the bridge, a small electrical current was sent to the speaker of each phone. However, none of the thirty phones inside the sky bridge rang. The phone wires to the speakers had been disconnected and then reconnected instead to small transistors that could be turned on by a mild electrical current. Each transistor, in turn, activated a detonator.[138]

At exactly 5:03 pm on 21 May 2012, the sky bridge of the Petronas Towers exploded in a ball of fire. The inferno eventually came crashing down to earth. There were over a hundred visitors on the bridge when it exploded. It came crashing down on fifty-four onlookers.

Tau'am did not wait to see the press coverage. He was on a Singapore Airlines flight that took him to the west coast of the United States. From Los Angeles, he took a United flight to reach his destination at Frederick County.

And the third angel sounded, and there fell a great star from the heavens, burning as if it were a lamp.

☥

Katra, Jammu & Kashmir, India, 2012

Nearly five-and-a-half million devotees paid homage to the Goddess in 2003: an average of 14,794 visits each day of the year. A pilgrimage to the holy shrine of Vaishno Devi was considered to be one of the holiest pilgrimages by one billion Hindus in the world. The holy cave of the divine Goddess was situated at an altitude of 5,200 feet. The pilgrims had to trek around twelve kilometres uphill from the base camp at Katra in order to reach the shrine.[139]

A virtual sea of humanity would make the trek during the holiest period of the year, Navratri, or the Festival of Nine Nights. The nine days were divided into three sets of three days each. Each set of three days would be used to worship three different manifestations of the Supreme Mother.[140]

On the first three days, the Goddess would be worshipped as the nurturer and the provider of spiritual and material wealth, Lakshmi. The next three days would be spent worshipping the divine feminine as Saraswati, the goddess of wisdom. Finally, the divine Mother would be worshipped as the force of destruction, Kali.

A Shiva temple was located about fifteen kilometres away from Katra. A spring ran from the rocks in a wooded grove and flowed into a holy rivulet that eventually merged with the Chenab river.

The truck-mounted water tank was one among hundreds that supplied drinking water to pilgrims. This one, however, was different. Instead of water, it contained a deadly cocktail consisting of cyanide, arsenic, mercury, parathion, sodium fluoroacetate, cadmium, sarin, sulphur mustard and dieldrin.

The accident was perfectly targeted—at the mouth of the river. It resulted in the immediate death of the driver. Kali was about to manifest her awesome powers of destruction that day on 21 June 2012. More than 500 pilgrims were killed and over 2,000 lay sick or critical in various hospitals due to the poisoned river water.

Bin Fadan was neither sick nor dead. He headed for the Indira Gandhi International Airport in New Delhi from where he caught a KLM flight through Amsterdam to New York. He then drove to Frederick County in an Avis rental car.

*. . .it fell upon one-third of the rivers, which became
undrinkable and killed many.*

🔱

Baghdad, Iraq, 2012

Camp War Eagle, initially used by the 1st Squadron, 2nd
Cavalry Regiment, was located in the Tisa Nissan district of
Baghdad. Conditions at Camp War Eagle had improved
dramatically over the years of occupation by American forces.
Air-conditioners and generators hummed all over the place. A
spanking new basketball court stood in the centre of the camp.
Payphones allowed the men to be in direct touch with their
families. New barracks were continuously being erected to
accommodate additional men.[141]

Unfortunately, these things did not help keep the men safe.
Almost all the residents of the camp had already had close
encounters with incoming explosives. Thousands of soldiers had
been injured in the sixty-acre camp, mostly when they were
walking towards the mess room. Luckily, there had been no
fatalities; not till today anyway.

They could not have envisioned Kader al-Zarqawi's men
launching rocket-propelled grenades and improvised explosive
devices at Bayji, Daura and Basra in simultaneous and
coordinated attacks.

At the same time, multiple cargo containers at various ports,
including Al Faw, Khawr Al Amaya, Mina Al Bakr, Umm Qasr,
and Al Basraha, exploded. Four of these ships contained
flammable liquids. Two of the flaming boats contained resins
and coatings including isocyanates, nitriles, and epoxy resins.
Winds began carrying thick black smoke and releasing toxic
chemicals and metals into the air.

The soldiers used to joke that the appropriate epitaph for
anyone serving at the camp would be: 'And when he gets to
heaven/To Saint Peter he will tell/ "Just another soldier reporting,
sir, I've done my time in hell!"'

196

Two hundred and thirty soldiers and more than a thousand civilians reported to Saint Peter on 21 July 2012. Job done, Kader al-Zarqawi left Baghdad by road in order to board a flight out of Istanbul. He had been told not to be late for the conference in Frederick County.

And a fourth angel sounded, and one-third of the sun, moon and stars was darkened so that one-third of the day became dark.

𐤈

Wyoming, USA, 2012

Shamoon Idris was dressed as a garbage-collector. In front of him was a large dustbin that could be rolled forward on a set of wheels. A close observer would have noticed that he was not collecting any garbage. The dustbin remained tightly shut. What exactly was he doing inside the Yellowstone National Park?

America's best-known national park was the centre of the tourist circuit as it was home to a large variety of wildlife including grizzly bears, wolves, bison and elk. The most important attraction, of course, was the 'Old Faithful' and a collection of the world's most extraordinary geysers and hot springs. Why was Shamoon here?

Some minutes later, Shamoon rolled the dustbin onto a boat as it sped into the centre of Yellowstone Lake. Having reached the pre-determined point, Shamoon donned a diving suit and threw the dustbin overboard. Instead of floating, the dustbin submerged itself and came to rest on the lakebed.

Scientific studies of volcanic activity at Yellowstone National Park had shown the existence of a massive volcanic bulge at the bottom of the lake.[142] Shamoon needed to ensure that the dustbin was correctly positioned on the hump and detonated before currents could move it elsewhere. Accuracy was the key.

The powerful bomb that exploded on top of the hump ruptured the bulge on the bottom of Yellowstone Lake and set in motion a chain reaction that tore apart the underground magma chamber. As the magma chamber erupted, the ground shook as portions of the park imploded into the caldera underneath and then exploded in a massive eruption of lava, embers, dust and soot.

21 August 2012. One thousand seven hundred and twelve dead and countless injured. Shamoon wasn't around. He had already reached Bozeman, Montana, from where he travelled to Hagerstown Regional Airport. He needed to be in Frederick County on time.

And the fifth angel sounded, and a star fell from heaven unto the earth and to him was given the key of a bottomless pit. And he opened the bottomless pit; and there arose a smoke like that of a great furnace and the atmosphere became black.

Jakarta, Indonesia, 2012

The Bung Karno Stadium, one of the world's largest, had been built in 1962. The stadium had a registered capacity of 100,000, but at times the audience could swell to over 120,000. Named after Sukarno, Indonesia's first President, the stadium was undergoing a huge renovation exercise to host the next Asia Cup. The Football Association of Indonesia, in the meantime, had reintroduced a national cup competition featuring seventy-four clubs within the country. The first match of the series was on 21 September 2012.[143]

Unfortunately, since half the stadium was under renovation, the fans who turned up for the match that day were herded together like cattle into the remaining usable half of the stadium. There was an air of excitement in the usable half of the stadium but cement-mixers lay silently in the area of the stadium under renovation.

As half-time was announced, the crowds started moving towards the toilets, which was when the mixers were mysteriously turned on. The anthrax spores were transported by aerosol delivery through a special spraying device built into the mixers.[144] As the spraying continued, bacilli anthracis were inhaled by thousands of spectators in the stadium. Hundreds died over the next few days.

The contracting firm providing the mixers was a small outfit called Bermis Bakti PT Mohammed Yusif, the owner of the contracting firm, held 100 per cent of the equity shares of his company; however, all his equipment had been procured on leases. The leases for the equipment were held by Samba, the Saudi-American Bank. The future cash flows from the leases had been discounted and securitised. The securities had been sold to a small investment trust in the British Virgin islands called the Isabel Madonna trust.

Yaqub Islamuddin was on a Garuda flight, musing, 'It's quite amazing, the things one can plan when one has time inside prison. But it's nice to be out. This conference in Frederick County will do me good.'

. . . and out of the smoke came locusts upon the earth . . .

New South Wales, Australia, 2012

The plains of New South Wales were quiet and meditative. The vast fields of wheat and cotton stretched endlessly and the population density was extremely low.

The quiet was about to be broken by a deafening buzzing. An isolated swamp created by the previous year's rains had been well cultivated by Adil Afrose. As he detonated a bomb in the centre of the swamp, the grasshoppers formed swarms that would travel more than 500 kilometres searching for food.

Weeks later, the Australian Plague Locust Commission reported that a single swarm over just one square kilometre had contained over fifty million locusts and had consumed eleven tonnes of vegetation every twenty-four hours. Tens of millions of dollars in damage had been done to crops, pastures, orchards, gardens and sports fields in a single day.[145] 21 October 2012. Adil was also flying, like the locusts. He was on a Qantas flight; desti-nation—Frederick County.

. . . and unto the locusts was given the power to hurt men that did not have the seal of God upon their foreheads.

⚔

Grozny, Chechnya, Russia, 2012

Yahya was in Argun Mosque coordinating efforts centrally. Soon, from 2,000 mosques across Chechnya, a battle cry was heard: '*Miyarsh Noxchi Che*! Long Live Free Chechnya!' Coinciding with the war cry, hundreds of Chechen rebels mounted their horses and charged upon the Russian base near Vedeno in the south of Chechnya led by Yahya Ali. A hundred and twelve Russian soldiers were killed. This was just the beginning.

On 21 November 2012, the Vnukovo Airlines flight bound for Moscow from Grozny was completely full. The plane, a Tupolev 154, took off at 8:40 am from Grozny and was scheduled to land in Moscow three hours later. Immediately prior to landing, Yahya and his two men took over the aircraft and diverted it to Istanbul. In Istanbul, they were joined by another colleague, Kader al-Zarqawi, who had arrived by road from Baghdad. They were provided passage to Prince Mohammed-bin-Abdel Aziz airport in Medina, Saudi Arabia.

When the flight arrived in Saudi Arabia, the four men held the 128 passengers hostage till a getaway vehicle was provided. As they sped away, they remote-triggered the device that had been stored in the overhead luggage rack of one the seats. Ninety-three dead, thirty-five injured.

The getaway vehicle took them to Kuwait, where they separated. Yahya switched identities and took an Emirates flight to the United States. He had done his job well. He deserved some rest in Frederick County.

And the sixth angel sounded, and was asked to let loose two hundred thousand horsemen to kill one-third of humanity.

༢༗

Waziristan, Pakistan-Afghanistan border, 2012

The Sheikh's Master, the beneficiary of the Isabel Madonna trust, was busy recording a DVD. He was seated on his rug, wearing his trademark camouflage jacket. The DVD would be released to the world on 21 December, in the midst of universal turmoil. The Sheikh watched his Master as he recorded his statement.

Praise be to Allah, who created the universe for his worshippers and commanded them to be just and permitted the wronged one to retaliate against the oppressor in kind. To proceed . . . peace be upon he who follows the guidance.

What has already transpired is merely a forerunner. The destruction of the Vallée Blanche glacier in France; the burning down of millions of dollars worth of natural resources in Bolivia; the destruction and devastation caused to the Three Gorges Dam in China; the massive oil spills in the English Channel; the blast at the Petronas Towers in Malaysia; the poisoning of river waters in India; the dramatic explosions of oil assets in Iraq; the volcanic eruptions in Wyoming; the anthrax attack in Jakarta; the plague of locusts in Australia; and the hijacking and blowing up of a Russian passenger plane that was headed out of Chechnya . . . these were mere appetisers. If you think that these events were hell, you have not yet seen the wrath of God. The main course is yet to come!

I say to all of you, accept the will of Allah and prevent your destruction. Give Muslims their rights, their lands, their oil, and their political power, otherwise we shall continue to rain fire and chaos upon you. Your security is in your own hands. And every state that doesn't play with our security has automatically guaranteed its own security. And Allah is our Guardian and Helper, while you have no Guardian or Helper. All peace be upon he who follows the Guidance. Be on your guard, for Armageddon is finally here!

Click. The Sheikh, who was behind the camera, shut it off and pulled out the recordable DVD. He efficiently sealed it in a 3M-Scotch cushioned envelope so that it could be delivered to Al-Jazeera television at the appropriate time. The Sheikh was wondering how he would meet his end of the deal. Commitments made within the Crux Decussata Permuta were not to be taken lightly. It was these commitments that had ensured the spread and growth of the two largest religions of the world, Christianity and Islam. He knew that his Master did not think the same way.

Chapter Nineteen

Goa, India, 2012

Vincent and Martha fell instantly in love with Goa. The place was filled with famous churches, including the Se Cathedral, the Church of St Anne at Talaulim Ilhas, the ruins of the Church of St Augustine, the Reis Magos Church built on the banks of the Mandovi river, the Basilica of Bom Jesus, the St Cajetan Church, the Church of St Paul, the Church of Mary Immaculate Conception, and the Church of St Francis of Assissi.

Vincent was pained to note that Goa's magnificent temples of Christianity were pretty much a legacy of ruthless Portuguese colonisation. Christianity had been forced upon the local population with religious zeal by the Portuguese, particularly during the Inquisition. This had involved a massive pogrom to destroy Muslim mosques and Hindu temples and had continued till the end of the Inquisition in 1812. Unfortunately, many of Goa's beautiful churches had been built on sites of former temples and mosques. The lands had been forcibly taken over by the Church.

Which wasn't surprising, thought Vincent. After all, Pope Leo X had said to King Manoel of Portugal in 1515, 'Receive this warlike sword in your always victorious and warlike hands . . . use your force, strength, and power against the fury of the infidels!'[146]

The first step Vincent and Martha decided to take was to attempt to decipher the document handed over by Terry to Vincent. The document said:

It is enough, O Lord, it is enough, the two angels said. Mastrilli, without doubt, made the best silver bed. But to carefully guard a secret of the dead, Ignatius's gold cup is better than a silver bed. The city is located between 15°48' and 14°53'54' north and between 74°20' and 73°40' east.

The problem lay in the latitude and longitude provided. It covered almost the whole of Goa. Hence this could mean almost any church in Goa.

Then it struck Vincent! The envelope in which Terry had handed over the documents to him had the words 'Bom Jesus' scrawled on it by Terry. Furthermore, the Church of Bom Jesus contained the tomb of the Spanish missionary, Saint Francis Xavier. It was claimed that the body remained in a permanent state of preservation within a silver casket constructed by Mastrilli. The reference to Mastrilli meant that the document they were searching for must have been stored in the Basilica of Bom Jesus. They needed to get to the Basilica immediately.

⚜

It was past 9 pm when Vincent and Martha arrived at the Basilica. The church was located in old Goa, which had been largely abandoned after the fall of Portuguese rule. All that remained were a few churches, a monastery and a convent. In the quiet of the night, they made their way inside the church. In the dim candlelight they together gasped at the beauty of the gilded altar, the extravagant frescoes and the intricate inlay work.

To the south of the church stood an airtight glass coffin ensconced in a silver casket designed and executed by a Florentine craftsman of the seventeenth century. The embalmed body of St Francis Xavier lay within. Under the casket was a pair of stone angels holding a message, '*Satis est, Domine, Satis est!*' Translated, it meant, 'It is enough, O Lord, it is enough!'

They began to look beneath the casket. 'Are you looking for this old parchment?' the voice resonated. They froze. It was a nun. Her feet shuffled along the marble floor as she walked towards them. 'You are searching for the documents hidden here by Alphonso de Castro, aren't you? Here, I have them,' she said as she threw the document in Vincent's face.

It was only when she was right beside him that he noticed the Japanese face and felt the cool hardness of the metal nub of a 9-mm pistol pressed against his ribs.

Martha looked on helplessly as Swakilki led Vincent out of the church and into a waiting car. The woman had been quietly firm: 'One false move and I'll kill him.'

After a few minutes of remaining frozen, Martha sprang into action. Swakilki had obviously known that they were after the original of the document handed over by Terry Acton to Vincent. She also had a copy of it in her possession. This meant that someone besides Terry had known of its existence. Moreover, Swakilki had followed them to Goa. There was only one person who had known why Vincent and Martha were in Goa—Thomas Manning! Vincent should never have trusted him!

This was a bigger conspiracy than they could handle. The local police would be of little help in this. Who could she turn to? Swakilki was a dangerous foe. 'For heaven's sake! Who can help me save Vincent?' muttered Martha under her breath. She then recalled her conversation with Terry Acton a couple of days before his death.

While it had been a well-known fact that Terry was researching various religions and was deeply involved in past-life therapy, what had generally not been known was that his research was sponsored by the Illuminati. Terry had been convinced that modern-day Christianity, as taught by the Roman Catholic Church, was far removed from the Gnostic spirituality of Christ. The Illuminati had believed that the findings from Terry's research could possibly neutralise the power of their primary foe—the

Roman Catholic Church. Terry had revealed to Martha that his Rhodes Scholarship and Skull & Bones connections had led him to the Illuminati; after all, the origin of Skull & Bones itself lay in the Bavarian Illuminati. And the contact point had been Terry's close friend from his Yale days—Stephen Elliot.

Martha remembered Stephen because he had visited Terry in London several times after the death of Terry's wife, Susan. Stephen had even asked Martha to help pick out a gift from Harrods for his fiancé, Alissa. She needed to get in touch with Elliot. She wondered how Alissa would react to these developments, but she realised that she had very little choice in the matter.

It was as she was racing towards the church door that she saw the document the nun had flung in Vincent's face before abducting him. It was lazily stretched out on the cool marble floor, not in the least bit concerned about the chaos that it had just caused.

⚕

New Delhi, India, 2012

RAW. The name sounded earthy and rough. That's because it was. RAW stood for 'Research and Analysis Wing' and was India's premier intelligence agency, which had over 12,000 agents operating around the world. The chief of RAW held the rather meek title of 'Secretary (R)' in the Cabinet Secretariat, which was part of the Indian Prime Minister's office. RAW's primary responsibility was that of gathering external intelligence. This role was complementary to that of its cousin, the Intelligence Bureau, which was responsible for gathering and analysing internal intelligence. The two organisations were meant to jointly report to the National Security Council, headed by the Prime Minister.[147]

Secretary (R) General Prithviraj Singh was pondering over the tip-off that he had received from his old friend in the SAS,

Stephen Elliot. Prithviraj was among the old-guard elitists within the security apparatus of India. Educated at Eton, with a Ph.D. in mathematics from Yale, the white-moustached, bow-tie wearing, Montecristo-smoking veteran was a gentleman in every sense of the word, except for his intellect, which was razor-sharp.

As a Yallie, he had excelled in Game Theory. He had delighted himself by not answering exam questions—he would instead write detailed and well-reasoned explanations on why there were inherent flaws in the framing of the questions. His intellectual arrogance had been a source of lively debate on the Yale campus.

He stared at his friend from Mossad, Zvi Yatom. Yatom had been involved in some of the Israeli intelligence agency's most successful operations. In 1981 he had spearheaded the destruction of Iraq's Osirak nuclear reactor. Some years later, Yatom had masterminded the assassination of Abu Jihad, Yasser Arafat's most loyal aide within the Fatah party.[148] Zvi had flown down to New Delhi from Tel Aviv to assist Prithviraj in figuring out exactly where the bomb could be headed.

Prithviraj was now wondering how he should brief the Prime Minister. A priest kidnapped in Goa by an international assassin on behalf of a group called the Crux Decussata Permuta, a group that had already succeeded in bumping off an English professor because of his anti-Church research! A nuclear device smuggled into India, a land of 3.28 million square kilometres and a population of 1.02 billion people, with no clear indication of where it was headed! It was like looking for a needle in a haystack!

He paused outside the Prime Minister's office door and then knocked twice. 'Enter!' came the voice from within. The general sighed, opened the door and walked in along with Zvi. The octogenarian Prime Minister accorded them his trademark smile, the one that had won him the last general election. Behind the smile was a Machiavellian streak that could turn foe into friend, defeat into victory and opposition into dust.

'What was so urgent, General Sahib?' asked the Prime Minister, using the respectful Indian suffix as he motioned both men to sit.

'Sir, we have reliable information from our American friends that the Lashkar-e-Toiba or a sub-group within the Lashkar has managed to procure a nuclear device, roughly of the capacity used at Hiroshima. The Pakistani and North Korean connection seems quite evident. The reason for the urgency is that this device, according to American intelligence, is already in Indian territory. Unfortunately, we have no indication of whether it is still on Indian soil or whether it is headed to some other destination such as Israel.' Brief. Concise. Matter-of-fact.

'What are our options?' asked the octogenarian. Zvi spoke up. 'It seems that this could be the work of Ghalib, sir. It is likely to be the twelfth attack in a series of attacks that have been happening on the 21st of each month this year, including the attack that India had to cope with in Katra. The key question is, who facilitated such a nuclear transaction with the Pakistanis? Our sources indicate, quite incredibly, the involvement of a fringe Christian group called the Crux Decussata Permuta that is using the nuclear deal as barter for something else.'

'What could that be?' asked the PM.

'There is one person who could have helped us answer that question. Professor Terry Acton, who obviously knew enough to get taken out by the Crux. According to our friend at the SAS, Stephen Elliot, Terry Acton's research was shared with a priest, Vincent Sinclair. Unfortunately, he was kidnapped last night in Goa. Efforts are on to locate him, although that's easier said than done. I need your clearance to deploy one of our four Rapid Action Divisions in order to help me trace him,' replied Prithviraj.

'You have it,' came the immediate response, 'but keep this matter under wraps, gentlemen'.

'We shall be as quiet as the dew!' retorted Prithviraj, taking a leaf out of Emily Dickinson's poem as he gently closed the heavy oak door of the PM's office.

Chapter Twenty

Mari, Indo-Pakistan border, 1898

The British Army was building a watchtower on a hill called Pindi Point when they noticed the old monument. If they had simply asked the locals, they would have been informed that it was a tomb called 'Mai Mari da Asthan'. The tomb had been placed in Jewish east-west orientation. This ruled out the possibility of the occupant being Muslim. It certainly could not be Hindu, since Hindus cremated their dead.

Translated, *Mai Mari da Asthan* meant 'The Final Resting Place of Mary'. It was from this particular tomb that the place had derived its name, Mari.[149] It was believed that when Jesus was on his way from Turkey to Kashmir, his mother, who was around seventy years old at the time, had died in Mari and been buried there.

This tomb, however, was not in dispute, unlike another one in Kashmir.

Kashmir, AD 1774

The dispute pertained to an old tomb located in Kashmir. The decree was finally issued by the High Court of Kashmir, under the seal and hand of the Grand Mufti.

The Seal of the Justice of Islam, Mulla Fazil, 1194 AH.
In this High Court of Justice, in the Department of Learning and Piety of the Kingdom.

Present: Rehman Khan, son of Amir Khan, submits that: the kings, the nobles, the ministers and the multitude come from all directions of the kingdom to pay their homage and offerings in cash and kind at the lofty and the holy shrine of Yuz Asaf, the Prophet, may God bless him.

Claims: That he is the only and absolute claimant, entitled to receive the offerings and utilise these, and none else has any right whatsoever on these offerings.

Prays: That a writ of injunction be granted to all those who interfere and that others be restrained from interfering with his rights.

Verdict: Now this court, after obtaining evidence, concludes as under. It has been established that during the reign of Raja Gopadatta, who built many temples and got repaired especially the Throne of Solomon on the hill of Solomon, Yuz Asaf came to the valley. Prince by descent, he was pious and saintly and had given up earthly pursuits. He spent all his time in prayer and meditation. The people of Kashmir having become idolaters after the great flood of Noah, God Almighty sent Yuz Asaf as a Prophet to the people of Kashmir. He proclaimed oneness of God till he passed away. Yuz Asaf was buried at Kanyar on the banks of the lake, and the shrine is known as Rozabal.

Orders: Since the shrine is visited by devotees, both high and common, and since the applicant, Rehman Khan, is the hereditary custodian of the shrine, it is ordered that he be entitled to receive the offerings made at the shrine as before, and no one else shall have any right to such offerings. Given under our hand, 11 Jamad-ud-sani, 1184 AH.

The Throne of Solomon, referred to in the judgment, was more commonly known as the Takhat Sulaiman and had been repaired in AD 78.

Kashmir, AD 78

The Takhat Sulaiman, the Throne of Solomon, was a magnificent temple located on the peak of a hill near the Dal Lake. There were four inscriptions on the structure.

The first of these inscriptions was, 'The mason of this pillar is Bihishti Zargar, Year fifty and four.'

The second inscription was, 'Khwaja Rukun, son of Murjan erected this pillar.'

The third inscription was, 'At this time Yuz Asaf proclaimed his prophethood. Year fifty and four.'[150]

And finally, the fourth inscription proclaimed, 'He is Jesus, Prophet of the Children of Israel.'

The same Yuz Asaf mentioned by Shaikh Sadiq in his writings.

Khorasan, Iran, AD 962

Shaikh Sadiq was dying. During his global travels, he had written several books, including *Ikmal-ud-Din*, in which he had written of the travels of Yuz Asaf:

> Then Yuz Asaf, after roaming about in many cities, reached that country which is called Kashmir. He travelled in it far and wide and stayed there and spent his remaining life there, until death overtook him, and he left the earthly body and was elevated towards the Light.

Shaikh Sadiq also wrote about some of the parables Yuz Asaf taught:

> When a sower goes forth to sow, some seeds fall by the wayside, and the birds pick up the seeds. Some fall upon stray land, and when the new stems reach the stony foundation they wither away. Some fall among thorns and grow not. But the seed that falls on good land grows and brings forth fruit.

Strikingly similar to the 'sower' parable of Jesus.

※

Srinagar, Kashmir, India, 2012

Barabbas was the name of the charming houseboat on the Dal Lake in Srinagar. It had a delightful cedar-panelled bedroom, with many conveniences of a luxury hotel. The boat had fine furniture, warm Kashmiri carpets, and modern bathroom fittings. It was moored at a location where one had a view of the beautiful lotus gardens of Kashmir. It had a balcony in the front, a lounge, dining room, pantry and three bedrooms with attached bathrooms.

Srinagar's thousand-odd houseboats were permanently moored in the Dal and Nagin lakes as well as in the river Jhelum. All houseboats in Srinagar, regardless of category, had highly personalised service. Not only was there a butler on every boat, the manager and his family, too, were never far away.

The owner of this particular boat was none other than Ghalib. He never stayed on it—he was mostly away travelling; the boat was usually used by his trusted aide and friend, Yehuda Moinuddin. Yehuda was also the junior assistant director of Archives, Archaeology, Research and Museums for Kashmir.

The owner of the boat had twelve 'children' scattered around the world. In Urdu, the number twelve was *barah* and the word for father was *abba*. This particular owner, Ghalib-bin-Isar, was affectionately called 'Bara-abba', the 'father of twelve'. Who else had twelve disciples?

※

Jerusalem, AD 27

Very early in the morning, the chief priests, including Caiaphas, with the elders, the teachers of the law and the whole Sanhedrin, reached a decision. They bound Jesus, led him away and handed him over to Pilate. 'Are you the king of the Jews?' asked Pilate.

'Yes, it is as you say,' Jesus replied.

The chief priests accused him of many things. So again Pilate asked him, 'Aren't you going to answer? See how many things they are accusing you of!' But Jesus made no reply, and Pilate was amazed. Now, it was the custom at the Feast to release a prisoner the people requested for. The crowd came up and asked Pilate to do for them what he usually did.

'Do you want me to release to you the king of the Jews?' asked Pilate, knowing that it was out of envy that the chief priests had handed Jesus over to him.

And the crowd shouted, 'Release Jesus Barabbas!'

Now, among the prisoners awaiting crucifixion that day, there was a man called Barabbas, whose first name was also Jesus. Some scholars believe the crowd was asking for the release of Jesus the prophet, who was also called Bar-abba (Son of the Father), and not the criminal.

Or Jesus Bara-abba, the father of twelve.

⚕

Langley, Virginia, USA, 2012

Stephen Elliot was here at headquarters in the middle of the night reading the information that had been sent to him by his mole, CIA Trois, several weeks earlier.

> *Boutros Ahmad* is the point man for South America. He was definitely involved in the Bolivia affair. Boutros is the Arabic form of the name Peter.

> *Kader al-Zarqawi* is head of Iraqi operations. 'Kader' means 'the strong one' in Arabic. This is similar to the name Andrew, which also means 'the strong man'.

> *Yahya Ali* is the kingpin of Chechnya operations. His original name was Dzhokar Raduev. Yahya is the Arabic form of the name John.

> *Yaqub Islamuddin* is the brains behind Jemaah Islamiyah and the Jakarta operation. Yaqub is the Arabic form of Jacob from which the name James is derived.

Shamoon Idris is the key operative of the Islamic Jehad Council in North America. Shamoon is the Arabic form of Simon.

Faris Kadeer is the chief of the East Turkestan Islamic Movement and coordinator of the Chinese sector. Faris means 'horseman' in Arabic. In Greek, the name Philip also means 'horseman'.

Bin Fadan is one of the key operatives of the Jaish-e-Mohammed's activities within India. Bin Fadan means 'son of the plough'. It should be noted that this has the same meaning as the name Bartholomew, which in Aramaic means 'son of the plough'.

Ataullah al-Liby is the kingpin of the French Intifada. Ataullah means 'gift from God' in Arabic. This is similar to the name Matthew which is derived from the Hebrew name Mattiyahu, meaning 'gift from God'.

Tau'am Zin Hassan is the main operative of the Darul Islam in Malaysia. Tau'am means 'twin' in Arabic. This is similar to the name Thomas, which is the Greek form of the Aramaic name Te'oma, which also means 'twin'.

Adil Afrose is chief commander of the Australian operation. Adil means 'one who acts justly' in Arabic, similar to James—'the just'.

Yehuda Moinuddin is the most trusted aide of Ghalib and is involved in the overall operations of the group. Yehuda is the Arabic form of the Hebrew name Judah, or Judas.

Fouad al-Noor is head of the group's activities in the UK. Fouad literally means 'heart' in Arabic. This is similar to the meaning of Thaddaeus, which is derived from the Aramaic word for 'heart'.

Ghalib-bin-Isar is leader of the Lashkar-e-Talatashar, the Army of Thirteen. The name Ghalib in Arabic means 'dominant' or 'conqueror'. In Arabic, the word 'bin' means 'son of'. The name 'Isar' can be traced back to Isar-el, the eastern Kabbalists' Sun God, from which the name 'Israel' was derived.[151]

214

So, Ghalib-bin-Isar would translate to 'dominant among the lineage of Isar'.

The person providing this information to Elliot was one of these thirteen people. His code name, CIA Trois, was an anagram for another word. Iscariot.

Yehuda Moinuddin, junior assistant director of Archives, Archaeology, Research and Museums for Kashmir, and trusted aide and friend to Ghalib, was Elliot's mole. Yehuda was the Arabic form of the Hebrew name Judah, the Greek form of which was Judas.

Judas Iscariot.

🔱

Jerusalem, AD 27

Then went one of the twelve, who was called Judas Iscariot, to the chief priests. And said to them: 'What will you give me, and I will deliver him unto you?' And they appointed him thirty pieces of silver.

Chapter Twenty-One

Mathura, north India, 3127 BC

The moon was in the constellation of Aldebaran and it was the eighth lunar day of the dark fortnight in 3127 BC.[152] The blessed virgin, Devaki, was about to deliver a baby boy; Krishna was to be his name. His birth had been heralded by the astral formation of a Rohini Nakshatra, a most auspicious astrological sequence.

Unfortunately, an old Brahmin had predicted to King Kansa, the ruler of Mathura, that a son born to Devaki would eventually destroy him. Kansa ordered the death of all male babies born on the day of Krishna's birth to prevent the prophecy from coming true. Luckily for Krishna, his father had been warned and fled with the child to Gokul where he could be brought up safely.

Hinduism has long worshipped the holy trinity of Brahma—the creator, Vishnu—the preserver, and Shiva—the destroyer. Krishna, it was believed, was the second entity in this trinity because he was an avatar of Vishnu. Much like the second entity in the trinity of the Father, the Son and the Holy Ghost. The name Krishna is sometimes also spelt '*Christna*'.

The entire story of Krishna was written in a Hindu epic of 1,00,000 verses some time before 500 BC.

Five hundred years before Christ. Sixty-six years after the Buddha.

Kapilavastu, Indo-Nepal border, 566 BC

Deep sleep produces strange dreams. Maya, the queen of Kapilavastu, had a dream that her soon-to-be-born son,

Siddhartha Gautama, was entering his virgin mother's womb on a white elephant on a full moon night in July.[153]

Soon after his birth, Siddhartha was examined by a group of Brahmins who predicted that the boy would be either a great king or a *Buddha*, an Enlightened One.

At the age of twenty-nine, he left his home and spent the next six years in meditation in the jungles. While meditating, he visualised thousands of his previous lives. He realised that all beings were subject to rebirth. Good actions led to good rebirths and bad actions led to bad rebirths. The place and nature of a rebirth was governed by one's deeds, or karma.

On 8 December, at the age of thirty-five, he found enlightenment after forty-nine days of penance in the wilderness. This was in spite of the devil tempting and taunting him repeatedly.

The Buddha probably knew that the devil would try the same tricks around six centuries later with someone else who fasted for forty days and forty nights in the Judean desert.

Judean desert, AD 26

Jesus was led by the Spirit into the desert to be tempted by the devil. After fasting for forty days and forty nights, he was hungry. The tempter came to him and said, 'If you are the Son of God, tell these stones to become bread.' He answered, 'It is written that man does not live on bread alone, but on every word that comes from the mouth of God.'

A thousand years earlier, the devil had offered much more than bread—he had offered the entire world.

Persia, 1000 BC

Satan offered him the entire world if he would forsake his worship of Ahura Mazda, the Lord of Wisdom.

He was born to a virgin. He received his calling at the age of thirty. The whole world rejoiced at his birth. He was baptised in a river. He astounded wise men with his wisdom.[154] He wandered about with his followers. He went into the wilderness where he was tempted by the evil one. He cast out demons. He restored the sight of a blind man. He revealed the mysteries of heaven, hell, judgement and salvation. He and his followers celebrated a sacred meal together.

No. He wasn't Jesus. His name was Zarathustra, the prophet of the Zoroastrian faith, whose deeds were written about almost 1,000 years before Jesus. Zarathustra was a thousand years too late.

Syria, 2000 BC

Tammuz would rise from his cave each morning, travel across the sky by day and return to his cave at night. He was a shepherd and healer. Tammuz soon died and descended into the lower world. However, his loving wife, Inanna, could not accept his death. She went in search of Tammuz. During Inanna's absence from earth, nature froze. When God heard the pleas of humans, Inanna was allowed to leave the netherworld along with Tammuz. The sad death and happy resurrection of Tammuz occurred every year thereafter. It corresponded with the cycle of nature: life died in autumn and was reborn in spring.

On what date had the virgin Myrrha given birth to little Tammuz? On 25 December.[155] Tammuz too was a thousand years too late.

Egypt, 3000 BC

Horus was born to the virgin, Isis, on 25 December in a manger.[156] His birth was announced by a star in the east. At the age of twelve, Horus taught in the temple and was baptised in the Eridanus by Anup, who was later beheaded.

Horus performed many miracles, including walking on water. He had twelve disciples, and was crucified on a tree amongst thieves. After his death, he was buried in a tomb from where he was resurrected and he ascended into heaven. He raised a man from the dead. The man was called El-Azar-Os.

Later, the Bible would also speak of a man raised from the dead—his name would be Lazarus.

2⟨⟩

Bethany, Judea, AD 27

Now there was a certain sick man, named Lazarus of Bethania, of the town of Mary and of Martha, her sister. Jesus therefore came and found that he had been four days already in the grave. And he asked, 'Where have you laid him?' They said to him, 'Lord, come and see.'

Jesus then went to the sepulchre. It was a cave; a stone was laid over it. Jesus said, 'Take away the stone.' And Jesus, lifting up his eyes, said, 'Father, I give Thee thanks that Thou hast heard me.'

Was it a ritual? Similar to another one in which Jesus would rise from the dead on a day which would then be celebrated as Easter Sunday? Possibly. After all, Easter Sunday had been celebrated from 600 BC onwards, almost 600 years before the resurrection.

2⟨⟩

Persia, 600 BC

Mithras, the Sun God, was born on 25 December. He was a wandering teacher and had twelve disciples. He performed many miracles. He was also called 'the good shepherd'. His sacred day was Sunday. He sacrificed the pleasures of life. Intense purity was demanded of his followers, who were baptised in blood. They usually had a communion supper of bread and wine.[157]

When he died, he was buried in a tomb. After a few days, he was resurrected. Mithras's resurrection was then celebrated each year. The date on which his resurrection was celebrated was Easter Sunday, a date that would later be associated with Jesus of Nazareth.

Judea, AD 23

Was he really Jesus of *Nazareth*? Or was he Jesus the *Nazarene*? In fact, after his return to Judea many years later, Jesus would be fit for initiation into the fold of the *Nazars* because of his strong educational background. Admission into the fold of the Nazars would make him a Nazarene. The word *nazar* itself was actually a derivative of *nazir*, which means *separate* in the Aramaic language. Nazirites were Jews who had taken special vows of dedication under the rules of which they would abstain for a specific period from alcohol, cutting hair or approaching corpses. The Urdu word *nazar* also means *to see* and thus Jesus was *one who could see*.

As a young disciple, he would be called a Chrestos during his probation. Having completed his probationary period, he would be anointed with oil and given the title of Christos, meaning 'the anointed one'.[158]

The end of the oath required immersion in water. Like the baptism of Jesus?

Jordan river, Judea, AD 26

In those days John the Baptist appeared, preaching in the desert of Judea. At that time, the people of Jerusalem, all Judea, and the entire region around Jordan were going to him and being baptised by him in the Jordan river as they acknowledged their sins.[159] He said, 'I am baptising you with water, for repentance, but the one who is coming after me is mightier than I. I am not worthy to carry his sandals.'

Thousands were baptised in the river. The same scene would be repeated in 2001.

⚎

Allahabad, north India, 2001

The thirty million people knew that this Kumbh Mela was special. This year the planets had come into a position that was very auspicious, occurring after 144 years.[160] A dip in the Ganges during the month-long festival would cleanse the human soul of all sins and enable escape from the cycle of rebirth.

The Kumbh Mela had been taking place every three years for thousands of years. A similar event had been seen in Jordan in AD 26. The origins of ritual immersion in water were fundamentally Indian, like the sacred ritual of marriage—Hieros Gamos.

⚎

Bethany, Judea, AD 27

She was making Jesus go through an ancient fertility ritual called Hieros Gamos, or 'the sacred marriage'.

In 1993, a book entitled *The Woman With the Alabaster Jar* by Margaret Starbird suggested that the anointing of Jesus by Mary Magdalene was carried out as part of a sacred marriage ritual. Starbird wrote:

> Jesus had a secret dynastic marriage with Mary of Bethany. She was a daughter of the tribe of Benjamin, whose ancestral heritage was the land surrounding the Holy City

of David, the city of Jerusalem. A dynastic marriage between Jesus and a royal daughter of the Benjamites would have been perceived as a source of healing to the people of Israel.

Perhaps the earliest verbal references attaching the epithet Magdala to Mary of Bethany's name had nothing to do with an obscure town in Galilee. In Hebrew, the epithet 'magdala' literally means tower, or elevated, great, magnificent . . . This meaning has particular relevance if the Mary so named was in fact the wife of the Messiah. It would have been the Hebrew equivalent of calling her Mary the Great.

In older sacred marriage rituals, a woman who represented the goddess and the land was wedded to the king. Their union symbolised many things, depending on the time and place such a ritual was practised, including the blessing of ongoing fertility, the rejuvenation of the land and the community soul, and the connection between humans and the Divine. Some of these old ceremonies included a ritualistic slaying of the king, either symbolically or literally, after he was married to the priestess-goddess. In the symbolic slayings, he would then rise again in a mystical resurrection echoing the cycles of death and rebirth evident in nature.[161]

The million-dollar question: if the anointing of Jesus was part of the sacred fertility ritual, could the crucifixion and resurrection also have been part of this same ritual?

So, was Jesus the bridegroom?

Cana, Galilee, AD 23

'They have no wine,' said Mary to Jesus.

And on the third day there was a marriage in Cana of Galilee; and the mother of Jesus was there. And both Jesus and his disciples were called to the marriage. And when they wanted wine, Mary, the mother of Jesus, said to him, 'They have no wine.'

Mary immediately ordered the servants to do whatever Jesus instructed. And Jesus told them to fill the pots with water up to the brim. He then asked them to draw wine from them and to serve the governor of the feast.

The servants served the wine. When the ruler of the feast tasted the water that had been made into wine, the governor called the bridegroom and said to him that most people served the good wine first and the lower grade wine later. The bridegroom, on the other hand, had done the reverse. His mother, Mary, had clearly been in charge. She was the hostess, without doubt. And the bridegroom had been Jesus.[162]

Bethany, Israel, AD 27

Christ loved her more than all the disciples and used to kiss her often on the mouth. According to the Gnostic Gospel of Philip, Mary Magdalene was the companion of the Saviour. But Christ loved her more than all the disciples and used to kiss her often on the mouth. The rest of the disciples were offended by it and expressed disapproval. They asked, 'Why do you love her more than all of us?'

The Saviour answered and said to them, 'Why do I not love you like her? When a blind man and one who sees are both together in darkness, they are no different from one another. When the light comes, he who sees will see the light, and he who is blind will remain in darkness . . .'[163] After all, he was Jesus the Nazarene, 'the one who could see'.

Mary anointed Jesus twice with nard. She once anointed his head. Another time she anointed his feet, later wiping them with her long hair. Nard was a fragrant ointment more commonly called spikenard and was part of a sacred marriage ritual practised by Hebrew, Sumerian and Egyptian priestesses who were also trained in music, healing, magic, chants, dance and herbal medicine. In the Old Testament's Song of Solomon, this act of anointing was carried out as an element of the marriage ceremony.

Lynn Picknett, a researcher of religious mysteries, would later write:

> In their time was a sublimely pagan rite that involved a woman anointing a chosen man both on the head and feet—and also on the genitals—for a very special destiny. This was the anointing of the sacred king, in which the priestess singled out the chosen man and anointed him, before bestowing his destiny upon him in a sexual rite known as the Hieros Gamos.

Mary Magdalene was effectively royalty from the tribe of Benjamin, and since Jesus was from the royal family of David, their marriage would have been a powerful dynastic alliance. It now became clear why Jesus was called the 'King of the Jews'. His title had not been merely a spiritual one, but also one that was temporal and political.[164]

In 1982, *Holy Blood, Holy Grail*, a book by Henry Lincoln, Michael Baigent and Richard Leigh, had come up with the theory that Mary Magdalene's womb had in fact been the Holy Grail which eventually carried the child of Jesus Christ.

In his book *King Jesus*, Robert Graves had suggested way back in 1946 that Jesus's ancestry and marriage would have been kept hidden from virtually all except a few in order to protect the bloodline.

So this was a temporal and earthly king. A good man, a great man who did good deeds, but simply a man nonetheless. How could he be made divine? Fast forward to AD 337.

⚚

Constantinople, AD 337

Roman Emperor Constantine lay on his deathbed. He had decided to be baptised into the Christian faith before his death.

After all, in AD 312, he had been able to defeat his rival for the imperial throne, Maxentius, only through Christian support.[165] During his lifetime, he had been sympathetic to the Christian cause but had essentially remained a sun worshipper. In fact, Constantine had ordered the judiciary to observe its weekly holiday on Sunday, which was the 'venerable day of the sun'. Christians, on the other hand, had continued to have their weekly rest on the Jewish Sabbath—Saturday. The Christians now fell in line with Constantine's edict and began observing their weekly rest on Sunday. This brought Christianity closer to existing Roman practice.

The birthday of Jesus, which till then had been celebrated on 6 December, was changed to 25 December. This was done in order to bring Christianity in line with the existing 25 December celebrations of the Roman festival of Natalis Invictus.

Christianity was now being marketed to a Roman audience. Jesus could not merely be a messiah or a teacher if he had to be marketed to the Romans; he had to be a God. One that was greater than the mythology of Mithras, Horus, Tammuz or Krishna. It was necessary to have a virgin birth, and it was imperative to have miracles. It was critical to have a resurrection. He needed to have a stature that was greater than Buddha or Zarathustra, who were merely messengers. Jesus had to be divine!

It also marked the end of the theory of reincarnation. As usual, Constantinople would be at the centre of it all.

Constantinople, Turkey, AD 553

'If anyone asserts the fabulous pre-existence of souls, and asserts the monstrous restoration which follows from it, let him be anathema,' shouted the church elders.[166]

Origen, the third-century Christian theologian (and pupil of Ammonius Saccas) had written that 'The soul has neither beginning nor end . . . it comes into this world strengthened by the victories or weakened by the defeats of its previous existence . . .'[167] This view was not uncommon. Early Christians seem to have believed that the soul existed even before the birth of a person. This was similar to several tenets of Greek, Buddhist and Hindu philosophy.

In AD 553, around three centuries after Origen's death, Emperor Justinian convened the Second Council of Constantinople. The Council passed the infamous resolution that 'If anyone asserts the fabulous pre-existence of souls, and asserts the monstrous restoration which follows from it, let him be anathema.'

That marked the end of the theory of reincarnation within Christianity, and the beginning of the marketing of Jesus. And no one knew how to design and market a package better than the French.

⚜

Lyons, France, AD 185

Irenaeus, the Bishop of Lugdunum in Gaul, had just written *Adversus Haereses*, or *Against Heresies*. In his work he refuted Gnostic teachings completely while strongly claiming that the four gospels that he espoused were the four pillars of the Church—these were the four Gospels of Matthew, Mark, Luke and John.

The Gospels that said that Jesus was born of a virgin, in a manger, with the star of Bethlehem hovering overhead. The same Gospels that said that Jesus had turned water into wine, that he had walked on water, and that he had raised a man from the dead. The same Gospels that stated that he had risen from the dead.

Serapis, Osiris, Horus, Hermes, Mercury, Imhotep, Krishna, Buddha, Mithras, Perseus, Theseus, Hercules, Bacchus, Hyacinth, Nimrod, Marduk, Tammuz, Adonis, Baal, Quetzalcoatl, Baldur, Tien, Attis, Hesus, Crite, Orisaoko, Mahavira and

Zarathustra, were just some of the gods, prophets, messengers, or angels who shared commonalities with Jesus Christ.[168]

They belonged to various time periods prior to Jesus and to various geographical spaces including Egypt, Greece, Persia, India, China, Babylonia and Mexico, among others. Some of them were born of virgins. Some were born in caves or mangers. Many of their births were heralded by astral formations. Some of them were visited by wise men. Indeed, there was a great deal of material available to create a story around the historical Jesus Christ.[169]

Often, they were in mortal danger and had to be taken away elsewhere, either for protection or into exile. Many of them had to overcome the temptations of the devil. Most of them performed miracles. Virtually all of them preached love and forgiveness. Some of them wandered with disciples.

Some of them rose from the dead.

Or remained alive under a shroud in Turin.

⚎

Turin, Italy, 1988

Anastasio was humiliated. It was 13 October 1988. He, the cardinal of Turin, Anastasio Alberto Ballestrero, was being compelled to tell the world that the Shroud of Turin was a hoax![170]

A group of eminent scientists had cut a small sample from the edge of the shroud and carried out carbon dating on it. The Roman Catholic Church was left with no alternative but to accept the finding that the Shroud of Turin was a hoax. It was a difficult position to accept, particularly in view of the fact that eight years earlier Pope John Paul II had kissed the same shroud in reverence.

Subsequently, several scientists would show that the original carbon dating had been flawed because the sample collection itself had been flawed. More important, the blood on the shroud had the rare blood group AB.

⚱️

Oviedo, Spain, 1988

The blood on the Sudarium was also the rare group AB. The Sudarium was a small, bloody cloth kept in a cathedral in Oviedo in Spain. It was believed that this garment had been used to cover the head of Jesus after his crucifixion. Unlike the patchy history of the shroud, the history of the Sudarium could be traced back to the first century. This meant that if one considered the Sudarium to be genuine, it also increased the odds of the shroud being genuine.[171]

⚱️

Was it possible that the shroud, while dating from the time of Jesus, could be from another crucifixion during the same period?

While it was true that the wounds would have been similar in all cases of crucifixion, the one factor that had been significantly different in the case of Jesus was the crown of thorns that the Roman soldiers had placed on his head. The shroud in Turin, as well as the Sudarium in Spain, clearly indicated head wounds caused by precisely such a crown.

According to the Gospels, 'Joseph brought a large linen cloth, took Jesus off the cross, wrapped him in the cloth and laid him in a tomb.' On Easter morning, this garment was found 'folded together on one side of the tomb' and would later reach Abgar V.

⚱️

King Abgar V ruled Edessa, an independent principality in southeastern Anatolia, around the time of Jesus's death. The king had been suffering from leprosy and heard that Jesus could heal lepers. He wrote to Jesus requesting him to visit Edessa, but Jesus was unable to go.

After the crucifixion of Jesus, it was believed that two disciples of Jesus had taken the shroud in which he had been buried to Edessa, and Abgar had been miraculously healed. Abgar became a devout follower and had the cloth affixed on top of one of the city's main gates. The cloth had been folded in such a way that only the face could be seen.

After Abgar's death, his kingdom gradually forgot about Jesus and reverted to older religious beliefs and customs. In AD 525, when the city walls were reconstructed, the shroud was rediscovered. It reached Constantinople around 420 years later and was finally moved to Turin in northern Italy in 1578.

Abgar V was lucky to have been healed. By the 'Leader of the Healed', Yuz Asaf?

It was in 1898 that the photographer, Secondo Pia, was able to see a negative film of the shroud, and this was even more remarkable. The negative, for the first time, actually showed in stunning detail the image that had been hidden within the garment.

The commonly accepted findings were that the image was definitely that of a crucified person. The bloodstains were real and were of the rare blood type AB. There were no brush strokes or pigments. The weave was typical of the Middle East. Examination of pollen taken from the shroud indicated the presence of pollen from plants specific to Palestine in the times of Jesus. Traces of coins minted by Pilate in AD 29 and AD 31 were found on the portion of the shroud that would have covered the eyes. Street dust was found in the area where the feet would have been. The image had been created from chemical saccharides, which were synthesised by the proximity of the cloth to the body.

According to the late Professor Bonte, who was the head of the department for forensic science at the University of Dusseldorf, ' . . . everything speaks for the fact that the blood circulation activity had not ceased yet'.

Several scientists now believe that the man under the shroud must have been alive, not dead.

Chapter Twenty-Two

The *Bhrigu Samhita* was an exceptionally long treatise that had been compiled in ancient India by a sage called Maharishi Bhrigu. The Maharishi had been the first person to compile half a million horoscopes of individuals to build a database for predictive astrology.[172]

Maharishi Bhrigu had collected details of the lives and events of half a million people along with their dates, times and places of birth. He and his disciples had then charted horoscopes for each of these people based on the planetary positions of the sun, moon, Mercury, Venus, Mars, Jupiter and Saturn, at the time of birth.

Using this extensive database, Maharishi Bhrigu had provided predictions and horoscope readings for each of the individuals. The result had been a database that held forty-five million permutations that could be used for predictive astrology.

During the Islamic conquests of India from the seventh century onwards, the invaders had looted these miraculous documents that had been lovingly preserved by the Brahmins. The destruction of the ancient Nalanda University in Maghada had further decimated the exhaustive work carried out under the Maharishi. Eventually, only around 1,00,000 horoscopes that had formed part of the original half-million database remained in India, and these were scattered all over the country. One chunk of this original lot remained with a Brahmin family in the dusty town of Hoshiarpur.

The heir to the prized treasure was Pandit Ramgopal Prasad Sharma, the world-famous astrologer who practised his art every alternate week at the Taj Mahal Hotel in Mumbai. He now sat under the banyan tree outside his ancestral home, poring over the parchments that constituted his life. He had a troubled expression on his face. In fact, he had not been able to sleep at night. He should never have sharpened his predictive skills to the extent that he had succeeded in doing; it only caused excessive worry.

His chance encounter with the man who had wanted the date reference from his ephemeris had troubled him. He had been on a routine visit to the divine Mother Goddess at Vaishno Devi in Jammu when this meeting had happened. He had immediately returned to Hoshiarpur to consult his *Bhrigu Samhita*. He was absolutely convinced. The end of the world was at hand.

He got up and walked to the post office. Pandit Ramgopal did not own a telephone. From the post office, he phoned one of his clients who was an important man in the Indian intelligence services. He needed him to arrange an audience with General Prithviraj Singh.

ॐ

New Delhi, India, 2012

'Your name begins with the letter "P". Your father's name begins with the letter "P". Your mother's name begins with the letter "P". The year of your birth sums up to twenty-two,' said Pandit Ramgopal Prasad Sharma.

Prithviraj. Padamraj. Parvathi. 1957. $1+9+5+7=22$. Prithviraj was stunned. He didn't know this man and yet this stranger seemingly knew lots about him.

'Who are you, sir?' enquired Prithviraj. 'And how do you know who I am?'

'My name is Pandit Ramgopal Prasad Sharma. I am from Hoshiarpur in Punjab, and I have travelled a great distance simply to meet you. I was not only able to predict when and where I would meet you, but also what you looked like. That's why I could find you.'

'Me? Why me?'

'Son, I think we had better sit down and talk. There are many things that will need to be explained.' Intrigued, General Prithviraj Singh led Pandit Ramgopal Prasad Sharma to the sitting area of his simple home.

'Tell me, Mr Sharma, who are you and how have you heard of me? More important, how did you track me down?'

'I need you to promise me something first,' said the wise old astrologer.

'And what is that?'

'I need you to promise me that you will keep an open mind and will not let your judgement be clouded by Western tendencies to treat the inexplicable as unscientific,' said Sharma matter-of-factly.

'Don't you think you are prejudging me? Anyway, I promise.'

'Fine. Now hear this. I am a Brahmin from Punjab. I have in my possession one of the oldest documents in Hindu history, the *Bhrigu Samhita*—a database of over half a million horoscopes that can accurately predict future events. If an original leaf containing the horoscope of an individual is available in the database, it will not only accurately recount the past and accurately predict the future, but will also reveal the date, time and place of consultation. Recently, when I was studying the *Bhrigu*, I stumbled across a horoscope that indicated that I would have to make a reading here in New Delhi, today, to you. This is why I am here,' said Sharma.

Prithviraj was baffled. 'But why did you specifically make the effort of locating me? What was the urgency?'

'You are the only person who has the power to save us from destruction, my son. On the winter solstice of 2012, the noonday sun exactly conjuncts the crossing point of the sun's ecliptic with the galactic plane, while also closely conjuncting the exact centre of the galaxy. This day occurs on 21 December 2012. Your horoscope indicates that you have the power to save a man of God who holds the key to the riddle.'

'Why should I believe you?' asked Prithviraj, rather irritably.

'You lost your father when you were fifteen, your mother when you were twenty-nine. Yours is an old soul that has been through many human lifetimes. This could be your final one, before you attain moksha. You have neither a brother nor sister. You were born and brought up in Punjab but studied in the West, possibly England, America, or both. Most important, you had a brother, for a while, in spirit.'

Prithviraj sat still, awestruck by the accuracy of Sharma's readings. Then he spoke, 'I never had a brother.'

'Yes, you did. Your mother produced a stillborn son in the seventh month of her pregnancy. He is the brother that you had in the spirit world who I am referring to. He is no longer in the spirit world—he has taken rebirth in some other family,' said Sharma confidently.

'Well, there's only one way to find out,' said Prithviraj, as he got up to use the phone to call his aunt, his mother's younger sister, who lived in Amritsar. She picked up the phone on the fourth ring.

'Auntyji,' he said, using the familiar Punjabi-Indian fusion term. 'Listen, I need to ask you something.'

'*Bolo puttar*. Go ahead, son.'

'Did Ma go through another pregnancy after I was born?'

'*Beta*, what's this about?'

'No time for explanations, Auntyji. Just tell me, please.'

'Okay. She went through a pregnancy, which turned out to be near fatal. The doctors were able to save her but not the child . . . a son.'

'And when did this happen, do you remember?'

'I think it was about a year or two after they had you.'

'The child was stillborn?'

'Unfortunately, yes. Your parents never told you because they did not want to burden you with something that they thought was of no relevance in your life.'

'How old was the baby?'

'I think the emergency C-section was done a couple of months before full term. However, the bone marrow transplant was successful.'

'Bone marrow?'

'Puttar, you had been diagnosed with thalassemia as an infant. The only solution was a bone marrow transplant from a sibling. That's why your parents had another child . . . to save you.'

Prithviraj was silent as he digested the enormity of this information. 'Thank you, Auntyji. I'll come and see you when I visit Amritsar in a few weeks.'

Prithviraj hung up. He looked over at the old man sitting calmly on the sofa, running the prayer beads through his fingers. He walked over to him.

'Fine. You're not a con. So what?'

'Son, the brother who died . . . he took on your karma to save you. You were destined to die, but he died for you instead. He has died or killed for you in previous lifetimes too. He has a karmic relationship with you.'

'Fine, but what does this have to do with 21 December?'

'Son,' began Sharma, 'I see utter destruction on that day. Clouds of poison. Total darkness. Dense smoke that suffocates everything in its path. A huge ball of fire that touches the skies. I see colossal human tragedy. But most important, I see a rainbow in the sky which tells me that there could be a way to avert this disaster.'

Prithviraj froze. 'Are you saying that there will be some sort of explosion or earthquake?'

'Worse! An earthquake would be putting it rather mildly. It seems like a manmade tragedy. More in the nature of a colossal bomb of some sort.'

'And I can avert this?' asked the general incredulously.

'Yes.'

'How?'

'Find the priest I met in Mumbai,' said Sharma.

'Vincent Sinclair? I'm already trying to locate him.'

'And son . . .'

'Yes.'

'That brother, who died for you . . .'

'Yes?'

'You will know when you have to return the favour.'

'Do you believe in destiny?' asked General Prithviraj Singh.

'*Unmeitte shinjiru?* heard Pandit Ramgopal.[173]

'What was that?' asked Pandit Ramgopal.

'Do you believe in destiny?' repeated the general.

'*Unmeitte shinjiru?* heard Ramgopal again.

Pandit Ramgopal Prasad Sharma got up.

He said excitedly, 'Prithviraj, there is a Japanese connection. I am sensing a dangerous woman. She has what is called a Paap-Katri Yog or a Vish-Kanya Yog. The force is feminine. Her moon is afflicted and surrounded by malevolent planets—Saturn, Mars as well as Rahu-Ketu. This makes her maniacal. She will not hesitate to kill. I had warned Vincent Sinclair about precisely this negative force.'

'Where can I find her?' asked the general.

Goa, India, 2012

Further away, towards the outskirts of Goa, Vincent surveyed his surroundings. The dim lighting and musty feel of the room gave the impression that this was a basement. Towering over him was Swakilki. Vincent squinted, trying to bring her face into focus. He tried adjusting his body and then realised that his hands and feet had been tied.

'You have been snooping!' barked Swakilki.

'What? No. Where am I? It's you . . .' began Vincent, recollecting the Japanese woman he had seen several times in passing.

Before he could complete his sentence, he felt a stinging slap across his face. 'Shut up!' she hissed. The venom in her voice was blood-curdling. 'Do not play games with me. You have been tracking a prey that you had no business to.'

Vincent was completely disoriented. He didn't have an answer. 'Look, I really do not know what you are talking about. I would like to cooperate, but I am lost. What *are* you talking about?'

Swakilki looked at him with contempt. 'My guest seems to have lost his memory. He seems to have forgotten his extended conversations with Brother Thomas Manning. He has conveniently forgotten his past-life sessions in London with Professor Terry Acton. Has he also forgotten the Bom Jesus papers that Acton gave him? I think he needs a jolt to be brought to his senses.'

Vincent couldn't believe what he was hearing. Thomas Manning had promised to keep his conversation confidential. And why was this woman aware of Terry Acton? How did she know of the Bom Jesus papers? Was there a conspiracy that was being covered up? Could Terry's research have made someone uncomfortable?

Vincent kept staring at Swakilki with a glazed expression on his face. In his brain, he kept seeing himself as the bodyguard killing Mama Anawarkhi to prevent her from plotting against the King Sapa Inca Pachacuti. Swakilki morphed into Mama Anawarkhi. She then morphed back into Swakilki. She then morphed into the Empress Wu Zhao, the evil power on the throne, as she shattered his limbs and placed him in a large wine urn to die a slow death in agony. Wu Zhao morphed back into Swakilki. Then back into Charlotte Lavoisier as she stabbed Jean-Paul Pelletier. He saw Sanson chopping off her head and then saw Swakilki chopping off Terry Acton's head. Swakilki then morphed into a woman who was . . . no, this was not possible . . . Mary Magdalene! As usual, she was blurred—he was seeing several Mary Magdalenes! He was going crazy! Then it was back to Swakilki.[174]

That was when he realised the full significance of Swakilki. He had several past-life connections with her, the present being just one among a series of lifetimes.

'Listen to me, please,' pleaded Vincent. 'I think I know what is happening. My interest in the subject that you spoke of is purely academic . . . why don't you tell me what you want and I'll see if I can fill in some of the blanks.'

'See how the mighty have fallen,' remarked Swakilki sarcastically as she grabbed a fistful of the hair on his head and breathed into his face. 'Now you listen to me . . . you will do exactly as I say . . . do I make myself clear? I will not have you meddling around.' Vincent nodded dumbly in fear as she left the room, the lock clicking firmly in place as she closed the door.

Vincent's arms and legs were hurting. She had used a rough twine rope to tie his arms behind his back. His legs were tied together at the ankles. He had been in the same position for several hours. His head was pounding and his throat was parched. He was unable to figure out where he was. The basement seemed unused and was dark, damp and musty. With the exception of the entrance door to the far right of the room, there were no other doors or windows. A lone, naked ten-watt light bulb hung from a cable in the ceiling, casting a dim light where he lay.

The door was suddenly flung open and the Japanese woman barged in. 'Dinner is served, Your Grace,' she remarked as she put a tin plate containing some rounds of naan and lentils in front of him, along with a plastic bottle of water.

'I can't eat with my hands tied,' mumbled Vincent and was treated to another stinging slap from Swakilki for being rude. 'You will speak when spoken to, am I clear?' she said to him. She untied Vincent's hands and pointed her Beretta 93R automatic at him. 'One false move and I'll blow your brains out!' she said. Vincent was not particularly hungry, but he knew he needed to preserve his strength. He wolfed down the food that had been offered with several gulps of water from the plastic bottle.

'Now, why don't you tell me what you were doing here? Trying to track down the family of Jesus?' demanded Swakilki.

'No . . . no . . . you've got it all wrong. I'm here with my aunt. She's an Indophile and wanted to experience the Navratri festival . . .' began Vincent. Swakilki cut him off.

'I know about your aunt. Don't bother me with the irrelevant stuff. You expect me to believe that after having seen Jesus in a previous life, after having seen him survive a crucifixion, after having discussed this with Manning, after having taken a set of Bom Jesus papers from Acton, after having reached Goa—the home of Bom Jesus—you are merely here on a holiday?' snapped Swakilki.

'Yes! Please believe me! Yes, I went through regression therapy. Yes, I saw Jesus. Yes, I did discuss the possibilities of a Jesus bloodline with Thomas. But no, I did not come to India to find anyone . . . I really do not know anything more,' pleaded Vincent.

'Hmm. I'll tell you what I'll do. I'm going to read you a bedtime story. See if you can recognise the book . . .'

Swakilki pulled out a couple of A4-size papers and began reading. 'Issa and Mary had a child by the name of Sara, who was born to them in India, but was later sent to Gaul with her mother. Issa remained in India, where he married a woman from the Sakya clan on the persistence of King Gopadatta, and had a son, Benissa. Benissa had a son, Yushua, who fathered Akkub. Akkub's son was Jashub. Abihud was the son of Jashub. Jashub's grandson was Elnaam. Elnaam sired Harsha, who sired Jabal, who sired Shalman. Shalman's son Zabbud converted to Islam. Zabbud fathered Abdul, who sired Haaroon. His child was Hamza. Omar was Hamza's son and he produced Rashid. Rashid's offspring was Khaleel . . . Does the passage ring a bell, Father Sinclair?' asked Swakilki.

Vincent replied hesitantly, 'Sure. It's from the *Tarikh-Issa-Massih*. Ah! I see now. You think I was playing detective?'

'Precisely, Mr Sherlock Holmes! That's exactly what you were doing,' exclaimed Swakilki triumphantly.

Vincent protested, 'But I only got to Khaleel. No further. In fact, I do not even know whether the book is reliable.' Vincent conveniently omitted mention of the Urdu version of the *Tarikh-Issa-Massih* that Martha had located which seemed to take the lineage further.

'Oh yes, it is reliable. Terry Acton had spent years researching the subject and would have assured you that it was completely reliable had his life not come to an abrupt end.'

'So are you telling me you know who is at the end of the Jesus lineage?' asked Vincent incredulously.

'Figure it out yourself, Father. You're the so-called research enthusiast, aren't you?' she retorted. 'I made it so easy for you. Pity you didn't bother to hang on to the papers that I gave you at the church!'

'No. It's not possible to figure out anything from those papers. The book that Terry Acton had in his possession, the *Tarikh-Issa-Massih*, only talks of sixteen generations after Jesus. Even taking a forty-year lifespan for each generation, we only have information for around 640 years after Jesus. The remainder of the story is not there!' he explained.

'Oh it's there, all right. Maybe you didn't quite look in the right place,' muttered Swakilki. 'In any case, enough! We have to now get rid of you,' said Swakilki to Vincent. 'Get ready, Father, you are going to see your Lord pretty darn soon! I normally kill my victims immediately. You are lucky that I have a soft corner for your aunt!'

Secretary (R), General Prithviraj Singh, had rolled into Goa with 100 elite troops and set up camp at the Fort Aguada Hotel. He was sitting in a makeshift communications room along with Zvi Yatom when Martha barged in, followed closely by Pandit Ramgopal Prasad Sharma. 'Please help us,' cried Martha. 'My nephew has been kidnapped.'

General Prithviraj Singh looked up at them irritably and said, 'Please let me do my job. We already have 100 men scattered across town doing nothing else but attempting to find Mr Sinclair.'

'Please, General Sahib!' The general saw Pandit Ramgopal Prasad Sharma's anxious expression. 'Panditji?' he asked. The general knew what the old man's expression indicated. 'Quick, Panditji. Do you know where we need to focus our search?'

'Satan! The devil!' said Pandit Ramgopal Prasad Sharma, while Martha continued to sob.

ॐ

The workers were busy constructing the huge effigy of the demon Ravana in the heart of Goa. This effigy, duly stuffed with firecrackers, would be set ablaze on Dussera day, the tenth day after the nine-day Hindu festival of Navratri. This particular effigy was impressive indeed. It scaled a height of forty-five feet and depicted Ravana with ten heads. The demon had a menacing scowl on all ten faces and stood holding his weapons with his feet astride a huge platform. The platform itself was around thirteen feet high.

The company that had been awarded the contract by the coordinating committee was a newcomer and was going the extra mile to please its clients. The contractor had imported the fireworks that would be used from China. This had roused the suspicions of RAW. Within the next thirty minutes, the town centre was cordoned off by the Rapid Action Division commanded by the general. In the centre of the cordoned-off area stood the devil . . . the demon king Ravana with his ten heads.

The general picked up his mobile phone and dialled the number of his counterpart in the CMG—the Crisis Management Group—a part of the DEA, the Department of Atomic Energy. 'I need a team here immediately,' he shouted as his men went about arresting the workers who were putting up the effigy of Ravana.

ॐ

Over the years that it had devoted to nuclear research, India had very little by way of nuclear detection technology. Its front

241

line of defence had primarily consisted of slightly more sophisticated Geiger counters. Unfortunately, these machines did a pathetic job of distinguishing highly enriched uranium, a dangerous element in a nuclear weapon, from naturally occurring radiation, which could be found in almost everything, including fertiliser and kitty litter. The other drawback was the fact that the enriched uranium used in a 'dirty bomb' would normally be encased in lead, thus resulting in very small amounts of radiation leakage.

Since 9/11, scientists at the Indian Department of Atomic Energy had been working on a new generation of equipment that could enhance uranium detection. These devices were engineered to detect all types of radiation in the first phase. In the second phase, advanced computing software was used to characterise the source and type of radiation. In fact, even a dirty bomb ensconced in a lead container would be detectable because some of the gamma rays would still escape the casing and this 'signature' would be identifiable by the software code that was being perpetually updated by software engineers working in a high-tech facility in Bangalore.[175]

The challenge would be to take the prototype and manufacture it in 'cookie-cutter' fashion so that it could be coupled with simple notebook computers that came with pre-loaded detection software. This mass manufacturing was still some years away.

In the meantime, the prototype was available with the Indian Institute of Technology in Mumbai. The general, through a word from the Prime Minister's office, had succeeded in requisitioning the equipment and having it door-delivered to him in Goa.

🔱

General Prithviraj Singh and Zvi Yatom were watching the Crisis Management Team from the Department of Atomic Energy disassemble the effigy of the demon king Ravana with his ten heads. 'Thank you, God, for making it quick and painless to locate the device,' Prithviraj thought to himself as he watched the men prise open the base platform that was meant to contain Vincent and the bomb. About an hour later, he was halfway through chewing one of his Montecristo cigars when the chief supervisor walked over to him. 'All clear,' he said. 'Nothing to fear.'

'So you disarmed the nuke?' asked the general.

'Nuke? Nah. Just routine Chinese firecrackers stuffed inside the effigy. No explosives at all. Not even semtex.' He paused. 'And General?'

'Yes.'

'You said that we may find a guy strapped inside . . .'

'Sure.'

'No such luck.'

'No nuke? No priest? Then where in God's name are they, and why did Pandit Ramgopal lead me to Satan?' asked the general just as his mobile phone started buzzing. It was Stephen Elliot from Langley.

The nightclub near Anjuna Beach was a really wild place. It had red walls, red lights and even a red floor. The lamps were three-pointed pitchforks that had candles on each of the spikes. In the centre was the dance floor on which women, scantily clad in dark red bikini outfits, gyrated to loud rave music. Smoke from joints and spliffs permeated the air as locals and hippies picked up strangers in the night.

The name of the nightclub was 'Shaitana'—the Indian word for 'devil'—'Satan'.

Vincent had been left there, drugged with pentobarbital, an Aum Shinrikyo speciality. In his hand was a note that read:

> *You have been left in Shaitana's red; without losing a hair on your head. I could destroy you—don't think I can't. For your life you should thank your aunt. What you search for does exist; but I pray you to desist! You think your*

search will treasure find? No, it's better to be blind. Some
secrets are better left alone! Why make the living into Skull
or Bone?

Rawalpindi, Pakistan, 2012

The home of Dawood Omar, who was not only Pakistan's
key nuclear research scientist but now also an important member
of Pakistan's largest religious political front, the Jamaat Islami,
was rather quiet at 5 am. He was fast asleep, jet-lagged from
his trip to Pyongyang to sell nuclear equipment subsidised by
Oedipus for Isabel Madonna.

That was when three dozen SAS agents broke down the
doors and captured the startled man as he was reaching for his
Kalashnikov. Dawood was a big fish indeed. The suspected
mastermind of several sensational terrorist acts around the world,
he had a $25-million price-tag on his head.

Stephen Elliot dug into Dawood Omar's laptop and was
struck with fear. On the hard disk was an Al-Qaeda plan to
create a series of nuclear hell storms throughout the United
States, Europe and Israel.[176]

Many hours of sleep deprivation later, Dawood began to
sing. He revealed to his interrogators that the 'American
Hiroshima' command structure reported not to Osama-bin-
Laden but to his deputy, a nameless and faceless man who was
simply known as the Sheikh. The Sheikh and his Master, Osama,
lived just a few hundred yards apart in Waziristan. The nuclear
deal had been paid for by a Christian group called the Crux
Decussata Permuta. Dr Abdul Qadeer Khan's University of
Leuven connections with Alberto Valerio had been used.

The one question that Dawood had been unable to answer
was what the Christians wanted in return for having arranged
the nuclear deal. He didn't need to tell them. Stephen Elliot
already knew.

Washington DC, USA, 2012

The 132 rooms, 35 bathrooms, 6 levels, 412 doors, 147 windows, 28 fireplaces, 8 staircases and 3 elevators of 1600 Pennsylvania Avenue constituted the highest security zone in the world.[177] In the West Wing of 1600 Pennsylvania Avenue stood the room built by the twenty-seventh President of the United States of America, William Howard Taft. Taft's preference for an oval-shaped room could be traced back to the days of George Washington, who had introduced the innovation in order to ensure that his guests could all stand equidistant from him.

The forty-fourth President of the United States of America sat inside the oval office listening to the security brief being presented by Stephen Elliot, head of the SAS, in the presence of the National Security Advisor. This President was known to have a short attention span, preferring short and crisp briefings. Patience was in short supply with this President, Oxford education notwithstanding.

This President's tenure had seen the ruthless reorganisation of the Department of Homeland Security, the most comprehensive rehaul of the federal government in a half-century, consolidating twenty-two agencies and 1,80,000 employees. This President meant business.

'So, what do we know?' asked the President.

'Well, we know that our "ally" in the war on terror, Pakistan, has been a key supplier. Funnily enough, this has happened without presidential sanction from Islamabad. It seems that the A.Q. Khan network has been independently in action through Dawood Omar. The Russians provided Bakatin to play the friendly broker. The device was smuggled into India using the Lashkar-e-Toiba network but has now crossed several international borders. Our sources tell us that there aren't eleven targets but twelve. All of the incidents occurring so far have been major attacks although not on the scale of a Hiroshima. I am given to understand that the twelfth attack may be nuclear and that the target may be Israel,' responded Stephen.

'Jesus! Where? Why?' asked the President.

'Tel Megiddo—the Bible had prophesied that the final military showdown of the world would happen in Megiddo . . . these guys want to prove the point that Armageddon is finally here. It's Islam vs the non-believers.'

'And do we know who these people are?'

'Ghalib-bin-Isar is head of the group. He takes his instructions from someone they call the Sheikh. He, in turn, seems to take instructions from Osama. It is the Crux Decussata Permuta connection that is confusing. We have never heard of these guys. What are they doing dealing with Islamic terrorists?'

'Who is this Ghalib chap?'

'He definitely trained under Osama. He has a tightly-knit pack of twelve stationed all over the world—India, the United States, England, Australia, France, South America, Malaysia, Indonesia, Russia, Iraq and China. They call themselves the "Lashkar-e-Talatashar". Translated into English, it means the "Army of Thirteen".'

'Do we have anyone inside?'

'Nope. We don't have a Judas as yet.'

The President was silent. The National Security Advisor thought for a moment and then asked Stephen rather crossly, 'Why don't we have human intelligence? I thought this was meant to be the highest priority at the agency!'

The President coughed and got up to leave the room for another scheduled event. A knowing glance was exchanged between the President and Stephen Elliot as the former walked out of the Oval Office.

Elliot had not bothered to keep the National Security Advisor informed of CIA Trois. He had, however, always given the President the full picture. The President recalled the BBC interview granted by the White House to Stephen Sackur four years earlier.

London, UK, 2008

Stephen Sackur of the BBC was interviewing the American President for *HardTalk*. The president was on a visit to England, having just won the presidential elections two months earlier.

Sackur: 'The head of the SAS was at Yale. Did you get to know him there?'

President: 'Yes.'

Sackur: 'It is rumoured that both of you were involved in Skull & Bones, the secret offshoot of the Illuminati.'

President: 'Well, if it's secret, how can I possibly talk about it?'

Sackur: 'But what does that mean for those who see something sinister in secret societies such as the Illuminati, the Rhodes Scholars or Skull & Bones? They say you are anti-Church.'

President (laughs): 'I am a practising Christian. Why would I be anti-Church?'

Sackur: 'They say you worry about the Church becoming too powerful . . . pursuing its own foreign policy. You want to keep Islam and Christianity at loggerheads so that oil prices remain high.'

President: 'Who are the "they" that you keep referring to?'

Sackur: 'It's a secret. Like your days as director in the CIA!'[178]

⚵

The American President had been director of the CIA prior to running for office.

This was around the time that the Norm Dixon story had appeared. 'How the CIA created Osama-bin-Laden,'[179] was the headline:

> How things change in the aftermath of a series of terrorist atrocities, the most despicable being the mass murder of more than 6,000 working people in New York

and Washington on 11 September. Bin-Laden, the 'freedom fighter' is now lambasted by US leaders and the Western mass media as a 'terrorist mastermind' and an 'evil-doer', yet the US government refuses to admit its central role in creating the vicious movement that spawned bin-Laden, the Taliban and Islamic fundamentalist terrorists that plague Algeria and Egypt, and perhaps the disaster that befell New York.

In April 1978, the People's Democratic Party of Afghanistan (PDPA) seized power in Afghanistan. The PDPA was committed to radical land reform that favoured the peasants, trade union rights, an expansion of education and social services, equality for women and the separation of church and state. The PDPA also supported strengthening Afghanistan's relationship with the Soviet Union.

Such policies enraged the wealthy semi-feudal land-lords, the Muslim religious establishment and the tribal chiefs. Washington, fearing the spread of Soviet influence to its allies in Pakistan, Iran and the Gulf states, immediately offered support to the Afghan Mujahideen, as the 'contra' force was known.

Between 1978 and 1992, the US government poured at least US$ 6 billion (some estimates range as high as $20 billion) worth of arms, training and funds to prop up the Mujahideen factions. Other Western governments, as well as oil-rich Saudi Arabia, kicked in as much again. Wealthy Arab fanatics, like Osama-bin-Laden, provided millions more.

Washington's policy in Afghanistan went far beyond simply forcing Soviet troops to withdraw; it aimed to foster an international movement to spread Islamic fanaticism into the Muslim Central Asian Soviet republics to destabilise the Soviet Union. The grand plan coincided with Pakistan military dictator General Zia-ul-Haq's own ambitions to dominate the region.

US-run Radio Liberty and Radio Free Europe beamed Islamic fundamentalist tirades across Central Asia, while paradoxically denouncing the 'Islamic revolution' that had toppled the pro-US Shah of Iran in 1979.

Washington's favoured Mujahideen faction was one of the most extreme, led by Gulbuddin Hekmatyar. The West's distaste for terrorism did not apply to this unsavoury 'freedom fighter'. Hekmatyar was notorious in the 1970s for throwing acid in the faces of women who refused to wear the veil. Hekmatyar was also infamous for his side trade in the cultivation of and trafficking in opium. Osama-bin-Laden was a close associate of Hekmatyar and his faction.

The Director of the CIA and later presidential candidate was unrepentant about the explosion in the flow of drugs: 'Our main mission was to do as much damage as possible to the Soviets . . . There was a fallout in terms of drugs, yes. But the main objective was accomplished. The Soviets left Afghanistan.'

It was this same CIA Director who had committed CIA support to a long-standing Pakistani Inter-Services Intelligence proposal to recruit volunteers from around the world to join the Afghan jihad. At least 100,000 Islamic militants flocked to Pakistan (some 60,000 attended fundamentalist schools in Pakistan without necessarily taking part in the fighting).

Soon, Osama-bin-Laden, one of twenty sons of a billionaire construction magnate, arrived in Afghanistan to join the jihad. An austere religious fanatic and business tycoon, bin-Laden specialised in recruiting, financing and training the estimated 35,000 non-Afghan mercenaries who joined the Mujahideen.

Osama has simply continued to do the job he was asked to do in Afghanistan during the jihad—fund, feed and train mercenaries. All that has changed is his primary customer. Then it was the ISI and, behind the scenes, the CIA. Bin-

Laden only became a 'terrorist' in the eyes of the US when he fell out with the Saudi royal family over its decision to allow more than 540,000 US troops to be stationed on Saudi soil following Iraq's invasion of Kuwait.

Chapter Twenty-Three

The lanky, olive-skinned Sheikh read the note that Ghalib had sent him upon reaching his destination. 'Praise be to Allah!' he exclaimed as he read Ghalib's note:

UOY.OT.HTAO.YM.MAMI.HO
OWT.MOTA.TA.MOTA.TIH.OT
HT33T.3HT.TA.MIA.HTUOM.3HT.TA.MIA
TA3H.TOH.3TIHW.HTIW.YAWA.MIH.TIH
3OW.OT.MIH.3IT.YOT.YM.HTIW.3YA
3WO.I.HTUOY.YM.MIHW.YHT.OT
3M.HTIW.TUO.MIH.HTIW.TUO
3M.3SIMOTA.OT.3MIT.YHT.TIAWA.I

'My Master's secret weapon is finally in place,' said the Sheikh in his usual hushed voice as his hands trembled with excitement.

Islamabad, Pakistan, 2012

The Aiwan-e-Sadr, the official residence of the President of Pakistan, lay in the centre of the city that had been meticulously planned and built by the Greek Constantinos Doxiadis. Islamabad, meaning 'the abode of Islam', was the capital city of Pakistan, located at the crossroads of Punjab and the North-West Frontier Province.[180] Ensconced inside the plush interiors of the Aiwan-e-Sadr sat the Iron Man of Pakistan. Born in Lahore to a lower-middle-class family, his parents could never have imagined in their wildest dreams that their son would one day become the President of Pakistan. This was the man who was supposedly at the forefront of the war on terror. This was also the man who had no qualms at waxing eloquent about enlightened moderation while enlisting the political support of Islamic hardliners.

The President was looking at the transcript of a secret phone conversation between the chief of Pakistan's Inter-Services Intelligence (ISI) and a Thuraya satellite phone somewhere in the Middle East being operated by a terrorist called Ghalib. His theory had been proved correct. His intelligence agencies continued to remain involved with Islamic terror groups despite his strict orders to the contrary. The problem was that this situation could not be wished away.

The President had earlier that day been officially briefed by his ISI chief, who had conveniently omitted to mention that a terrorist called Ghalib was running loose somewhere in the Middle East with a nuclear bomb. The phone tap transcript seemed to indicate that this Ghalib and his team were taking orders from someone called the Sheikh. The main worry was that the bomb in question might be of Pakistani origin. That damned Dawood Omar!

During the phone conversation, the ISI chief had been trying to convince Ghalib to give himself up to Stephen Elliot of the SAS! How dare he! Was the ISI chief's salary being paid by the Pakistan Government or by those American bastards? Apparently, the deal had been brokered by the Russians, who had been funded by a right-wing Christian group called the Cux Decussata Permuta. The ironic fact was that no one seemed to be too concerned about the nuclear weapon. All parties wanted Ghalib.

'Why is this man so important to all of them?' thought the Pakistani leader as he sipped his evening scotch and soda.

Goa, India, 2012

The scotch, soda and ice in their hotel room were a welcome relief. Vincent's reunion with Martha had been an emotional one. The ordeal he'd been through only reinforced the importance of friends and family. He also realised the enormity of what he had learned from Swakilki.

'Vincent, are you all right? We were worried sick about you,' said Martha as she sobbed. 'I really thought I'd lost you forever.'

Vincent hugged Martha. 'Relax, Nana. The worst is behind us. There is a reason that we made this trip. If we hadn't come here, we would never have come face-to-face with this dangerous woman. And if I hadn't met her, I would never have realised the importance of what I'd seen in my past-life regressions with Terry and you.'

'And what is that?' asked Martha nervously. She looked somewhat dishevelled from the hours of anxious waiting and searching.

'I need to take my quest to its logical conclusion. That was the reason for my meeting Terry. Destiny took me to London, to Mumbai and to Goa. Maybe it now needs to take me elsewhere.' Vincent was exhausted but highly charged.

Martha looked at him helplessly. 'I'm scared, Vincent. You nearly lost your life. I'm not sure whether I want you to take this matter any further. You're lucky she spared your life . . . and she's left a warning note in your hand.'

'You are my lucky charm, Nana! Didn't you read the note? She spared me because she likes you! Incredible! But Nana, really, this isn't about me. It's about something that has been one of the world's greatest mysteries—something that one cannot simply leave unresolved. The greatest story ever told, the bestseller of the world, ended with an unsolved riddle. I now have a chance to fit the final piece into the jigsaw puzzle. Now, please show me the document you found on the floor of the Bom Jesus Basilica.'

The document was old and yellow and was written on in Portuguese in flowing ink, customary of eighteenth-century manuscripts.

I, Alphonso de Castro, tinham chegado em Goa para dar um ímpeto mais adicional ao Inquisition em 1767. Eu fui requisitado fazer uma lista exhaustive dos textos antigos que tinham sido encontrados nos repousos, temples, igrejas, mosques e synagogues dos Hindus, Thomas Cristãos, os muçulmanos e os Jews de Sephardic . . .

Vincent began to translate the document into English:

'I, Alphonso de Castro, arrived in Goa ostensibly to give further impetus to the Inquisition in 1767. I was ordered to make an exhaustive list of ancient texts that had been found in the homes, temples, churches, mosques and synagogues of the Hindus, the Thomas Christians, the Muslims and the Sephardic Jews. Any texts that did not suit the sensibilities of the Roman Catholic Church were to be destroyed by me. While I was going through an old set of manuscripts discovered in the bowels of the Church of Bom Jesus, I found this particular document.

The Church of Bom Jesus had existed well before 1559—as a mosque. Within one of the pillars that had been discarded in favour of non-Islamic stonework was a cavity. This cavity contained a bundle of documents that had been written in Urdu. These documents had been found by a Hindu construction worker, Lakshman Powale, at the site where the mosque was being torn down to make way for the church.

The bundle was immediately transferred to the archives of the Portuguese viceroy, where it continued to sit till it was taken up for cataloguing by me nineteen years later. The bundle contained eleven texts, of which ten were earmarked by me for destruction. The eleventh one was deliberately not catalogued by me. It was called the *Tarikh-Issa-Massih*.

Through fear for my life, I felt it would be better for me to leave the document in India prior to my departure for Lisbon today. I am determined to store the document in a place where it will be preserved so that it may be discovered by future generations; they may then know the truth.

Tonight, my ship sets sail for Lisbon. Oh Heavenly Father, please forgive me for disturbing Saint Francis Xavier. Since he has the miraculous powers of preserving himself, I believe that under his safekeeping, this document will also remain preserved. 23 April 1770.'

Remember: It is enough, O Lord, it is enough, the two angels said. Mastrilli without doubt made the best silver bed. But to carefully guard a secret of the dead. Ignatius's gold cup is better than a silver bed.

'Do you understand what this means?' said Vincent excitedly. 'It means that the original *Tarikh-Issa-Massih* was found by Alphonso de Castro and hidden away in the Bom Jesus Basilica!'

'But Vincent, this document was already with the Japanese woman. If she had found this, she would certainly have found the original *Tarikh-Issa-Massih* too,' reasoned Martha.

'You're right,' said Vincent. 'The document will be long gone by now. In fact, it is probably tucked away in some secret archive of the Vatican by now.'

Their deliberations were interrupted by General Prithviraj Singh, Zvi Yatom and Pandit Ramgopal Prasad Sharma.

'Father Sinclair, I understand that you have been through a harrowing experience. Unfortunately, I do not have the luxury of giving you time to recuperate. We need to talk immediately!' commanded the general.

Vincent did not notice the general keenly eyeing the Alphonso de Castro letter that Vincent was holding.

Chapter Twenty-Four

All of them sat inside Prithviraj's makeshift office at the Fort Aguada Hotel. Prithviraj began, 'I must tell you that the past few days have put me in turmoil. I have always believed that there is no substitute for good old-fashioned detective work. Unfortunately, the circumstances of the last year are only now beginning to get pieced together.'

Zvi Yatom took over. 'We now know for a fact that Ghalib-bin-Isar and his twelve commandos have carried out terrorist acts all over the world in the past eleven months. Each of these has been timed to occur on the twenty-first of each month. Twenty-first December is just a week away. We expect this will be the mother of all the acts.'

There was stillness in the room as everyone digested this information. The general resumed. 'We now also know for a fact that a nuclear weapon has been obtained by these terrorists and that it has transited through India. The American President, the Pakistani President and the Indian Prime Minister have been in communication with one another and it seems that Ghalib plans to use the device somewhere in the Middle East. We would have been able to pinpoint his exact location from his satellite phone if the conversation he had with his handlers in the ISI had been a bit longer.

'We are re-examining the interrogation that is being conducted on Dawood Omar, a key Osama-bin-Laden operative in Pakistan. We also know that the nuclear weapon transaction was facilitated by a Russian intelligence operative, Lavrenty Edmundovich Bakatin.' Prithviraj looked around him; there was complete, rapt attention.

'The question my colleagues and I asked our counterparts in the CIA was: why would a fringe group within the Church, calling itself the Crux Decussata Permuta, be willing to pay huge sums of cash to Pakistani scientists and North Korean contractors on behalf of a group of Islamic terrorists unless they had something significant to gain? Even today, we are not clear as to what the actual barter involves.

'What I can tell you is that this bunch of terrorists has modelled itself along the lines of Jesus Christ and his twelve disciples. All these men trained together in Afghanistan under Osama-bin-Laden's henchmen. Each of them has executed a major terrorist act on the twenty-first of each month,' explained the general.

'Now, the question that you might ask is: how do we fit into any of this? Well, we know that Father Sinclair was meant to be killed. We now also know that the kidnapper was Swakilki, an international assassin who has been keeping herself under the radar and evading arrest. We also know that she takes her instructions from the Crux Decussata Permuta. The death of Professor Terry Acton and the attempt on Father Sinclair are related. Since both these gentlemen were digging into the bloodline of Jesus Christ, it obviously made someone within the Vatican, or the Crux, or Opus Dei, very uncomfortable. It is thus possible that Ghalib may actually be a descendant of the historical Jesus.

'We have tried working with information from our friends in the office of the secretary-general of CESIS, the Italian intelligence services, and the IAB in Japan, and have come to some conclusions. These are:

'One. Swakilki, a Japanese national, has links with the Roman Catholic Church because she lived as an orphan at the Holy Family Home, an Osaka orphanage.

'Two. A regular visitor there was Alberto Valerio, who held the position of secretary for the Congregation for the Oriental Churches, at which time he travelled extensively within the Orient. His connection to the Priestly Society of the Holy Cross is now known. He possibly also heads the Crux Decussata Permuta.

'Three. Swakilki was initially under the influence of the Aum Shinrikyo cult and committed several crimes with her partner Takuya, till such time as she killed him too. Subsequently, Swakilki Herai has carried out assignments for Valerio only.

'Four. Brother Thomas Manning, who resides mostly in Switzerland, was the banking contact who ensured that Russia received the requisite doses of cash to ensure the freedom of the erstwhile Iron Curtain countries from the Soviet Union. This was done through Bakatin, who also had excellent connections with Al-Qaeda, more particularly someone known as the "Sheikh", who probably reports to a higher Master, possibly Osama.

'Five. After the war on terror, Osama-bin-Laden went into hiding in the Waziristan district of the tribal regions on the Pakistan–Afghanistan border. His new focus was to support local Islamic terror groups with ideology and cash. He wanted to expand his activities by creating local franchises. One of these was the Lashkar-e-Toiba in Pakistan. When, as a fallout of the war on terror, the Lashkar-e-Toiba was banned by the Americans, they spun off the ultra-elite Lashkar-e-Talatashar, or the Army of Thirteen, with Ghalib as the head.

'Six. In the last 11 months, the group has carried out eleven attacks in different parts of the world. Each attack has been on the twenty-first, leading us to believe that the big one will be on 21 December this year.

'Seven. We know that a nuclear weapon is in the hands of Ghalib and that the Crux Decussata Permuta have played a role in making this possible. Valerio, Dawood Omar and A.Q. Khan, Pakistan's head of nuclear research, studied at the University of Leuven in Belgium around the same time. Thus, it is quite possible that they were friends. We believe that Ghalib is taking his instructions from Osama-bin-Laden's right-hand man, the Sheikh.

'This is where you come into the picture, Father Vincent Sinclair. We need your help to understand why elements within the Crux Decussata Permuta would be willing to risk a nuclear war for the sake of Ghalib. Is he truly of the lineage of Jesus Christ? Moreover, what is the significance of 21 December, particularly at Tel Megiddo?'

No one noticed that Martha's knuckles had gone completely white.

၂၄

Vincent sat stunned and motionless as he heard the general give his speech. Memories of 11 September 2001 came flooding back. He had been in the staff room of Stepinac High School along with his friend, the permanently unshaven janitor, Ted Callaghan. The television had been turned on in the staff room.

Then on that day, at 8:46 am, American Flight 11 from Boston had crashed into the North Tower. Seventeen minutes later, at 9:03 am, United Flight 175 from Boston had crashed into the South Tower.[181]

Vincent and Martha attended Mass at St Patrick's Cathedral on Sunday, five days after the attack on the World Trade Centre. Cardinal Egan decided to hold Mass for all those who had died in the tragedy.

Two thousand people turned up.

After the memorial Mass was over, Vincent walked over to Thomas Manning and said, 'I need to talk to you.' Thomas had nodded. Martha left them alone, and Thomas and Vincent strolled over to Murray's Bagels on 6th Avenue. They bought a couple of bagels with a variety of cream cheeses and settled down at a table. 'So, what's all this I hear about you and Opus Dei? An Opus Dei-connected FBI agent was arrested and they're saying he was a parishioner at your church,' Vincent asked.

'Vincent, you know I value our friendship. I want you to know that I had nothing to do with that FBI agent who was arrested. He simply attended prayers at St Catherine's, the same church in which I preached. Period.'

'Point taken. Are you a member of Opus Dei?'

259

'What is this? An inquisition?' asked Thomas, visibly irritated. 'Vincent . . . look . . .'

'Just answer the question, Thomas! I need to know.'

'No. I am not Opus Dei. And I promise you—that's the absolute truth.'

It *was* the truth. He was not Opus Dei.

He was Crux Decussata Permuta.

The group was deliberating on what the general had just told them. 'Martha, you have regressed your patients into the past, but isn't it possible to progress them into the future? Some gurus, such as Weiss, have indicated that our futures are variable, which means that the choices we make in the present could determine the quality of our future,' said Vincent.[182]

Martha thought about it before replying. 'Well, progression is not very different from regression. The problem is that it is difficult to distinguish between fact and fantasy. What if one sees something in the future that may not be true? It could do irreparable damage to the psyche of the patient.'

'Could you progress me?' he asked.

'Sure. But I don't feel very comfortable doing it. You must understand that hypnotic projection is the exact opposite of regression and implies projecting the mind into the future. The purpose would be to see what will happen in the future or what is likely to happen in the future. If this is crazy to a "normal" mind, consider the basic fact that the human mind can not only regress or progress but can also move sideways. Take the concept of dreams; isn't it possible to dream through the passage of an entire year in a matter of an hour?'

'So why won't you progress me if it could tell us something critical?' demanded Vincent.

'If the mind "sees" an event happening often enough, there is a strong possibility that such an event would eventually play itself out as a self-fulfilling prophecy. I don't want to put you in that situation, Vincent.'

Pandit Ramgopal Prasad nodded his agreement. He said to Vincent, 'Son, your future is not a predetermined one. That is the essence of Hindu philosophy. Even though there is always a "most probable" scenario, it is definitely in our hands to change the outcome via our actions. That is the basis of karma.'

Vincent was adamant. 'We are living in a moment of crisis. We need to do something dramatic that may help us. I think I can live with the consequences.'

'Okay, Vincent, you win. What do you want to see?' asked Martha helplessly.

'Do we have a bloodline of Jesus here in India? Is it Ghalib? Is he the anti-Christ? Does he have a bomb? Where is it? Where do they plan to set it off? Will the world tomorrow be a better place than the world today? Will there even be a world left tomorrow?' Vincent was on a roll.

'I get the picture, Vincent,' remarked Martha caustically. 'Let's get you settled. Please understand that projection can be either directive or non-directive. Directive progression is better suited for curing ailments or traumas. My progression will be non-directive, in which you will be free to choose the path yourself. Understood?'

'Sure.'

'Why don't you settle down comfortably on the bed and let me pull this chair near you. Comfortable?' Vincent nodded as he settled onto the hotel bed. Martha pulled up the chair beside him while the others continued to remain seated on the floor cushions.

'Okay, settle back into the pillow and begin to relax . . . that's right . . . just . . . relax.' The voice was soothing, reassuring, but firm. She continued, 'Just relax, and concentrate on my voice. You have absolutely nothing to do right now. You don't need to move. Just relax.'

She continued with the same soothing voice, 'Now drift deeper with every breath you take. Feel your body getting heavier and sinking down further. You're comfortable and relaxed, but you're heavy and sinking. Deeper. Deeper. Okay. Now I want you to allow your mind to drift back in time . . . drift back to this morning . . . drift back to last night . . . drift back to last week . . . to your high-school days . . . drift back to your infancy . . . drift back beyond your infancy . . . that's right.' Martha now began to probe with gentle questions.

'Where are you now?'

'Yerushalem.'

'And what do you see around you?'

'Temple fires. It's night. I can see Caiaphas and the Sanhedrin assembled, judging Jesus. They are irritable because no reliable witnesses are coming forth with evidence against Jesus.'

'Anyone familiar from your present life?'

'Thomas Manning.'

'Who is he?'

'He is Caiaphas—poisoning the minds of those assembled against Jesus. In this life too, he continues to seek vengeance.'

'Anyone else?'

'The Japanese woman who kidnapped me. Swakilki. She's present. She's Mary Magdalene!'

'Anyone else?'

'You, Nana!'

'What am I doing?'

'You're Mary Magdalene!'

'You're confused Vincent . . .' began Martha nervously. She tried to switch tracks. 'Anyone else there?'

'Another woman—I don't know her. She's Mary Magdalene!'

'Vincent, you seem to think everyone is Mary. Let's move on . . . now what's happening?'

'I can see Jesus and three women walking towards Damascus . . . I can only see their backs.'

'Why Damascus?'

'Damascus is a stronghold of the Essenes. He can remain hidden and protected there till they decide where to go.'

'Vincent, I will now count forward from one to five. You will feel yourself floating forward along a continuum of time into a lifetime ahead with each number . . . one . . . two . . . three . . . four . . . five . . . Okay, Vincent, where are you?'

'Megiddo.'

'In Israel?'

'Yes.'

'Who are you?'

'A Roman soldier—my name is Antonius.'

'What are you doing?'

'I am searching for a fugitive. The fugitive is a Roman soldier. His name is Gaianus.'

'Why are you after him?'

'He is a secret Christian. All Christians are enemies of the state!'

'What can you learn from this?'

'I persecuted Christians in my former life. Destiny has made me a Christian priest in my present one.'

'I will again count forward from one to five. Float forward . . . one . . . two . . . three . . . four . . . five . . . Okay, Vincent, where are you?'

'China. I am an advisor to the Emperor Gaozong. The chief concubine, Wu Zhao, has seized the throne and wants to eliminate me. Luckily, she has not succeeded, even though she has crippled me.'

'Anyone familiar?'

'Yes . . . It's her, the evil Wu Zhao who is my captor—she's Swakilki!'

'Counting forward from one to five. You will move forward in time . . . one . . . two . . . three . . . four . . . five . . . Okay, Vincent, where are you?'

'I'm an Inca warrior protecting Sapa Inca Pachacuti. I am the bodyguard for Mama Anawarkhi, the wife of Sapa Inca Pachacuti.'

'You like her?'

'No. I am killing her. I have to. She is plotting against the Sapa Inca. She's Swakilki!'

'Anyone else familiar?'

'Yes. General Prithviraj. He is the Sapa Inca. I protected him. That's why he is protecting me!'

'I will again count forward from one to five. You will move forward in time . . . one . . . two . . . three . . . four . . . five . . . Okay, Vincent, where are you?'

'It's 1794. I'm in France. The guillotine is bloody with the heads that have rolled.'

'Anyone you recognise?'

'The woman, Charlotte Lavoisier, she is being guillotined; she looks like Swakilki. Her executioner, Sanson, looks like Terry Acton. He takes her head in one life . . . she will take his in another.'

'Counting forward . . . one . . . two . . . three . . . four . . . five . . . Okay, Vincent, where are you?'

'I'm a doctor in London. World War Two is going on. I am working for the Red Cross. I can see the Sossoon home, which is a supply depot.'

'Anyone familiar?'

'Clementine Sossoon. She is very sick . . . cancer. Her face is like yours, Nana. Wait. It *is* you, Nana! I took care of you, that's why you love me so much. Isn't that so?'

Martha smiled as she continued: 'Counting forward . . . one . . . two . . . three . . . four . . . five . . . where are you?'

'In the backyard of my parents' home in New York. My dad and I are playing catch in the backyard. My mom is barbequing hot dogs in the corner.'

'Moving forward . . . one . . . two . . . three . . . four . . . five . . . where are you?'

'At my parents' funeral. It's raining. I cannot make out whether my face is wet because of my tears or on account of the rain.'

'Moving forward . . . one . . . two . . . three . . . four . . . five . . . where are you?'

'In captivity. Swakilki is holding me prisoner. She leaves me inside a windowless toilet in the Shaitana nightclub. It's stifling hot inside.'

'Moving forward . . . one . . . two . . . three . . . four . . . five
. . . where are you?'

'Back in Megiddo.'

'What are you doing?'

'I am at a kibbutz in Israel. The hill that overlooks the valley
of the kibbutz is where the final showdown will happen.'

'Where is this hill located?'

'Very close to the intersection of Highway 65 and 66. Nearby
is a large prison holding many Palestinians who have been
arrested for terrorism against the Israeli state.'

'What do you see?'

'A mosaic.'

'What sort of mosaic?'

'It belongs to an ancient church. It was uncovered recently.
It belongs to the third century. It has a sign. It says that Gaianus
donated his own money to build this church.'[183]

'The same Gaianus you saw earlier? The one you were
chasing when you were a Roman soldier?'

'It's him!'

'Who?'

'Him! Gaianus! Ghalib!'

'What else do you see?'

'Little boy.'

'Who?'

'A bomb. It looks like the one used in Hiroshima. It was
called Little Boy.'

'Are you sure?' asked Martha.

'Yes.'

'Anyone familiar near the bomb?'

'This can't be! No! You?'

'Relax—Vincent. Who are you seeing?'

'Jesus! Gaianus! Ghalib!'

'You see Jesus?'

'أنت! ماذا تفعل؟ اعتقد هذا ما يفعله العالم! يي'[184]

'Vincent. I need you to float above the scene. Speak to me
in English, not Arabic!' instructed Martha.

'Hey, you! What are you doing? Think of what this will do to the world!'

'Who is saying this? To whom?'

Blank. Vincent was completely quiet.

Martha realised she had reached a blind spot. She continued, 'Moving forward . . . one . . . two . . . three . . . four . . . five . . . where are you?'

'I can't say. It's deserted here. No food. No water. Corpses and vultures. It's as if the world has been laid waste by fire.'

'Is it war? Famine?'

'I warned everyone that religious polarisation was going to get us nowhere. No one listened. See what happened. We now have nothing left to fight over.'

'Can you identify the date?' asked Martha.

'An extremely close conjunction of the winter solstice sun with the crossing point of the galactic equator and the ecliptic path of the sun.'

'When is that, do you know?'

'21 December 2012.'

Pandit Ramgopal Prasad Sharma nodded; the very date that he had seen as the end of the world.

'What can you see?'

'The radiation produced by the explosions has destroyed all the vegetation.'

'What else?'

'Burning trees. Burning grass. Rivers and oceans of blood. Complete darkness.'

'Can you see anyone else?'

'I can see him.'

'Who?'

'The man who started it. The man who finished it.'

'What did he start or finish?'

'The end of the world.'

Waziristan, Pakistan-Afghanistan border, 2012

The Sheikh needed to reconfirm the contents of Ghalib's note. He asked his loyal attendant to fetch him his mirror. When this was in front of him, he held the note up and re-read it from the mirror image:

OH.IMAM.MY.OATH.TO.YOU
TO.HIT.ATOM.AT.ATOM.TWO
AIM.AT.THE.MOUTH.AIM.AT.THE.TEETH
HIT.HIM.AWAY.WITH.WHITE.HOT.HEAT
AYE.WITH.MY.TOY.TIE.HIM.TO.WOE
TO.THY.WHIM.MY.YOUTH.I.OWE
OUT.WITH.HIM.OUT.WITH.ME
I.AWAIT.THY.TIME.TO.ATOMISE.ME

Chapter Twenty-Five

Herr Egloff, the investment advisor from Bank Leu, was sitting in the dining room of his chalet near Lake Aegiri consuming his usual breakfast of Birchermuesli mixed with fruit and yoghurt. This particular batch had been made with chopped filberts, chopped almonds, sweetened wheat germ, rolled oats, dried currants, and dried apricots. Herr Egloff attributed his good health to this wonderful concoction that had been invented by the renowned Swiss Dr Bircher-Benner.

The other reason for Herr Egloff's good health was the excellent state of his clients' portfolios. More specifically, the portfolio managed for Brother Thomas Manning. A single-sheet summary lay on the dining table.

Next to it lay an unsigned draft press release. It spoke about a nuclear threat in the heart of the Middle East. The fallout of such an event would be a reduction in the production and supply of oil in the region. Prices would further rise. Brother Manning would be pleased.

Crude Oil Future Contract Number One that he had purchased for his clients at $51.06 per barrel was now trading at $203.11 per barrel.

He had made a similar investment for his biggest client, a radical outfit called the UNL Militia. Herr Egloff did not ask too many questions about where the money came from. It was just one of the reasons for his tremendous success.

Before doing anything else, he had an important assignment to carry out for His Eminence. He transferred $30,000 from the Oedipus account to that of Iscariot. He then took a phone call from Washington DC and transferred a million dollars from the UNL Militia to Iscariot.

ᛟ

Jerusalem, AD 27

Then went one of the twelve, who was called Judas Iscariot, to the chief priests. And said to them: 'What will you give me, and I will deliver him unto you?' And they appointed him thirty pieces of silver.

ᛟ

Srinagar, Kashmir, India, 2012

She had come here to Srinagar to meet him. It had taken several months of effort to finally get him to agree on a deal. He was the junior assistant director of Archives, Archaeology, Research and Museums for Kashmir. His name was Yehuda Moinuddin a.k.a. CIA Trois a.k.a. Iscariot a.k.a. Judas.

As such, he had complete access to the former director's work—the work of Dr Fida M. Hassnain. A person listed in the Who's Who of archaeology and having complete control over the entire body of ancient Kashmiri documents. One of Dr Hassnain's bestselling books had been *A Search for the Historical Jesus*, written in 1994. This phenomenal work of scholarship had contained tonnes of painstaking and verifiable research to prove that Jesus had not died on the cross and that he had spent the latter part of his life in Kashmir.

Yehuda had worked in this heady environment of scholarship and research for quite some time. Over many years he had absorbed each and every little detail that was available regarding the Jesus-in-Kashmir theory.

However, there was one extremely important difference between him and Dr Hassnain. Dr Hassnain was a true scholar. He was a Sufi, a mystical proponent of Islam, and was never out

269

to discredit Jesus or the Christian faith. In fact, it was his love for Jesus Christ that made him want to distinguish fact from fiction. Yehuda Moinuddin, on the other hand, was a different matter. He was one of the key members of the Lashkar-e-Talatashar. He was Ghalib's most trusted aide, who managed all the financial matters of the group and lived on the houseboat *Barabbas* that belonged to Ghalib.

He was sitting in the balcony of the houseboat moored on the Dal Lake sipping a cup of kahwa, a delicate Kashmiri tea flavoured with saffron and almonds. 'I must find him before Vincent Sinclair and the others can reach him,' Swakilki said to him.

'I have spent the last two years researching everything there is to research on the subject. I already know whatever there is to know. I simply need to lead you to him. For that you must pay me my price.'

Swakilki handed over a thin white envelope containing a slip with an account number at the Bank Leu, Zurich. Yehuda Moinuddin took it and looked at the slip eagerly. Thirty thousand dollars. He smiled a sly smile of satisfaction. 'I won't confirm with Egloff because I trust you,' he said.

Swakilki shot back, 'You won't confirm because I can kill you.' He laughed. 'No, you won't. I'm the only one who can take you to him,' he said as he thought of the last meal he had with Ghalib.

Duly washed, they sat down and were served the lamb. Ghalib took the hot naan and, breaking it into pieces, lovingly served it to his men. He then spoke to Yehuda, 'In Srinagar, there is a Japanese woman looking for me. You will go, find her, and tell her that you will deliver me to her.'

🕉

The trip westwards from Srinagar towards the Poonch district of Kashmir, along the Indo-Pakistan line of control, is very scenic.

One necessarily has to travel through what is commonly called the 'Valley of Kashmir', a strip that is about eighty miles long and thirty-five miles wide, straddling the river Jhelum at an average elevation of 5,500 feet. Looking at the verdant hills and orchards and endless miles of swaying chinar trees, Swakilki found it difficult to understand how Bill Clinton could have called this 'the most dangerous place on earth'.

The rugged India-made Mahindra Commander 650, an extremely basic 4x4, was ideal for the difficult roads that they were traversing. Yehuda was at the wheel. Swakilki sat on the uncomfortable bench seat in the rear of the vehicle wearing an Afghan burqa that covered her entirely from head to toe. Swakilki was looking forward to finally being able to see the man in person.

⚶

Vatican City, 2012

'One can never trust Muslims!' shouted His Eminence Alberto Cardinal Valerio. Brother Thomas Manning was silent as he listened to Valerio venting his anger.

'We transfer funds from our Oedipus trust to the Isabel Madonna trust. We convince Dawood Omar to part with the first bomb of the series, only to be told that Osama plans to use Ghalib as the trigger! God curse his soul to eternal damnation!' he thundered. Silence greeted him.

'Don't you have anything to say? Do you realise what could happen to the Church if word got out?' he demanded furiously.

'Your Eminence . . .' began Thomas Manning.

'Yes. Say whatever you want quickly!'

'Does it matter whether Ghalib is delivered to us alive or dead?' asked Manning delicately.

'What do you mean?' asked Valerio.

'Well, wasn't the intention of this exercise to prevent word from getting out that Christ had not died on the cross and that he had not been resurrected. Wasn't it our intention to ensure that the story we have fed our faithful flock for centuries remains intact?'

His Eminence wanted to be angry; instead, he smiled at Manning's logical mind.

⚜

Maryland, USA, 2012

Stephen Elliot and Prithviraj Singh were with their friend from Mossad, Zvi Yatom. They were not alone. Around fifty people were in the darkened room along with them. The poorly lit room had walls that were padded in dark velvet. The sweet smell of incense pervaded the atmosphere. The room was accessed through a single passageway, the entrance to which was camouflaged by a portrait of Benjamin Franklin, painted in 1759 by Benjamin Wilson. Inside the secret hall, one could observe in the dim light, thirteen passages that led to thirteen separate rooms. Each of these rooms was used for very specific ceremonies.

The Grand Master spoke. '*Achaita*, divine revelation. Rome will pass away, Jerusalem will burn and the reason will become broken. And my Law, the Law of Zión, will be acclaimed by the whole of humanity.'[185]

'Achaita!' said all those gathered in unison.

'Oh Illuminated, Brothers and Sisters of the Great Hidden Lodge, of the Night, of the Star, of the Light! Zión is the Law!'

'Achaita!'

'Elevate and proclaim the Light, and break the chains of death, with the force Zión, oh Illuminated. I am the creator of worlds. I am the Great Architect of the Universe. Nations and governors are dust in front of me!'

'Achaita!'

'The next centuries and millennia will only know one word: Zión. And one Law: Zión. The next millennia will be of freedom and light, life and creation, love and kindness, under the Law of Zión, the Law of the Eternal One!'

'Achaita!'

'Proclaim Zión, oh Illuminati, and lead the slaves to the footpath of freedom. The brave ones will be free and eternal, to image and similarity of God. The cowardly ones will die forgotten and surrounded in their chains of ignorance and sin!'

'Zión! Zión! Zión! Zión! Zión! Zión! Zión! Zión! Zión! Zión! Zión! Zión!'

The Grand Master, dressed in scarlet robes, thrust the knife into the dummy that had been placed on the large black granite slab in the centre of the room.

'Zión! Zión! Zión! Zión! Zión! Zión! Zión! Zión! Zión! Zión! Zión! Zión!'

After the dummy had been 'sacrificed', each member went up to the Grand Master, bowing and kissing the Grand Master's ring. As they kissed it, they swore their allegiance to *Novus Ordem Seclorum*, the New World Order.

'We have lost our colleague Terry Acton to the forces of the evil Church. Fear not! His sacrifice was not in vain. As we speak, the forces of Islam and the forces of Christianity are positioning themselves for the greatest conflict ever. At the end of this conflict, they will both destroy themselves. And then will arise the New World Order—the power of the Illuminati!'

Ceremony over, the Grand Master retreated through the secret passageway till it ended at the secret door that was camouflaged on the other side by the painting. The Grand Master placed both palms on the scanners by the sides of the entrance and waited till the door swung open.

The forty-fourth President of the United States of America then went and settled down behind the antique desk in the study of the official 125-acre retreat in the centre of Catoctin Mountain Park in Frederick County, Camp David.

The forty-fourth President, the SAS director Stephen Elliot, RAW chief Prithviraj Singh and Mossad operative Zvi Yatom were all peas from the very same pod.

The Illuminati.

Chapter Twenty-Six

Tel Megiddo, Israel, 2012

Ghalib surveyed the area. El-Azhar was very familiar with the site. He had brought along with him all the required ordinance maps that outlined every inch of the territory. El-Azhar told Ghalib not to worry as they parked the truck inside a small thicket so that it would not attract too much attention. El-Azhar asked Ghalib to wait while he surveyed the caves to determine the exact location that would be ideally suited to their purpose. Ghalib would continue observing El-Azhar from a distance, using night-vision binoculars. He would wait desperately for the next four days while El-Azhar continued to remain invisible. Ghalib was worried. Could something have happened to him? Just as he was about to break protocol and go searching for him, he saw an extremely tired and fatigued El-Azhar emerge from one of the very small openings along the slope of the hill. Ghalib lifted his eyes to the heavens and exclaimed, '*Ma sha' Allah!* I thank the all-merciful Allah for having heard my prayers! El-Azhar lives to tell me his story!'

Bethany, Judea, AD 27

Now, there was a certain man sick, named Lazarus, of Bethany. Jesus therefore came and found that he had been four days already in the grave. And said: 'Where have you laid him?' It was a cave; and a stone was laid over it. Jesus said: 'Take away the stone.' They took, therefore, the stone away. And Jesus lifting up his eyes, said: 'Father, I give thee thanks that thou hast heard me.'

⚜

Tel Megiddo, Israel, 2012

Ghalib's arrest by Zvi Yatom was quick and effortless. El-Azhar had done his job well by tipping them off. Within a few minutes Ghalib had been surrounded. The problem was that his truck, containing the alleged device, had disappeared.

The Israeli state gave the police blanket powers to arrest suspected terrorists, carry out communication intercepts, and severely curtail freedom of expression. In high-risk areas, search warrants could be done away with and the authorities were free to periodically ban communications through mobile phones or cyber cafés.

It was a classic chicken-and-egg story. Which came first—the terrorist or torture? Hard-line Islamic terrorist groups claimed that thousands had been tortured by the Israeli state whereas the authorities claimed that they had no other way to deal with people who saw nothing wrong in killing innocent women and children in schools, hospitals and restaurants. The greater the terrorist menace, the more aggressive were the police and army in questioning suspects and, consequently, the higher the levels of torture and interrogation. But each suspect that emerged from the jails, innocent or not, became sympathetic to the terrorist cause.

⚜

Tel Megiddo, Israel, 2012

He was strapped naked in a prostrate position on a table and interrogated, while the soles of his feet were whacked repeatedly till the bones began to crumble.

275

Ghalib merely whispered, 'The person who participates in holy battles in Allah's cause will be recompensed by Allah . . . will be admitted to Paradise if he is killed in battle as a martyr . . . *Bismillah, i-rahman, i-rahim*, in the name of Allah, most gracious, most merciful, *Sibhana man halalaka lil dabh*, praise be upon he who has made me suitable for slaughter.'

⚛

Jerusalem, AD 27

The Roman soldiers stripped Jesus and proceeded to tie his hands tightly to the post above him. The flagellum was made from a combination of individual leather pieces, bone and lead. Two soldiers, one on either side, carried out the task. While the Jews had an upper limit of forty lashes, the Romans had no such limit. The flagellum struck the skin of his back, shoulders and legs with maximum impact. With each progressive lash, the whip not only cut through the skin but also through tissue, capillaries, veins and muscles.

⚛

Tel Megiddo, Israel, 2012

The High Purity Germanium (HPGe) detector that Zvi Yatom had succeeded in obtaining from Tel Aviv was cleverly able to identify radioactive materials from their 'natural signatures'— because all radioactive substances continued to emit gamma rays, x-rays, alpha particles, beta particles, or neutrons.[186] The machine had already sounded several alerts. The first alert had flashed on the screen.

Thorium-234. 24.1 days. Beta, Gamma, X-ray.

It had turned out to be a huge fertiliser warehouse on the edge of a neighbouring field. The radioactive thorium was a key component of fertiliser and had a 'half-life' of 24.1 days. The half-life was the amount of time it took for half of the atoms in the given radioactive substance to decay.[187] The next alert was near the kibbutz. It turned out to be the x-ray department of the kibbutz hospital. Zvi was looking at the notebook computer's screen as it flashed another message.

Potassium-40. 1.28 billion years. Beta (1.3-MeV), Gamma.

Wrong number again. It was a truckload of bananas being transported to the local market from the kibbutz.

Another message flashed:

Thorium-232. 14.1 billion years. Alpha, x-rays.

'Yes! We may have found it!' shouted Zvi triumphantly as he ordered the patrol vehicles of the unit to head in the northerly direction pinpointed by the map on the screen. The signal became stronger and then suddenly stopped. They were in a granite quarry! Radiation was quite obviously going to be high owing to the high uranium and thorium content of the granite stone.

'Turn back!' he ordered. 'Let's move towards the hill.'

As the convoy progressed, the earlier computer message reappeared.

Thorium-232. 14.1 billion years. Alpha, x-rays.

Zvi Yatom stopped his jeep and peered over the shoulder of the technician operating the infernal radiation detector. 'What is it?' he asked.

The operator looked up at him and said, 'Sir, this area is the local scrapyard. Disused metal objects are brought here and are re-used for welding. The thoriated tungsten welding rods emit radiation. That's the signature we seem to be picking up.'

Zvi was exasperated. The damn computer was identifying fertiliser, granite quarries, bananas, x-ray machines, welding rods and everything other than the damn bomb. 'Carry on towards the excavation site,' he ordered, 'that's our best bet.'

Suddenly, the screen came alive.

Uranium-235. 700 million years. Alpha, x-rays.

They had it! Uranium-235 gave off alpha rays, which had a half-life of 700 million years. They were close to a source of enriched uranium. There was no alternative. They would have to evacuate the area immediately.

⚱

Waziristan, North-West Frontier Province, 2012

'*Shukran li-l-láh!* Thanks be to Allah!' cried the Sheikh. 'Even though he is in the clutches of the Jewish scum, he has not forgotten his duty. Where is he?'

The messenger spoke up. 'I am given to understand that he has been whisked away to the Tel Megiddo prison nearby, where the Mossad agents are interrogating him.'

'Rascals! They would whore their own mothers to achieve their aims. So what do we do about the truck that is sitting there? The detonation codes are only with Ghalib.'

'Uh . . . Sheikh . . . It seems that he has already sent those to you in a previous dispatch.'

'Ah!' remarked the Sheikh. 'Ghalib, my jihadi, you have made me proud.'

'Err . . . Sheikh . . . why do the rascals want Ghalib?'

'It's a very long story. It begins in Jerusalem . . .'

⚱

Vatican City, 2012

His Eminence was very clear. Successive American presidents had used Islam to counter the power of the Church while continuing to maintain a façade of innocence. Illuminati bastards! They needed to be taught a lesson.

The phone buzzed. Thomas Manning. He was speaking rather softly. The cardinal's face turned red as he heard Manning's words, ' . . . captured . . . Megiddo . . . Mossad . . . no truck . . . in custody . . .'

His Eminence could control himself no longer. He screamed at Manning, 'Don't you realise what has happened? I wanted

278

Ghalib alive! I compromised by allowing you to give him to me dead. The one man who could shake the very foundations of our beloved Church is now in the custody of people who would like nothing better . . . those sons of whores, the Illuminati!'

Balakote, Indo-Pakistan border, 2012

It was 11pm when they reached Balakote. Yehuda was tired, but Swakilki remained alert and excited—like a hunter before the kill. Yehuda pointed out Ghalib's tent from the distance. Swakilki took out the sharp Nepali kukri from its sheath under her burqa and held it lovingly in her right hand. She then stealthily moved towards Ghalib's tent.

She could make out the dim light of a kerosene lamp inside, but there were no voices. Obviously, he was asleep. She slit open the tent near the base and crawled in.

'Welcome Swakilki!' boomed the voices of Stephen Elliot and Prithviraj Singh as they quickly wrestled the knife out of her hand and held her at gunpoint.

Standing some distance away, Yehuda smiled to himself. His Illuminati masters had paid him much better than the crumbs thrown his way by His Eminence. One could not compare the paltry 30,000 transferred from Oedipus to Iscariot with the one million transferred from the UNL Militia to Iscariot. UNL Militia was just an anagram of the name of another organisation, the Illuminati.

Yehuda got back into his Mahindra Commander 650 jeep and started the long drive back to Srinagar. He needed to catch an international flight to meet his compatriots, who were already in Frederick County.

Priobskoye, Siberia, 2012

Zvi Yatom was speaking on a secure line with Stephen Elliot and Prithviraj Singh. With Ghalib in Israeli custody and with Swakilki in Indian custody, it seemed that the two key protagonists were now under their control.

'So, is the truck in place?' asked Stephen.

'Yes. The detonation will be triggered from Waziristan on 21 December 2012 by the Sheikh. He has the detonation sequence. He thinks Ghalib has managed to plant the device in Megiddo. He does not know that the entire truck has been secretly airlifted to Priobskoye,' explained Zvi.

Discovered in 1982, the Priobskoye oilfield occupied an area of 5,466 square kilometres in the Khanty-Mansiysk Autonomous District of Western Siberia. It was Russia's largest oilfield. After Saudi Arabia and the United States, Russia was now the third largest oil producer in the world.[188] The explosion would decimate Russian oil production, leaving the largest oil reserves in the hands of Saudi Arabia and America—oil reserves owned mostly by Illuminati-controlled companies. Killing many birds with one stone was the specialty of the Illuminati.

Chapter Twenty-Seven

Vincent and Martha were inside the Basilica of Bom Jesus. Vincent was determined not to give up so easily. He had with him the piece of paper that Swakilki had flung at his face on the night of his kidnapping. He looked at the last line:

> *Remember: It is enough, O Lord, it is enough, the two angels said. Mastrilli without doubt made the best silver bed. But to carefully guard a secret of the dead, Ignatius' gold cup is better than a silver bed.*

And then, the penny dropped! The tomb of St Francis Xavier was a three-tiered bier that had been financed by the Duke of Tuscany in exchange for the pillow on which St Francis Xavier's head had lain for several years after his demise. On top, lay the silver casket containing Xavier's remains. The casket had been assembled by local silversmiths under the guidance of Father Marco Mastrilli. The casket was crowned by a cross with the figures of two angels holding the message '*Satis est, Domine, satis est*', meaning 'It is enough, O Lord, it is enough!' These words were believed to have been the most common utterance of Saint Francis Xavier. What the lines seemed to suggest was that the secret was not with the angels or inside the casket, but with St Ignatius.

Vincent looked towards the main altar of the church. The Blessed Sacrament that had earlier been kept on the main altar under the statue of St Ignatius was now preserved in a gold tabernacle. The infant Jesus was shown under the protection of

St Ignatius of Loyola, the founder of the Society of Jesus. The statue of St Ignatius was almost three metres high. *But to carefully guard a secret of the dead, Ignatius' gold cup is better than a silver bed.*

The infant Jesus was dressed in white and was superimposed on a red background. Vincent knew he would have to climb up on the altar to check it more thoroughly. As he stood up to balance himself, he took the support of the massive gilded goblet upon which the statues had been supported. He was shocked to find that it was entirely hollow. *Ignatius' gold cup is better than a silver bed.*

He stood on his toes to peer inside the mammoth goblet and began feeling within its inner surface for any inconsistencies. The inner surface was smooth, unlike the heavily engraved outer surface. Suddenly his hand felt a crack. It was not a natural formation. It was a straight line. As his hands moved down the straight line, he found another line running at 90 degrees to the first. On a hunch, he followed the next line to find yet another. He was right! There was an inner secret panel!

'Just what do you think you are doing?' the voice echoed through the depths of the church. Vincent and Martha turned around in shock. It was Father Dias, the priest, extremely agitated to find that his altar and sacraments were being desecrated. Vincent hastily scrambled down and apologised, 'I am sorry, Father. I am also a priest and had heard so much about Bom Jesus that I wanted to observe the baby Jesus from as close as possible. Please accept my apologies.'

'If you are a man of God, then you should know better than to be disrespectful to the traditions of the Church!' argued Father Dias. However, his tone had mellowed. 'I will forgive you just this once. Please be more careful in future.'

The two culprits beat a hasty retreat. Once outside the church, Martha asked Vincent anxiously, 'Why were you so engrossed with the goblet? Did you find anything?'

Vincent replied, 'There was a secret panel inside it. As I was feeling around inside, the Father's voice jolted me and I ended up pressing on it very hard, mostly out of fright. I had no idea that the panel had a spring action and that this little piece of parchment would fall into my hand!'

'Ah! I see. That's why you could afford to be so apologetic,' commented Martha sarcastically. The two of them looked at the delicate parchment in Vincent's hands. It read:

Do Ieste-Occidental ou Nort-Sul Que diferença faz? Rozabal de Kanyar dorme quietamente, porque Yuz Asaf não é uma falsificação. Tentativa 34.09° N 74.79° E.

Translated to English, it meant:

East-west or north-south. What difference does it make? Rozabal of Kanyar sleeps quietly, because Yuz Asaf is no fake. Try 34.09° N 74.79° E.

༒

Srinagar, Kashmir, India, 2012

The onset of winter in idyllic Kashmir meant that the days were gradually getting shorter. Even though it was only three in the afternoon, it felt like night was rapidly falling. Icy winter winds, having wafted through the numerous apple and cherry orchards of the area, brought a spicy and refreshing aromatic chill to Vincent's nostrils. The leather jacket and lambswool pullover underneath it were his only comfort as he knelt at the tomb to pray. Martha had stayed back in Goa, but Vincent had refused to lose another day.

He rubbed his hands together to keep warm as he took in the sight of the four glass walls, within which lay the wooden sarcophagus. The occupant of the tomb, however, was residing below in an inaccessible crypt. Standing in front of a Muslim cemetery, the tomb was located within an ordinary and unassuming structure with whitewashed walls and simple wooden fixtures.

The sign outside informed visitors that the Rozabal tomb in the Kanyar district of old Srinagar contained the body of a person called Yuz Asaf. Local land records acknowledged the existence of the tomb since AD 112.

The word 'Rozabal', derived from the Kashmiri term 'Rauza-Bal', meant 'Tomb of the Prophet'. According to Muslim custom, the gravestone had been placed along the north-south axis; however, a small opening revealed the true burial chamber beneath. Here one could see the sarcophagus of Yuz Asaf. It lay along the east-west axis as per Jewish custom.

East-west or north-south. What difference does it make? Rozabal of Kanyar sleeps quietly, because Yuz Asaf is no fake.

Nothing was out of the ordinary in this place. Nothing—except for the carved imprint of a pair of feet near the sarcophagus. The feet were normal human feet. Normal—except for the fact that they bore marks on them: marks that coincided with puncture wounds from a crucifixion. Crucifixion had never been practised in Asia, so it was quite obvious that the resident of the tomb had undergone this ordeal elsewhere in some distant land.

Vincent respectfully took off his shoes and walked inside the simple structure. The old caretaker looked up at him and smiled, 'Ah! You have finally come.'

Vincent was too shocked to speak. He regained his composure and then said, 'I think you are mistaking me for someone else, sir.'

'No. I know who you are. You are the genie.'

Vincent was convinced that the old man had gone senile. 'What?' he asked.

'The genie. The one who will reveal all. The one who bore the cross of Yuz Asaf. Your work is not yet finished. The last visit here was by a Russian man. Dmitriy Novikov was his name. He found a document here. It was written in Aramaic and was buried in a copper tube by the side of Hazrat Yuz Asaf,' said the wrinkled face.

'So why have you been waiting for me?' asked Vincent.

'Because he left the original as well as a translation for you.'

'But Novikov would have been here in 1887. That's 125 years ago. He could not possibly have met you.'

'Ah. You are right. He met my great-grandfather, who was the grandson of Rehman Khan. Our family has been caring for this site over many generations. We have fought legal battles to remain in custody of this shrine.'

The Seal of the Justice of Islam, Mulla Fazil, 1194 A.H. In this High Court of Justice, in the Department of Learning and Piety of the Kingdom.

Present: Rehman Khan, son of Amir Khan, submits that: the kings, the nobles, the ministers and the multitude come from all directions of the kingdom to pay their homage and offerings in cash and kind at the lofty and the holy shrine of Yuz Asaf, the Prophet, may God bless him.

Claims: That he is the only and absolute claimant, entitled to receive the offerings and utilise these, and none else has any right whatsoever on these offerings.

Prays: That a writ of injunction be granted to all those who interfere and others be restrained from interfering with his rights.

'And the document?'

'Here. Take it. It is now your responsibility. My ancestors and I have done our duty,' he said emphatically as he handed over an extremely old copper tube to Vincent.

Vincent carefully unscrewed the cap and gently pulled out three documents. One was a very thin and old papyrus written in a language that he could not understand. The other two documents, while aged, were in good condition and were written in English. One of the newer documents was a letter:

I, Dmitriy Novikov, set out on a historical quest to determine whether Jesus had lived in India. When I succeeded in my efforts, I was branded a liar and a traitor.

What I revealed to the world was only one part of my story: the translations of the documents I discovered at the monastery in Hemis that spoke about a young boy, Issa, who had fled Judea to come and live and learn in India.

But as I dug deeper, I realised that the manuscripts were merely a very small piece of the puzzle. There was a wealth of information available from multiple Hindu and Buddhist sources. Those led me to the Church of Bom Jesus where I found the clues provided by Alphonso de Castro, and finally to Rozabal, where Castro had buried the document that he had discovered entitled the *Tarikh-Issa-Massih*, or *The History of Jesus the Messiah*.

It was here that I discovered that the four Gospels of the Roman Catholic faith do not do justice to the wealth of knowledge that Jesus Christ, our Lord, had imparted to mankind. While many more gospels, including Gnostic ones, will be discovered in the due course of history, I am sure that the accompanying document was written by Yuz Asaf before his death in Kashmir around AD 115.

Upon reading it, I immediately realised that it contained teachings and observations, as well as prophecies, and that these were meant for another yet to come. It was not for me to reveal these to the world, but for someone else still to come—the genie. The caretakers of Yuz Asaf's tomb are the guardians of the sacred remains of Yuz Asaf and I believe that Rehman Khan's family will be able to identify the genie correctly.

The fact that you are reading this document means that the chosen person is you. Please use it wisely.

Dmitriy Novikov, Srinagar, 21 May 1887

The letter was accompanied by the papyrus as well as what seemed to be an English translation of its contents that had possibly been done by Castro or Novikov:[189]

> In the reign of Shalivahana, the king. Tidings of peace to Kashmir did I bring. Issa-Massih and Miryai, my wife; bearing La Sara Kali, oh delicate life. My deeds, words and

spirit were completely pure, Yuz-Asaf was my name that in this land endured. Born of a virgin, son of God, plucking for truth the pea from the pod. I helped the king repair the Solomon throne; grateful king put my name in stone. But twelve years later I told my wife, how I fear for our daughters' lives. Take them away to the land of Gaul, so that my blood may course through the veins of all. Here in Kashmir, I can live alone, and when I die, I'll rest skull and bone. I am Krestos, the Christ, the anointed one; I have travelled my life and can no longer run. I am not worthy of titles, honours, or grace; the one who is worthy is the mirrored face. Stand by the mirror and look at yourself; you are the anointed, within yourself. Simon of Cyrene was greater than I; he bore the cross of a passerby. He is worthy of the knowledge that I convey, this document will rest till it's again his day. One day the stone of Rozabal will rise, and will expose the treachery and the lies. Over this document will be earth and stones; and a decaying pile of skull and bones. Who says pagan gods are fake? For heartfelt prayer, the stone will shake. The power is within you, don't you see? How does it matter if it's also in me? Why would I make water into wine, when water quenches the thirst just fine? Why would I make a blind man see, when those who have eyes cannot feel me? Why would I walk on water, I pray, when a boatman could take me most of the way? The real miracle is in knowing yourself, and understanding the Brahman, the endless, the self. Brahma and Abraham are one and the same; glorious and endless— an eternal flame. Illuminating light is peace not power; it is this sort of madness that brings down the tower. And comprehending the wonder and miracle of life, the end is not the end, even with a knife. Prophets will write of the anti-Christ, whose tongue will evil and hate entice. My children will lose their lives over me, my chosen twelve shall die, so it shall be. There is no anti-Christ divined. The anti-Christ is in your heart and mind. December twenty-

first, two-thousand and twelve, no end is near, no further delve. Because there is no beginning and no end; it's an endless road without a bend. You take great pains to search for me, when I am within you, it's plain to see. I need no temples and mortar and stone; I need only your awareness of spirit alone. Miracles are things that happen each day; the greatest is the blessing when you pray. You are my genie, revealing me; use these verses as a key. Take my shekels in your hand, see the pyramid in the sand. See it better than the all-seeing eye, see it better than the bird up high. Count the steps up to the top, count the leaves and fruit in the crop. Count the arrows to put them in slumber, count your armour of equal number. And when they have fallen, riddled with scars, make sure that they count the number of stars. And when death knocks and destiny brings, shade and fan them with my wings. My plumes on both sides will protect, count them over to be correct. Count the language inside the beak, count the language above the peak, now count me and my apostles meek. And when you emerge and see the trees, please do consider what will make you free. Thirteen Cycles. One and Three. The Maya called it the Sacred Tree. I just call it the Sacred Three. Brahma, Vishnu and Shiva are Three. Lakshmi, Kali and Saraswati. The third eye that the Hindus see. The lines of a triangle in trinity. Christian, Muslim, Illuminati. The first two fight, the third waits to see. How much destruction can there possibly be?

Vincent fell to the ground and kissed the pages reverentially. He then hastened to the market where he could get the precious document photocopied. Photocopying done, he started walking towards the bus terminal, hoping that he could catch the bus out of Srinagar into Delhi. He was so completely absorbed in his own private little world that he did not notice General Prithviraj Singh coming up behind him till he felt the Mauser pressed against his back.

Chapter Twenty-Eight

'Well done, Father Sinclair. I knew I was right to involve you in this matter. We finally have the document that the Illuminati has spent the last few hundred years searching for!' exclaimed Prithviraj Singh, while continuing to hold the gun against Vincent's spine.

'You, General, are no better than Osama-bin-Laden. The terrorist, in fact, is merely a pawn that you move on your Illuminati chessboard!' hissed Vincent.

'So you think I am evil, huh? And what about Opus Dei? What about the Crux Decussata Permuta? Do you think that any religion other than Catholicism would have been allowed to survive on earth if they had their way? And what about the true believers of Islam? You think they would have left non-believers alone? We are the only force that could keep these forces in check! How dare you judge me!' thundered the general.

Vincent shot back, 'You cannot fight fire with fire. The best way to fight a fire is with water, General. Instead, you and your cronies have been throwing in fuel to keep the fires raging. It has been in your interest to keep the fires of hatred burning. Your approach is a thin veil that hides your greed for money and power. It is the powerful elite of this world that has created the Osamas of the world to further their own self-interest. You are a hypocrite!'

'Why are we arguing? We're both after the same thing. We have found it. Let us revel in the find,' said the general.

'But why should this document be of importance to you?' asked Vincent.

'Because it is the very basis on which the Illuminati was founded. This document that you call the *Tarikh-Issa-Massih*, is actually the *Gnostic Gospel of Jesus*. It was written by Jesus sometime in the last few days of his life. When he was in Kashmir.'

'But I thought that the Illuminati was a recent creation. The Bavarian Illuminati came into existence only in 1776. How can you say this document could have anything to do with your organisation?'

'Father Sinclair, let me explain. Jesus did not die on the cross. In fact, his suspension on the cross was merely a "ritual slaying" that had to be performed by Mary Magdalene, the high priestess, as part of the sacred Hieros Gamos.'

'How does this concern you or the Illuminati?'

'Jesus had already said that the illuminating light came from within. He was a great yogi, a great guru. But this aspect of his teaching would not have created a great religion. How would the Church have controlled its flock? So what did they do? They branded Mary Magdalene a prostitute. They "killed" Jesus on the cross. Instead of explaining the resurrection of the soul, they created the resurrection of Jesus's body. Instead of the ancient yogic trinity of the creator, nurturer and destroyer, they created the Christian trinity of the Father, Son and Holy Ghost. Most important, salvation was to be obtained only through their Church!'

'I still don't get it.'

'Wake up, Father! Jesus talks in his gospel of opposites. Good must have bad. Hot must have cold. Positive must have negative. Male must have female, and so on. We, the Illuminati, decided that Christ must have an anti-Christ. This anti-Christ will bring down the Roman Catholic Church, once and for all!'

'But the same gospel that we have just found says that there is no anti-Christ! It says that illuminating light should be used for wisdom and inner peace, not power!'

'Ah! You now know why I need that document. I need to destroy it!' shouted Prithviraj.

'The words of Jesus have been twisted and perverted throughout history. You plan to do exactly that. I will not let history repeat itself!'

'Then you must die!'

🔱

Waziristan, Pakistan-Afghanistan border, 2012

The Sheikh was looking at the message sent by Ghalib containing the detonation sequence. He re-read the words without a mirror once again and then proceeded to ignore all the characters other than 'O' and 'I':

UOY.OT.HTAO.YM.MAMI.HO
OWT.MOTA.TA.MOTA.TIH.OT
HT33T.3HT.TA.MIA.HTUOM.3HT.TA.MIA
TA3H.TOH.3TIHW.HTIW.YAWA.MIH.TIH
3OW.OT.MIH.3IT.YOT.YM.HTIW.3YA
3WO.I.HTUOY.YM.MIHW.YHT.OT
3M.HTIW.TUO.MIH.HTIW.TUO
3M.3SIMOTA.OT.3MIT.YHT.TIAWA.I

The resultant series was:

00010 00010 101 01111 001101 01010 10110 100111.

These were binary numbers, just the sort used by computers to transmit data. He took a pen and began to convert the binary numbers to standard decimal numbers.[190] The result:

2-2-5-15-13-10-22-39

He now had before him the detonation sequence. He picked up the Thuraya satellite phone that would communicate with the device and began to carefully punch in the digits. The digits entered by him were transported to the geostationary Inmarsat satellite from where they would be bounced back to another phone on earth. That phone would activate the bomb. Not in Priobskoye, Siberia, as imagined by Zvi Yatom.

But in the rocky landscape of Waziristan, just a hundred yards away from where the Sheikh stood.

⚏

The fireball from the x-ray-heated air sent a shockwave in all directions at the speed of sound. The frugal houses scattered in the arid and remote frontier simply dissolved. The circle of destruction was around one mile. Everything that was flammable burst into flame, glass products and sand melted into molten glass, and any humans were instantly vaporised by the blinding light, accompanied by radiant heat from the fireball near ground zero.

Around 2,000 people would be killed directly from the blast at the hypocenter and an equal number would be injured. The future impact would include nuclear fallout, cancer, and deformed or stillborn babies.

The damage would have been much greater if the bomb had been detonated in a populated area. The hilly region of the North-West Frontier Province used by the Sheikh and his Master was in the middle of nowhere.

The Sheikh and his Master were now simply vapour in the air.

⚏

Frederick County, Maryland, USA, 2012

Yehuda smiled a quiet smile of satisfaction. The whole world thought Judas had betrayed Jesus. How ridiculous! Judas, in fact, had been the chosen one. The one who would perform the final act of an elaborate ritual. Ensuring that the nuclear device exploded near the Sheikh and his Master—this had been Yehuda's final act of obedience to his own master, Ghalib.

292

From the port at Pipavav, the truck containing the device had headed to Jammu. The truck had proceeded along the interstate Punjab-Kashmir border westwards and had stopped short of the town of Rajouri on the Indian side. From here it had crossed over into Pakistani territory and, a few hours later, reached Mirpur.

The truck had then moved northwards to Muzaffarabad and from there westwards to Mansehra. From Mansehra it had headed in a gentle southwesterly direction towards Peshawar in the North-West Frontier Province of Pakistan, where it had waited to cross the Khyber Pass.

Before crossing the Khyber Pass, it had unloaded the 'construction jig' near Waziristan and continued towards Jalalabad on its long journey to Tel Megiddo.

Yehuda remembered Ghalib taking him aside one day and reciting to him the Islamic Hadith of Tirmidhi. 'And God's messenger said: "In the last times men will come forth who will fraudulently use religion for worldly ends and wear sheepskins in public to display meekness. Their tongues will be sweeter than sugar, but their hearts will be the hearts of wolves."'[191] He had then quoted the Qur'an 6:112: 'Thus have We appointed unto every Prophet an adversary—devils of humankind and jinn—who inspire in one another plausible discourse through guile.'

Ghalib had then said to Yehuda, 'It is in your destiny to be called a traitor. It is in my destiny to be called a terrorist. Why not make the best of the situation? It is better that both these men, the Sheikh and his evil Master, are destroyed, even if it means that we die in the process.'

'But why do you want me to betray you by taking money from Oedipus and the UNL Militia?' Yehuda had asked.

'I have a value. Isn't it better that the money is used to ensure that other orphaned children such as myself are not made into future terrorists? Think of the number of schools that could be established that would counter the actions of the madrasas. Yehuda, I was literally brainwashed into believing that my only duty was to die for Islam—is that any way to bring up a child? This will be my one good deed towards attaining paradise!'

'But, Barabba, why are we allowing these eleven events to happen all over the world? Why can't we stop them?'

'It is not in our control. You think that the instructions are from me?'

'Then from whom are they? The Sheikh? His Master?'

'Yehuda, my friend, you have a lot to learn. You follow my orders. I follow the Sheikh's orders. The Sheikh follows his Master's orders. Whose orders does the Master follow?'

'I am not sure.'

'The Illuminati, my friend. You think that Islamic terrorism just happened one day without immense financial backing? Call them the CIA, the SAS, even the American presidency—all Illuminati. It has been in the Illuminati's interest to keep the fires burning. It ensures that Illuminati-controlled companies make money. It ensures that defence contractors get orders in Iraq. It ensures that the Catholic Church as well as puppet regimes of the Middle East are kept in check. It keeps India focused on Kashmir, Pakistan focused on India, China focused on Tibet, Russia focused on Chechnya, and the world focused on Osama.'

'I still do not understand why you want me to ask El-Azhar to betray you. This is going too far.'

'It is vital. Everyone needs me dead. It is vital that they think I am in custody. If this impression is not created accurately, the final result will not be what we want. These are very intelligent people! They have used me as an anti-Christ to artificially fulfil the third prophecy of Nostradamus. They need to be handled very carefully.'

And then he had told him to 'betray' him to the Japanese woman.

Sitting in his suite at the charming Country Inn on Frederick Road, he was feeling quite proud of himself for having followed Ghalib's instructions flawlessly. He was now here to meet all the other eleven, and to explain to them the final words of Ghalib.

There was a knock on the door.

'Who is it?' he asked, as he headed towards the door.

'Room service,' came the reply.

The waiter brought the tray and placed it on the coffee table in the sitting area. Yehuda thanked the waiter and signed the room service bill, adding a generous tip. He always ensured that his tips were generous when he was travelling abroad; it made the damned white man feel inferior! He started to hand back the leather folder containing the signed bill and the tip when he became aware that the waiter was now behind him.

The sudden tightening of a rope around his neck was when he realised that the tip had been of no use.

New Delhi, India, 2012

The Japanese woman was sitting in Tihar.

Tihar Jail, the largest prison in South Asia,[192] was located in the western sector of Delhi, about eight kilometres away from Chanakyapuri, the diplomatic area of the Indian capital. It was one of the largest prison complexes in the world and comprised eight prisons in the Tihar Complex. With a total population of around 13,160 prisoners against a sanctioned prison capacity of 5,648, it was also one of the most overcrowded prisons in the world. There were eight jail blocks in the complex numbered CJ-1 to CJ-8. The lodging arrangement in the various blocks, located over 400 acres, was according to the court cases, and then according to alphabetical ordering of names. Swakilki was in CJ-6, the women's block.

A special facility was provided to foreigners to have interviews with the diplomats of their countries on any working day between

4 pm and 5 pm. The Japanese representative was meeting Swakilki in the office of the deputy superintendent of the jail, located near the entrance. His demeanour was polite and respectful. Typically Japanese.

'*Konbanwa,*' he said to her. '*O genki desu ka?*' he enquired to find out how she was.

'*Hai, genki desu,*' replied Swakilki. 'I am fine.'

'Do you need anything?' he enquired.

'I need to confess. Get me a priest,' she said simply.

'Bless me, Father, for I am about to sin. It has been a month since my last confession.'

'My child, I cannot absolve you of a sin that has not yet been committed.'

'Yes, but I am about to kill a man. And I have already sinned.'

'How can you say that? You have not yet killed him, and you call it a sin?'

'I should have killed my father years ago. That is my sin— not having killed him yet. Oh, my God, I am heartily sorry for having offended Thee. I firmly resolve, with the help of Thy grace, to sin no more. Amen.'

There was a startled pause. The priest recovered and continued, 'But why would you want to kill your own father, my child?'

Swakilki began.

'My mother had always brought me up to believe that I had inherited unusual powers. Unfortunately, I lost her at the age of six and many of my childhood memories were repressed.'

'Do go on.'

'Among the repressed memories were those of my mother's death; as well as memories of my father. I now remember the man who used to visit our house often. My mother used to say that I was descended from a long line of high priestesses . . . my father would laugh and say that he would prove her wrong.'

'And?'

'He had her killed. He made it look like a gas leak. He had me orphaned to teach the protectors of the divine feminine a lesson.'

'What is his name?'

'Alberto Valerio.'

'And yours?'

'Swakilki. It's derived from Sara Kali.'

'How do you know this?'

'I had forgotten that my lineage was far older than that of the Church. In Goa, I secretly met a Hindu priest, Pandit Ramgopal Prasad Sharma. He is a proponent of the *Bhrigu Samhita*. By merely looking at me, he told me of a little girl born in Kashmir. She was bestowed great power by the divine Goddess and her mother, Mary Magdalene. She left India when she was twelve.'

'So how is this connected to you?'

'Her name was La Sara Kali.'

ॐ

Les Saintes-Maries-de-la-Mer, France, AD 42

In the town of Les Saintes-Maries-de-la-Mer in France, each 23-to-25 May is celebrated in honour of St Sarah, also known as La Sara Kali.[193] The festival has its roots in an event that had happened here in AD 42. A boat had arrived here carrying Mary Magdalene along with a twelve-year-old, dark-skinned child. The name 'Sarah' was the equivalent of 'princess' in Hebrew. Joseph of Arimathea was the protector of the Sangraal, the royal bloodline of Jesus and Mary. The chalice that carried this bloodline was the 'Holy Grail', the womb of Mary Magdalene.

Hence the festival for La Sara Kali.

Mary Magdalene was the bearer of the *sangraal*, the old French word that translates into the commonly accepted *holy grail*. But when the word *sangraal* was broken into two words, *sang* and *raal*, the phrase now meant *blood royal* in old French. Mary Magdalene had brought this royal blood to the coast of France in AD 42.

The marriage between Jesus and Mary Magdalene had resulted in the fusion of two royal Jewish bloodlines. Jesus was of the House of David and descended from King Solomon, king of the Jews. Mary Magdalene was of the royal House of Benjamin. The political implication of such a union was undeniable, since it meant the very real potential threat of political upheaval if ever an attempt was made to restore the lineage of Jewish kings.

The arrival of La Sara Kali in France did precisely that. The Jesus-Mary bloodline was carried forward in the form of the Merovingian dynasty, which remained perpetually at odds with the papacy. From the fifth to the eighth centuries, the Merovingian dynasty of kings ruled Europe and, from the Middle Ages until the present day, most of Europe's monarchs were Merovingians.

In AD 679, the Roman Catholic Church collaborated with the Carolingian dynasty to assassinate and remove the Merovingian King Dagobert II.[194] Having Mary Magdalene's bloodline as rulers was heresy!

The removal of the Merovingian kings ended with the coronation of Charlemagne, who became the Holy Roman Emperor in AD 800. Shrewdly enough, Charlemagne and the Carolingians married Merovingian wives in order to ensure the continuation of their dynasty. This resulted in the continuation of the Merovingian bloodline among the royalty of Europe.

The Merovingian dynasty also continued to perpetuate itself in a direct line from Dagobert II through his son Sigisbert IV. From this bloodline came Godfroi de Bouillon, who formed the Knights Templar, as well as the Prieuré de Sion with a view to recapturing Jerusalem and restoring the royal bloodline of Jesus and Mary Magdalene to the throne in 1099.

The bloodline continued down to Marie de Saint-Claire who became Grand Master of the Priory in 1220. The Saint-Clair surname was derived from the locality, Saint-Clair-sur-Elle in Normandy. A branch of this family would eventually reach

Scotland many years later, along with William the Conqueror.
Many centuries later, some of them would emigrate to America.
Their family name would be Sinclair.

Chapter Twenty-Nine

The President was at the official 125-acre retreat in the centre of Catoctin Mountain Park in Frederick County. Seated on an oversized leather Lazy-Boy in front of a roaring fire, the President was listening angrily to a briefing from Stephen Elliot. 'We never knew that the truck that was transported to Priobskoye aboard the CH-54 contained a dummy. The dummy had been radiated to ensure that it gave off the same nuclear signature. The bastard had already removed and placed the real one near Waziristan.'

'We needed Osama-bin-Laden to remain alive. His presence justified many other actions on our part, including the continued American presence in Pakistan,' said the President.

'The immediate problem that we now have to deal with is Ghalib. If he starts singing to the world about how the Illuminati controlled his puppet-strings all these years, the repercussions would be severe . . . particularly in view of the elections . . .' added Stephen, rather unnecessarily.

The President adjusted the Cartier wristwatch that covered the little tattoo on her wrist.

'There are only two possible actions. Illuminate or Eliminate! Tell Zvi to handle it!' said President Alissa Elliot, the forty-fourth President of the United States of America, and the very first woman to hold the position.

President Alissa Elliot remembered her years as a Rhodes Scholar in Oxford as well as the chance meeting with Stephen Elliot who had happened to be Terry Acton's best friend. It had been natural for her to find common ground with Stephen. The secret society of Rhodes and Yale's Skull & Bones were cousins, in a sense. Both wanted to control and rule the world secretly.

Alissa Elliot had been born Alissa Kaetzel in 1964, just a year before Terry Acton. Her childhood in Illinois had been a happy one. She had excelled at sports, remained active in her local church, and been a member of the National Honor Society. Her mother encouraged and motivated her to push herself hard and to make her own choice of career.

As an undergraduate at Yale, Alissa managed to mix academic excellence with school government. In 1993, she was selected as a Rhodes Scholar to study politics and government at Oxford. The first few months resulted in an enduring friendship with Terry. Terry moved on to Yale while Alissa had stayed on at Oxford to complete her M.Phil.

While on a visit to New Haven to meet Terry, Alissa had been introduced to Stephen and the connection was instantaneous. They had married just a year after Terry lost his wife Susan in a tragic car accident.

Alissa had always been interested in public service and politics. She would go on to serve two terms as a representative to Congress from Illinois. She would then be appointed to a series of high-level positions: ambassador to the United Nations, chief of the US Liaison Office in the People's Republic of China and director of the Central Intelligence Agency. Along the way, Alissa succeeded in building up terrific relationships with the rich and famous. By the time she entered the presidential race she had already created a campaign war chest exceeding $340 million.

Stephen Elliot had followed her dutifully while he built his own career within the SAS.

North America, AD 34

In present-day India stands the country's smallest state, Nagaland. The state derives its name from the original ancient rulers of India, the Nagas. The word naga, literally means 'snake'. The Nagas were rulers who wore a serpent crown on their foreheads. They became extremely powerful because of their ability to build ships that could travel long distances. These rulers worshipped the Hindu God Vishnu, who was depicted as travelling on an eagle, Garuda. Garuda was always shown holding a snake in its beak.

When the Spaniards first reached the Americas, they noticed that most American Indians worshipped a deity called Quetzalcoatl.[195] The Aztecs told the arriving Spaniards that, many centuries earlier, a divine priest by the name of Quetzalcoatl had visited them from a foreign land very far away. He was described as a bearded white man, wearing a robe with cross symbols embroidered on the front. Had the Spaniards dug a little deeper they would have realised that the name Quetzalcoatl was actually a combination of *quetzalli*, a brightly-coloured Mesoamerican bird, and *coatl*, meaning serpent. Garuda with the snake in its beak![196]

The ancient visit of Quetzalcoatl would subsequently be recorded by the Book of Mormon which took this story as proof of Jesus having visited America. It was partly correct. The descendants of Quetzalcoatl in America were actually descendants of the Nagas, a ruling clan that had also held sway over one of India's most important kingdoms, the kingdom of Maghada, the spiritual home of Mary Magdalene.

Over the years these descendants would merge into the American population. The name *Quetzalcoatl* would get corrupted to *Kate-Zahl* and eventually to *Kaetzel*. Alissa Kaetzel.

Tel Megiddo, Israel, 2012

Sometime in 2005, Israeli archaeologist Yotam Tepper had excavated the ruins of a church dating back to the third century, a period of history when Christians were still being persecuted by Rome.[197] Yotam Tepper would find a large mosaic with a Greek inscription consecrating the church to Jesus Christ. The mosaic was in surprisingly good condition. The mosaic had images of fish, an ancient Christian symbol. Experts seemed to be inclined to believe that the site could possibly be the oldest Christian church in Israel.

The ruins were located within the boundaries of the military prison in which Ghalib was being held. An inscription inside the church ruins spoke of a Roman soldier, Gaianus, who had contributed money to have the mosaic executed.

Just under the inscription lay the lifeless body of Ghalib-bin-Isar. Gaianus from another lifetime. His hands were outstretched on either side and his feet were tied together. He had been crucified. Paradise awaited. Actually, a coffin and an international flight waited to take his body to its final resting place.

New Delhi, India, 2012

The judicial process in India was notorious for delays. Swakilki was awaiting trial before the Tis Hazari Courts of Delhi. Bittu Singh, her jailer, had been easy to bribe. Bittu had found out that she was to be taken to court in an armoured van at 11am. The walk from her cell to the van was approximately 200 metres and involved going through two security gates at varying intervals.

She felt the sharp two-inch miniature Nozaki knife inside her clenched fist that was now bleeding from holding it. The knife had been helpfully procured by Bittu. Swakilki was just ten feet away from the van, duly cuffed and chained to her handlers. Suddenly, she lunged for the guard on the left and deftly brought the Nozaki to his throat. Swakilki held the knife to her handler's throat and hissed, 'I will not hesitate to kill you if anyone moves!'

Still holding the knife to his throat, she deftly bent down and with her free hand reached for the keys that dangled from his belt as the other handler looked on helplessly. She pulled off the entire ring and expertly unlocked the chains that were holding her in captivity. She threw the keys to the ground and held the guard in a vice-like grip from behind, all the while keeping the knife firmly in contact with the skin of his neck.

The sirens were blaring; the alarm had been sounded. All inmates were automatically locked into whichever sectors they were currently in. The perimeter gate had also been locked automatically. Guard reinforcements were running to the spot to secure the area, but they were hesitant to take a shot, given that their colleague was still in her captivity.

Swakilki quickly shoved him into the passenger seat of the van and clambered into the driver's seat. She picked up the 9-mm pistol that had fallen on the ground from the guard's holster and held it to her handler's head with her right hand as she revved the engine.

The vehicle was a Tata diesel right-hand drive vehicle, tough, sturdy and ideal for Indian roads. She pressed her foot on the clutch, shifted the manual gearshift with her left hand, and slammed her foot on the accelerator. The truck lunged forward towards the outer perimeter gate.

One of the guards stood his ground in front of the gate and pointed his rifle at her, but it was too late. The truck knocked him down and ran him over before the gate came crashing down. Instant karma.

⚷

Vatican City, 2012

His Eminence Alberto Cardinal Valerio was uncharacteristically worried. He paced up and down the marble floors of his office. Brother Thomas Manning watched him as he shuffled along, hands clenched together behind his back.

'Why haven't we heard from Swakilki yet?' he asked as he sat down behind his desk. Almost immediately, he began tapping the dark wood irritably. His patience was running out.

The last few days had been very tiring. The capture of Swakilki was not good news. It left Father Vincent Sinclair free to nose around. Moreover, who knew what she herself might reveal in captivity? The news of the death of Ghalib, however, had come as welcome relief. Damn the Illuminati! Creating an Islamic Jesus to appear as an anti-Christ! Jesus!

While Valerio had not really been happy to stitch together the nuclear deal for the Sheikh's Master, he had later realised that the location of the proposed destruction worked to his advantage. A nuclear explosion in Megiddo would prove the literal truth behind the words of the Bible. Continued success for Ghalib would mean increased Islamic terror around the world. Valerio was quite happy if there was stepped-up Islamic radicalism all over the world. It would only make Christians much more vulnerable, making them infinitely more devout. In fact, history recorded the Christian crusades as being an outcome of early Islamic victories.

Now, however, Valerio was justifiably furious. He did not know that Swakilki had escaped. He felt that his objectives were coming unstuck. Instead of getting their target, their agent Swakilki was now in custody. The complications and their repercussions were just too hideous to contemplate, particularly if she began talking about the Crux Decussata Permuta.

'So . . .' he continued. Thomas Manning looked up from the deep burgundy armchair that he was ensconced in. 'So, you mean to tell me that we do not have the ability to get her out? Nor do we have the means of shutting up Vincent Sinclair?' asked His Eminence.

'We do have the means, Your Eminence. Unfortunately, this has now become a battle between the Crux Decussata Permuta and the Illuminati.'

'What power do the Illuminati have in that region?'

'Well, India presently has excellent relations with the current administration in the White House . . . and we all know that the White House is dominated by the Illuminati.'

'But why? What can they possibly want with Vincent Sinclair?'

'Your Eminence! How can you even ask a question like that? It should be abundantly clear that the primary goal of the Illuminati over so many centuries has been to discredit the Church. They would use Vincent Sinclair to do precisely that!'

'The American President's public image is that of a God-fearing Christian—a born-again.'

'Born again as an Illuminati. Not as a Christian!'

'The Church is an institution that has been built over 2,000 years. We cannot let it be destroyed. The Illuminati be damned! Now they have got their illegitimate offspring, those Satan-worshippers, Rhodes and Skull & Bones to do their evil work!' shouted His Eminence.

He got up abruptly and walked out of the room. He was on his way to the Archivio Segreto Vaticano, the Secret Archives of the Vatican. Thomas Manning hastily got up to follow him. They quickly reached the entrance to the archives through the Porta S. Anna in via di Porta Angelica. They hurried inside and their conversation became hushed. 'What exactly are we looking for, Your Eminence?' whispered Manning.

His Eminence Alberto Cardinal Valerio looked Thomas Manning straight in the eye and said softly, 'Damage control. In the event that anything comes to light from the Bom Jesus papers, it is vital that it be discredited immediately.'

'And how would we do that?' asked Manning.

'Vincent and others will try to poke holes in the fundamental pillars of the Roman Catholic Church. Jesus did not die on the cross. There was no resurrection. He married Mary Magdalene. Mary had children.'

'So?'

'Our archives contain a family tree. A tree that talks about Mary Magdalene and her lineage till the present day. And just as the Priory of Sion has been attempting to protect Mary's bloodline, our group has been doing everything possible to destroy it, discredit it, discard it! That's how I came into contact with Aki Herai,' said Valerio.

'Who?' asked Manning.

'Swakilki's mother. She was descended from one of Mary Magdalene's daughters. I impregnated her—I broke my vows for the greater good,' explained Valerio.

'Why?' asked a bewildered Manning.

Valerio thought for a moment before replying. 'I thought that if I could get Mary Magdalene's bloodline to become staunchly Roman Catholic, discarding its beliefs in the sacred feminine, I would have achieved the greatest victory ever for our glorious Church. Swakilki does not know this.'

'But what about the theory that Mary and her child were taken to France by Joseph of Arimathea? Isn't this at odds with the official position that there were no children?' asked Manning.

'Officially speaking, there was no offspring. Off the record, yes, there was a bloodline. The problem with acknowledging the bloodline was that one would have to accept that Jesus had married Mary Magdalene. If one accepted that, then one might also have to accept that the crucifixion was nothing else but a pagan rite, part of the sacred marriage ritual, Hieros Gamos.'

'So the bloodline continued in France?'

'No. The sacred powers of the divine feminine could only be passed down from one female member to another. Mary Magdalene herself had derived these powers from a long lineage that could be traced back to the empire of Ashoka the Great, who had sent his missionaries to Egypt. Do you know the name of Ashoka's empire in India?'

'No. How is it relevant?'

'Ashoka's empire was called "Maghada".[198] Can you now understand why Mary was Mary *Maghada*-lene? It was obvious that Jesus and Mary would go to India after having escaped death in Jerusalem.[199] Over the next 2,000 years, the bloodline of the sacred feminine would travel all over the world, including Maghada in India, France, Japan and North America.'

'And Ghalib? Was he descended from this bloodline?' asked Manning incredulously.

'That was precisely the trick played on us by the Illuminati. Ghalib and his followers were an illusion. There was certainly a bloodline left in India by Mary Magdalene, but that was not Ghalib and his band of thugs! By creating an illusion that a descendant of Jesus Christ was now living in India as a terrorist, the Illuminati would succeed in bringing shame and dishonour to the Church. Precisely what they wanted.'

'But the *Tarikh-i-Kashmir* spoke of Jesus having married a woman, Marjan of the Sakya clan, at the insistence of King Shalivahana . . . it also spoke of several generations of children thereafter . . .'

'My dear Thomas, *Marjan* is merely another derivative of *Mary*. As regards the *Sakya* clan, you may not know this, but the Buddha was called *Sakya Muni*. Mary Magdalene herself was descended from a sacred lineage. So, what was being said was that Jesus married Mary Magdalene, nothing more, nothing less.'

'But why talk of a son of Jesus called Benissa, and his children, then?'

'Think about it, Thomas. Ben merely means "son of", so Benissa means "son of Issa". A little too convenient! No, the line spoken about was fictitious. You know why? To draw attention away from the real bloodline, that of La Sara Kali.'

'But they could still discredit the Church if they get lucky on the Bom Jesus trail. Even if there is no Ghalib as an anti-Christ, the Bom Jesus papers could still show that Jesus did not die on the cross and that there was no resurrection.'

'Yes. And that's why we need Vincent Sinclair out of Illuminati hands and in our own.'

'And the Islamic connection? Why did the Sheikh cooperate with you? Why was he willing to follow instructions conveyed by me to Bakatin?'

'Because it suited both of us. Just like Saladin the Great and Richard the Lionheart of the Crusades, we had to reach an uneasy agreement. He was happy to let Ghalib's men do their worst because it furthered his caliphate aims, even though the actions were Illuminati-financed.'

'No, no . . . why was he willing to give up Ghalib?'

'Because he knew that Ghalib was not of the bloodline of Jesus. He struck a good deal with us. Genuine nuclear weapons for a fake anti-Christ!'

'And we were willing to allow a nuclear holocaust for a fake anti-Christ?'

'Well, a nuclear explosion at Megiddo suited me fine. The other eleven events also suited me. They only strengthened the claim that the biblical prophecies were true.'

'So, for all this time, the Church has known that Jesus had actually married Mary Magdalene?'

'It was a ritual. Jesus had a secret dynastic marriage with Mary, who was a daughter of the tribe of Benjamin. It was a royal dynastic marriage of King Jesus. In such sacred marriage rituals, the Goddess and land would be wedded to the king. The Goddess would bring him wealth. She would then take care of him as a nurturer. This would be followed by a ritualistic symbolic slaying of the king, when the Goddess would manifest her destructive force.'

'So did she actually slay him?'

'No. The slaying was symbolic. After the slaying, the king would be resurrected, depicting the multiple cycles of birth, death and rebirth.'

'But was Jesus actually crucified?'

'Well, that's really the core issue. If Jesus went through a sacred fertility ritual with Mary Magdalene, Hieros Gamos, then isn't it possible that the crucifixion and resurrection could have also been mere rituals? In fact, the raising of Lazarus from the dead could also have been a similar ritual.'

'So you don't believe that Jesus died on the cross?'

'Well, all indications are that he did not. Why did he faint when he was given a sponge of vinegar? He should have revived. His fainting indicates that he was deliberately drugged. Why were his legs not broken when that would have accelerated his death? Why was Joseph of Arimathea allowed to take down his body? Why were herbs such as aloe vera and myrrh used to heal his wounds if he was dead? Why were there Essene monks inside the cave? I'd say that there's enough evidence to indicate that he did not actually die.'

'If he did not die on the cross, then where did he go?'

'Well, indications are that he went to India. Jesus had derived many of his teachings from Essene and Buddhist thought. Mary's sacred powers and rituals were also from there, from Maghada. Also, Kashmir was a land that had been occupied by one of the ten lost tribes of Israel. It would have been logical for him to return to his spiritual roots. Moreover, the discoveries by Dmitriy Novikov, Nicholas Notovich and other explorers in the late 1800s seemed to give further credence to the theory, leading to the discovery of the Rozabal tomb in Srinagar.'

'But one can't actually prove that the tomb is that of Jesus, can one?'

'No. But consider this. Even though the burial chamber is Islamic north-south, the actual body is placed along the Jewish east-west. The word *Rozabal* is thought to have been derived from the Kashmiri term *Rauza-Bal*, meaning *Tomb of the Prophet*. But what if the term is derived from *Rose-a-bal?* You know about the Rosslyn Chapel in Paris, right? It was dedicated by the Priory of Sion to Mary Magdalene. The sign outside the chapel reads *Roslin*. This ancient spelling is derived from the *Rose Line* meridian on which the chapel sat or from the *Line of the Rose*— the ancestral lineage of Mary Magdalene. In Kashmir, it is assumed that the word *bal* means *place,* what is often forgotten is that *bal* also translates in Urdu to *hair*—a single strand of hair, a single line! Isn't it possible that Rozabal has exactly the same meaning as Roslin—the *Line of the Rose?*'

'So the Roman Catholic Church has known this all along?'

'I'd say yes. The early years of the Christian faith were extremely difficult for the faith. There were multiple versions of Christianity being propounded. The Gospels were not merely the four canonical ones but also the various Gnostic ones such as those of Thomas, Philip and Mary. Furthermore, Christianity needed a wider audience in Rome, and to that extent, it had to be brought more in line with existing pagan beliefs. Christmas Day. Easter Day. Weekly rest on Sunday. Resurrection. The divine nature of Jesus. These were elements that were liberally borrowed from various other characters and stories including those of Krishna and Buddha. How many people today realise that the Hindu god Krishna's mother was *Yeshu*-dha, the mother of Yeshua? Who recalls that Buddha's wife was *Yeshu*-dhara, the wife of Yeshua? Given the circumstances, what the Church fathers did was not wrong. It was the need of the hour to make the Christian religion sustainable, acceptable, marketable.'

'And Alphonso de Castro's discovery threatened to bring it all down?'

'Alphonso de Castro was an imbecile! He was sent to Goa to strengthen the Inquisition. Instead, he meddled with ancient texts and books. Unfortunately, he could not be recalled immediately because of his father's influence over the Portuguese royal family.'

'Why did he not go public with his find?'

'Well, I think he intended to but was dissuaded by his father. His father arranged a meeting for Castro with the Pope, and some secret deal was struck. The document went into the archives and Castro's family never ever had to work again—they were made wealthy forever. Castro left church life and settled down in England, where he married a young girl by the name of Patricia Kaetzel. Their son, Herbert Castro, entered the lucrative opium trade between India and China. He soon became well acquainted with Samuel Russel, who had established Samuel Russel & Co. for trading opium between Turkey and China. Some years later, a cousin of Samuel, William, helped set up the Skull & Bones society at Yale, a de facto chapter of the Bavarian Illuminati.'[200]

'Ah. So the Illuminati has always had access to Castro's secrets?'

'Unfortunately, yes.'

'Your Eminence, you seem to know virtually everything. I, your brother in the Crux Decussata Permuta, have never questioned your directions or motivations—but this seems to be asking me to go beyond the line of duty.'

'Let me share a little secret with you. In the immediate aftermath of the death of Jesus, Mary Magdalene attempted to take over the leadership of the Christian faith by telling the other disciples that Jesus had communicated several matters to her alone. Quite naturally, both St Peter and St Andrew were not in agreement with her.'

'That is common knowledge.'

'Yes, but the Knights Templar and the Priory of Sion took it upon themselves to protect the bloodline of Mary Magdalene and protect the powers of the sacred feminine. It was precisely to counter the Priory that the Crux Decussata Permuta was created. As you know, *crux* is Latin for *cross*, *decussata* implies the X-shaped cross, and *permuta* means *inverted*. As you also know, St Peter was crucified in Rome upon an inverted cross and St Andrew was crucified in Achaea on an X-shaped cross. The loyalists of Andrew and Peter decided that they needed to protect the Catholic Church from the pagan and Gnostic influences of Mary Magdalene and her continuing bloodline and created a secret society for this purpose. This would be called the Crux Decussata Permuta, of which you and I are loyal members.'

'Yes. But we never get to meet other members,' said Manning.

'That's because you and I are the last surviving members of the Crux Decussata Permuta,' said Valerio.

'There's no one else?'

'One died just recently. He also wore the pendant secretly.'

'Who?'
'The Sheikh.'

Jerusalem, 1192

The great Saladin had become Master of Jerusalem in 1187. Pope Gregory VIII reacted hastily and commissioned Richard the Lionheart to mount the third Crusade to recapture the holy city. Richard marched on Jerusalem in 1192 but he and his army were plagued by fever, hunger and thirst.

He appealed to Saladin to provide him with food and water. And Saladin obliged, but on one condition. Richard would need to convert to Islam.

A negotiated settlement was eventually reached. Five of Richard's ten men belonging to the secret Crux Decussata Permuta offered themselves for conversion.[201] They would allow themselves to be converted instead of Richard. Deal struck, Saladin remembered his duty to help the needy as a devout Muslim. He sent frozen snow and fresh fruit to revive Richard and his men.

Richard eventually sued for a truce with Saladin under which Christian pilgrims would be free to visit the holy city without being troubled in any way by Saladin's Muslim brothers. They would be watched over by five Muslim guards—the members of the Crux Decussata Permuta who had been converted from Christianity to Islam.

The five converted Muslim men in Saladin's camp and the remaining five Christian men in Richard's camp continued to operate the Crux Decussata Permuta secretly. It suited them to have a secret organisation with a foot in both camps, Islam and Christianity.

Islamic conquests encouraged devout behaviour among Christians and vice versa. Muslims and Christians alike saw each other as lesser evils than the 'sins' of paganism, polytheism, abortion, and homosexuality. A secret alliance between Christianity and Islam had matured.

♆

'So who exactly was the Sheikh? Osama-bin-Laden?' asked Manning.

'No. Osama was a creation of the Illuminati. He created world terror and made the Illuminati ever more powerful around the world—in positions of government, banking, business, military and politics. He gave the Americans an excuse to police the world.'

'And the Sheikh?'

'The Sheikh was descended from the original five members of the Crux Decussata Permuta who had been converted to Islam by Saladin. All along, he tried to cooperate with us . . . unfortunately, his Master's cooperation was always with the Illuminati.'

His Eminence did not notice the two ropes snaking around his ankles. They suddenly tightened into two nooses and he was yanked off his feet. The ropes had been individually pulled from a terrace above. In less than a minute, he was dangling upside down. Each ankle was firmly in a noose and his legs were spread apart because of the distance between the two ropes. Seen from a distance, his body looked like an 'X', but upside down, feet up, arms down. Crux Decussata Permuta.

The single sniper bullet wound to his genitals caused immense bleeding and by the time Manning was able to get help and bring his body down, he had already bled to death.

Swakilki had avenged the death of her mother.

Chapter Thirty

Stephen Elliot, Prithviraj Singh and Zvi Yatom were back in the darkened room of padded velvet. The Grand Master, Alissa Elliot, spoke: 'Achaita, divine revelation. Rome will pass away, Jerusalem will burn and the reason will become broken. And my Law, the Law of Zión, will be acclaimed by the whole of humanity.'

'Achaita!' said all those gathered in unison.

'Oh illuminated, brothers and sisters, see what we have before us!'

'Achaita!'

The Grand Master, dressed in scarlet robes, held the knife close to Vincent's heart. Vincent had been placed on the large black granite slab in the centre of the room.

'Elevate and proclaim the Light! The last of the Crux Decussata Permuta is finished. We have created an abundance of wealth by keeping the world in fear! Achaita!'

'The truth must emerge. And the Church must crumble.'

'Zión! Zión! Zión! Zión! Zión! Zión! Zión! Zión! Zión! Zión! Zión! Zión! Zión!'

As Prithviraj saw the Grand Master's golden knife aimed at Vincent's heart, he saw a vision of Pandit Ramgopal Prasad Sharma flash before him.

'Son. The brother who died, took on your karma to save you. You were destined to die and he died for you. He has died or killed for you in previous lifetimes too. He has a karmic relationship with you . . .'

'Find the priest, my son . . .'

'And son . . . that brother, who died for you . . . You will know when you have to return the favour . . .'

The next few seconds were a blur. Prithviraj pulled out his .357 Magnum pistol and took a shot at the Grand Master. The consequences came in slow motion.

Because of the dark robes of the Grand Master, the blood was not visible to the others in the room. They were still chanting, 'Zión! Zión! Zión!'

In the din, no one heard the shot. The Grand Master's right hand, which was holding the golden knife, fell limply to one side while the knife fell on the granite platform upon which Vincent had been tied down. Prithviraj lunged forward, grabbed the knife and desperately started cutting loose the ropes that held Vincent prisoner.

'Run!' he shouted. Vincent was dazed. He remained frozen. Prithviraj used the knife to give Vincent a deep gash on his thigh, just to shock him into action. 'Run!' he shouted again.

This time Vincent got up and started moving towards the passageway. But it was too late. Stephen Elliot, Zvi Yatom and countless others had pulled out their guns and were shooting madly towards the table. Prithviraj went down in a flurry of bullets.

The karmic debt had been settled. *'And son . . . that brother, who died for you . . . You will know when you have to return the favour . . .'*

The confusion that followed bought Vincent some time. There were thirteen passageways. He blindly ran into one of them.

🔱

Vincent ran madly through the passage that led to an equally dark room. He froze when he looked at the sight before him.

In front of him was a clear glass pane with a 'shop window' display behind it, dimly illuminated. The rest of the room was dark so as to ensure that the entire focus was on the window. Behind the window was a corpse. The corpse had been mounted for display on an upside-down cross. The body was that of Boutros Ahmad, Ghalib's point man for South America.

The room had two exits other than the central passageway through which Vincent had entered. One was to the left of the display window and the other to the right of it. Vincent dashed through the left exit. It took him through a curving passage, equally dark and forbidding.

Within thirty seconds, he found himself in another room, identical to the first. The macabre display in this room was even more ghoulish. Behind the glass pane was a corpse that had been arranged neatly on a bed. Prior to placing the body on the bed, it was evident that the body had been fried in oil. It belonged to Yahya Ali, Ghalib's trusted lieutenant in Chechnya.

Vincent's instincts were now on full alert. He could hear voices. The panic caused by the shooting of the Grand Master and the retaliation on Prithviraj had taken the attention off him, at least for a few moments. He had to find a way out of this nightmarish catacomb.

The third, fourth and fifth rooms were no better. In one of them, Vincent found the body of Yaqub Islamuddin, Ghalib's Jemaah Islamiyah operative in Jakarta, arranged on a chair with his head placed separately and neatly on a table nearby. The next room contained Kader Al-Zarqawi, Ghalib's head of Iraq operations, crucified on an 'X'-type cross. He had not been nailed, but tied to it with his legs prised apart, causing a much slower and more painful death.

Vincent was going mad. He wanted to vomit. He doubled up to puke and felt like he was expelling all his guts. As he came up for air, he was hit by an even more ghastly sight. In front of him lay the body of Shamoon Idris, Ghalib's key operative of the Islamic Jehad Council in North America, sawed in half with the battleaxe still positioned in his torso. The aim—to recreate an accurate visual description of the manner of death—had been achieved perfectly.

Vincent screamed in terror as he fled through the passageway. It was of no use. The next room contained the crumpled corpse of Fouad al-Noor, head of the group's activities in England. He lay crumpled in a corner with a gaping wound in his side. He had been pierced with a lance.

By now Vincent had reached a point of no return. Terror had made him numb. He observed the body of Faris Kadeer, Ghalib's chief of the East Turkestan Islamic Movement, hanging upside down on a cross with a spear having split open his thigh. The sight of Ataullah al-Liby, Ghalib's kingpin of the French Intifada, was unbearable. His body lay on a stone platform with a spear through his stomach, guts spilling out across the stone.

The display of the corpse of Tau'am Zin Hassan, Ghalib's manager within the Darul Islam in Malaysia, was positively benign, when compared with the others. His display had been organised in a manner such that he was seated on a chair, clutching a dart that had pierced his heart.

Vincent lost count of the number of dungeon-like rooms he had run through. The sight that greeted him in this one was the worst of all. Bin Fadan, Ghalib's Jaish-e-Mohammed representative in India, had been arranged so that he was clutching his own skin. He had been skinned alive.

Vincent felt faint. What was this place? How could they do this to human beings? He looked up and saw the body of Adil Afrose, Ghalib's chief commander of the Australia operation. His body lay separated from his legs, which had been viciously broken. He had then been clubbed and stoned to death, evidenced by a massive rupture to his skull.

The next room contained the lifeless body of Yehuda, trusted aide to Ghalib, hanging from a noose around his neck. Vincent ran through the exit and reached the thirteenth room. It contained the body of Ghalib. He lay crucified on a Roman cross, with a crown of thorns on his head.[202]

The Illuminati had made sure their grand plan would never be revealed to the world. The Lashkar-e-Talatashar was dead. The anti-Christ and his flock of twelve were dead. Vincent finally passed out.

Rome, AD 67

Peter lay dead on an upside-down cross. He had journeyed through Gaul and Britain before being imprisoned for nine months at Mamertime. He was crucified on the orders of the Roman Emperor at Nero's circus. He had requested that it be done upside down so that the manner of his death would not be the same as that of his master.[203]

Patras, Achaea, AD 69

Andrew, the first apostle of Christ, had travelled through southern Russia, Byzantium, Thrace, Macedonia and Greece. In Greece, he was crucified in Sebastopolis by Aegeas, the governor of the Edessences, on his refusal to denounce Christ. The cross that he was crucified on was an 'X', not a 'T'. He was not nailed but corded to the cross, causing much more suffering than normal. He died after three days.[204]

Jerusalem, Judea, AD 44

James had returned to Jerusalem after travelling to Spain and Portugal. On 2 January, AD 40, the Virgin Mary had appeared before him on the bank of the Ebro River. James had then returned to Judea, where he had been decapitated by King Herod Agrippa I himself.

Patmos, Turkey, AD 110

John preached in Russia and Iran until he was exiled to Patmos, off the Turkish coast. He died in his bed at an old age, having worn out his body. He had been plunged into boiling hot oil by the Romans but had somehow survived the ordeal.

✣

Hieropolis, Phrygia, AD 66

Philip had succeeded in saving the life of the Roman proconsul's sick wife. This miracle had made her convert to Christianity. The political fallout was the wrath of the proconsul who told Philip, 'Denounce Jesus and save your life.' Philip answered, 'Accept Jesus and save your soul.' He was pierced through the thigh and then crucified upside down till he died. His daughters were killed along with him in the same manner.

✣

Albana, Armenia, AD 68

Bartholomew had journeyed through Turkey, Iran, India, Ethiopia, Persia and Egypt before reaching Armenia. Here he was 'skinned alive' and subsequently beheaded.

✣

Mylapore, south India, AD 72

Thomas Didymus was praying in the woods outside his hermitage when a hunter who belonged to the Govi clan aimed his poisoned dart and hit Thomas. The wound was critical and St Thomas died on 21 December, AD 72.

✣

Ethiopia, AD 60

Matthew spent twenty-three years preaching in Ethiopia,

Macedonia, Persia and Egypt. His death was ordered by King Hircanus, who sent his men to run a spear through him.

$$2⅟\complement$$

Ardaze, Armenia, AD 65

Thaddæus had spent many years preaching in Mesopotamia. He was killed under Abgarus, king of the Edessenes in Berytus, by a lance through his side.

$$2⅟\complement$$

Caistor, Lincolnshire, Britain, AD 61

Simon Zelotes spent his life in Mauritania and Africa before he was martyred in Britain by a halberd, a battleaxe on a long pike handle. He was sawn in half.

$$2⅟\complement$$

Jerusalem, AD 33

The 'treasurer' of the twelve disciples, Judas Iscariot, flung the thirty pieces of silver that he had accepted for betraying Jesus at the feet of the Sanhedrin. He then went out and hanged himself. The money was not accepted by the priests because it was 'blood money' and was, instead, used to purchase a plot of land for burying the poor.

$$2⅟\complement$$

Jerusalem, AD 62

James the Just was killed because he did not deny the Lord. Ananias, the high priest, tried to force James to deny the Lord, but when he would not, he was thrown off the pinnacle of the temple, which caused his legs to break. He was then clubbed to death.

⚜

Alexandria, Egypt, AD 61

Mark, the evangelist interpreter of Peter, was dragged through the city of Alexandria for more than two days. His flesh was entirely raked off and hung from his body like rags. He died from loss of blood.

⚜

Rome, AD 67

Paul, originally known as Saul, one of the main persecutors of Christians, who had a change of heart when Jesus appeared before him in Damascus, was beheaded in Rome under the orders of Nero.

⚜

Washington DC, USA, 2012

The CNN newswoman was saying, 'Seventy-two hours ago, the President was accidentally shot and fatally wounded during a weekend hunting and camping trip with friends while in Maryland. The shooting occurred at about 5:30 pm on Saturday. Her husband, SAS director Stephen Elliot, who had been with the President when the accident happened, said that investigations were ongoing, but that all indications were that it was certainly an accident.'

The newswoman continued, 'The President's Secret Service detail rushed with emergency medical assistance but death was almost immediate. The autopsy at Bethesda Naval Hospital

322

confirmed that the cause of death was a shot from a .357 Magnum, which is sometimes used for deer hunting.'

The panoramic views of Camp David gave way to footage of the coffin lying in state as she continued. 'The body of the President was placed in the East Room of the White House from where it was sent on a horse-drawn caisson to the Capitol to lie in state. Thousands lined up outside the Capitol building to pay their last respects to the departed leader. Heads of government and heads of state from over a hundred countries are expected to attend the state funeral on Tuesday. After a funeral service at St Matthew's Cathedral, the late President will be laid to rest at Arlington National Cemetery in Virginia. The vice-president has assumed full executive powers and has declared Monday to be a national day of mourning.'

The commentary went on. 'The late President Alissa Kaetzel Elliot is survived by her husband, Stephen Elliot, SAS director. Her alma maters, Yale and Oxford, are also observing a day of mourning. Viewers will recall that Alissa had met her husband-to-be while he was a student at Yale.'

⚍

Vincent felt as though he were falling through space. Actually, he was. As he fainted inside the thirteenth room containing Ghalib's body, the impact of his fall activated a secret panel in the carpeted floor. Vincent fell through the hole like a sack of potatoes and landed with a thud in a brightly lit room.

Squinting, he saw that the room was wholly white. The entire ceiling was flooded with pure white fluorescent lighting. Even the floor was covered in dazzling white tiles. The room seemed to be some kind of memorial. The stark walls bore framed black and white photographs of Presidents, prime ministers, generals, businessmen, actors, scientists and diplomats. Loyal and committed members of the Illuminati down the ages.

At one end was a door without a handle. Vincent tiptoed towards it and inspected it. He then tried nudging it open but found that it was an armoured door that was firmly sealed shut. On the right side of the door was a numerical keypad that probably controlled access through the door. Just above the keypad was the reverse side of a single one-dollar bill, duly laminated. Vincent looked at it, confused, until it struck him! The back of the American one-dollar bill was an entirely Illuminati-sponsored image! He pulled out the crumpled copy of the document that he had discovered at the Rozabal shrine from his inside pocket.

You are my genie, revealing me; use these verses as a key. Vincent thought to himself. Could it be? Could it actually be used as a key? He had nothing to lose. *Take my shekels in your hand, see the pyramid in the sand. See it better than the all-seeing eye, see it better than the bird up high. Count the steps up to the top, count the leaves and fruit in the crop.*

Vincent looked at the one-dollar bill, the modern world's shekel. There indeed was a pyramid. The pinnacle of the pyramid had a single 'all-seeing' eye. Next to it was the American bald eagle—the bird up high. Vincent began counting the steps on the pyramid. Thirteen. The eagle was holding two branches in its talons. One branch had leaves and the other had fruit. Vincent counted the leaves and the fruit. Thirteen each!

Count the arrows to put them in slumber, count your armour of equal number. And when they have fallen, riddled with scars, make sure that they count the number of stars. And when death knocks and destiny brings, shade and fan them with my wings. My plumes on both sides will protect, count them over to be correct.

Vincent looked more closely at the eagle's talons. It was also holding arrows. Vincent counted them. Thirteen! The eagle also held an armoured shield. Vincent counted the armoured bars on the shield. Thirteen! Above the eagle was a cloud containing stars. By now, Vincent knew what to expect; nevertheless, he counted the stars. Surprise, surprise . . . thirteen! He then looked at the eagle's wings. He carefully counted the plumes on each side, right and left. Thirteen each.

Count the language inside the beak. Count the language above the peak. Then count me and my apostles meek.

Vincent looked at the eagle's beak. It was holding a banner that read 'E Pluribus Unum', meaning 'Out of Many, Emerges One'. Thirteen letters. He then saw the Latin motto above the pyramid's peak, 'Annuit Coeptis', meaning 'God has favoured our undertaking'. Thirteen letters again.

Jesus and his twelve apostles. Thirteen.

Vincent hurriedly punched 13 into the numeric keypad and watched the door slide open silently.

The First Continental Congress had requested that Benjamin Franklin, along with a team, develop the Great Seal for the United States. It took them four years to accomplish this task and another two years to get it approved. The back of the United States' one-dollar bill bears this seal that depicts a pyramid. Very few would notice that the pyramid on the bill was a Masonic symbol, a pyramid of 13 progressive levels. The number 13 was present not only in the 13 steps of the pyramid. There were 13 stars above the eagle, 13 bars on the shield, 13 leaves on the branch, 13 fruits, 13 arrows.[205] Just like the army created by the Illuminati to terrorise the world. The Lashkar-e-Talatashar. Or the Army of Thirteen. The base of the pyramid had the year 1776 inscribed on it. The American public thought it was the year in which the American Declaration of Independence had been signed.

Actually, it was the beginning of the final cycle of the Maya Long Count calendar. More important, it was the year in which Adam Weishaupt created the Illuminati. The base of the pyramid bore the motto '*Novus Ordo Seclorum*' which, from Latin, translates to 'New Order of the Ages'. Much like the objectives of the Illuminati. Creating a new world order and ruling it.

Talpiot, Israel, 1980

Had Vincent looked more closely at the one-dollar bill he would have noticed something else that was extremely important. The pyramid's peak was a triangle with an all-seeing eye.

'At about 11 in the morning of 28 March 1980, with the Christian season of Lent already a month old and almost over, first light entered a tomb, beneath the treads of a bulldozer. On this exceptionally beautiful Friday, the entire south face of the tomb's antechamber fell away to reveal what looked for all the world like a doorway; carved above it was a symbol that none of the construction crew had ever seen before.'[206]

Inside the tomb, archaeologists found ten ossuaries, limestone boxes that had served as first-century coffins. Six had inscriptions, including 'Jesus, son of Joseph', two 'Mary's and 'Judah, son of Jesus'.

Subsequent research would cast substantial doubt on the genuineness of the tomb as the final resting place of Jesus and his family. Many would say that Talpiot was a hoax perpetuated to embarrass the Church. Not too many people were worried that the symbol above the tomb looked much like the Illuminati symbol of the all-seeing eye within the peak of a pyramid depicted on the American one-dollar bill.

Chapter Thirty-One

Thomas Manning was in the corridors of the Ospedale Bambino Gesu, the hospital within the Vatican premises. His Eminence had been rushed to the hospital, but had been pro-nounced dead a few hours later. Manning had been pacing up and down the corridors for more than three hours. A kindly nurse, Sister Maria Esperanza, a beautiful young nun of mixed blood, brought the immensely fatigued man a cup of steaming hot espresso. Thomas did not know that Sister Maria Esperanza had a special recipe for espresso.

She would grind the best Lavazza beans, using a good burr grinder. She would then fill the double shot filter basket without pressing the ground coffee down. She would level off the loose ground coffee by sliding a straight finger across the top. Then she would expertly 'tamp' the coffee, using a solid handheld tamper and around thirty pounds of force. Having fitted the filter handle, she would extract the steaming hot espresso shot into the cup that already contained her special ingredient, a spoonful of 1080.

Compound 1080, or sodium monoflouroacetate, was a water-soluble chemical used primarily to kill coyotes. It was a colourless, odourless, tasteless poison. One teaspoon could kill up to a hundred adult humans. There was no antidote.[207]

Sister Maria Esperanza made the best coffee in town. The funny thing was that no one in the hospital knew her name. Brother Thomas Manning was unable to thank her for the coffee before he died.

Swakilki didn't care. She slipped out of the nurse's uniform, got back into her own clothes, mounted her Honda Spazio scooter, and headed over to Leonardo da Vinci Airport.

ᛉ

Islamabad, Pakistan, 2012

He was sitting inside the Aiwan-e-Sadr, the official residence of the President of Pakistan. The President was looking at the transcript of a phone conversation between the chief of Pakistan's Inter-Services Intelligence and Stephen Elliot of the SAS.

'Why is this man so important to them?' he had wondered about Ghalib some nights earlier, as he sipped his evening scotch and soda. Now he knew.

His goddamned chief of intelligence and those American bastards wanted to justify their extended presence in Pakistan by ensuring that trouble continued to be stirred up by the likes of Osama and the Sheikh. Enough!

He decided that it was time to have a scotch and soda in the evening with the deputy director of the ISI.

ᛉ

The Directorate for Inter-Services Intelligence, known as the ISI, wielded immense power in Pakistan. The ISI was responsible for surveillance, interception and espionage, as well as the security of Pakistan's nuclear programme. The ISI's power had been consolidated in 1988 when the Pakistani military dictator, President Zia ul-Haq, had commenced Operation Tupac—an action plan for the control of Kashmir. The ISI had been responsible for creating and training at least six major militant organisations, with approximately between 5,000 and 10,000 armed men of Indian-Kashmiri origin, who would plague Indian authorities for the next few decades.[208]

The ISI chief ran his organisation ruthlessly. Under him, his deputy director in charge of the political, external and general

329

divisions had to be constantly on call. The ISI chief was a veteran. Under him, the ISI had played a pivotal role in the CIA-sponsored Mujahideen war to push the Soviets out of Afghanistan in the 1980s. The CIA had assigned the responsibility of training and money distribution to the ISI, which had trained about 83,000 Afghan Mujahideen and sent them off to Afghanistan to fight. The CIA had then decided to use the ISI to promote the smuggling of heroin into Afghanistan with a view to turning the resident Soviet troops into addicts. The ISI chief had executed the plan with his usual ruthless precision. He had even ensured the takeover of Afghanistan by the radical Islamic Taliban regime after the fall of the Soviet-backed government in Kabul in 1992. His rise had been partly due to the constant backing and support of an equally enthusiastic director of the CIA, the late President of the United States of America, Alissa Kaetzel Elliot. He had enjoyed an extremely cosy relationship with Stephen Elliot of the SAS too.

This particular ISI chief had to go. His deputy director was the man for the job.

🛕

The ISI chief was escorting Stephen Elliot and Zvi Yatom from the Pindh Ranjha International Airport to their suite at the luxurious Islamabad Serena Hotel in his Hummer. His boss, the Pakistani President, had been very specific about holding the meeting with the American and the Israeli here in Islamabad.

It was around 6 pm when the blast occurred. An improvised bomb containing TNT had been placed against the left underside of the vehicle, near the gasoline tank and the rear passenger seat. This ensured that the gas tank explosion would eliminate all the occupants. The trigger was via a pager.

The deputy director phoned the President to convey to him the tragic news regarding the death of the three men inside the Hummer.

Maryland, USA, 2012

Vincent had hurriedly punched 13 into the numeric keypad and watched as the door slid silently open. In front of him was a long tunnel. It had been built out of reinforced concrete on all sides. It was unpainted, but a single cable along the length of the roof supplied power to the hundreds of naked light bulbs that ran endlessly in a straight line.

Ignoring his fatigue, Vincent began jogging towards the end of the tunnel. It was tiring because the tunnel had an upward incline. After about half an hour, which seemed like an eternity, Vincent reached a solid whitewashed concrete wall with an equally white door.

On the white background was painted the German phrase: '*Wer war der thor, wer weiser, bettler oder kaiser? Ob arm, ob reich, im tode gleich.*'

Under it was an English equivalent: 'Who is the fool? Who is the wise? Who is the beggar or king likewise. Wizened fools and beggars on thrones. All underneath are just skull and bones.' It was the motto of the Bavarian Illuminati, established in 1776. The same year, 1776, was alluded to at the base of the pyramid on the American one-dollar note. The same year that marked the beginning of the final cycle of the Mayan calendar.

Next to the door was another numeric keypad. Above it was a small laminated sign that had the following words very neatly laser-printed: 'Please enter your room number.' Vincent didn't need to do the calculation! He had always wondered what the significance of Room Number 322 of the Skull & Bones society was. Vincent quickly punched in 3-2-2. It was his lucky day. The lock clicked and Vincent was able to push the door open.

Vincent looked around. He was somewhere in the forested Catoctin Mountain Park along the eastern rampart of the Appalachian Mountains.[209] He was standing in a lush verdant forest along one of the mountain slopes. He turned around to look at the door through which he had exited a few moments earlier. It was virtually impossible to discern, quite ingeniously hidden away in the slope.

'It's probably used by all those lunatics to enter and exit the ceremonial chambers without being observed,' thought Vincent as he carefully trudged along to get to the main road and onwards to civilisation.

He felt inside his pocket for the photocopy of the Rozabal document that he had managed to secretly keep in spite of the original being snatched away by General Prithviraj Singh in Srinagar. It wasn't there! It had obviously slipped out sometime during his escape from the Illuminati headquarters. The Illuminati now had the original as well as the photocopy somewhere on their premises.

ᘐᐸᶜ

Katra, Jammu, India, 2012

The Trikuta Mountain, where the Vaishno Devi shrine was located, had a single base but three peaks. Hence the name *tri-kuta*, meaning 'three peaks'. Three women were walking up the slope of the mountain toward the place where they would be able to access the holy cave that eventually led to the shrine itself. On an average, 5.4 million devotees paid homage to the divine Mother Goddess each year, trekking nearly twelve kilometres from the base till they reached the holy shrine at an altitude of 5,200 feet.

This particular shrine had no statues. The three heads that were worshipped by devotees were natural rock formations. The uniqueness of this formation was that although emanating from one single rock form, each head was distinctly different from the other two in colour and texture; hence each would be worshipped as a different manifestation of the divine Mother.

The three women seemed quite comfortable with each other. Swakilki, Alissa and Martha were on their way to reacquainting themselves with the powers of the cult of the sacred feminine.

ᘐᐸᶜ

In the centre stood the divine Mother in gold. The golden goddess was considered to be the source of wealth and prosperity. She was supposed to enhance the qualities of inspiration and effort in her devotees. Her name was Lakshmi.

To the left stood the divine Mother in white. The white goddess was considered to be the source of all creation, knowledge, wisdom, righteousness, art, spiritualism and piety. Her name was Saraswati.

To the right stood the divine Mother in black. She represented the quality associated with the darker and unknown realms of life. Since human knowledge about life was rather limited, and given the fact that man continued to remain in the dark about most of it, the black goddess was the basic source of all that was mystical and unknown to man. The black goddess was supposed to guide her devotees in conquering the forces of darkness. Her name was Kali.

Hindus believed that all human beings contained attributes of the three divine Mothers and that their behaviour was determined by the attributes that were predominant in their nature. But they also believed that in order to lead a meaningful life, a proper balance among these three was necessary and that any exaggerated trait spelt danger.

This was the significance of the number 13. One supreme being and three manifestations.

The holy trinity.

Lakshmi Saraswati Kali.

La Sara Kali.

Not just an anagram, but an indication of membership of a very exclusive club. The cult of the sacred feminine.

New York, USA, 2012

Vincent was on a flight back to New York when he remembered the most important words from the Gospel of Jesus:

And when you emerge and see the trees. Please do consider what will make you free. Thirteen Cycles. One and Three. The Mayan called it the Sacred Tree. I just call it the Sacred Three. Brahma, Vishnu and Shiva are Three. Lakshmi, Kali and Saraswati. The third eye that the Hindus see. The lines of a triangle in trinity. Christian, Muslim, Illuminati. The first two fight, the third waits to see. How much destruction can there possibly be?

That was when the shekel dropped!

Mary Magdalene herself had studied the ancient occult sciences as a temple priestess in Maghada and had derived her powers from the three manifestations of the divine Goddess. Lakshmi, Saraswati and Kali.

And when she reached France, her daughter had been called La Sara Kali because she represented not only the bloodline of Jesus and Mary but also the continuation of the cult of the sacred feminine. Her name represented all three elements of the trinity: *La*-kshmi, *Sara*-swati and *Kali*.

Then he remembered the visions from his projection with Martha in Goa:

'Where are you now?'

'Yerushalem.'

'And what do you see around you?'

'Temple fires. It's night. I can see Caiaphas and the Sanhedrin assembled, judging Jesus. They are irritable because no reliable witnesses are coming forth with evidence against Jesus.'

'Anyone familiar from your present life?'

'Thomas Manning.'

'Who is he?'

'He is Caiaphas—poisoning the minds of those assembled against Jesus. In this life too, he continues to seek vengeance.'

'Anyone else?'

'The Japanese woman who kidnapped me. Swakilki. She's present. She's Mary Magdalene!'

'Anyone else?'

'You, Nana!'

'What am I doing?'

'You're Mary Magdalene!'

'You're confused Vincent . . . anyone else there?'

'Another woman—I don't know her. She's Mary Magdalene!'

'Vincent, you seem to think everyone is Mary. Let's move on . . . now what is happening?'

'I can see Jesus and three women walking towards Damascus . . . I can see only their backs.'

Vincent realised how foolish he had been! He had seen Mary Magdalene, the high priestess of Maghada, surrounded by the three manifestations of the sacred feminine: the creator, the nurturer, the destroyer.

After all, Mary Magdalene herself was a supremely powerful personification of Shakti, the divine power of the sacred feminine. Just like every woman ever!

⚶

Les Saintes-Maries-de-la-Mer, France, AD 42

In the town of Les Saintes-Maries-de-la-Mer in France, each 23 to 25 May was celebrated in honour of St Sarah, also known as La Sara Kali. The festival had its roots in an event that had occurred here in AD 42. A boat had arrived carrying Mary Magdalene along with her daughter, La Sara Kali.

Mary's ancient occult powers had been derived from the divine feminine. The divine Mother would be worshipped on Navratri, the Festival of Nine Nights. On the first three days, the supreme feminine would be worshipped as the nurturer and the provider of spiritual and material wealth, Lakshmi. The next three days would be spent worshipping the divine feminine as

Saraswati, the goddess of wisdom. Finally, the divine Mother would be worshipped as the force of destruction, Kali.

Over the next 2,000 years, the powers of the divine feminine would continue to be handed down from mother to daughter in an unbroken chain, creating a sacred cult of the divine feminine. Each woman who was a member would bear a tattoo symbolising the three manifestations of the feminine trinity.

This unbroken chain of the feminine cult had eventually reached three women: Martha Sinclair, Swakilki Herai and Alissa Elliot and, by a grand design of the universe, each had developed and exhibited a single prominent dimension of the divine Mother.

Martha Sinclair was a descendant of the Saint-Clair family that had been descendants of the French Merovingian kings in whom ran the blood of Mary Magdalene through La Sara Kali. Martha had spent years studying meditation, yoga and spirituality. She had become a vast repository of knowledge, much like Saraswati.

Alissa Elliot had been born Alissa Kaetzel and was descended from the bloodline of Quetzalcoatl, a Naga king who had reached the shores of North America in ancient times. He was married to the second branch of the Mary Magdalene family tree, having settled in Mary Magdalene's spiritual home, Maghada. Alissa had used every opportunity to further her political and financial ambitions. She had reached the pinnacle of power and wealth. Just like Lakshmi.

Swakilki Herai had derived her name from the village of Shingo, which in ancient times used to be called *Herai*. The name *Herai* itself had been derived from the word *Heburai*, meaning *Hebrew*. It was one more place that the family tree of Mary Magdalene had reached. Swakilki Herai, through a twist of fate, had become the deadly destroyer. Because of her several misspent lives, her karma had been skewed, and she had killed again and again.

The three women were the Rozabal Line—the unbroken chain of the sacred feminine cult, handed down by Mary Magdalene, the high priestess of Maghada.

ॐ

Katra, Jammu, India, 2012

The three women emerged from the temple and walked out into the sunlight.

'I don't understand why you had to kill so many people before you came to your senses,' Martha said to Swakilki. 'I kept looking at you again and again, each time we would bump into each other—in London, in Mumbai and in Goa. I was trying to tell you that you were quite unnecessarily taking on the burden of bad karma for your future lives. I hope you are repentant—it will be good for your soul.'

'Yes. I do repent and I know that it will take me several lifetimes to wash away my accumulated sins, but I cannot understand why she had to terrorise the entire world to further her powers,' said Swakilki, pointing at Alissa. 'Martha, did Stephen ever tell you how ambitious Alissa was?'

'Let's not argue,' said Alissa. 'I do not wish to draw attention to ourselves. I am supposed to have died and been buried in Virginia. I wonder who's been placed inside the casket . . . probably poor Prithviraj. In any case, what about Martha? For years she never let anyone know the extent of the spiritual knowledge she had attained. Poor Vincent would keep debating theology with her, completely oblivious of his aunt's awesome powers.'

'You're right,' said Martha. 'Why do men continue to think that their power emanates from the Father, Son and Holy Ghost, when it is the divine Mother who pretty much decides everything? That she is Shakti, the female energy that powers the universe?'

Swakilki spoke up. 'I know that I shall take many births before I can pay off the debts of my sins, but I also know that if it were not I doing what I did, it would have been someone else. The karmic cycle goes on and on endlessly.'

'And the good and bad, hot and cold, positive and negative, white and black, love and hate, man and woman, and so many other opposites are merely manifestations of the same divine,' offered Alissa.

As they neared the end of the pathway, they saw a familiar figure trailing a few steps behind them. Vincent had decided to follow them, after all. The women were surprised to see him. 'Vincent dear,' said Martha, as she reached out to hug him. Vincent backed off.

'Why didn't you tell me?' he asked, full of hurt. Martha realised that he genuinely felt betrayed. She paused and thought for a moment before she spoke.

'How could I tell you that the three of us were women chosen by our bloodline to carry forward the cult of the sacred feminine? How could I tell you that our battle with the Crux Decussata Permuta was nothing but the age-old battle between the genders? How could I tell you that Mary Magdalene was not great only because of Jesus, but that Jesus was great also because of her? How could I tell you about the extent of Mary Magdalene's knowledge, power and high principles?' asked Martha.

Alissa spoke up and recited the Gospel of Philip to Vincent. *'Christ loved her more than all the disciples and used to kiss her often on the mouth. The rest of the disciples were offended by it and expressed disapproval. They asked, "Why do you love her more than all of us?" The Saviour answered and said to them, "Why do I not love you like her: When a blind man and one who sees are both together in darkness, they are no different from one another. When the light comes, he who sees will see the light, and he who is blind will remain in darkness."*

Vincent, the light is in *gnosis*, knowing yourself. This light is available to all, but some are blind and cannot spot it. The ones who can see it are the ones who are trully blessed! It is precisely because so many people continue to remain blind that groups such as the Crux Decussata Permuta, the Illuminati, Islamic terrorists, Hindu hardliners, Jewish fundamentalists, Aum Shinrikyo and Opus Dei continue to flourish.'

Vincent looked at Swakilki. 'And Swakilki? A killer who took several innocent lives? How is this following the teachings of the sacred feminine? How can this be good?'

Swakilki hung her head and said softly but purposefully, 'None of us can take a life, Vincent. Our birth and death is in the hands of the Supreme. We are mere puppets. The strings are pulled from elsewhere.'

'No. I cannot accept that. It is wrong to take life. You cannot justify your actions by saying you were merely a puppet!'

'I agree with you, Vincent. I cannot and will not be able to distance myself from my actions—that's what karma is all about. Terry Acton beheaded me at the guillotine in France. I got to do the same to him in the present life. You killed me, Mama Anwarkhi, the Sapa Inca's wife. I had the task of punishing you when I was Wu Zhao. Takuya electrocuted me at Sing-Sing and I electrocuted him in this life. You died for Prithviraj as his infant brother, and he died for you at the hands of the Illuminati. There is never any action without an equal and opposite reaction. The pendulum is in perpetual motion,' explained Swakilki.

Martha stepped in. 'You once thought persecuting Christians was the right thing to do, when you were Antonius, an ordinary Roman soldier. You went after Gaianus because he was a Christian sympathiser. In this life you had to understand what it meant to be a good Christian. Right?'

'I still can't understand why you would help the Illuminati,' asked Vincent, turning his attention to Alissa.

'Elementary, my dear Vincent,' said Alissa, lightly. 'Why was Swakilki willing to operate as an agent of the Crux Decussata Permuta? Being part of it was the only way to finish it.'

'But the Illuminati is not finished,' argued Vincent.

'Isn't it?' asked Alissa. 'Prithviraj, Zvi and Stephen Elliot, my late husband, are all dead. Ghalib and his tribe of twelve are dead. Osama and the Sheikh are dead. Who's left?'

ASHWIN SANGHI

Realisation was beginning to slowly dawn on Vincent, but he had to ask. 'So are all three of you descendants of Mary Magdalene?'

Martha smiled. She then answered, 'Well, yes. All of us do have her blood. But that's not all that unites us. What unites us is the sacred power that Mary passed down to her daughters.'

'Daughters? I thought that Mary had one daughter, La Sara Kali, who went to France with her mother.'

Martha explained. 'She had three daughters, my dear. One went to France. The other went to Japan. The third was sent back to Maghada, Mary's spiritual home, from where future Naga kings took the bloodline to America. Having been a priestess who worshipped the sacred feminine, it was quite obvious that she would name her daughters after the three manifestations of the sacred feminine, Lakshmi, Saraswati and Kali. The name La Sara Kali is not the name of one daughter but the collective name of three daughters.'

'So are all three of you the three manifestations of the Supreme Mother?' asked Vincent incredulously.

'No. Every human being is a manifestation of one or more elements of the Mother. We are not divine, Vincent. Our purpose is merely to ensure that the supremacy of the sacred feminine is not lost,' said Swakilki. She paused. 'Vincent, have you ever thought about the six-pointed Star of David . . . you know, the sacred symbol of Judaism? Have you ever wondered why it has six points and is formed by the intersection of two triangles?'

Vincent did not reply. He knew an answer was on its way.

His silence paid off. 'Well, as you know, the female form is often represented by the chalice or an inverted triangle. This is often thought to resemble the womb. The male form is represented as the opposite, an upright triangle. This is thought to symbolically represent the phallus. In Hinduism, female energy is represented by the trinity of Lakshmi-Saraswati-Kali and male energy is represented by the trinity of Brahma-Vishnu-Shiva. Both the male and female trinities are representative of the Creator-Nurturer-Destroyer.' Vincent digested the information as she made him visualise it.

Martha continued, 'The supreme force—call this force God, if you like—is simply a combination of all these manifestations. Male and female energy. Imagine what would happen if you made the two triangles overlap? *Voila!* You would have the Star of David—a representation of the one universal being into whom we all must merge!'

Vincent was dumbstruck. He thought about what his aunt had just told him, but doubts still lingered. 'So why don't Hindus also worship the Star of David?' he asked.

'Actually Vincent, they do—only in a slightly different form. Imagine that you took each triangle and literally "opened" each one out before making them overlap. What would you get? The Hindu Swastika! Same concept, just slightly different geometry!'

Martha continued. 'In fact, the two triangles are present even in the most striking Illuminati symbol. The American dollar!'

'But why would Jews have symbology derived from India? Why would the lost tribes of Israel run to India? Why would Mary Magdalene come to India? Why would Jesus settle down in India? Why?' asked Vincent.

Alissa took up the challenge. 'Well, in Judaism, Abraham is the father of the Israelites, blessed and chosen by God. Historians have placed Abraham at around 1950 BC. Jews and Christians alike believe they are descendants of Abraham's son, Isaac. On the other hand, Muslims believe that they are descended from Ishmael, Abraham's other son. The key question is quite obvious. Who exactly was Abraham? According to the Book of Genesis, Abraham was the son of Terah, who was from Ur in Sumer. Abraham's wife was Sara. In Hinduism, you have Brahma and his consort, Saraswati. Isn't it possible that Abraham and Brahma were one and the same person? Also consider the fact that Abraham's father was Terah. Do you know that in India, *terah* means thirteen?' asked Alissa.

Vincent looked sceptical. Swakilki took over. 'One supreme entity and three manifestations. In any case, the *Sumerian* civilisation to which Abraham belonged was actually the *Somarian* civilisation. The Sumerians were essentially moon-worshippers. In Hinduism, the god of nectar or ambrosia was *Soma*. The crescent moon was considered to be the cup from which the gods drank the divine nectar, and hence the Hindu moon god was known as *Soma*-natha. The first day of the week, Monday, is called *Somavara*, or "the day of the moon" by Hindus. Is it surprising that the word 'Monday' itself should mean "day of the moon"? Essentially, the Sumerian and Indian civilisations were one and the same. These were one and the same people, Vincent . . . and Abraham was one of them! Is it surprising then that Mary Magdalene or Jesus would have had a spiritual connection to India?

Martha interjected. 'Mesopotamia and India were indeed inhabited by the same people, Vincent. Zoroaster, the founder of the Zoroastrian faith, was born around 628 BC, somewhere near an area called Ravy, in modern-day Iran, the region of Mesopotamia. He is supposed to have written the *Gathas*, the holy Zoroastrian scriptures, in the ancient language of Avestan. On the other hand, the ancient Hindu book of knowledge—the *Rig Veda*—had been written almost 700 years earlier in Sanskrit. Now, Vincent, here's a verse from Avestan: *'Təm amavantəm yazatəm, surəm damohu scvistəm'*. You'll be shocked when I recite the corresponding verse from the Vedas in Sanskrit: ' *Tam amavantam yajatam, suram dhamasu savistham*'. Almost identical!'

Vincent was bewildered. It was too much to absorb. Martha spoke once again. 'Vincent, in Hinduism, there were two groups of deities, the *devas* and the *asuras*. Do you know that in Zoroastrianism too, there were two groups of deities—the *daevas* and the *ahuras*! The Mesopotamians and the Indians were one and the same people!'

'And what about Mary Magdalene? Was she descended from the divine Mother? Could she be considered a manifestation or incarnation of the sacred feminine?' asked Vincent.

Swakilki replied, 'Vincent, recall the final words mentioned in the document that you retrieved from Rozabal. *The power is within you, don't you see? How does it matter if it's also in me? I am not worthy of titles, honours, or grace; the one who is worthy is the mirrored face. Stand by the mirror and look at yourself; you are the anointed, within yourself. The real miracle is in knowing yourself, and understanding the Brahman, the endless, the self.* Mary Magdalene was a manifestation of sacred power, but so are we all! It's just that we don't realise it. Each one of us is God. We are simply rivers and streams that merge into the ocean. The essential ingredient that constitutes the rivers as well as the ocean into which they must merge is the same—water. In Hindu philosophy, Shiva and Vishnu are opposites, but consider this. If one takes only the first segment of each name, we have *Shiv* and *Vish*, which are simply the same word flipped around! Essentially, we are all made of the same stuff!'

It was Alissa who took over this time. 'Mary Magdalene must certainly have been one of the best students of the sacred feminine cult. Jesus and Mary met while he was studying in India. She was descended from the royal house of Benjamin and he was from the royal house of David. A union was not only natural, but also a powerful statement—a political alliance and a union with a clear intent to rule. Thus, when Jesus was called *King of the Jews*, it was not merely a spiritual title, it was also meant as a political one. This political element was seen as a threat by the Romans, and hence the need to crucify Jesus. The Romans had been quite happy to allow the Jews to manage their own religious affairs. There was no need to interfere. The intervention happened because of political reasons, not religious ones,' explained Alissa.

'But I saw three Marys with Jesus in my visions,' said Vincent. 'How was that possible? There was only one Mary Magdalene.'

'A hypnotic trance is similar to a meditative trance—in each of them one's mind becomes pure and it becomes possible to perceive the presence of the divine. You simply saw the divine Mother, not Mary Magdalene. You saw the Mother in her three manifestations,' explained Martha, 'and given that all three of us have elements of those traits within us, you simply saw our faces as representative of each of those forms'.

'I still cannot understand why the world did not end. I saw it in my visions—the end of the world. I saw Hell!'

Swakilki took over. 'No. Vincent, there is no Heaven, and there is no Hell. Your soul drifts in and out of each lifetime and, depending upon your karma, a given lifetime can be Heaven or Hell. And as for the end of the world . . . the world is also subject to karma. When one world ends, another begins. The destruction you saw was merely the nuclear explosion in Waziristan—not the end of the world.'

'So what should I believe? Are all religions bad? Should I give up my religious work?' asked a bewildered and confused priest, one who seemed to have lost the very ground that he was standing on.

'On the contrary, all religions are fundamentally good. Judaism asks one to believe with perfect faith that the Creator, Blessed be His Name, rewards those who keep His commandments and punishes those that transgress them. How can a religion that establishes rules for good behaviour be bad?' asked Swakilki.

'Christianity teaches us that love is patient; love is kind; love is not envious or boastful or arrogant or cruel. It does not insist on its own way; it is not irritable or resentful; it does not rejoice in wrongdoing, but rejoices in the truth. It bears all things, believes all things, hopes all things, endures all things. Tell me, Vincent, how can a religion that teaches us to love be bad?' asked Alissa.

'Islam enjoins its followers to give food, out of love for Allah, to the poor, the orphan and the slave, while saying, "We feed you only for Allah's pleasure—we desire from you neither reward nor thanks." How can a religion that asks people to be charitable be bad?' asked Martha.

'Hinduism teaches us that the doer who performs necessary actions unattached to their consequences and without love or hatred is of the nature of the quality of truth. How can a religion that teaches one to do one's duty be bad?' asked Swakilki.

'Buddhism tell us that the kind of seed sown will produce that kind of fruit. Those who do good will reap good results. Those who do evil will reap evil results. If you carefully plant a good seed, you will joyfully gather good fruit. How can a religion that tells us to do good deeds be bad?' asked Alissa.

'There is something good to be found in all faiths, Vincent. The problem has never been belief but the deliberate misinterpretation and misuse of it,' said Swakilki thoughtfully. 'And yet, all humankind believes redemption awaits us when our souls arise and merge with that Greatest Soul of all. That is the true resurrection. If this universal oneness could be understood by all, there would be no conflict at all!'

Vincent suddenly saw a light at the end of the long, dark, tunnel of violence he'd been running through, scared, for an eternity, it seemed to him. He fell to his knees before the three women. When he looked up again, there was only One.

Notes, Acknowledgements and References

[1] The Rozabal Tomb does exist. See *Jesus Lived in India: His Unknown Life Before and After the Crucifixion* by Holger Kersten, Penguin, 2001.

[2] The Lashkar-e-Toiba does exist. The Lashkar-e-Talatashar is fictional.

[3] Inspired by speeches of Osama-bin-Laden, although not attributed to him. See *Messages to the World: The Statements of Osama-bin-Laden* edited by Bruce Lawrence, translated by James Howarth, Verso, 2005.

[4] The words used in both English and Latin for confession have been taken from an online article on the subject located at http://en.wikipedia.org/wiki/Confession

[5] Bank Leu is indeed the oldest Swiss bank. The character of Egloff, however, is fictional.

[6] The character Dmitriy Novikov is fictional. However, his achievements are based upon the real-life figure of Nicolas Notovitch, the nineteenth-century explorer/researcher, who wrote *The Unknown Life of Jesus Christ*, Leaves of Healing Publications, 1990.

[7] As recounted in *Jesus Lived in India: His Unknown Life Before and After the Crucifixion* by Holger Kersten, Penguin, 2001.

[8] Much of the Islamic rituals and customs are taken from *The Absolute Essentials of Islam* by Faraz Rabbani, White Thread Press.

[9] Taken from an online article by Shachi Rairikar at http://www.organiser.org/dynamic/modules.php?name=Content&pa=showpage&pid=69&page=17

[10] See *Ghost Wars: The Secret History of the CIA, Afghanistan, and Bin Laden, from the Soviet Invasion to September 10th, 2001* by Steve Coll, Penguin, 2004.

[11] Asahara Shoko is fact. A very well-written online biography is available at http://religiousmovements.lib.virginia.edu/nrms/aums.html. Takuya is fictional.

[12] http://en.wikipedia.org/wiki/Yigal_Amir

[13] A great deal of information was derived on this subject from *The Jesus Papers* by Michael Baigent, Harper, 2006.

[14] While Opus Dei and the Priestly Society of the Holy Cross are real in every sense, the Crux Decussata Permuta is purely fictional.

[15] Throughout this book, I have utilised travel information such as flight numbers, arrival and departure information, etc. The process of getting this information was effortless because of www.travelocity.com

[16] A wealth of information about the Archdiocese of New York, the seminaries and the cardinals is available online at their official website http://www.archny.org/

[17] I have extensively used the online Bible resources provided at http://www.biblegateway.com/

[18] The entire joke was taken from http://www.positiveatheism.org/writ/drlaura.htm

[19] A great deal of information on the White House, historical and biographical information on American Presidents, etc., was obtained at http://www.whitehouse.gov/history/presidents/al16.html

[20] http://www.forgotten-ny.com/CEMETERIES/Hidden%20cemeteries/hidcem.html

[21] See *The Light on Pranayama: The Yogic Art of Breathing* by B.K.S. Iyengar, Crossroad General Interest, 1985.

[22] See *The Art of Living: Vipassana Meditation: As Taught by S.N. Goenka* by William Hart, Harper San Francisco, 1987.

[23] I found excellent discussions on the issue of reincarnation theory in Christianity online at http://www.comparativereligion.com/reincarnation3.html

[24] http://www.britannica.com/ebc/article-9372767

[25] A wonderful history of the East End of London and Lesney's Matchbox Factory is to be had at http://www.eastlondonhistory.com/lesney.htm

[26] See *Cecil Rhodes* by Sarah Gertrude Millin, Simon Publications, 2001.

[27] See *America's Secret Establishment: An Introduction to the Order of Skull & Bones* by Antony C. Sutton, Trine Day.

[28] See http://www.conspiracyarchive.com/NWO/Illuminati.htm

[29] The Spiritualist Association of Great Britain does exist. The Association has an online presence at http://www.sagb.org.uk/

[30] See *Many Lives, Many Masters: The True Story of a Prominent Psychiatrist, His Young Patient, and the Past Life Therapy that Changed Both Their Lives* by Dr Brian Weiss, Warner Books.

[31] I used several sources to build a 'hypnosis script' but an excellent one was available online at http://hypnoticworld.com/scripts/problem_rsolution.asp

[32] See http://www.brown.edu/Administration/Chaplains/Communities/Descriptions/hinduism.html

[33] See *Karma and Reincarnation: The Wisdom of Yogananda, Volume 2* by Paramhansa Yogananda, Crystal Clarity Publishers.

[34] A good commentary on the guilt felt by modern Christians in regard to past-life therapy and issues of reincarnation has been written by Dr Michael G. Millett and is available online at http://www.elevated.fsnet.co.uk/index-page14.html

[35] Tibetan phrases taken from http://www.geocities.com/Athens/Academy/9594/tibet.html

[36] For a detailed account of the historical search for the Dalai Lama, you may visit http://www.tibet.com/DL/discovery.html

[37] Detailed astrological and astronomical issues around the birth of Jesus have been taken from http://www.math.nus.edu.sg/aslaksen/gem-projects/hm/0203-1-18-bethlehem.pdf

[38] See http://www.channel4.com/history/microsites/H/history/e-h/herod01.html

[39] The itinerary of the holy family when they left Bethlehem can be found at http://weekly.ahram.org.eg/2005/724/tr6.htm

[40] See an interesting article on the origins of ritual immersion in water by Prof. M.M. Ninan located at http://www.acns.com/~mm9n/Baptism/601.htm

[41] Asoka. *Encyclopædia Britannica*. Encyclopædia Britannica Online. 17th June 2007 <http://www.britannica.com/eb/article-9009884>.

[42] Ptolemy II is mentioned in the Edicts of Ashoka as a recipient of the Buddhist proselytism of Ashoka, although no Western historical record of this event remains. See http://en.wikipedia.org/wiki/Ptolemy_II_Philadelphus

[43] See http://en.wikipedia.org/wiki/Baudhayana. 'The most notable of the rules in the *Baudhâyana Sulba Sutra* says: A rope stretched along the length of the diagonal produces an area which the vertical and horizontal sides make together. If this refers to a rectangle, it is the earliest recorded statement of the Pythagorean theorem.'

[44] See *Pythagoras and the Story Behind the Croton Crown* by Adi Kanga & Sam Kerr. It can be found online at www.vohuman.org/Article/Pythagoras%20and%20the%20story%20behind%20the%20Croton%20Crown.htm

[45] From *Chrishna to Christ* by Raymond Bernard, Health Research, 1961.

[46] British Library, Online Gallery of Sacred Texts, http://www.bl.uk/onlinegallery/sacredtexts/deadseascrolls.html

[47] *The Complete World of the Dead Sea Scrolls* by Philip R. Davies, Thames & Hudson, 2002.

[48] *The Gnostic Discoveries: The Impact of the Nag Hammadi Library* by Marvin Meyer, Harper San Francisco, 2006.

[49] *The Refutation of All Heresies, Book One* by Antipope Hippolytus, Kessinger Publishing, 2004.

[50] *Saving the Savior: Did Christ Survive the Crucifixion?* by Abubakr Ben Ishmael Salahuddin, Tree of Life Publications, 2001.

[51] See http://en.wikipedia.org/wiki/Gondophares

[52] See http://www.indianchristianity.com/html/chap4/
chapter4c.htm which says: 'Different reports of this tradition have
come down to us. The earliest is recorded by Marco Polo, and
that of Bishop John de Marignolli comes next. We reproduce
them from Yule's Marco Polo, 2nd ed., and his Cathay and the
Way Thither. Marco Polo (ut supr., vol.ii.p.340): "Now I will tell
you the manner in which the Christian brethren who keep the
church relate the story of the Saint's death. They tell the Saint
was in the wood outside his hermitage saying his prayers, and
round about him were many peacocks, for these are more
plentiful in that country than anywhere else. And one of the
idolaters of that country being of the lineage of those called Govi
that I told you of, having gone with his bow and arrows to shoot
peafowl, not seeing the Saint, let fly an arrow at one of the
peacocks; and this arrow struck the holy man on the right side,
insomuch that he died of the wound, sweetly addressing himself
to his creator. Before he came to that place where he thus died,
he had been in Nubia, where he converted much people to the
faith of Jesus Christ."'

[53] See http://www.sol.com.au/kor/7_01.htm which says:
'Further clues are cited from The Apocryphal Acts of Thomas,
and the Gospel of Thomas which are of Syrian origin and have
been dated to the 4th Century AD, or possibly earlier. They are
Gnostic Scriptures and despite the evidence indicating their
authenticity, they are not given credence by mainstream
theologians. In these texts Thomas tells of Christ's appearance in
Andrapolis, Paphlagonia (today known as in the extreme north of
Anatolia) as a guest of the King of Andrappa. There he met with
Thomas who had arrived separately. It is at Andrapolis that Christ
entreated Thomas to go to India to begin spreading his
teachings.'

[54] See a contemporary news item online regarding Balakote at
http://jammu-kashmir.com/archives/archives2002/
kashmir20020615a.html

[55] I found an excellent source for Qur'an research at http://
quod.lib.umich.edu/k/koran/ an electronic version of The Holy
Qur'an, translated by M.H. Shakir, Tahrike Tarsile Qur'an, Inc.,
1983. Most references in the book regarding the Qur'an are
taken from here.

[56] http://en.wikipedia.org/wiki/Sermon_on_the_Mount

[57] See the Kashmir Information Directory at http://www.samawar.com/content/view/7/20/

[58] See http://www.plantnames.unimelb.edu.au/Sorting/Nardostachys.html

[59] See the history of Buckingham Palace at Royal Residences located online at http://www.royal.gov.uk/OutPut/Page568.asp

[60] Actually, the Royal College of Psychiatrists is located at No.17, not No.18, Belgrave Square. Also, the last tenant before the college was Lady Leontine Sassoon, not Lady Clementine Sossoon. Actual history about No. 17 Belgrave Square is located on the College's website at http://www.rcpsych.ac.uk/college/archives/history/historyofbelgravesquare.aspx

[61] The Vipassana Research Institute, see http://www.vri.dhamma.org/

[62] The Lord's Prayer in Aramaic was taken from http://www.godswillministries.com/prayers.html

[63] A description of what Jerusalem looked like during the time period of Jesus was obtained from an excellent article in *Time* magazine. It can be accessed online at http://www.time.com/time/2001/jerusalem/cover.html

[64] For sake of efficiency, I extensively used Babel Fish's online translation service and found it to be excellent. I cannot be certain of the accuracy of the final translations and if there are any errors, I crave forgiveness. The Babel Fish translator can be used online at http://babelfish.altavista.com/tr

[65] See the BBC story on this scientific discovery at http://news.bbc.co.uk/1/hi/health/3929471.stm

[66] See Sloan-Kettering's website to find out about the scientific properties of myrrh. Go to http://www.mskcc.org/mskcc/html/69309.cfm

[67] See http://www.beercook.com/prochefs/markdorber.htm

[68] See http://www.tombofjesus.com/indonesian/core/majorplayers/crucifixion/crucifixion-p2.htm

[69] *Black Potatoes: The Story of the Great Irish Famine, 1845-1850* by Susan Campbell Bartoletti, Houghton Mifflin, 2005.

[70] http://www.forgotten-ny.com/STREET%20SCENES/middlevillage/middlevillage.html

[71] http://members.virtualtourist.com/m/b6eb4/a8f71/ for a history of Einsiedeln

[72] http://www.hps.com/~tpg/ukdict/ukdict-8.html

[73] For further reading regarding the guillotine and the French Revolution, visit Jørn Fabricius' excellent site at http://www.guillotine.dk

[74] Based loosely on the historical Marie Anne Charlotte de Corday D'Armant who was beheaded in 1793 at the guillotine for having murdered Jean-Paul Marat.

[75] Excellent background information on the Inca empire at http://en.wikipedia.org/wiki/Sapa_Inca

[76] Background information on the historical figure of Wu Zhao can be accessed at http://www.womenofchina.cn/people/women_in_history/3594.jsp

[77] A full chronology of Jesus's actions post-crucifixion were taken from http://www.westarinstitute.org/Periodicals/4R_Articles/Easter/Chronology/chronology.html

[78] See *The Meaning of Shinto* by J.W.T. Mason, Trafford Publishing, 2006.

[79] See the website of the International Center for Reiki Training at http://www.reiki.org/

[80] See *Muhammad: A Biography of the Prophet* by Karen Armstrong, Harper San Francisco, 1993.

[81] See a paper entitled 'Jesus in Islam' by the Islamic Centre of Rochester at http://theicr.org/Jesus%20in%20Islam.pdf

[82] See *Irenaeus Against Heresies* by Irenaeus, Kessinger Publishing, 2004.

[83] See details of this recorded encounter at http://www.tombofjesus.com/core/majorplayers/the-tomb/the-tomb-p3.htm

[84] See *Jesus in India: Being An Account of Jesus' Escape from Death on the Cross and His Journey to India* by Hazrat Mirza Ghulam Ahmad, Fredonia Books, 2004.

[85] The actual BBC report can be read at http://news.bbc.co.uk/ 2/hi/south_asia/4400957.stm

[86] See *A Long and Uncertain Journey: The 27,000 Mile Voyage of Vasco Da Gama* by Joan Elizabeth Goodman, Mikaya Press, 2001.

[87] http://www.keralachurch.com/ main_left_right.php?cmd=keralachristianity

[88] See *The Goa Inquisition: Being a Quarter Centenary Commemoration Study of the Inquisition of India* by Anant Kakba Priolkar, South Asia Books.

[89] http://www.christianaggression.org/ item_display.php?type=ARTICLES&id=1111142225

[90] http://www.newadvent.org/cathen/04610a.htm

[91] There is no book called the *Tarikh-Issa-Masih*. There is reference at http://www.tombofjesus.com/core/majorplayers/ the-tomb/the-tomb-p7.htm#marriageandchildren to an old 'Persian work entitled the *Negaris-Tan-i-Kashmir*, in which an account of Jesus's marriage is contained. We will continue trying to get hold of it, and the reader can check from time to time at the website to see if that document has been obtained . . . We have contacted various people, attempting to get hold of this work, including the English translation of the relevant portions. This might be a difficult task, but we are determined to put every effort into securing it. In the meantime, we reproduce below an excerpt from Andreas Faber Kaiser's *Jesus Died in Kashmir*, in which Kaiser relates a conversation he had with Mr Basharat Saleem, a man who claims to be a living descendant of Jesus Christ: 'He told me that to his knowledge the only written source on this subject [of Jesus's marriage] was the *Negaris-Tan-i-Kashmir*, an old Persian book that had been translated into Urdu, and that relates that King Shalewahin (the same king as met and conversed with Jesus in the mountains) told Jesus that he needed a woman to take care of him, and offered him his choice of fifty. Jesus replied that he did not need any and that no one was obliged to work for him, but the king persisted until Jesus agreed to employ a woman to cook for him, look after his house and do his washing. Professor Hassnain told me that the woman's name was Maryan, and that the same book says that she bore Jesus children.'

[92] 'God give me strength to save this book' in Portuguese.

[93] See *Was Jesus a Buddhist?* at http://www.thezensite.com/non_Zen/Was_Jesus_Buddhist.html

[94] See *The Security Organs of the Russian Federation* at http://www.psan.org/document551.html

[95] Loosely based on real-life FBI agent Robert Hanssen who spied for the Russians at the behest of Opus Dei. See http://www.foxnews.com/story/0,2933,27409,00.html

[96] Dr Dawood Omar's character is based loosely on A.Q. Khan, the founder of Pakistan's nuclear programme. He actually did attend the University of Leuven. See profile at http://www.ias-worldwide.org/profiles/prof85.htm

[97] See WMD Insights on Pakistan's nuclear programme and the arrest of A.Q. Khan at http://www.wmdinsights.com/I3/G1_SR_AQK_Network.htm

[98] Read the actual *Washington Quarterly* article at http://www.twq.com/05spring/docs/05spring_albright.pdf

[99] Detailed description of Salah taken from http://www.islamawareness.net/Salah/

[100] See *Saladin: a Benevolent Man, Respected by both Muslims & Christians* by the Institute of Arabic & Islamic Studies at http://www.islamic-study.org/Saladin%20(Salahu%20ad-Deen).htm

[101] Taken from an actual CNN story. See http://www.cnn.com/2005/WORLD/europe/04/19/pope.tuesday/index.html

[102] Read the actual article at http://www.benadorassociates.com/article/13899

[103] See http://www.pipavav.com/a_in.html

[104] See *A Failure of Imagination (Intelligence, WMDs, and 'Virtual Jihad')* by Scott Atran, Centre National de la Recherche Scientifique, Paris, France and the University of Michigan, Ann Arbor located at http://www.sitemaker.umich.edu/satran/files/atran-sct-0406.pdf

[105] See *Nostradamus: The Complete Prophecies* by John Hogue, Element Books, 1997.

[106] Read *Time* magazine's article on the French Intifada at http://www.time.com/time/world/article/0,8599,1127429,00.html

[107] See http://warfare2050.blogspot.com/2007/04/warfare-2050-dictionary-la-triple.html

[108] Centre for Defense Information: http://www.cdi.org/terrorism/etim.cfm

[109] Uighur phrase for 'Perfect!'

[110] See http://www.globalsecurity.org/military/world/para/ji.htm

[111] http://www.globalsecurity.org/security/profiles/jaish-e-mohammed.htm

[112] All planetary positions calculated on http://www.ephemeris.com/ephemeris.php

[113] Character loosely based on Abu Musab Al-Zarqawi. See http://www.globalresearch.ca/articles/CHO405B.html

[114] Arabic for 'son of a bitch'.

[115] http://www.jihadwatch.org/archives/004849.php

[116] Character loosely based on Abu Bakar Bashir, the actual founder of Jemaah Islamiyah. Profile of J.I. from Council on Foreign Relations at http://www.cfr.org/publication/8948/

[117] http://www.dfat.gov.au/facts/muslims_in_australia.html

[118] Character loosely based on Shamil Basayev, Chechen warlord. See information at http://topics.nytimes.com/top/reference/timestopics/people/b/shamil_basayev/index.html

[119] http://www.socialpages.com.pk/137/art.asp

[120] Durand Line. *Encyclopædia Britannica*. Retrieved on 23 June 2007 from Encyclopædia Britannica Online: http://www.britannica.com/eb/article-9031550

[121] See *The How & Why of the Mayan End Date in 2012 A.D.* by John Major Jenkins at http://www.levity.com/eschaton/Why2012.html

[122] http://www.specialoperations.com/Domestic/CIA/SAS/Default.html

[123] The tour itinerary and material are taken from Benny Kurien's actual tour of Kerala. Read the information at http://www.earthfoot.org/p2/in013.htm

[124] See *Jesus Died in Kashmir: Jesus, Moses and the Ten Lost Tribes of Israel* by Andreas Faber Kaiser, Gordon & Cremonesi, 1977.

[125] Bahrdt, Carl Friedrich. *Encyclopædia Britannica*. Retrieved in 2007 from Encyclopædia Britannica Online: http://www.britannica.com/eb/article-9011796

[126] See Swoon Hypothesis at http://www.answers.com/topic/swoon-hypothesis

[127] The relevant passages of the *Nathanamavali* can be accessed at Atma Jyoti Ashram's website http://www.atmajyoti.org/sw_unknown_life.asp

[128] *Guardian of the Dawn* by Richard Zimler, Delta, 2005.

[129] Richard Zimler's interview by Rediff.com is located at http://in.rediff.com/news/2005/sep/14inter1.htm

[130] http://www.answering-islam.de/Main/Intro/islamic_jesus.html

[131] See the article regarding Thiaoouba Prophecy at http://thiaoouba.com/tomb.htm

[132] See *The Book of Revelation (The Smart Guide to the Bible Series)* by Daymond R. Duck and Larry Richards, Thomas Nelson, 2006.

[133] http://www.chamonet.com/faq.php?id_faq_type=43

[134] http://www.powerlabs.org/chemlabs/deflagrants.htm

[135] Background information on the Three Gorges Dam taken from http://en.wikipedia.org/wiki/Three_Gorges_Dam

[136] See http://www.acfnewsource.org/science/bomb_prevention.html

[137] See Great Buildings Online at http://www.greatbuildings.com/buildings/Petronas_Towers.html

[138] http://www.textually.org/textually/archives/cat_cell_phones_used_by_terrorists.htm

[139] See Shri Mata Vaishno Devi Shrine Board's website at http://www.maavaishnodevi.org/

[140] My thanks to Sadiq M. Alam (Mystic Saint), whose blog http://mysticsaint.blogspot.com/2008/05/earthly-mother-extra-ordinary-teaching.html gave me some wonderful ideas regarding the sacred feminine.

[141] http://www.globalsecurity.org/military/world/iraq/baghdad-monuments.htm

[142] http://www.armageddononline.org/content/view/25/49/

[143] See details of Bung Karno Stadium at http://www.worldstadiums.com/stadium_menu/stadium_list/100000.shtml

[144] http://www.pbs.org/wgbh/nova/bioterror/agen_anthrax.html

[145] http://news.nationalgeographic.com/news/2004/11/1130_041130_locusts.html

[146] http://www.goacom.org/overseas-digest/Religion/Christianity&Europe/church-crusades,colonial%20backing&no-salvation-outside-church.html

[147] Information on Indian intelligence agencies at http://www.fas.org/irp/world/india/raw/index.html

[148] Information on the exploits of Mossad taken from http://www.answers.com/topic/mossad

[149] For more information on Mary's purported burial site see the article 'Mai Mari da Asthan' by Mohamed Elmasry at http://www.despardes.com/articles/deco5/121305-virgin-mary-elmasry.asp

[150] See *The Fifth Gospel: New Evidence from the Tibetan, Sanskrit, Arabic, Persian and Urdu Sources About the Historical Life of Jesus Christ After the Crucifixion* by Fida Hassnain and Dahan Levi, Ahtisham Fida, Blue Dolphin, 2006.

[151] A wealth of etymological information on various English and Arabic names was taken from http://www.behindthename.com/

[152] From the *Shrimad-Bhagavatam* we learn that Lord Krishna appeared on earth when the Moon was in the constellation of Rohini (Aldebaran) and the eighth lunar day of the dark fortnight (Krishna Ashtami), 125 years before the advent of the Age of Kali (which began on 18 February 3102 BC, which works out to 12-13

July 3127 BC), according to Glenn Smith at http://
www.swaveda.com/articles.php?mnthyr=&action
=show&id= 59&comment= Comment&PHPSESSID=
62d5c9a1147aa21f70e24b089dbc1fee

[153] See *The Berzin Archives* at http://www.berzinarchives.com/
web/en/archives/approaching_buddhism/teachers/
lineage_masters/life_shakyamuni_buddha.html

[154] See *Wilson's Almanac* on gods and men with similarities to
Jesus at http://www.wilsonsalmanac.com/jesus_similar.html

[155] See *The World's Sixteen Crucified Saviors* at http://
www.infidels.org/library/historical/kersey_graves/16/

[156] See article 'Born of a Virgin on December 25th: Horus, Sun
God of Egypt' by S. Acharya at http://www.truthbeknown.com/
horus.html

[157] See *Daughters of the Inquisition: Medieval Madness: Origins
and Aftermaths* by Christina Crawford Seven Springs, 2003.

[158] See 'Who Was the Real Jesus?' by David Pratt at http://
ourworld.compuserve.com/homepages/dp5/jesus.htm

[159] http://www.answers.com/topic/john-the-baptist

[160] http://www.hinduismtoday.com/archives/2004/1-3/36-
37_lore.shtml

[161] See *The Woman with the Alabaster Jar: Mary Magdalen and
the Holy Grail* by Margaret Starbird, & Co., 1993.

[162] See *The Christ Conspiracy: The Marriage of Jesus* by Rhawn
Joseph, at http://brainmind.com/
MarriageOfJesusChristConspir.pdf

[163] http://altreligion.about.com/library/graphics/
bl_smarymagdalen.htm

[164] See *The Templar Revelation: Secret Guardians of the True
Identity of Christ* by Lynn Picknett and Clive Prince, Touchstone,
1998.

[165] http://www.roman-empire.net/decline/constantine-index.html

[166] See 'Pope Arrested for Believing in Reincarnation' at http://
reluctant-messenger.com/reincarnation-pope.htm

[167] *Origen De Principiis* by Origen, published by Kessinger Publishing, 2004.

[168] One of the best books on this subject is *The Christ Conspiracy—The Greatest Story Ever Sold* by Acharya S., Adventures Unlimited Press, 1999.

[169] My thanks to Neelen Patten who runs the blog jesusofeastandwest.blogspot.com for drawing my attention to the BBC documentary on YouTube: http://www.videosift.com/video/Did-Jesus-Die-BBC-4-Documentary

[170] See http://www.shroud.com/menu.htm

[171] See *The Jesus Conspiracy: The Turin Shroud and the Truth About Resurrection* by Holger Kersten and Elmar R. Gruber, Element Books, 1994.

[172] http://www.answers.com/topic/bhrigu-samhita

[173] Japanese for 'Do you believe in destiny?'

[174] If one accepts Margaret Starbird's notion of Hieros Gamos, i.e., in older sacred marriage rituals, a woman who represented the Goddess and the land was wedded to the king. Some of these old ceremonies included a ritualistic slaying of the king, either symbolically or literally, after he was married to the priestess-goddess. In the symbolic slayings, he would then rise again in a mystical resurrection echoing the cycles of death and rebirth evident in nature. To that extent, it would be perfectly legitimate for Mary Magdalene to be 'killing' Jesus.

[175] See http://www.eurekalert.org/features/doe/2004-09/ddoe-rdo091604.php

[176] Loosely based on Khalid Sheikh Mohammed, the Al-Qaeda kingpin arrested in Rawalpindi. See story at http://timesofindia.indiatimes.com/articleshow/1205101.cms

[177] http://www.whitehouse.gov/history/facts.html

[178] Inspired by an actual interview given by George W. Bush to BBC *HardTalk*'s Stephen Sackur.

[179] Edited version of an original story by Norm Dixon that first appeared in the *Green Left Weekly*. The full article can be accessed at http://www.conspiracyarchive.com/NWO/CIA_Created_Osama.htm

[180] http://en.wikipedia.org/wiki/Islamabad

[181] Culled from http://www.usatoday.com/news/graphics/ 9_11sequenceofevents/flash.htm

[182] See *Same Soul, Many Bodies: Discover the Healing Power of Future Lives through Progression Therapy* by M.D. Brian L. Weiss, Simon & Schuster, 2005.

[183] The oldest church in the world has actually been discovered at the site. See http://www.haaretz.com/hasen/pages/ ShArt.jhtml?itemNo= 641806&contrassID =2&subContrassID = 15&sbSubContrassID=0&listSrc=Y

[184] Arabic for 'You! What are you doing? Think what this will do to the world.'

[185] Script taken from http://conspiracycentral.info/ index.php?showforum=11

[186] See http://www.scielo.br/pdf/bjp/v33n2/a07v33n2.pdf

[187] All radiation data taken from http://www.hc-sc.gc.ca/ewh- semt/alt_formats/hecs-sesc/pdf/pubs/water-eau/doc-sup- appui/radiological_characteristics/radiological- radiologiques_e.pdf

[188] http://www.yukos.com/EP/Priobskoe_Oil_Field.asp

[189] The verses are fictitious and have been composed by the author.

[190] I took the help of a very convenient calculator at http:// mistupid.com/computers/binaryconv.htm

[191] See *A Manual of Hadith* by Muhammad Ali, Ahmaddiyya Anjuman Ishaat, 1990.

[192] Information on Tihar Jail taken from http://tiharprisons.nic.in/ html/infra.htm

[193] See http://www.answers.com/topic/saint-sarah

[194] http://www.christian-forum.net/lofiversion/index.php/ t18866.html

[195] My thanks to M. Michael Crown for drawing my attention to the story of Quetzalcoatl and Glenn Kimball's site.

[196] See article by Gene D. Matlock at http://www.viewzone.com/ snake.html

[197] See news article in *The Christian Century* at http:// findarticles.com/p/articles/mi_m1058/is_24_122/ai_n15923405

[198] Maghada, see http://www.everything2.com/index.pl?node=Magadha

[199] See *Jesus in Kashmir, The Lost Tomb* by Suzanne Olsson, Olsson Books, 2007.

[200] Samuel is fiction but William is not. He was the founder of Skull & Bones. More about him at http://www.theforbiddenknowledge.com/hardtruth/the_russell_bloodline.htm

[201] This is speculation that some conversions must have happened. See http://users.rcn.com/jonathan02/muslimhistory.pdf for a brief note on conversion to Islam being a common practice in Islamic conquests.

[202] I was inspired by by the novel *Messiah* by Boris Starling in which a serial killer finds victims and kills them in exactly the same manner as the apostles died. You will notice, however, that there is a huge difference in the details.

[203] I found an excellent summary on 'The Apostles and Historical Figures of the Church' at http://www.imt.net/~gedison/apostle.html

[204] Also see http://www.christianhomesite.com/cherryvale/text/apostles.htm, http://www.gotquestions.org/apostles-die.html, http://www.direct.ca/trinity/disciples.html, http://www.ccel.org/bible/phillips/CN500APOSTLES%20FATE.htm, http://www.shrinesf.org/apostles.htm

[205] Read about the Illuminati influences on the American One Dollar Bill in an interesting article 'Satan on our Dollar' at http://www.jesus-is-savior.com/Evils%20in%20Government/Federal%20Reserve%20Scam/satan_on_our_dollar.htm

[206] See *The Jesus Family Tomb, The Discovery, the Investigation, and the Evidence That Could Change History* by Simcha Jacobovici and Charles Pellegrino, Harper San Francisco.

[207] Properties of Compound 1080 taken from http://www.dpiw.tas.gov.au/inter.nsf/WebPages/RPIO-4ZM7CX?open

[208] See http://www.globalsecurity.org/intell/world/pakistan/isi.htm

[209] http://usparks.about.com/od/lodging/l/blcatoctinother.htm